JOHN BROWN

Born 23rd September 1810 at Biggar, Lanarkshire, where his father was minister of the
Burgher Church. He was educated at the High
School and the University of Edinburgh; served
his apprenticeship under James Syme, and took
his medical degree in 1833. Thereafter, with
one short interval of two years as an assistant
at Chatham, he practised as a physician in
Edinburgh. He died on 11th May 1882.

JOHN BROWN

Rab and his Friends

AND OTHER PAPERS AND ESSAYS

INTRODUCTION BY
W. L. RENWICK

DENT: LONDON
EVERYMAN'S LIBRARY
DUTTON: NEW YORK

824'8 BRo

NO. *116*

ISBN: 0 460 00116 7

INTRODUCTION

JOHN BROWN was born in the Lanarkshire village of Biggar
in 1810, the son, grandson and great-grandson of notable
ministers of a Seceder Church. His mother died in 1816.
When he was twelve his father was elected to a church in
Edinburgh, where he attended the High School and then the
medical faculty of the university. On qualifying, he was for
two years an assistant in Chatham, and returned to Edinburgh
and his father's house to scrape together a practice of his
own, succeeding well enough to marry the beautiful girl to
whom he had been engaged for eight or nine years. Thereafter
his life was entirely in Edinburgh, where he died in 1882.

The influences on him were strong and lasting. In a review
of a local history he proclaimed himself, with some zest, 'a
Biggar callant', and it may be that the memory of those
early surroundings bred in him, in spite of the prevalent
taste for the more picturesque Highlands, the love of the
green, rounded Lowland hills so evident in, for instance,
'Minchmoor' and 'Enterkin'. Of his mother he wrote in
later life, 'I lost my mother forty-four years ago, and I have
never ceased to feel her loss'. It was not that his father
neglected him. On the contrary, he kept the boy by him,
and taught him well and assiduously. This was the stable
thing in his experience. His father meant everything to him,
and there is no more heartfelt tribute of love and reverence
from son to father than the 'Letter to Dr Cairns' which he
contributed to the biography he was asked to assist. It
goes far beyond the mere gossip of reminiscence that Cairns
probably expected.

The change from 'that shrewd and sturdy *auld-farrant*
capital of the Upper Ward' to the capital of Scotland was
not catastrophic. The High School continued the solid
classical education in which his father had grounded him.
What mattered was that it gave him also a circle of friends
of his own age and of comparable background; for friendliness
was in his nature and a mainspring of his life ever after. The
household of the widowed man absorbed in his studies cannot
have been the liveliest place for a boy to grow up in, and it
was as well that the change came no later than at the age of
twelve.

The next powerful influence was that of the surgeon James Syme, to whom he was apprenticed, as was still the custom, when he enrolled in the medical faculty of the university. Syme had his own hospital in Minto House, and gave his students a sound training in anatomy and the opportunity of assisting in his theatre—no small opportunity, since he was a master operator. Brown had no desire to specialize in surgery, and preferred general practice. He was, however, profoundly impressed by Syme's gift as a clinician. During his time in Chatham, he met a serious outbreak of cholera, and though he faced it with great courage, the feeling of helplessness in its treatment may have reinforced the diffidence with which he met the problems of practice in later life. It may have been the classical description of cholera that attracted him to Sydenham. His professional creed is expounded in his essay 'Locke and Sydenham'—the careful study of the individual case, the rigid application of strict logic to the observed symptoms in the light of knowledge of the human body; the avoidance of preconceptions bred of tradition and theory; and the minimum of interference with the body's natural functions. These two were the masters Brown preached to all students; and behind them towered the dominant figures of his father and his teacher. Research and experiment did not attract him. Syme may have been exploring new ways in his theatre, but, being almost inarticulate (as Brown describes him), he could not explain his methods or intentions, so that the apprentice was thrown back on observation.

Like his great fellow townsman Sir Walter Scott—the comparison would have flattered him—Brown tended to look back rather than forward. In the present, what mattered was the individual: in ecclesiastical affairs, Voluntaryism as against State and Establishment; in politics, Liberalism; in all things, freedom from the constraint of generalizations. Nor should the practitioner, in life or in practice, rely too much on mechanical aids like stethoscopes or laboratory tests. Healing was an art, not a science, but a native instinct, trained but not achieved by cultivation and experience. Above all, it demanded sympathy with the individual sufferer. The sensitiveness that made him shrink from distressing scenes in Dickens and other novelists, and the personal sorrow of his wife's death after years of decay, brought on a nervous breakdown in 1866. He was therefore in no condition to share in the excitements of antisepsis and anaesthesia, though the great exponents were his near neighbours in Edinburgh. The condition recurred, and persisted as a settled melancholy, until a year or two before his death.

All this sounds very negative, but there was more in his

life. Reading, naturally, was a habit in his father's son. He found refreshment in Virgil and Homer, and strength in philosophy—Plato, and even more in Aristotle and in the seventeenth-century thinkers. In a letter of 1873 he wrote: 'Wordsworth was a revelation to me. I read the *Excursion* when I was eighteen, and was a different man from that time; he added a precious seeing to the eye and to the mind.' Nor was it an uncritical admiration. He remarked on the prosaic patches in Wordsworth as on the over-elaborate parts of Tennyson. He could understand and appreciate Clough and Crabbe, and the power of genius in Byron. Browning 'has genius, true poetic genius, but he kills it with hard consonantal words, and philosophy and metaphysics, and obscurity and endlessness'. So also with the novelists: '*Alton Locke*, a book which is my especial horror as being one of the "tremendous" school of literature, everything at its highest pitch—words, sentiments, politics, character (if it deserves the name), conversation, all bursting most uncomfortably from excess of meaning (or its intention) and fury.' George Eliot's views on religion naturally offended him; her determined cerebration repelled him. 'She is an anatomist, and in order to be so she must either get her subjects dead to begin with, or kill them. . . . I would say that G. Eliot has *enormous* talent, sometimes intensified into almost genius, but that her books are manufactured, not *born*. She sets herself to do them, possesses, is not possessed by their Life.' It is 'romantic' criticism, as we might expect from a disciple of Wordsworth; but there is something in it. He missed in her the apparently unconscious creation of character, above mere 'truth to life', the thing Samuel Butler claimed for 'Don Quixote, Mr Pickwick and Others', the entry into real existence of people who were born, not manufactured, the consummate creation he found in Fielding, in Scott, in Jane Austen, in Charlotte Brontë, even (with reservations) in Mrs Gaskell. Personal acquaintance doubtless clouded his judgment of the two great men novelists of the day. In 1871 he wrote to Lady Minto: 'I am afraid I don't like Forster's Life of Dickens. I dislike the personal essence of both men, while I admire the unique genius of the one and the grandiose talent of the other. Dickens was at the core hard and egotistic, intensely. How different from poor soft-hearted, great-natured Thackeray. I read *his* books more than ever. Dickens I cannot re-read, and yet he was infinitely the greater genius in the true sense, in which he is what never was before or will be again.' Earlier he had written: 'I wearied of Thackeray's winking (as some-body else said) constantly to the reader and telling you his think about his peoples. But what a quantity of good matter in that book [*The Newcomes*], and what a thoroughly good style. Have you read *Little Dorrit* No. 1? Nothing more Dickensish could be, in good and bad. Dickens is a child of genius, but only a child; he never progresses, never improves, never studies, never restrains.' Both criticisms could be maintained in 1855, but the bias is clear in 1873: 'My reasons for saying he [Dickens] was hard-hearted are—1st, my personal knowledge of him many years ago, and my seeing then his intense, adamantine egoism. 2nd, the revelation of his nature given so frankly . . . in [Forster's] Life. . . . He was a man softest outside, hardest at the core.' It may be disputed, but Brown is good evidence.

Neither his love of books, old and new, his moral and religious faith, nor his professional opinions on medical practice, strong though they all were, led him to begin writing himself, but an unrelated taste. He was interested in painting and had friends among artists all his life, and in 1846 Hugh Miller invited him to contribute an article on the Scottish Academy exhibition. With his usual diffidence he was about to refuse, but to his practical wife the twenty pounds which accompanied the offer was too useful a windfall to let slip. In spite of her persuasion, he was unhappy about it, but it must have attracted enough attention in Edinburgh to encourage him. An Edinburgh man was naturally interested in an exhibition of Raeburn's portraits, and acquaintance with John Leech, through Thackeray, helped him to write a good obituary notice.

'My two cardinal vices,' he wrote to his friend Dick, 'are a tendency to preaching and fine writing, and something which in anyone else I would call affection.' From such vices he was freed when he indulged another of his personal idiosyncracies, his love of dogs. There was no weak sentimentalism about his feeling for dogs. He saw them as individuals, in their canine nature. If, as Isaac Watts said, 'Dogs delight to bark and bite, for God hath made them so', we must take them as they come. If fighting and cat-killing are part of their nature, we can only observe the fact. It is all in the great inscrutable scheme of Nature, and men shall see and rejoice: in dogs and landscapes and the works of the masters, and in humankind. His suspicion of theories combined with his visual sense in 'Dick Mihi', which not only indulged his pleasure in the looks of a terrier but gave him 'the chance of a good-humoured bit of banter upon Darwin's stuff of natural selection'. The point of 'Our Dogs' is that dogs are individuals, to be appreciated for their individuality. Good looks and good breeding are to be prized, but the judgment of the dog show is not final. Character matters most. Jessie the collie is beautiful and purebred, but the interesting thing about her is her disappearance every

morning to help the drovers in the market; there she was
following the nature of her kind. And if the character or
appearance was comic, so much the better to a born humorist.
There was nothing satirical in Brown's humour. It is like
Chaucer's, the humane enjoyment of people and things as
they are; and it could play most freely and best among dogs,
where preaching would be out of place. He admired spirit,
in a good horse as his father did, in a small school friend of
his half-sister, in a well-bred terrier, or in a mongrel. The
virtue of 'Our Dogs' lies in the pleasure he took in them,
which gave his portraits that clarity and economy as well as
zest and conviction.

People, of course, come first, and the claims of religion and
morality have to be observed, for they are the foundations
of the behaviour and daily intercourse among people. It
was not a question of mindless regulation, as we are taught
by the critics of 'Victorianism' to believe. The general
practitioner knew too much of human frailties both physical
and moral, and knew also what these same critics ignore, the
fineness of spirit that makes people worth caring for. Thus a
reminiscence of Hugh Miller's shows that spark of quality
still shining among tragic wreckage in 'Her Last Half-Crown',
a thing calling not only for charity, but for something like
pride in nature of humankind. The two are not divorced,
nor, as both Thackeray and Carlyle proclaimed, are they
divorced from humour. 'Rab and his Friends' is his best
work because everything comes into it. The centre of it is a
memory of his apprentice days with Syme, twenty-eight
years before, a never-forgotten revelation of human spirit
among simple folk, worthy of reverence along with the
reverence due to the great thinkers and artists. And—such
is the oddity of literary experience—what might have been
an occasion of mere sentiment or preaching is saved by the
appearance of the dog among the suffering people. The
Howgate carrier doubtless had a guard-dog for his cart—that
was usual—and it may have been a specimen that caught
the eye of the dog-loving young man; but whether the
sequence ran as it is told, from a casual fight seen in the
street by a couple of schoolboys to the tragic tenderness of
the scene in Syme's hospital, is another matter. Brown
should be given credit for his literary sense. The dog's
instinctive share in the sorrow of the human beings, the
feeling that Rab could do nothing that mirrors the helplessness of the young man, and even the great surgeon, deepens
the emotion and adds a strange breadth to the situation;
and the boys among the little crowd in the street set it all in a
proper distance and perspective, with no fear of its drifting
into a sermon like the comic picture of 'Jeems the Doorkeeper'.

Mr Frank Gent has shown how this same imagination appears in 'Pet Marjorie'. Marjorie Fleming did live; her diary can be seen in the National Library of Scotland, Edinburgh; Sir Walter Scott may have met her; but Mr Frank Gent has shown that the idyllic picture is a product of Brown's imagination. Brown's sympathetic humour had been caught by a published description of Marjorie Fleming and her journals; as in 'Rab and his Friends' but less seriously, he needed a setting; he probably also wanted to commemorate, somewhere and somehow, the well known and much admired figure of the great writer he had seen in his youth; and in this sketch he combined them. Facts scarcely mattered. Brown's literary fancy was in charge. Miss Stirling Graham's confession of 'impersonations' required less wrapping up. She was still alive, and Brown knew her well. The essay was originally a preface to a public reprint of her privately printed version, and there was little place for Brown's imagination. The object is Miss Graham's. What Brown did was to give a clear picture of the society in which she carried out her vivid little plays.

Brown's reputation is not broadly based, but with the 'Letter to Dr Cairns', 'Locke and Sydenham', 'Rab and his Friends', and perhaps 'Our Dogs', it is solid and secure. Further reading in *Horæ Subsecivæ*, and in his letters, strengthens the impression, and it is one that should make us pause before we accept the image of the smug, self-confident, impervious 'Victorianism' commonly promulgated earlier in this century. And that is a good thing.

Edinburgh, 1969.   W. L. RENWICK.

BIBLIOGRAPHY

A short bibliography is printed on page 30 and the dates of first publication of the essays in the present selection are given in the list of contents on page 31.

PREFACE TO FIRST SERIES OF
"HORÆ SUBSECIVÆ"

In that delightful and provoking book, *The Doctor,*
etc., Southey says: "'Prefaces,' said Charles Blount,
Gent., 'Prefaces,' according to this flippant, ill-
opinioned, and unhappy man, 'ever were, and still
are, but of two sorts, let the mode and fashions vary
as they please,—let the long peruke succeed the godly
cropt hair; the cravat, the ruff; presbytery, popery; and
popery, presbytery again,—yet still the author keeps to his
old and wonted method of prefacing; when at the beginning of his book he enters, either with a halter round
his neck, submitting himself to his readers' mercy whether
he shall be hanged or no, or else, in a huffing manner,
he appears with the halter in his hand, and threatens
to hang his reader, if he gives him not his good word.
This, with the excitement of friends to his undertaking,
and some few apologies for the want of time, books, and
the like, are the constant and usual shams of all scribblers,
ancient and modern.' This was not true then," says
Southey, "nor is it now." I differ from Southey, in thinking there is some truth in both ways of wearing the halter.
For though it be neither manly nor honest to affect a
voluntary humility (which is after all, a sneaking vanity,
and would soon show itself if taken at its word), any
more than it is well-bred, or seemly to put on (for it
generally is put on) the "huffing manner," both such
being truly "shams,"—there is general truth in Mr.
Blount's flippancies.

Every man should know and lament (to himself) his
own shortcomings—should mourn over and mend, as he
best can, the "confusions of his wasted youth;" he
should feel how ill he has put out to usury the talent
given him by the great Taskmaster—how far from being
"a good and faithful servant;" and he should make this

rather understood than expressed by his manner as a writer; while at the same time, every man should deny himself the luxury of taking his hat off to the public, unless he has something to say, and has done his best to say it aright; and every man should pay not less attention to the dress in which his thoughts present themselves, than he would to that of his person on going into company.

Bishop Butler, in his Preface to his Sermons, in which there is perhaps more solid living sense, than in the same number of words anywhere else, says, after making the division between " obscurity " and " perplexity and confusion of thought,"—the first being in the subject, the others in its expression,—" confusion and perplexity are, in writing, indeed without excuse, because any one may, if he pleases, know whether he understands or sees through what he is about, and it is unpardonable in a man to lay his thoughts before others, when he is conscious that he himself does not know whereabouts he is, or how the matter before him stands. *It is coming abroad in disorder, which he ought to be dissatisfied to find himself in at home.*"

There should therefore be in his Preface, as in the writer himself, two elements. A writer should have some assurance that he has something to say, and this assurance should, in the true sense, not the Milesian, be modest.

My objects, in this volume of odds and ends, are, among others—

I. To give my vote for going back to the old manly intellectual and literary culture of the days of Sydenham, Arbuthnot, and Gregory; when a physician fed, enlarged, and quickened his entire nature; when he lived in the world of letters as a freeholder, and reverenced the ancients, while, at the same time, he pushed on among his fellows, and lived in the present, believing that his profession and his patients need not suffer, though his *horæ subsecivæ* were devoted occasionally to miscellaneous thinking and reading, and to a course of what is elsewhere called "fine confused feeding," or though, as his Gaelic historian says of Rob Roy at his bye hours, he be "a man of incoherent transactions." As I have said, system is not always method, much less progress.

II. That the study in himself and others of the human understanding, its modes and laws as objective realities, and his gaining that power over mental action in himself and others, which alone comes from knowledge at first-hand, is one which every physician should not only begin in youth, but continue all his life long, and which in fact all men of sense and original thought do make, though it may lie in their minds, as it were, unformed and without a tongue.

III. That physiology and the laws of health are the interpreters of disease and cure, over whose porch we may best inscribe *hinc sanitas*. That it is in watching Nature's methods of cure [1] in ourselves, and in the lower animals,—and in a firm faith in the self-regulative, recuperative powers of nature, that all our therapeutic intentions and means must proceed, and that we should watch and obey this truly Divine voice and finger, with reverence and godly fear, as well as with diligence and worldly wisdom—humbly standing by while He works, guiding, not stemming or withdrawing His current, and acting as His ministers and helps. Not, however, that we should go about making every man, and above all, every woman, his and her own doctor, by making them swallow a dose of science and physiology, falsely so called.

---

[1] "'That there is no curing diseases by art, without first knowing how they are to be cured by nature,' was the observation of an ancient physician of great eminence, who very early in my life superintended my medical education, and by this axiom all my studies and practice have been regulated."— Grant on Fevers, Lond. 1771. An admirable book, and to be read still, as its worth, like that of nature, never grows old, *naturam non pati senium*. We would advise every young physician who is in practice, to read this unpretending and now little-known book, especially the introduction. Any "ancient physician," and the greater his eminence and the age the better, so that the eminence be real, who takes it up, will acknowledge that the author had done what he said, made "this axiom" the rule of his life and doctrine.

There is much mischievous nonsense talked and acted on, in this direction. The physiology to be taught in schools, and to our clients the public, should be the physiology of common sense, rather than that of dogmatic and minute science; and should be of a kind, as it easily may be, *which will deter from self-doctoring*, while it guides in prevention and conduct; and will make them understand enough of the fearful and wonderful machinery of life, to awe and warn, as well as to enlighten.

Much of the strength and weakness of Homœopathy lies in the paltry fallacy, that every mother, and every clergyman, and " loose woman," as a wife friend calls the restless public old maid, may know when to administer *aconite*, *arsenicum*, and *nux*, to her child, his entire parish, or her " circle." Indeed here, as elsewhere, man's great difficulty is to strive to walk through life, and through thought and practice, in a straight line; to keep *in medio*—in that golden mean, which is our true centre of gravity, and which we lost in Eden. We all tend like children, or the blind, or the old, or the tipsy, to walk to one side, or wildly from one side to the other : one extreme breeds its opposite. Hydropathy sees and speaks some truth, but it is as in its sleep, or with one eye shut, and one leg lame; its practice does good, its theory is sheer nonsense, and yet it is the theory that its masters and their constituents doat on.

If all that is good in the Water-Cure, and in Rubbing, and in Homœopathy, were winnowed from the false, the useless, and the worse, what an important and permanent addition would be made to our operative knowledge,—to our powers as healers; and here it is, where I cannot help thinking that we have, as a profession, gone astray in our indiscriminate abuse of all these new practices and nostrums : they indicate, however coarsely and stupidly, some want in us. There is in them all something good, and if we could draw to us, instead of driving away from us, those men whom we call, and in the main truly call, quacks,—if we could absorb them with a difference, rejecting the ridiculous and mischievous much, and adopting and sanctioning the valuable little, we and the public would be all the better off. Why should not "the Faculty" have under their control and advice, and at their command, rubbers, and shampooers, and water men, and milk men, and grape men, and cudgelling men, as they have cuppers, and the like, instead of giving them the advantage of crying out "persecution," and quoting the martyrs of science from Galileo downwards.

IV. As my readers may find to their discontent, the natural, and, till we get into "an ampler æther and diviner air," the necessary difference between speculative science and practical art is iterated and reiterated with much persistency, and the necessity of estimating medicine more as the Art of healing than the Science of diseased action and appearance,[1] and its being more teachable and

---

[1] When the modern scientific methods first burst on our medical world, and especially, when morbid anatomy in connexion with physical signs (as distinguished from purely vital symptoms, an incomplete, but convenient distinction), the stethoscope, microscope, &c., it, as a matter of course, became the rage to announce with startling minuteness what was the organic condition of the interior—as if a watchmaker would spend most of his own time and his workmen's, in debating on the beautiful ruins of his wheels, instead of teaching himself and them to keep the *totum quid* clean, and going, and winding it up before it stopped. Renowned clinical professors would keep shivering, terrified, it might be dying, patients sitting up while they exhibited their powers in auscultation and pleximetry, &c., the poor students, honest fellows, standing by all the while and supposing this to be their chief end; and the same eager, admirable, and acute performer, after putting down everything in a book, might be seen moving on to the lecture-room, where he told the same youths *what they would find on dissection,* with more of minuteness than accuracy, deepening their young wonder into awe, and begetting a rich emulation in all these arts of diagnosis,—while he forgot to order anything for the cure or relief of the disease ! This actually happened in a Parisian hospital, and an Englishman, with his practical turn, said to the lively, clear-headed professor, " But what are you going to give him?" " Oh !" shrugging his shoulders, " I quite forgot about that;" possibly little was needed, or could do good, but that little should have been the main thing, and not have been shrugged at. It is told of another of our Gallic brethren, that having discovered a specific for a skin disease, he pursued it with such keenness on the field of his patient's surface, that

better by example than by precept, insisted on as one of the most urgent wants of the time. But I must stick to this. Regard for, and reliance on a person, is not less necessary for a young learner, than belief in a principle, or an abstract body of truth; and here it is that we have given up the good of the old apprenticeship system, along with its evil. This will remedy, and is remedying itself. The abuse of *huge classes* of mere hearers of the law, under the *Professor*, has gone, I hope, to its utmost, and we may now look for the system breaking up into small bands of doers acting under the *Master*, rather than multitudes of mere listeners.

Connected with this, I cannot help alluding to the crying and glaring sin of *publicity*, in medicine, as indeed in everything else. Every great epoch brings with it its own peculiar curse as well as blessing, and in religion, in medicine, in everything, even the most sacred and private, this sin of publicity most injuriously prevails.

he perished just when it did. On going into the dead-house, our conqueror examined the surface of the subject with much interest, and some complacency—not a vestige of disease or life—and turning on his heel, said, "*Il est mort guéri!*" Cured indeed! with the disadvantage, single, but in one sense infinite, of the man being dead; dead, with the advantage, general, but at best finite, of the *scaly tetter* being cured.

In a word, let me say to my young medical friends, give more attention to steady common observation—the old Hippocratic ἀκρίβεια, exactness, literal accuracy, precision, niceness of sense; what Sydenham calls the natural history of disease. *Symptoms* are universally available; they are the voice of nature: *signs*, by which I mean more artificial and refined means of scrutiny—the stethoscope, the microscope, &c.—are not always within the power of every man, and with all their help, are additions, not substitutes. Besides, the best natural and unassisted observer—the man bred in the constant practice of keen discriminating insight—is the best man for all instrumental niceties; and above all, the faculty and habit of gathering together the entire symptoms, and selecting what of these are capital and special; and trusting in medicine as a tentative art, which even at its utmost conceivable perfection, has always to do with variable quantities, and is conjectural and helpful more than positive and all-sufficient, content with *probabilities*, with that measure of uncertainty which experience teaches us attaches to everything human and conditioned.

Every one talks of everything and everybody, and at all
sorts of times, forgetting that the greater and the better
—the inner part, of a man, is, and should be private—
much of it more than private.   Public piety, for instance,
which means the looking after the piety of others and
proclaiming our own—the Pharisee, when he goes up to
the temple to pray, looking round and criticising his
neighbour the publican, who does not so much as lift up
his eyes, even to heaven—the watching and speculating
on, and judging (scarcely ever with mercy or truth) the
intimate and unspeakable relations of our fellow-creatures
to their infinite Father, is often not co-existent with the
inward life of God in the soul of man, with that personal
state, which alone deserves the word piety.

So also in medicine, every one is for ever looking after,
and talking of everybody else's health, and advising and
prescribing either his or her doctor or drug, and that

Here are the candid and wise words of Professor Syme:—"In
performing an operation upon the living body, we are not in
the condition of a blacksmith or carpenter, who understands
precisely the qualities of the materials upon which he works,
and can depend on their being always the same.   The varieties
of human constitution must always expose our proceedings to
a degree of uncertainty, and render even the slightest liberties
possibly productive of the most serious consequences; so that
the extraction of a tooth, the opening of a vein, or the removal
of a small tumour, has been known to prove fatal.   Then it
must be admitted that the most experienced, careful, and
skilful operator may commit mistakes; and I am sure that
there is no one of the gentlemen present who can look back
on his practice and say he has never been guilty of an error."
This is the main haunt and region of his craft.   This it is
that makes the rational practitioner.   Here again, as in
religion, men now-a-days are in search of a sort of fixed
point, a kind of demonstration and an amount of certainty
which is plainly not intended, for from the highest to the
lowest of these compound human knowledges, "*probability*,"
as the wise and modest Bishop of Durham says, "is the rule
of life;" it suits us best, and keeps down our always budding
self-conceit and self-confidence.   Symptoms are the body's
mother-tongue; signs are in a foreign language; and there is
an enticing, absorbing something about them, which, unless
feared and understood, I have sometimes found standing in
the way of the others, which are the staple of our indications
always at hand, and open to all.

wholesome modesty and shame-facedness, which I regret to say is now old-fashioned, is vanishing like other things, and is being put off, as if modesty were a mode, or dress, rather than a condition and essence. Besides the bad moral habit this engenders, it breaks up what is now too rare, the old feeling of a family doctor—there are now as few old household doctors as servants—the familiar, kindly, welcome face, which has presided through generations at births and deaths; the friend who bears about, and keeps sacred, deadly secrets which must be laid silent in the grave, and who knows the kind of stuff his flock is made of, their " constitutions "—all this sort of thing is greatly gone, especially in large cities, and much from this love of change, of talk, of having everything explained,[1] or at least named, especially if it be in Latin, of running from one " charming " specialist to another; of doing a little privately and dishonestly to one's-self or the children with the globules; of going to see some notorious great man without telling or taking with them their old family friend, merely, as they say, " to satisfy their mind," and of course, ending in leaving, and affronting, and injuring the wife and good man. I don't say these evils are new, I only say they are large and active, and are fast killing their opposite virtues. Many a miserable and tragic story might be told of mothers, whose remorse will end only when they themselves lie beside some dead and beloved child, whom they, without thinking, without telling the father, without meaning anything, have, from some such grave folly, sent to the better country, leaving themselves desolate and convicted. Publicity, itching ears, want of reverence for the unknown, want of trust in goodness, want of what we call faith, want of gratitude and fair dealing, on the part of the public; and on the part of the profession, cupidity, curiosity, restlessness,

---

[1] Dr. Cullen's words are weighty : " Neither the acutest genius, nor the soundest judgment, will avail in judging of a particular science, in regard to which they have not been exercised. *I have been obliged to please my patients sometimes with reasons, and I have found that any will pass, even with able divines and acute lawyers; the same will pass with the husbands as with the wives.*"

ambition, false trust in self and in science, the lust and haste to be rich, and to be thought knowing and omniscient, want of breeding and good sense, of common honesty and honour, these are the occasions and results of this state of things.

I am not however a pessimist, I am, I trust, a rational optimist, or at least a meliorist. That as a race, and as a profession, we are gaining, I don't doubt; to disbelieve this, is to distrust the Supreme Governor, and to miss the lesson of the time, which is, in the main, enlargement and progress. But we should all do our best to keep of the old what is good, and detect, and moderate, and control, and remove what of the new is evil. In saying this, I would speak as much to myself as to my neighbours, It is in vain, that γνῶθι σεαυτόν (know thyself), is for ever descending afresh from heaven like dew, and silent dew; all this in vain, if ἔγωγε γιγνώσκω (I myself know, I am as a god, what do I not know!) is for ever speaking to us from the ground and from ourselves.

Let me acknowledge—and here the principle or habit of publicity has its genuine scope and power—the immense good that is in our time doing by carrying Hygienic reform into the army, the factory, and the nursery—down rivers, and across fields. I see in all these great good; but I cannot help also seeing those private personal dangers I have spoken of, and the masses cannot long go on improving if the individuals deteriorate.

There is one subject which may seem an odd one for a miscellaneous book like this, but in which I have long felt a deep and deepening concern. To be brief and plain, I refer to *man-midwifery*, in all its relations, professional, social, statistical, and moral. I have no space now to go into these fully. I may, if some one better able does not speak out, on some future occasion try to make it plain from reason and experience, that the management by accoucheurs, as they are called, of natural labour, and the separation of this department of the human economy from the general profession, *has been a greater evil than a good;* and that we have little to thank the Grand Monarque for, in this as in many other things, when to conceal the shame of the gentle La Vallière, he sent for M. Chison.

Any husband or wife, any father or mother, who will look at the matter plainly, may see what an inlet there is here to possible mischief, to certain unseemliness, and worse. Nature tells us with her own voice what is fitting in these cases; and nothing but the omnipotence of custom, or the urgent cry of peril, and terror, and agony, what Luther calls *miserrima miseria*, would make her ask for the presence of a man on such an occasion, when she hides herself, and is in travail. And as in all such cases, the evil reacts on the men as a special class, and on the profession itself.

It is not of grave moral delinquencies I speak, and the higher crimes in this region; it is of affront to Nature, and of the revenge which she always takes on both parties, who actively or passively disobey her. Some of my best and most valued friends are honoured members of this branch; but I believe all the real good they can do, and the real evils they can prevent in these cases, would be attained, if instead of attending—to their own ludicrous loss of time, health, sleep, and temper, some 200 cases of delivery every year, the immense majority of which are natural, and require no interference, but have nevertheless wasted not a little of their life, their patience, and their understanding—they had, as I would always have them do, and as any well-educated resolute doctor of medicine ought to be able to do, confined themselves to giving their advice and assistance to the *sage femme* when she needed it.

I know much that may be said against this—ignorance of midwives; dreadful effects of this, &c.; but to all this I answer, take pains to educate carefully, and to *pay well*, and treat well these women, and you may safely regulate ulterior means by the ordinary general laws of surgical and medical therapeutics. Why should not "Peg Tamson, Jean Simson, and Alison Jaup" [1] be sufficiently educated and paid to enable them to conduct victoriously the normal obstetrical business of "Middlemas" and its region,

[1] *Vide* Sir Walter Scott's *Surgeon's Daughter*.

leaving to Gideon Gray the abnormal, with time to cultivate his mind and his garden, or even a bit of farm, and to
live and trot less hard than he is at present obliged to do.
Thus, instead of a man in general practice, and a man, it
may be, with an area of forty miles for his beat, sitting for
hours at the bed-side of a healthy woman, his other patients
meanwhile doing the best or the worst they can, and it may
be, as not unfrequently happens, two labours going on at
once; and instead of a timid, ignorant, trusting woman—
to whom her Maker has given enough of "sorrow," and
of whom Constance is the type, when she says, "I am
sick, and capable of fears; I am full of fears, subject to
fears; I am a woman, and therefore naturally born to
fears," being in this hour of her agony and apprehension
—subjected to the artificial misery of fearing the doctor
may be too late, she might have the absolute security
and womanly hand and heart of one of her own sex.

This subject might be argued upon statistical grounds,
and others; but I peril it chiefly on the whole system
being *unnatural*. Therefore, for the sake of those who
have borne and carried us, and whom we bind ourselves
to love and cherish, to comfort and honour, and who
suffer so much that is inevitable from the primal curse,
and for its own sake, let the profession look into this
entire subject in all its bearings, honestly, fearlessly, and
at once. Child-bearing is a process of health; the excep-
tions are few indeed, and would, I believe, be fewer if we
doctors would let well alone.

One or two other things, and I am done. I could have
wished to have done better justice to that noble class of
men—our country practitioners, who dare not speak out
for themselves. They are underpaid—often not paid at
all—underrated, and treated in a way that the commonest
of their patients would be ashamed to treat his cobbler.
How is this to be mended? It is mending itself by the
natural law of starvation, and descent *per deliquium*.
Generally speaking, our small towns had three times too
many doctors, and, therefore, each of their Gideon Grays
had two-thirds too little to live on; and being in this state

of chronic hunger they were in a state of chronic anger at each other not less steady, with occasional seizures more active and acute; they had recourse to all sorts of shifts and meannesses to keep soul and body together for themselves and their horse, whilst they were acting with a devotion, and generally speaking, with an intelligence and practical beneficence, such as I know, and I know them well, nothing to match. The gentry are in this, as in many country things, greatly to blame. They should cherish, and reward, and associate with those men who are in all essentials their equals, and from whom they would gain as much as they get; but this will right itself as civilized mankind return as they are doing, to the country, and our little towns will thrive now that lands change, lairds get richer, and dread the city as they should.

The profession in large towns might do much for their friends who can do so little for themselves. I am a voluntary in religion, and would have all State churches abolished; but I have often thought that if there was a class that ought to be helped by the State, it is the country practitioners in wild districts; or what would be better, by the voluntary association of those in the district who have means—in this case creeds would not be troublesome. However, I am not backing this scheme. I would leave all these things to the natural laws of supply and demand, with the exercise of common honesty, honour, and feeling, in this, as in other things.

The taking the wind out of the rampant and abominable quackeries and patent medicines, by the State withdrawing altogether the protection and sanction of its stamp, its practical encouragement (very practical), and giving up their large gains from this polluted and wicked source, would, I am sure, be a national benefit. Quackery, and the love of being quacked, are in human nature as weeds are in our fields; but they may be fostered into frightful luxuriance, in the dark and rich soil of our people, and not the less that Her Majesty's superscription is on the bottle or pot.

I would beg the attention of my elder brethren to what I have said on Medical Reform and the doctrine of free

competition. I feel every day more and more its importance and its truth. I rejoice many ways at the passing
of the new Medical Bill, and the leaving so much to the
discretion of the Council; it is curiously enough almost
verbatim, and altogether in spirit, the measure Professor
Syme has been for many years advocating through good
and through bad report, with his characteristic vigour and
plainness. Holloway's Ointment, or Parr's Pills, or any
such *monstra horrenda*, attain their gigantic proportions
and power of doing mischief, greatly by their having
Governmental sanction and protection. Men of capital
are thus encouraged to go into them, and to spend thousands a year in advertisements, and newspaper proprietors
degrade themselves into agents for their sale. One can
easily see how harmless, if all this were swept away, the
hundred Holloways, who would rise up and speedily kill
nobody but each other, would become, instead of one huge
inapproachable monopolist; this is the way to put down
quackery, by ceasing to hold it up. It is a disgrace to our
nation to draw, as it does, hundreds of thousands a year
from these wages of iniquity.

I have to apologize for bringing in *Rab and his
Friends*. I did so, remembering well the good I got
from them long ago, as a man and as a doctor. It let me
see down into the depths of our common nature, and feel
the strong and gentle touch that we all need, and never
forget, which makes the world kin; and it gave me an
opportunity of introducing, in a way which he cannot
dislike, for he knows it is simply true, my old master and
friend, Professor Syme, whose indenture I am thankful I
possess, and whose first wheels I delight in thinking my
apprenticeship purchased, thirty years ago. I remember
as if it were yesterday, his giving me the first drive across
the west shoulder of Corstorphine Hill. On starting, he
said, " John, we'll do one thing at a time, and there will
be no talk." I sat silent and rejoicing, and can remember
the very complexion and clouds of that day and that
matchless view : *Damyat* and *Benledi* resting couchant at
the gate of the Highlands, with the huge Grampians, *immane pecus*, crowding down into the plain.

This short and simple story shows, that here, as everywhere else, personally, professionally, and publicly, reality is his aim and his attainment. He is one of the men—they are all too few—who desire to be on the side of truth more than to have truth on their side; and whose personal and private worth are always better understood than expressed. It has been happily said of him, that he never wastes a word, or a drop of ink, or a drop of blood; and his is the strongest, exactest, truest, immediatest, safest intellect, dedicated by its possessor to the surgical cure of mankind, I have ever yet met with. He will, I firmly believe, leave an inheritance of good done, and mischief destroyed, of truth in theory and in practice established, and of error in the same exposed and ended, such as no one since John Hunter has been gifted to bequeath to his fellow-men. As an instrument for discovering truth, I have never seen his perspicacity equalled; his mental eye is *achromatic*, and admits into the judging mind a pure white light, and records an undisturbed, uncoloured image, undiminished and unenlarged in its passage; and he has the moral power, courage, and conscience, to use and devote such an inestimable instrument aright. I need hardly add, that the story of *Rab and his Friends* is in all essentials strictly matter of fact.

There is an odd sort of point, if it can be called a point, on which I would fain say something—and that is an occasional outbreak of sudden, and it may be felt, untimely humorousness. I plead guilty to this, sensible of the tendency in me of the merely ludicrous to intrude, and to insist on being attended to, and expressed : it is perhaps too much the way with all of us now-a-days, to be for ever joking. *Mr. Punch*, to whom we take off our hats, grateful for his innocent and honest fun, especially in his Leech, leads the way; and our two great novelists, Thackeray and Dickens, the first especially, are, in the deepest and highest sense, essentially humorists,—the best, nay, indeed the almost only good thing in the latter, being his broad and wild fun; Swiveller, and the Dodger, and Sam. Weller, and Miggs, are more impressive far to my taste than the melo-dramatic, utterly unreal Dombey, or his strumous and hysterical son, or than all the latter dreary trash of Bleak House, etc.

My excuse is, that these papers are really what they profess to be, done at bye-hours. *Dulce est desipere*, when in its fit place and time. Moreover, let me tell my young doctor friends, that a cheerful face, and step, and neckcloth, and button-hole, and an occasional hearty and kindly joke, a power of executing and setting agoing a good laugh, are stock in our trade not to be despised. The merry heart does good like a medicine. Your pompous man, and your selfish man, don't laugh much, or care for laughter; it discomposes the fixed grandeur of the one, and has little room in the heart for the other, who is literally self-contained. My Edinburgh readers will recall many excellent jokes of their doctors—" Lang Sandie Wood," Dr. Henry Davidson our *Guy Patin* and better, &c.

I may give an instance, when a joke was more and better than itself. A comely young wife, the " cynosure " of her circle, was in bed, apparently dying from swelling and inflammation of the throat, an inaccessible abscess stopping the way; she could swallow nothing; everything had been tried. Her friends were standing round bed in misery and helplessness. " *Try her wi' a compliment*," said her husband, in a not uncomic despair. She had genuine humour, as well as he; and as physiologists know, there is a sort of mental tickling which is beyond and above control, being under the reflex system, and instinctive as well as sighing. She laughed with her whole body and soul, and burst the abscess, and was well.

Humour, if genuine (and if not, it is not humour), is the very flavour of the spirit, its rich and fragrant *ozmazome*—having in its aroma something of everything in the man, his expressed juice: wit is but the laughing flower of the intellect or the turn of speech, and is often what we call a " gum-flower," and looks well when dry. Humour is, in a certain sense, involuntary in its origin in one man, and in its effect upon another; it is systemic, and not local.

Sydney Smith, in his delightful and valuable *Sketches*

of Lectures on Moral Philosophy, to which I have referred,
makes a touching and impressive confession of the evil to
the rest of a man's nature from the predominant power
and cultivation of the ludicrous. I believe Charles Lamb
could have told a like, and as true, but sadder story. He
started on life with all the endowments of a great, ample,
and serious nature, and he ended in being little else than
the incomparable joker and humorist, and was in the true
sense, " of large discourse." [1]

[1] Many good and fine things have been said of this wonderful and unique genius, but I know none better or finer than
these lines by my friend John Hunter of Craigcrook. They
are too little known, and no one will be anything but pleased
to read them, except their author. The third line might have
been Elia's own :—

> " . . . . Humour, wild wit,
> Quips, cranks, puns, sneers,—with clear sweet thought profound ;—
> *And stin ing jests. with honev for the wound ;—*
> The subtlest lines of ALL fine powers, split
> To their last films, then marvellously spun
> In magic web, whose million hues are ONE ! "

I knew one man who was almost altogether and absolutely
comic, and yet a man of sense, fidelity, courage, and worth,
but over his entire nature the comic ruled supreme—the late
Sir Adam Ferguson, whose very face was a breach of solemnity ; I daresay, even in sleep he looked a wag. This was
the way in which everything appeared to him first, and often
last too, with a serious enough middle.

I saw him not long before his death, when he was of great
age and knew he was dying ; there was no levity in his
manner, or thoughtlessness about his state ; he was kind, and
shrewd as ever ; but how he flashed out with utter merriment
when he got hold of a joke, or rather when it got hold
of him, and shook him, not an inch of his body was free of
its power—it possessed him, not he it. The first attack was
on showing me a calotype of himself by the late Adamson (of
Hill and Adamson ; the Vandyke and Raeburn of photo-
graphy), in the corner of which he had written, with a hand
trembling with age and fun, " Adam's-sun *fecit* "—it came
back upon him and tore him without mercy.

Then, his blood being up, he told me a story of his uncle,
the great Dr. Black the chemist ; no one will grudge the
reading of it in my imperfect record, though it is to the
reality, what reading music is to hearing it.

Dr. Black, when Professor of Chemistry in Edinburgh

It only remains now for me to thank my cousin and life-long friend, John Taylor Brown, the author of the tract on *St. Paul's Thorn in the Flesh*. I am sure my readers will thank me not less heartily than I now do him. The theory that the thorn of the great apostle was an affection of the eyes is not new; it will be found in Hannah More's Life, and in Conybeare and Howson; but his argument and his whole treatment, I have reason to believe, from my father and other competent judges, is thoroughly original; it is an exquisite monograph, and to me most

University, had a gruff old man as his porter, a James Alston. James was one of the old school of chemistry, and held by phlogiston, but for no better reason than the endless trouble the new-fangled discoveries brought upon him in the way of apparatus.

The professor was lecturing on Hydrogen Gas, and had made arrangements for showing its lightness, what our preceptor, Dr. Charles Hope, called, in his lofty way, its "principle of absolute levity." He was greatly excited, the good old man of genius. James was standing behind his chair, ready and sulky. His master told his young friends that the bladder he had filled with the gas, must on principle, ascend; but that they would see practically if it did, and he cut the string. Up it rushed, amid the shouts and upturned faces of the boys, and the quiet joy of their master; James regarding it with a glum curiosity.

Young Adam Ferguson was there, and left at the end of the hour with the rest, but finding he had forgotten his stick, went back; in the empty room, he found James perched upon a lofty and shaky ladder, trying, amid much perspiration, and blasphemy, and want of breath to hit down his enemy, who rose at each stroke—the old battling with the new. Sir Adam's reproduction of this scene, his voice and screams of rapture, I shall never forget.

Let me give another pleasant story of Dr. Black and Sir Adam, which our Principal (Dr. Lee) delights to tell; it is merely its bones. The doctor sent him to the bank for £5 —four in notes, and one in silver; then told him that he must be paid for his trouble with a shilling, and next proceeded to give him good advice about the management of money, particularly recommending a careful record of every penny spent, holding the shilling up before him all the time. During this address, Sir Adam was turning over in his mind all the trash he would be able to purchase with the shilling, and his feelings may be imagined when the doctor finally put it into his waistcoat pocket.

instructive and striking. Every one will ask why such a man has not written more—a question my fastidious friend will find is easier asked than answered.

This Preface was written, and I had a proof ready for his pencil, when I was summoned to the death of him to whom I owe my life. He had been dying for months, but he and I hoped to have got and to have given into his hands a copy of these *Horæ*, the correction of which had often whiled away his long hours of languor and pain. God thought otherwise. I shall miss his great knowledge, his loving and keen eye—his *ne quid nimis*—his sympathy —himself. Let me be thankful that it was given to me *assidere valetudini, fovere deficientem, satiari vultu, complexu.*

Si quis piorum manibus locus; si, ut sapientibus placet, non cum corpore extinguuntur magnæ animæ; placide quiescas!

Or, in more sacred and hopeful words, which, put there at my father's request, may be found at the close of the paper on young Hallam: "O man greatly beloved, go thou thy way till the end; for thou shalt rest, and stand in thy lot at the end of the days."

It is not for a son to speak what he thinks of his father so soon after his death. I leave him now with a portrait of his spiritual lineaments, by Dr. Cairns,—which is to them what a painting by Velasquez and Da Vinci combined would have been to his bodily presence.

"As he was of the Pauline type of mind, his Christianity ran into the same mould. A strong, intense, and vehement nature, with masculine intellect and unyielding will, he accepted the Bible in its literal simplicity as an absolute revelation, and then showed the strength of his character in subjugating his whole being to this decisive influence, and in projecting the same convictions into other minds. He was a believer in the sense of the old Puritans, and, amid the doubt and scepticism of the nineteenth century, held as firmly as any of them by the doctrines of atonement and grace. He had most of the idiosyncrasy of Baxter, though not without the contemplation of Howe. The doctrines of Calvinism, mitigated but not renounced, and received simply as dictates of Heaven, without any effort or hope to bridge over their

inscrutable depths by philosophical theories, he translated into
a fervent, humble, and resolutely active life.

"There was a fountain of tenderness in his nature as well
as a sweep of impetuous indignation; and the one drawn out,
and the other controlled by his Christian faith, made him at
once a philanthropist and a reformer, and both in the highest
departments of human interest.   The union of these ardent elements, and of a highly devotional temperament, not untouched
with melancholy, with the patience of the scholar, and the
sobriety of the critic, formed the singularity and almost the
anomaly of his personal character.   These contrasts were
tempered by the discipline of experience; and his life, both
as man and a Christian, seemed to become more rich, genial,
and harmonious as it approached its close."—*Scotsman*,
October 20th.

                                                          J. B.

23, Rutland Street,
    October 30, 1858.

PREFACE TO THE SECOND SERIES
OF "HORÆ SUBSECIVÆ"

In making my bow, with this Second Series, I don't go
the length of the man (an ancestor, I suppose, of Uriah
Heep) of whom Robert Hall tells, "that he was for ever
begging pardon of all flesh for being in the body;" but
I sincerely wish this volume had been better than it is, or
half as good as I wished it to be.   There have been many
reasons for this; some good, some bad.   Perhaps my wish
was not strong enough to condense itself into will, and
maybe could was not commensurate with would; or, as it
is in the last line of an odd doggrel verse that comes into
my head as I write—

> "I wud nut lyv all ways,
>   I wud nut ef I cud;
> But, I kneed nut fret about it,
>   'Caws I cudn't ef I wud."

These Hours must, I fear, appear to many *Subseciviores*

—idler than ever; and some of the studies—browner than brown. I had intended to sober them by two professional papers—one, on the Doctrine and Practice of Prevention in Medicine; and the other, on the Management of Convalescence, how to make the most of it; but these must wait for that season which we may hope Felix of old did after all encounter, and they will. For what is not mine, I am sure all my readers will thank me; and thank still more the kind friend who has, through my importunity, allowed me to steal so much of her " Mystifications," which I am mistaken greatly if my readers do not relish and value. I have, by the kindness of Dr. Cairns, appended my letter to him, which forms a supplementary chapter to his admirable Memoir of my father. I somehow wished it, lame and imperfect and wandering as it is, to be in these Hours. It is little else than an expansion, and often, I fear, a dilution of the noble passage, by the same friend and brother, which closes the Preface to the First Series. May my father's Master, and his, deal kindly with him, as he has dealt with the dead!

February, 1861.

SELECT BIBLIOGRAPHY

ESSAYS. *Horæ Subsecivæ*, vol. i, 1858; vol. ii, 1861; vols. i and ii, 1862 (edited by A. Dobson, 1907); vol. iii, 1882. The Everyman selection draws on all three volumes; particulars will be found on the Contents page. *On the Deaths of Rev. John McGilchrist, John Brown and John Henderson*, 1860. *Health. Five Lay Sermons to Working People*, 1862.

LETTERS. Edited by J. Brown and D. W. Forrest, 1907.

BIOGRAPHY AND CRITICISM. A. Lang, 'Dr John Brown', in *Century Illustrated Monthly Magazine*, Feb. 1883; E. T. Maclaren, *Dr John Brown and his Sister, Isabella*, 1889; 1896 (as *Dr John Brown and his Sisters Isabella and Jane*); D. Masson, 'Dr John Brown', in *Edinburgh Sketches and Memories*, 1892; A. Peddie, *Recollections of Dr John Brown, with a Selection from his Correspondence*, 1893; J. T. Brown, *Dr John Brown. A Biography and a Criticism*, 1903; Frank Gent, 'Marjorie Fleming and Her Biographers', (*Scottish Historical Review*, Oct. 1947); Douglas Guthrie, *Janus in the Doorway*, 1963.

CONTENTS

" *If thou be a severe, sour-complexioned man, then I here disallow thee to be a competent judge.*"—IZAAK WALTON.

" *Non ulla nobis pagina gratior*
Quam quæ severis ludicra jungere
Novit, fatigatamque nugis
Utilibus recreare mentem."
DR. JOHNSON.

" *The treatment of the illustrious dead by the quick, often reminds me of the gravedigger in Hamlet, and the skull of poor defunct Yorick.*"—W. H. B.

" *A lady, resident in Devonshire, going into one of her parlours, discovered a young ass, who had found its way into the room, and carefully closed the door upon himself. He had evidently not been long in this situation before he had nibbled a part of Cicero's Orations, and eaten nearly all the index of a folio edition of Seneca in Latin, a large part of a volume of La Bruyère's Maxims in French, and several pages of Cecilia. He had done no other mischief whatever, and not a vestige remained of the leaves that he had devoured.*"—PIERCE EGAN.

" *Ce fagotage de tant si diverses pièces, se faict en cette condition: que je n'y mets la main, que lors qu'une trop lasche oysifveté me presse.*"—MICHEL DE MONTAIGNE.

" *Who made you?*" was asked of a small girl. She replied, " *God made me that length,*" indicating with her two hands the ordinary size of a new-born infant; " *and I growed the rest mysel'.*" This was before Topsy's time, and is wittier than even " *'Spects I growed,*" and not less philosophical than Descartes' nihil with Leibnitz's nisi as its rider.

RAB AND HIS FRIENDS

FOUR-AND-THIRTY years ago, Bob Ainslie and I were coming up Infirmary Street from the High School, our heads together, and our arms intertwisted, as only lovers and boys know how, or why.

When we got to the top of the street, and turned north, we espied a crowd at the Tron Church. " A dog-fight!" shouted Bob, and was off; and so was I, both of us all but praying that it might not be over before we got up! and is not this boy-nature? and human nature too? and don't we all wish a house on fire not to be out before we see it? Dogs like fighting; old Isaac says they " delight " in it, and for the best of all reasons; and boys are not cruel because they like to see the fight. They see three of the great cardinal virtues of dog or man— courage, endurance, and skill—in intense action. This is very different from a love of making dogs fight, and enjoying, and aggravating, and making gain by their pluck. A boy—be he ever so fond himself of fighting, if he be a good boy, hates and despises all this, but he would have run off with Bob and me fast enough: it is a natural, and a not wicked interest, that all boys and men have in witnessing intense energy in action.

Does any curious and finely-ignorant woman wish to know, how Bob's eye at a glance announced a dog-fight to his brain? He did not, he could not see the dogs fighting; it was a flash of an inference, a rapid induction. The crowd round a couple of dogs fighting, is a crowd, masculine mainly, with an occasional active, compassionate woman, fluttering wildly round the outside, and using her tongue

and her hands freely upon the men, as so many
"brutes;" it is a crowd annular, compact, and
mobile; a crowd centripetal, having its eyes and
its heads all bent downwards and inwards, to one
common focus.

Well, Bob and I are up, and find it is not over:
a small, thoroughbred, white bull-terrier, is busy
throttling a large shepherd's dog, unaccustomed to
war, but not to be trifled with.   They are hard at it;
the scientific little fellow doing his work in great
style, his pastoral enemy fighting wildly, but with
the sharpest of teeth and a great courage.   Science
and breeding, however, soon took their own; the
Game Chicken, as the premature Bob called him,
working his way up, took his final grip of poor
Yarrow's throat,—and he lay gasping and done for.
His master, a brown, handsome, big young shepherd
from Tweedsmuir, would have liked to have knocked
down any man, "drunk up Esil, or eaten a cro-
codile," for that part, if he had a chance: it was no
use kicking the little dog; that would only make him
hold the closer.   Many were the means shouted out
in mouthfuls, of the best possible ways of ending it.
"Water!" but there was none near, and many
shouted for it who might have got it from the well
at Blackfriars Wynd.   "Bite the tail!" and a large,
vague, benevolent, middle-aged man, more anxious
than wise, with some struggle got the bushy end
of *Yarrow's* tail into his ample mouth, and bit it
with all his might.   This was more than enough for
the much-enduring, much-perspiring shepherd, who,
with a gleam of joy over his broad visage, delivered
a terrific facer upon our large, vague, benevolent,
middle-aged friend,—who went down like a shot.

Still the Chicken holds; death not far off.   "Snuff!
a pinch of snuff!" observed sharply a calm, highly-
dressed young buck, with an eye-glass in his eye.
"Snuff, indeed!" growled the angry crowd, affronted
and glaring.   "Snuff! a pinch of snuff!" again
observes the buck, but with more urgency; whereon

were produced several open boxes, and from a mull which may have been at Culloden, he took a pinch, knelt down, and presented it to the nose of the Chicken. The laws of physiology and of snuff take their course; the Chicken sneezes, and Yarrow is free!

The young pastoral giant stalks off with Yarrow in his arms,—comforting him.

But the Chicken's blood is up, and his soul unsatisfied; he grips the first dog he meets, but discovering she is not a dog, in Homeric phrase, he makes a brief sort of *amende,* and is off. The boys, with Bob and me at their head, are after him; down Niddry Street he goes, bent on mischief; up the Cowgate like an arrow—Bob and I, and our small men, panting behind.

There, under the large arch of the South Bridge, is a huge mastiff, sauntering down the middle of the causeway, as if with his hands in his pockets : he is old, grey, brindled; as big as a little Highland bull, and has the Shakesperian dewlaps shaking as he goes.

The Chicken makes straight at him, and fastens on his throat. To our astonishment, the great creature does nothing but stand still, hold himself up, and roar—yes, roar; a long, serious, remonstrative roar. How is this? Bob and I are up to them. *He is muzzled!* The bailies had proclaimed a general muzzling, and his master, studying strength and economy mainly, had encompassed his huge jaws in a home-made apparatus, constructed out of the leather of some ancient *breechin.* His mouth was open as far as it could; his lips curled up in rage—a sort of terrible grin; his teeth gleaming, ready, from out the darkness; the strap across his mouth tense as a bowstring; his whole frame stiff with indignation and surprise; his roar asking us all round, "Did you ever see the like of this?" He looked a statue of anger and astonishment, done in Aberdeen granite.

We soon had a crowd: the Chicken held on.
"A knife!" cried Bob; and a cobbler gave him his
knife: you know the kind of knife, worn away
obliquely to a point, and always keen. I put its
edge to the tense leather; it ran before it; and then!
one sudden jerk of that enormous head, a sort of
dirty mist about his mouth, no noise,—and the bright
and fierce little fellow is dropped, limp, and dead.
A solemn pause; this was more than any of us had
bargained for. I turned the little fellow over, and
saw he was quite dead: the mastiff had taken him by
the small of the back like a rat, and broken it.

He looked down at his victim appeased, ashamed,
and amazed; snuffed him all over, stared at him, and
taking a sudden thought, turned round and trotted
off. Bob took the dead dog up, and said, "John,
we'll bury him after tea." "Yes," said I; and was
off after the mastiff. He made up the Cowgate at
a rapid swing: he had forgotten some engagement.
He turned up the Candlemaker Row, and stopped
at the Harrow Inn.

There was a carrier's cart ready to start, and a
keen, thin, impatient, black-a-vised little man, his
hand at his grey horse's head, looking about angrily
for something. "Rab, ye thief!" said he, aiming a
kick at my great friend, who drew cringing up, and
avoiding the heavy shoe with more agility than
dignity, and watching his master's eye, slunk dis-
mayed under the cart,—his ears down, and as much
as he had of tail down too.

What a man this must be—thought I—to whom
my tremendous hero turns tail! The carrier saw the
muzzle hanging, cut and useless, from his neck, and
I eagerly told him the story, which Bob and I always
thought, and still think, Homer, or King David, or
Sir Walter, alone were worthy to rehearse. The
severe little man was mitigated, and condescended
to say, "Rab, my man, puir Rabbie,"—whereupon
the stump of a tail rose up, the ears were cocked,
the eyes filled, and were comforted; the two friends

were reconciled. " Hupp !" and a stroke of the whip were given to Jess; and off went the three.

Bob and I buried the Game Chicken that night (we hadn't much of a tea) in the back-green of his house, in Melville Street, No. 17, with considerable gravity and silence; and being at the time in the Iliad, and, like all boys, Trojans, we called him, of course, Hector.

Six years have passed,—a long time for a boy and a dog : Bob Ainslie is off to the wars; I am a medical student, and clerk at Minto House Hospital.

Rab I saw almost every week, on the Wednesday; and we had much pleasant intimacy. I found the way to his heart by frequent scratching of his huge head, and an occasional bone. When I did not notice him he would plant himself straight before me, and stand wagging that bud of a tail, and looking up, with his head a little to the one side. His master I occasionally saw; he used to call me " Maister John," but was laconic as any Spartan.

One fine October afternoon, I was leaving the hospital, when I saw the large gate open, and in walked Rab, with that great and easy saunter of his. He looked as if taking general possession of the place; like the Duke of Wellington entering a sub-dued city, satiated with victory and peace. After him came Jess, now white from age, with her cart; and in it a woman, carefully wrapped up,—the carrier leading the horse anxiously, and looking back. When he saw me, James (for his name was James Noble) made a curt and grotesque " boo," and said, " Maister John, this is the mistress; she's got a trouble in her breest—some kind o' an income we're thinkin'."

By this time I saw the woman's face; she was sitting on a sack filled with straw, her husband's plaid round her, and his big-coat, with its large white metal buttons, over her feet. I never saw a more unforgetable face—pale, serious, *lonely*,[1] delicate, sweet, without being what we call fine. She looked sixty, and had on a mutch, white as snow, with its black ribbon; her silvery smooth hair setting off her dark-grey eyes—eyes such as one sees only twice or thrice in a lifetime, full of suffering, but full also of the overcoming of it; her eye-brows black and delicate, and her mouth firm, patient, and contented, which few mouths ever are.

As I have said, I never saw a more beautiful countenance, or one more subdued to settled quiet. "Ailie," said James, "this is Maister John, the young doctor; Rab's freend, ye ken. We often speak aboot you, doctor." She smiled, and made a movement, but said nothing; and prepared to come down, putting her plaid aside and rising. Had Solomon, in all his glory, been handing down the Queen of Sheba at his palace gate, he could not have done it more daintily, more tenderly, more like a gentleman, than did James the Howgate carrier, when he lifted down Ailie, his wife. The contrast of his small, swarthy, weatherbeaten, keen, worldly face to hers—pale, subdued, and beautiful—was something wonderful. Rab looked on concerned and puzzled, but ready for anything that might turn up,—were it to strangle the nurse, the porter, or even me. Ailie and he seemed great friends.

"As I was sayin', she's got a kind o' trouble in her breest, doctor; wull ye tak' a look at it?" We walked into the consulting-room, all four; Rab grim and comic, willing to be happy and confidential if cause could be shown, willing also to be quite the reverse, on the same terms. Ailie sat down, undid her open gown and her lawn handkerchief round her neck, and,

[1] It is not easy giving this look by one word; it was expressive of her being so much of her life alone.

without a word, showed me her right breast. I looked at and examined it carefully,—she and James watching me, and Rab eyeing all three. What could I say? there it was, that had once been so soft, so shapely, so white, so gracious and bountiful, " so full of all blessed conditions,"—hard as a stone, a centre of horrid pain, making that pale face, with its grey, lucid, reasonable eyes, and its sweet resolved mouth, express the full measure of suffering overcome. Why was that gentle, modest, sweet woman, clean and lovable, condemned by God to bear such a burden?

I got her away to bed. " May Rab and me bide?" said James. " *You* may; and Rab, if he will behave himself." " I'se warrant he's do that, doctor;" and in slunk the faithful beast. I wish you could have seen him. There are no such dogs now : he belonged to a lost tribe. As I have said, he was brindled, and grey like Aberdeen granite; his hair short, hard, and close, like a lion's; his body thick set, like a little bull —a sort of compressed Hercules of a dog. He must have been ninety pounds' weight, at the least; he had a large blunt head; his muzzle black as night; his mouth blacker than any night, a tooth or two—being all he had—gleaming out of his jaws of darkness. His head was scarred with the records of old wounds, a sort of series of fields of battle all over it; one eye out, one ear cropped as close as was Archbishop Leighton's father's—but for different reasons,— the remaining eye had the power of two; and above it, and in constant communication with it, was a tattered rag of an ear, which was for ever unfurling itself, like an old flag; and then that bud of a tail, about one inch long, if it could in any sense be said to be long, being as broad as long—the mobility, the instantaneousness of that bud was very funny and surprising, and its expressive twinklings and winkings, the intercommunications between the eye, the ear, and it, were of the subtlest and swiftest. Rab had the dignity and simplicity of great size; and having fought his way all along the road to absolute

supremacy, he was as mighty in his own line as Julius
Cæsar or the Duke of Wellington; and he had the
gravity [1] of all great fighters.

You must have often observed the likeness of certain men to certain animals, and of certain dogs to
men.   Now, I never looked at Rab without thinking
of the great Baptist preacher, Andrew Fuller.[2]   The
same large, heavy, menacing, combative, sombre,
honest countenance, the same inevitable eye, the same
look,—as of thunder asleep, but ready,—neither a
dog nor a man to be trifled with.

Next day, my master, the surgeon, examined Ailie.
There was no doubt it must kill her, and soon.   It
could be removed—it might never return—it would
give her speedy relief—she should have it done.   She
curtsied, looked at James, and said, " When?"   " To-
morrow," said the kind surgeon, a man of few words.
She and James and Rab and I retired.   I noticed
that he and she spoke little, but seemed to anticipate
everything in each other.   The following day, at noon,
the students came in, hurrying up the great stair.
At the first landing-place, on a small well-known
black board, was a bit of paper fastened by wafers,
and many remains of old wafers beside it.   On the
paper were the words, " An operation to-day. J. B.
Clerk."

---

[1] A Highland game-keeper, when asked why a certain
terrier, of singular pluck, was so much graver than the other
dogs, said, " Oh, Sir, life's full o' sairiousness to him—he
just never can get enuff o' fechtin'."

[2] Fuller was in early life, when a farmer lad at Soham,
famous as a boxer; not quarrelsome, but not without " the
stern delight " a man of strength and courage feels in the
exercise. Dr. Charles Stewart, of Dunearn, whose rare gifts
and graces as a physician, a divine, a scholar, and a gentleman, live only in the memory of those few who knew and
survive him, liked to tell how Mr. Fuller used to say, that
when he was in the pulpit, and saw a buirdly man, he would
instinctively draw himself up, measure his imaginary antagonist, and forecast how he would deal with him, his hands
meanwhile condensing into fists. He must have been a hard
hitter if he boxed as he preached—what " The Fancy " would
call " an ugly customer."

Up ran the youths, eager to secure good places: in they crowded, full of interest and talk. " What's the case?" " Which side is it?"

Don't think them heartless; they are neither better nor worse than you or I: they get over their professional horrors, and into their proper work; and in them pity—as an *emotion,* ending in itself or at best in tears and a long-drawn breath, lessens, while pity as a *motive,* is quickened, and gains power and purpose. It is well for poor human nature that it is so.

The operating theatre is crowded; much talk and fun, and all the cordiality and stir of youth. The surgeon with his staff of assistants is there. In comes Ailie: one look at her quiets and abates the eager students. That beautiful old woman is too much for them; they sit down, and are dumb, and gaze at her. These rough boys feel the power of her presence. She walks in quickly, but without haste; dressed in her mutch, her neckerchief, her white dimity shortgown, her black bombazeen petticoat, showing her white worsted stockings and her carpet-shoes. Behind her was James, with Rab. James sat down in the distance, and took that huge and noble head between his knees. Rab looked perplexed and dangerous; for ever cocking his ear and dropping it as fast.

Ailie stepped up on a seat, and laid herself on the table, as her friend the surgeon told her; arranged herself, gave a rapid look at James, shut her eyes, rested herself on me, and took my hand. The operation was at once begun; it was necessarily slow; and chloroform—one of God's best gifts to his suffering children—was then unknown. The surgeon did his work. The pale face showed its pain, but was still and silent. Rab's soul was working within him; he saw that something strange was going on,—blood flowing from his mistress, and she suffering; his ragged ear was up, and importunate; he growled and gave now and then a sharp impatient yelp; he would have liked to have done something to that man. But James had him firm, and gave him a glower from

time to time, and an intimation of a possible kick;—
all the better for James, it kept his eye and his mind
off Ailie.

It is over : she is dressed, steps gently and decently
down from the table, looks for James; then, turning
to the surgeon and the students, she curtsies,—and
in a low, clear voice, begs their pardon if she has behaved ill.   The students—all of us—wept like children; the surgeon happed her up carefully,—and,
resting on James and me, Ailie went to her room,
Rab following.   We put her to bed.   James took off
his heavy shoes, crammed with tackets, heel-capt and
toe-capt, and put them carefully under the table, saying, "Maister John, I'm for nane o' yer strynge nurse
bodies for Ailie.   I'll be her nurse, and on my stockin'
soles I'll gang about as canny as pussy."   And so he
did; and handy and clever, and swift and tender as
any woman, was that horny-handed, snell, peremptory
little man.   Everything she got he gave her : he seldom slept; and often I saw his small, shrewd eyes
out of the darkness, fixed on her.   As before, they
spoke little.

Rab behaved well, never moving, showing us how
meek and gentle he could be, and occasionally, in his
sleep, letting us know that he was demolishing some
adversary.   He took a walk with me every day, generally to the Candlemaker Row; but he was sombre
and mild; declined doing battle, though some fit cases
offered, and indeed submitted to sundry indignities;
and was always very ready to turn, and came faster
back, and trotted up the stair with much lightness,
and went straight to *that* door.

Jess, the mare—now white—had been sent, with
her weather-worn cart, to Howgate, and had doubtless
her own dim and placid meditations and confusions,
on the absence of her master and Rab, and her
unnatural freedom from the road and her cart.

For some days Ailie did well.   The wound healed
"by the first intention;" as James said, "Oor Ailie's
skin's ower clean to beil."   The students came in

quiet and anxious, and surrounded her bed. She said she liked to see their young, honest faces. The surgeon dressed her, and spoke to her in his own short kind way, pitying her through his eyes, Rab and James outside the circle,—Rab being now reconciled, and even cordial, and having made up his mind that as yet nobody required worrying, but, as you may suppose, *semper paratus.*

So far well: but, four days after the operation, my patient had a sudden and long shivering, a "groofin'," as she called it. I saw her soon after; her eyes were too bright, her cheek coloured; she was restless, and ashamed of being so; the balance was lost; mischief had begun. On looking at the wound, a blush of red told the secret: her pulse was rapid, her breathing anxious and quick, she wasn't herself, as she said, and was vexed at her restlessness. We tried what we could. James did everything, was everywhere; never in the way, never out of it; Rab subsided under the table into a dark place, and was motionless, all but his eye, which followed every one. Ailie got worse; began to wander in her mind, gently; was more demonstrative in her ways to James, rapid in her questions, and sharp at times. He was vexed, and said, " She was never that way afore; no, never." For a time she knew her head was wrong, and was always asking our pardon—the dear, gentle old woman: then delirium set in strong, without pause. Her brain gave way, and that terrible spectacle,

> " The intellectual power, through words and things,
>   Went sounding on its dim and perilous way;"

she sang bits of old songs and Psalms, stopping suddenly, mingling the Psalms of David, and the diviner words of his Son and Lord, with homely odds and ends and scraps of ballads.

Nothing more touching, or in a sense more strangely beautiful, did I ever witness. Her tremulous, rapid, affectionate, eager Scotch voice,—the swift, aimless, bewildered mind, the baffled utterance, the bright and perilous eye; some wild words, some household cares, something for James, the names of the dead, Rab called rapidly and in a "fremyt" voice, and he starting up, surprised, and slinking off as if he were to blame somehow, or had been dreaming he heard. Many eager questions and beseechings which James and I could make nothing of, and on which she seemed to set her all and then sink back ununderstood. It was very sad, but better than many things that are not called sad. James hovered about, put out and miserable, but active and exact as ever; read to her, when there was a lull, short bits from the Psalms, prose and metre, chanting the latter in his own rude and serious way, showing great knowledge of the fit words, bearing up like a man, and doating over her as his "ain Ailie." "Ailie, ma woman!" "Ma ain bonnie wee dawtie!"

The end was drawing on: the golden bowl was breaking; the silver cord was fast being loosed—that *animula, blandula, vagula, hospes, comesque,* was about to flee. The body and the soul—companions for sixty years—were being sundered, and taking leave. She was walking, alone, through the valley of that shadow, into which one day we must all enter, —and yet she was not alone, for we know whose rod and staff were comforting her.

One night she had fallen quiet, and as we hoped, asleep; her eyes were shut. We put down the gas, and sat watching her. Suddenly she sat up in bed, and taking a bedgown which was lying on it rolled up, she held it eagerly to her breast,—to the right side. We could see her eyes bright with a surprising tenderness and joy, bending over this bundle of clothes. She held it as a woman holds her sucking child; opening out her night-gown impatiently, and holding it close, and brooding over it, and murmuring foolish little words, as over one whom his mother comforteth, and who is sucking, and being satisfied. It was pitiful and strange to see her wasted dying look, keen and yet vague—her immense love. " Preserve me!" groaned James, giving way. And then she rocked back and forward, as if to make it sleep, hushing it, and wasting on it her infinite fondness. " Wae's me, doctor; I declare she's thinkin' it's that bairn." " What bairn?" " The only bairn we ever had; our wee Mysie, and she's in the Kingdom, forty years and mair." It was plainly true: the pain in the breast, telling its urgent story to a bewildered, ruined brain; it was misread and mistaken; it suggested to her the uneasiness of a breast full of milk, and then the child; and so again once more they were together, and she had her ain wee Mysie in her bosom.

This was the close. She sunk rapidly; the delirium left her; but as she whispered, she was clean silly; it was the lightening before the final darkness. After having for some time lain still—her eyes shut, she said " James!" He came close to her, and lifting up her calm, clear, beautiful eyes, she gave him a long look, turned to me kindly but shortly, looked for Rab but could not see him, then turned to her husband again, as if she would never leave off looking, shut her eyes, and composed herself. She lay for some time breathing quick, and passed away so gently, that when we thought she was gone, James, in his old-fashioned way, held the mirror to her face. After a long pause, one small spot of dimness was breathed out; it vanished away, and never returned, leaving the blank clear darkness of the mirror without a stain. " What is our life? it is even a vapour, which appeareth for a little time, and then vanisheth away."

Rab all this time had been full awake and motionless: he came forward beside us: Ailie's hand, which James had held, was hanging down; it was soaked with his tears; Rab licked it all over carefully, looked at her, and returned to his place under the table.

James and I sat, I don't know how long, but for some time,—saying nothing: he started up abruptly,

and with some noise went to the table, and putting
his right fore and middle fingers each into a shoe,
pulled them out, and put them on, breaking one of
the leather latchets, and muttering in anger, " I never
did the like o' that afore !"

I believe he never did ; nor after either.   " Rab !"
he said roughly, and pointing with his thumb to the
bottom of the bed.   Rab leapt up, and settled himself ; his head and eye to the dead face.   " Maister
John, ye'll wait for me," said the carrier ; and disappeared in the darkness, thundering down stairs in
his heavy shoes.   I ran to a front window : there
he was, already round the house, and out at the gate,
fleeing like a shadow.

I was afraid about him, and yet not afraid ; so I
sat down beside Rab, and being wearied, fell asleep.
I awoke from a sudden noise outside.   It was November, and there had been a heavy fall of snow.
Rab was in *statu quo ;* he heard the noise too, and
plainly knew it, but never moved.   I looked out ; and
there, at the gate, in the dim morning—for the sun
was not up, was Jess and the cart,—a cloud of steam
rising from the old mare.   I did not see James ; he
was already at the door, and came up the stairs, and
met me.   It was less than three hours since he left,
and he must have posted out—who knows how?—to
Howgate, full nine miles off ; yoked Jess, and driven
her astonished into town.   He had an armful of
blankets, and was streaming with perspiration.   He
nodded to me, spread out on the floor two pairs of
old clean blankets, having at their corners, " A. G.,
1794," in large letters in red worsted.   These were
the initials of Alison Græme, and James may have
looked in at her from without—unseen but not un-
thought of—when he was " wat, wat, and weary,"
and had walked many a mile over the hills, and seen
her sitting, while " a' the lave were sleepin' ;" and
by the firelight putting her name on the blankets for
her ain James's bed.   He motioned Rab down, and
taking his wife in his arms, laid her in the blankets,

and happed her carefully and firmly up, leaving the
face uncovered; and then lifting her, he nodded again
sharply to me, and with a resolved but utterly miserable face, strode along the passage, and down stairs,
followed by Rab.   I also followed, with a light; but
he didn't need it.   I went out, holding stupidly the
light in my hand in the frosty air; we were soon at the
gate.   I could have helped him, but I saw he was not
to be meddled with, and he was strong, and did not
need it.   He laid her down as tenderly, as safely,
as he had lifted her out ten days before—as tenderly
as when he had her first in his arms when she was
only " A. G.,''—sorted her, leaving that beautiful
sealed face open to the heavens; and then taking Jess
by the head, he moved away.   He did not notice me,
neither did Rab, who presided alone behind the cart.

I stood till they passed through the long shadow of
the College, and turned up Nicolson Street.   I heard
the solitary cart sound through the streets, and die
away and come again; and I returned, thinking of
that company going up Libberton brae, then along
Roslin muir, the morning light touching the Pentlands and making them like on-looking ghosts; then
down the hill through Auchindinny woods, past
" haunted Woodhouselee;'' and as daybreak came
sweeping up the bleak Lammermuirs, and fell on his
own door, the company would stop, and James would
take the key, and lift Ailie up again, laying her on
her own bed, and, having put Jess up, would return
with Rab and shut the door.

James buried his wife, with his neighbours mourning, Rab inspecting the solemnity from a distance.
It was snow, and that black ragged hole would look
strange in the midst of the swelling spotless cushion
of white.   James looked after everything; then rather
suddenly fell ill, and took to bed; was insensible when
the doctor came, and soon died.   A sort of low fever
was prevailing in the village, and his want of sleep,
his exhaustion, and his misery, made him apt to take
it.   The grave was not difficult to re-open.   A fresh

fall of snow had again made all things white and
smooth; Rab once more looked on, and slunk home
to the stable.

And what of Rab? I asked for him next week at
the new carrier's who got the goodwill of James's
business, and was now master of Jess and her cart.
"How's Rab?" He put me off, and said rather
rudely, "What's *your* business wi' the dowg?" I
was not to be so put off. "Where's Rab?" He, getting confused and red, and intermeddling with his
hair, said, "'Deed, sir, Rab's deid." "Dead! what
did he die of?" "Weel, sir," said he, getting redder,
"he didna exactly die; he was killed. I had to brain
him wi' a rack-pin; there was nae doin' wi' him. He
lay in the treviss wi' the mear, and wadna come oot.
I tempit him wi' kail and meat, but he wad tak'
naething, and keepit me frae feedin' the beast, and
he was aye gur gurrin', and grup gruppin' me by the
legs. I was laith to mak' awa wi' the auld dowg,
his like wasna atween this and Thornhill,—but 'deed,
sir, I could do naething else." I believed him. Fit
end for Rab, quick and complete. His teeth and his
friends gone, why should he keep the peace and be
civil?

DICK *MIHI*, OR *CUR*, WHY?

Being vestiges of the Natural History of the Creation of a Highland Terrier; with a new rendering of "*de cespite vivo*," and a theory of BLACK and TAN.

"The reader must remember that my work is concerning the aspects of things only."—RUSKIN.

THE MYSTERY OF BLACK
AND TAN

We,—the *Sine Quâ Non*, the Duchess, the Sput-chard, the Dutchard, the Ricapicticapic, Oz and Oz, the Maid of Lorn, and myself,—left Crieff some fifteen years ago, on a bright September morning, soon after daybreak, in a gig. It was a morning still and keen : the sun sending his level shafts across Strathearn, and through the thin mist over its river hollows, to the fierce Aberuchil Hills, and searching out the dark blue shadows in the corries of Benvor-lich. But who and how many are " we "? To make you as easy as we all were, let me tell you we were four ; and are not these dumb friends of ours persons rather than things? is not their soul ampler, as Plato would say, than their body, and contains rather than is contained? Is not what lives and wills in them, and is affectionate, as spiritual, as immaterial, as truly removed from mere flesh, blood, and bones, as that soul which is the proper self of their master? And when we look each other in the face, as I now look in Dick's, who is lying in his " corny " by the fireside, and he in mine, is it not as much the dog within looking from out his eyes—the windows of his soul—as it is the man from his?

The *Sine Quâ Non*, who will not be pleased at being spoken of, is such an one as that vain-glorious and chivalrous Ulric von Hütten—the Reformation's man of wit, and of the world, and of the sword, who slew Monkery with the wild laughter of his *Epistolæ Obscurorum Virorum*—had in his mind when he wrote thus to his friend Fredericus Piscator (Mr. Fred. Fisher), on the 19th May, 1519, " *Da mihi*

51

uxorem, Friderice, et ut scias qualem, venustam, adolescentulam, probe educatam, hilarem, verecundam, patientem." "*Qualem,*" he lets Frederic understand in the sentence preceding, is one "*quâ cum ludam, quâ jocos conferam, amœniores et leviusculas fabulas misceam, ubi sollicitudinis aciem obtundam, curarum œstus mitigem.*" And if you would know more of the *Sine Quâ Non*, and in English, for the world is dead to Latin now, you will find her name and nature in Shakspere's words, when King Henry the Eighth says, "go thy ways."

The Duchess, alias all the other names till you come to the *Maid of Lorn*, is a rough, gnarled, incomparable little bit of a terrier, three parts Dandie-Dinmont, and one part—chiefly in tail and hair—cocker: her father being Lord Rutherfurd's famous "Dandie," and her mother the daughter of a Skye, and a lighthearted Cocker. The Duchess is about the size and weight of a rabbit; but has a soul as big, as fierce, and as faithful as had Meg Merrilees, with a nose as black as Topsy's; and is herself every bit as game and queer as that delicious imp of darkness and of Mrs. Stowe. Her legs set her long slim body about two inches and a half from the ground, making her very like a huge caterpillar or hairy *oobit*—her two eyes, dark and full, and her shining nose, being all of her that seems anything but hair. Her tail was a sort of stump, in size and in look very much like a spare fore-leg, stuck in anywhere to be near. Her colour was black above and a rich brown below, with two dots of tan above the eyes, which dots are among the deepest of the mysteries of Black and Tan.

This strange little being I had known for some years, but had only possessed about a month. She and her pup (a young lady called *Smoot*, which means smolt, a young salmon), were given me by the widow of an honest and drunken—as much of the one as of the other—Edinburgh street-porter, a native of Badenoch, as a legacy from him and a fee from her for my attendance on the poor man's deathbed. But my first sight of the Duchess was years before in Broughton Street, when I saw her sitting bolt upright, begging, imploring, with those little rough fore leggies, and those yearning, beautiful eyes, all the world, or any one, to help her master, who was lying " mortal " in the kennel. I raised him, and with the help of a ragged Samaritan, who was only less drunk than he, I got Macpherson—he held from Glen Truim—home; the excited doggie trotting off, and looking back eagerly to show us the way. I never again passed the Porters' Stand without speaking to her. After Malcolm's burial I took possession of her; she escaped to the wretched house, but as her mistress was off to Kingussie, and the door shut, she gave a pitiful howl or two, and was forthwith back at my door, with an impatient, querulous bark. And so this is our second of the four; and is she not deserving of as many names as any other Duchess, from her of Medina Sidonia downwards?

A fierier little soul never dwelt in a queerer or stancher body : see her huddled up, and you would think her a bundle of hair, or a bit of old mossy wood, or a slice of heathery turf, with some red soil underneath; but speak to her, or give her a cat to deal with, be it bigger than herself, and what an incarnation of affection, energy, and fury—what a fell unquenchable little ruffian !

The Maid of Lorn was a chestnut mare, a broken-down racer, thoroughbred as Beeswing, but less fortunate in her life, and I fear not so happy *occasione mortis:* unlike the Duchess, her body was greater and finer than her soul; still she was a ladylike creature, sleek, slim, nervous, meek, willing, and fleet. She had been thrown down by some brutal half-drunk Forfarshire laird, when he put her wildly and with her wind gone, at the last hurdle on the North Inch at the Perth races. She was done for, and bought for ten pounds by the landlord of the Drummond Arms, Crieff, who had been taking as

much money out of her, and putting as little corn
into her as was compatible with life, purposing to
run her for the Consolation Stakes at Stirling. Poor
young lady, she was a sad sight—broken in back, in
knees, in character, and wind—in everything but
temper, which was as sweet and all-enduring as
Penelope's or our own Enid's.

Of myself, the fourth, I decline making any
account. Be it sufficient that I am the Dutchard's
master, and drove the gig.

It was, as I said, a keen and bright morning, and
the S. Q. N. feeling chilly, and the Duchess being
away after a cat up a back entry, doing a chance
stroke of business, and the mare looking only half
breakfasted, I made them give her a full feed of meal
and water, and stood by and enjoyed her enjoyment.
It seemed too good to be true, and she looked up
every now and then in the midst of her feast, with a
mild wonder. Away she and I bowled down the
sleeping village, all overrun with sunshine, the dumb
idiot man and the birds alone up, for the ostler was
off to his straw. There was the S. Q. N. and her
small panting friend, who had lost the cat, but had
got what philosophers say is better—the chase.
"*Nous ne cherchons jamais les choses, mais la re-
cherche des choses,*" says Pascal. The Duchess
would substitute for *les choses—les chats.* Pursuit,
not possession, was her passion. We all got in, and
off set the Maid, who was in excellent heart, quite
gay, pricking her ears and casting up her head, and
rattling away at a great pace.

We baited at St. Fillans, and again cheered the
heart of the Maid with unaccustomed corn—the
S. Q. N., Duchie, and myself, going up to the beautiful rising ground at the back of the inn, and lying
on the fragrant heather, looking at the Loch, with
its mild gleams and shadows, and its second heaven
looking out from its depths, the wild, rough mountains of Glenartney towering opposite. Duchie, I
believe, was engaged in minor business close at hand,

and caught and ate several large flies and a humble-bee; she was very fond of this small game.

There is not in all Scotland, or as far as I have seen in all else, a more exquisite twelve miles of scenery than that between Crieff and the head of Lochearn. Ochtertyre, and its woods; Benchonzie, the head-quarters of the earthquakes, only lower than Benvorlich; Strowan; Lawers, with its grand old Scotch pines; Comrie, with the wild Lednoch; Dunira; and St. Fillans, where we are now lying, and where the poor thoroughbred is tucking in her corn. We start after two hours of dreaming in the half sunlight, and rumble ever and anon over an earthquake, as the common folk call these same hollow, resounding rifts in the rock beneath, and arriving at the old inn at Lochearnhead, have a *tousie* tea. In the evening, when the day was darkening into night, Duchie and I,—the S. Q. N. remaining to read and rest,—walked up Glen Ogle. It was then in its primeval state, the new road non-existent, and the old one staggering up and down and across that most original and Cyclopean valley, deep, threatening, savage, and yet beautiful—

> " Where rocks were rudely heaped, and rent
> As by a spirit turbulent;
> Where sights were rough, and sounds were wild,
> And everything unreconciled;"

with flocks of mighty boulders, straying all over it. Some far up, and frightful to look at, others huddled down in the river, *immane pecus*, and one huge unloosened fellow, as big as a manse, up aloft watching them, like old Proteus with his calves, as if they had fled from the sea by stress of weather, and had been led by their ancient herd *altos visere montes*— a wilder, more "unreconciled" place I know not; and now that the darkness was being poured into it, those big fellows looked bigger, and hardly "canny."

Just as we were turning to come home—Duchie unwillingly, as she had much multifarious, and as usual fruitless hunting to do—she and I were startled by seeing a dog *in* the side of the hill, where the soil had been broken. She barked and I stared; she trotted consequentially up and snuffed *more canino*, and I went nearer : it never moved, and on coming quite close I saw as it were the *image* of a terrier, a something that made me think of an idea *un*realized; the rough, short, scrubby heather and dead grass, made a colour and a coat just like those of a good Highland terrier—a sort of pepper and salt this one was—and below, the broken soil, in which there was some iron and clay, with old gnarled roots, for all the world like its odd, bandy, and sturdy legs. Duchie seemed not so easily unbeguiled as I was, and kept staring, and snuffing, and growling, but did not touch it,—seemed afraid. I left and looked again, and certainly it was very odd the *growing* resemblance to one of the indigenous, hairy, low-legged dogs, one sees all about the Highlands, terriers, or earthy ones.

We came home, and I told the S. Q. N. our joke. I dreamt of that visionary terrier, that son of the soil, all night; and in the very early morning, leaving the S. Q. N. asleep, I walked up with the Duchess to the same spot. What a morning ! it was before sun-rise, at least before he had got above Benvorlich. The loch was lying in a faint mist, beautiful exceedingly, as if half veiled and asleep, the cataract of Edinample roaring less loudly than in the night, and the old castle of the Lords of Lochow, in the shadow of the hills, among its trees, might be seen

"Sole sitting by the shore of old romance."

There was still gloom in Glen Ogle, though the beams of the morning were shooting up into the broad fields of the sky. I was looking back and down, when I heard the Duchess bark sharply, and then give a cry of fear, and on turning round, there was she with as much as she had of tail between her legs, where I never saw it before, and her small Grace, without noticing me or my cries, making down

to the inn and her mistress, a hairy hurricane. I
walked on to see what it was, and there in the same
spot as last night, in the bank, was a real dog—no
mistake; it was not, as the day before, a mere surface or *spectrum*, or ghost of a dog; it was plainly
round and substantial; it was much developed since
eight P.M. As I looked, it moved slightly, and as it
were by a sort of shiver, as if an electric shock (and
why not?) was being administered by a law of nature;
it had then no tail, or rather had an odd amorphous look
in that region; its eye, for it had one—it was seen
in profile—looked to my profane vision like (why not
actually?) a huge blaeberry (*vaccinium Myrtillius*, it is
well to be scientific) black and full; and I thought,—
but dare not be sure, and had no time or courage to
be minute,—that where the nose should be, there
was a small shining black snail, probably the *Limax
niger* of M. de Férussac, curled up, and if you look
at any dog's nose you will be struck with the typical
resemblance, in the corrugations and moistness and
jetty blackness of the one to the other, and of the
other to the one. He was a strongly-built, wiry,
bandy, and short-legged dog. As I was staring upon
him, a beam—Oh, first creative beam !—sent from
the sun—

> " Like as an arrow from a bow,
>   Shot by an archer strong "—

as he looked over Benvorlich's shoulder, and piercing a cloudlet of mist which clung close to him, and
filling it with whitest radiance, struck upon that eye
or berry, and lit up that nose or snail : in an instant
he sneezed (the *nisus* (*sneezus?*) *formativus* of the
ancients); that eye quivered and was quickened, and
with a shudder —such as a horse executes with that
curious muscle of the skin, of which we have a mere
fragment in our neck, the *Platysma Myoides*, and
which doubtless has been lessened as we lost our distance from the horse-type—which dislodged some dirt
and stones and dead heather, and doubtless endless
beetles, and, it may be, made some near weasel open

his other eye, up went his tail, and out he came, lively, entire, consummate, *warm*, wagging his tail, I was going to say like a Christian, I mean like an ordinary dog. Then flashed upon me the solution of the *Mystery of Black and Tan* in all its varieties: the body, its upper part grey or black or yellow, according to the upper soil and herbs, heather, bent, moss, etc.; the belly and feet, red or tan or light fawn, according to the nature of the deep soil, be it ochrey, ferruginous, light clay, or comminuted mica slate. And wonderfullest of all, the DOTS of TAN above the eyes—and who has not noticed and wondered as to the philosophy of them?—*I saw made* by the two fore feet, wet and clayey, being put briskly up to his eyes as he sneezed that genetic, vivifying sneeze, and leaving their mark, for ever.

He took to me quite pleasantly, by virtue of "natural selection," and has accompanied me thus far in our "struggle for life," and he, and the S. Q. N., and the Duchess, and the Maid, returned that day to Crieff, and were friends all our days. I was a little timid when he was crossing a burn lest he should wash away his feet, but he merely coloured the water, and every day less and less, till in a fortnight I could wash him without fear of his becoming a *solution*, or fluid extract of dog, and thus resolving the mystery back into itself.

The mare's days were short. She won the Consolation Stakes at Stirling, and was found dead next morning in Gibb's stables. The Duchess died in a good old age, as may be seen in the history of "Our Dogs." The S. Q. N., and the parthenogenesic earth-born, the *Cespes Vivus*—whom we sometimes called Joshua, because he was the Son of None (Nun), and even Melchisedec has been whispered, but only that, and Fitz-Memnon, as being as it were a son of the Sun, sometimes the Autochthon αὐτόχθονος; (indeed, if the relation of the *coup de soleil* and the blaeberry had not been plainly causal and effectual, I might have called him *Filius Gunni*, for at the very moment of that shudder, by which he leapt out of non-life into life, the Marquis's gamekeeper fired his rifle up the hill, and brought down a stray young stag,) these two are happily with me still, and at this moment she is out on the grass in a low easy-chair, reading Emilie Carlen's *Brilliant Marriage*, and Dick is lying at her feet, watching, with cocked ears, some noise in the ripe wheat, possibly a chicken, for, poor fellow, he has a weakness for worrying hens, and such small deer, when there is a dearth of greater. If any, as is not unreasonable, doubt me and my story, they may come and see Dick. I assure them he is well worth seeing.

OUR DOGS

.

"The misery of keeping a dog, is his dying so soon; but to be sure, if he lived for fifty years, and then died, what would become of me?"—Sir Walter Scott.

"There is in every animal's eye a dim image and gleam of humanity, a flash of strange light through which their life looks out and up to our great mystery of command over them, and claims the fellowship of the creature if not of the soul."—Ruskin.

OUR DOGS

I was bitten severely by a little dog when with my mother at Moffat Wells, being then three years of age, and I have remained " bitten " ever since in the matter of dogs. I remember that little dog, and can at this moment not only recall my pain and terror —I have no doubt I was to blame—but also her face; and were I allowed to search among the shades in the cynic Elysian fields, I could pick her out still. All my life I have been familiar with these faithful creatures, making friends of them, and speaking to them; and the only time I ever addressed the public, about a year after being bitten, was at the farm of Kirklaw Hill, near Biggar, when the text, given out from an empty cart in which the ploughmen had placed me, was " Jacob's dog," and my entire sermon was as follows :—" Some say that Jacob had a black dog (the *o* very long), and some say that Jacob had a white dog, but *I* (imagine the presumption of four years !) say Jacob had a brown dog, and a brown dog it shall be."

I had many intimacies from this time onwards— Bawtie, of the inn; Keeper, the carrier's bull-terrier; Tiger, a huge tawny mastiff from Edinburgh, which I think must have been an uncle of Rab's; all the sheep dogs at Callands—Spring, Mavis, Yarrow, Swallow, Cheviot, &c.; but it was not till I was at college, and my brother at the High School, that we possessed a dog.

TOBY

Was the most utterly shabby, vulgar, mean-looking cur I ever beheld : in one word, *a tyke*. He had

not one good feature except his teeth and eyes, and
his bark, if that can be called a feature. He was
not ugly enough to be interesting; his colour black
and white, his shape leggy and clumsy; altogether
what Sydney Smith would have called an extraordinarily ordinary dog : and, as I have said, not even
greatly ugly, or, as the Aberdonians have it, *bonnie
wi' illfauredness*. My brother William found him
the centre of attraction to a multitude of small black-
guards who were drowning him slowly in Lochend
Loch, doing their best to lengthen out the process,
and secure the greatest amount of fun with the
nearest approach to death. Even then Toby showed
his great intellect by pretending to be dead, and thus
gaining time and an inspiration. William bought
him for twopence, and as he had it not, the boys
accompanied him to Pilrig Street, when I happened
to meet him, and giving the twopence to the biggest
boy, had the satisfaction of seeing a general engagement of much severity, during which the twopence disappeared; one penny going off with a very
small and swift boy, and the other vanishing hopelessly into the grating of a drain.

Toby was for weeks in the house unbeknown to
any one but ourselves two and the cook, and from
my grandmother's love of tidiness and hatred of dogs
and of dirt, I believe she would have expelled " him
whom we saved from drowning," had not he, in
his straightforward way, walked into my father's
bedroom one night when he was bathing his feet, and
introduced himself with a wag of his tail, intimating
a general willingness to be happy. My father
laughed most heartily, and at last Toby, having got
his way to his bare feet, and having begun to lick
his soles and between his toes with his small rough
tongue, my father gave such an unwonted shout of
laughter, that we—grandmother, sisters, and all of
us—went in. Grandmother might argue with all
her energy and skill, but as surely as the pressure of
Tom Jones' infantile fist upon Mr. Allworthy's fore-

finger undid all the arguments of his sister, so did Toby's tongue and fun prove too many for grandmother's eloquence. I somehow think Toby must have been up to all this, for I think he had a peculiar love for my father ever after, and regarded grandmother from that hour with a careful and cool eye.

Toby, when full grown, was a strong, coarse dog: coarse in shape, in countenance, in hair, and in manner. I used to think that, according to the Pythagorean doctrine, he must have been, or been going to be a Gilmerton carter. He was of the bull-terrier variety, coarsened through much mongrelism and a dubious and varied ancestry. His teeth were good, and he had a large skull, and a rich bark as of a dog three times his size, and a tail which I never saw equalled—indeed it was a tail *per se;* it was of immense girth and not short, equal throughout like a policeman's baton; the machinery for working it was of great power, and acted in a way, as far as I have been able to discover, quite original. We called it his ruler.

When he wished to get into the house, he first whined gently, then growled, then gave a sharp bark, and then came a resounding, mighty stroke which shook the house; this, after much study and watching, we found was done by his bringing the entire length of his solid tail flat upon the door, with a sudden and vigorous stroke; it was quite a *tour de force* or a *coup de queue*, and he was perfect in it at once, his first *bang* authoritative, having been as masterly and telling as his last.

With all this inbred vulgar air, he was a dog of great moral excellence—affectionate, faithful, honest up to his light, with an odd humour as peculiar and as strong as his tail. My father, in his reserved way, was very fond of him, and there must have been very funny scenes with them, for we heard bursts of laughter issuing from his study when they two were by themselves : there was something in him that took that grave, beautiful, melancholy face.

One can fancy him in the midst of his books, and sacred work and thoughts, pausing and looking at the secular Toby, who was looking out for a smile to begin his rough fun, and about to end by coursing and *gurrin'* round the room, upsetting my father's books, laid out on the floor for consultation, and himself nearly at times, as he stood watching him —and off his guard and shaking with laughter. Toby had always a great desire to accompany my father up to town; this my father's good taste and sense of dignity, besides his fear of losing his friend (a vain fear!), forbade, and as the decision of character of each was great and nearly equal, it was often a drawn game. Toby ultimately, by making it his entire object, triumphed. He usually was nowhere to be seen on my father leaving; he however saw him, and lay in wait at the head of the street, and up Leith Walk he kept him in view from the opposite side like a detective, and then, when he knew it was hopeless to hound him home, he crossed unblushingly over, and joined company, excessively rejoiced of course.

One Sunday he had gone with him to church, and left him at the vestry door. The second psalm was given out, and my father was sitting back in the pulpit, when the door at its back, up which he came from the vestry, was seen to move, and gently open, then, after a long pause, a black shining snout pushed its way steadily into the congregation, and was followed by Toby's entire body. He looked somewhat abashed, but snuffing his friend, he advanced as if on thin ice, and not seeing him, put his fore-legs on the pulpit, and behold there he was, his own familiar chum. I watched all this, and anything more beautiful than his look of happiness, of comfort, of entire ease when he beheld his friend,— the smoothing down of the anxious ears, the swing of gladness of that mighty tail,—I don't expect soon to see. My father quietly opened the door, and Toby was at his feet and invisible to all but himself : had he sent old George Peaston, the "minister's man," to put him out, Toby would probably have shown his teeth, and astonished George. He slunk home as soon as he could, and never repeated that exploit.

I never saw in any other dog the sudden transition from discretion, not to say abject cowardice, to blazing and permanent valour. From his earliest years he showed a general meanness of blood, inherited from many generations of starved, bekicked, and down-trodden forefathers and mothers, resulting in a condition of intense abjectness in all matters of personal fear; anybody, even a beggar, by a *gowl* and a threat of eye, could send him off howling by anticipation, with that mighty tail between his legs. But it was not always so to be, and I had the privilege of seeing courage, reasonable, absolute, and for life, spring up in Toby at once, as did Athené from the skull of Jove. It happened thus :—

Toby was in the way of hiding his culinary bones in the small gardens before his own and the neighbouring doors. Mr. Scrymgeour, two doors off, a bulky, choleric, red-haired, red-faced man—*torvo vultu*—was, by the law of contrast, a great cultivator of flowers, and he had often scowled Toby into all but non-existence by a stamp of his foot and a glare of his eye. One day his gate being open, in walks Toby with a huge bone, and making a hole where Scrymgeour had two minutes before been planting some precious slip, the name of which on paper and on a stick Toby made very light of, substituted his bone, and was engaged covering it, or thinking he was covering it up with his shovelling nose (a very odd relic of paradise in the dog), when S. spied him through the inner glass door, and was out upon him like the Assyrian, with a terrific *gowl*. I watched them. Instantly Toby made straight at him with a roar too, and an eye more torve than Scrymgeour's, who, retreating without reserve, fell prostrate, there is reason to believe, in his own lobby. Toby contented himself with proclaiming his victory at the

door, and returning finished his bone planting at his
leisure; the enemy, who had scuttled behind the glass-
door, glaring at him.

From this moment Toby was an altered dog. Pluck
at first sight was lord of all; from that time dated
his first tremendous deliverance of tail against the
door, which we called "come listen to my tail."
That very evening he paid a visit to Leo, next door's
dog, a big, tyrannical bully and coward, which its
master thought a Newfoundland, but whose pedigree
we knew better; this brute continued the same
system of chronic extermination which was inter-
rupted at Lochend,—having Toby down among his
feet, and threatening him with instant death two or
three times a day. To him Toby paid a visit that
very evening, down into his den, and walked about,
as much as to say "Come on, Macduff!" but Macduff did not come on, and henceforward there was an
armed neutrality, and they merely stiffened up and
made their backs rigid, pretended each not to see
the other, walking solemnly round, as is the manner
of dogs. Toby worked his new-found faculty
thoroughly, but with discretion. He killed cats,
astonished beggars, kept his own in his own garden
against all comers, and came off victorious in several
well-fought battles; but he was not quarrelsome or
foolhardy. It was very odd how his carriage
changed, holding his head up, and how much
pleasanter he was at home. To my father, next to
William, who was his Humane Society man, he remained stanch. And what of his end? for the misery
of dogs is that they die so soon, or as Sir Walter
says, it is well they do; for if they lived as long as
a Christian, and we liked them in proportion, and
they then died, he said that was a thing he could not
stand.

His exit was miserable, and had a strange poetic
or tragic relation to his entrance. My father was
out of town; I was away in England. Whether it
was that the absence of my father had relaxed his

power of moral restraint, or whether through neglect of the servant he had been desperately hungry, or most likely both being true, Toby was discovered with the remains of a cold leg of mutton, on which he had made an ample meal;[1] this he was in vain endeavouring to plant as of old, in the hope of its remaining undiscovered till to-morrow's hunger returned, the whole shank bone sticking up unmistakably. This was seen by our excellent and Radamanthine grandmother, who pronounced sentence on the instant; and next day, as William was leaving for the High School, did he in the sour morning, through an easterly *haur*, behold him " whom he saved from drowning," and whom, with better results than in the case of Launce and Crab, he had taught, as if one should say " thus would I teach a dog,"—dangling by his own chain from his own lamp-post, one of his hind feet just touching the pavement, and his body preternaturally elongated.

William found him dead and warm, and falling in with the milk-boy at the head of the street, questioned him, and discovered that he was the executioner, and had got twopence, he—Toby's every morning's crony, who met him and accompanied him up the street, and licked the outside of his can— had, with an eye to speed and convenience, and a want of taste, not to say principle and affection, horrible still to think of, suspended Toby's animation beyond all hope. William instantly fell upon him, upsetting his milk and cream, and gave him a thorough licking, to his own intense relief ; and, being late, he got from Pyper, who was a martinet, the customary palmies, which he bore with something approaching to pleasure. So died Toby: my father said little, but he missed and mourned his friend.

There is reason to believe that by one of those

---

[1] Toby was in the state of the shepherd boy whom George Webster met in Glenshee, and asked, " My man, were you ever fou'?" " Ay, aince "—speaking slowly, as if remembering—" Ay, aince." " What on?" " Cauld mutton !"

curious intertwistings of existence, the milk-boy was that one of the drowning party who got the penny of the twopence.

WYLIE

Our next friend was an exquisite shepherd's dog; fleet, thin-flanked, dainty, and handsome as a small greyhound, with all the grace of silky waving black and tan hair. We got him thus. Being then young and keen botanists, and full of the knowledge and love of Tweedside, having been on every hill top from Muckle Mendic to Hundleshope and the Lee Pen, and having fished every water from Tarth to the Leithen, we discovered early in spring that young Stewart, author of an excellent book on natural history, a young man of great promise and early death, had found the *Buxbaumia aphylla*, a beautiful and odd-looking moss, west of Newbie heights, in the very month we were that moment in. We resolved to start next day. We walked to Peebles, and then up Haystoun Glen to the cottage of Adam Cairns, the aged shepherd of the Newbie hirsel, of whom we knew, and who knew of us from his daughter, Nancy Cairns, a servant with Uncle Aitken of Callands. We found our way up the burn with difficulty, as the evening was getting dark; and on getting near the cottage heard them at worship. We got in, and made ourselves known, and got a famous tea, and such cream and oat cake!—old Adam looking on us as " clean dementit " to come out for " a bit moss," which, however, he knew, and with some pride said he would take us in the morning to the place. As we were going into a box bed for the night, two young men came in, and said they were " gaun to burn the water." Off we set. It was a clear, dark, starlight, frosty night. They had their leisters and tar torches, and it was something worth seeing— the wild flame, the young fellows striking the fish coming to the light—how splendid they looked with the light on their scales, coming out of the darkness —the stumblings and quenchings suddenly of the lights, as the torch-bearer fell into a deep pool. We got home past midnight, and slept as we seldom sleep now. In the morning Adam, who had been long up, and had been up the " *Hope* " with his dog, when he saw we had wakened, told us there was four inches of snow, and we soon saw it was too true. So we had to go home without our cryptogamic prize.

It turned out that Adam, who was an old man and frail, and had made some money, was going at Whitsunday to leave, and live with his son in Glasgow. We had been admiring the beauty and gentleness and perfect shape of Wylie, the finest colley I ever saw, and said, " What are you going to do with Wylie?" " 'Deed," says he, " I hardly ken. I canna think o' selling her, though she's worth four pound, and she'll no like the toun." I said, " Would you let me have her?" and Adam, looking at her fondly—she came up instantly to him, and made of him—said, " Ay, I wull, if ye'll be gude to her;" and it was settled that when Adam left for Glasgow she should be sent into Albany Street by the carrier.

She came, and was at once taken to all our hearts, even grandmother liked her; and though she was often pensive, as if thinking of her master and her work on the hills, she made herself at home, and behaved in all respects like a lady. When out with me, if she saw sheep in the streets or road, she got quite excited, and helped the work, and was curiously useful, the being so making her wonderfully happy. And so her little life went on, never doing wrong, always blithe and kind and beautiful. But some months after she came, there was a mystery about her : every Tuesday evening she disappeared; we tried to watch her, but in vain, she was always off by nine P.M., and was away all night, coming back next day wearied and all over mud, as if she had travelled far. She slept all next day. This went on for some months and we could make nothing of it. Poor dear creature, she looked at us wistfully when she came in, as if she would have told us if she could, and was especially fond, though tired.

Well, one day I was walking across the Grass-market, with Wylie at my heels, when two shepherds started, and looking at her, one said, " That's her; that's the wonderfu' wee bitch that naebody kens." I asked him what he meant, and he told me that for months past she had made her appearance by the first daylight at the " buchts " or sheep pens in the cattle market, and worked incessantly, and to excellent purpose, in helping the shepherds to get their sheep and lambs in. The man said with a sort of transport, " She's a perfect meeracle; flees about like a speerit, and never gangs wrang; wears but never grups, and beats a' oor dowgs. She's a perfect meeracle, and as soople as a maukin." Then he related how they all knew her, and said, " There's that wee fell yin; we'll get them in noo." They tried to coax her to stop and be caught, but no, she was gentle, but off; and for many a day that " wee fell yin " was spoken of by these rough fellows. She continued this amateur work till she died, which she did in peace.

It is very touching the regard the south-country shepherds have to their dogs. Professor Syme one day, many years ago, when living in Forres Street, was looking out of his window, and he saw a young shepherd striding down North Charlotte Street, as if making for his house : it was midsummer. The man had his dog with him, and Mr. Syme noticed that he followed the dog, and not it him, though he contrived to steer for the house. He came, and was ushered into his room; he wished advice about some ailment, and Mr. Syme saw that he had a bit of twine round the dog's neck, which he let drop out of his hand when he entered the room. He asked him the meaning of this, and he explained that the magistrates had issued a mad-dog proclamation, commanding all dogs to be muzzled or led on pain of death. "And why do you go about as I saw you did before you came in to me?" "Oh," said he, looking awkward, "I didna want Birkie to ken he was tied." Where will you find truer courtesy and finer feeling? He didn't want to hurt Birkie's feelings.

Mr. Carruthers of Inverness told me a new story of these wise sheep dogs. A butcher from Inverness had purchased some sheep at Dingwall, and giving them in charge to his dog, left the road. The dog drove them on, till coming to a toll, the toll-wife stood before the drove, demanding her dues. The dog looked at her, and, jumping on her back, crossed his fore-legs over her arms. The sheep passed through, and the dog took his place behind them, and went on his way.

RAB

Of Rab I have little to say, indeed have little right to speak of him as one of "our dogs;" but nobody will be sorry to hear anything of that noble fellow. Ailie, the day or two after the operation, when she was well and cheery, spoke about him, and said she would tell me fine stories when I came out, as I promised to do, to see her at Howgate. I asked her how James came to get him. She told me that one day she saw James coming down from Leadburn with the cart; he had been away west, getting eggs and butter, cheese and hens for Edinburgh. She saw he was in some trouble, and on looking, there was what she thought a young calf being dragged, or, as she called it, "haurled," at the back of the cart. James was in front, and when he came up, very warm and very angry, she saw that there was a huge young dog tied to the cart, struggling and pulling back with all his might, and as she said

" lookin' fearsom." James, who was out of breath and temper, being past his time, explained to Ailie, that this " muckle brute o' a whalp " had been worrying sheep, and terrifying everybody up at Sir George Montgomery's at Macbie Hill, and that Sir George had ordered him to be hanged, which, however, was sooner said than done, as " the thief " showed his intentions of dying hard. James came up just as Sir George had sent for his gun ; and as the dog had more than once shown a liking for him, he said he " wad gie him a chance ;" and so he tied him to his cart. Young Rab, fearing some mischief, had been entering a series of protests all the way, and nearly strangling himself to spite James and Jess, besides giving Jess more than usual to do. " I wish I had let Sir George pit that charge into him, the thrawn brute," said James. But Ailie had seen that in his fore-leg there was a splinter of wood, which he had likely got when objecting to be hanged, and that he was miserably lame. So she got James to leave him with her, and go straight into Edinburgh. She gave him water, and by her woman's wit got his lame paw under a door, so that he couldn't suddenly get at her, then with a quick firm hand she plucked out the splinter, and put in an ample meal. She went in some time after, taking no notice of him, and he came limping up, and laid his great jaws in her lap : from that moment they were " chief," as she said, James finding him mansuete and civil when he returned.

She said it was Rab's habit to make his appearance exactly half-an-hour before his master, trotting in full of importance, as if to say, " He's all right, he'll be here." One morning James came without him. He had left Edinburgh very early, and in coming near Auchindinny, at a lonely part of the road, a man sprang out on him, and demanded his money. James, who was a cool hand, said, " Weel a weel, let me get it," and stepping back, he said to Rab, " Speak till him, my man." In an instant Rab

was standing over him, threatening strangulation if
he stirred.   James pushed on, leaving Rab in charge;
he looked back, and saw that every attempt to rise
was summarily put down.   As he was telling Ailie
the story, up came Rab with that great swing of his.
It turned out that the robber was a Howgate lad, the
worthless son of a neighbour, and Rab knowing him
had let him cheaply off; the only thing, which was
seen by a man from a field, was, that before letting
him rise, he quenched (*pro tempore*) the fire of the
eyes of the ruffian, by a familiar Gulliverian application of Hydraulics, which I need not further particu-
larize.   James, who did not know the way to tell
an untruth, or embellish anything, told me this as
what he called " a fact *positeevely*."

WASP

Was a dark brindled bull-terrier, as pure in blood
as Cruiser or Wild Dayrell.   She was brought by my
brother from Otley, in the West Riding.   She was
very handsome, fierce, and gentle, with a small, compact, finely-shaped head, and a pair of wonderful
eyes—as full of fire and of softness as Grisi's; indeed she had to my eye a curious look of that wonderful genius—at once wild and fond.   It was a fine
sight to see her on the prowl across Bowden Moor,
now cantering with her nose down, now gathered
up on the top of a dyke, and with erect ears, looking
across the wild like a moss-trooper out on business,
keen and fell.   She could do everything it became a
dog to do, from killing an otter or a polecat, to
watching and playing with a baby, and was as docile
to her master as she was surly to all else.   She was
not quarrelsome, but " being in," she would have
pleased Polonius as much, as in being " ware of
entrance."   She was never beaten, and she killed on
the spot several of the country bullies who came out
upon her when following her master in his rounds.

She generally sent them off howling with one snap, but if this was not enough, she make an end of it.

But it was as a mother that she shone; and to see the gipsy, Hagar-like creature nursing her occasional Ishmael—playing with him, and fondling him all over, teaching his teeth to war, and with her eye and the curl of her lip daring any one but her master to touch him, was like seeing Grisi watching her darling "*Gennaro*," who so little knew why and how much she loved him.

Once when she had three pups, one of them died. For two days and nights she gave herself up to trying to bring it to life—licking it and turning it over and over, growling over it, and all but worrying it to awake it. She paid no attention to the living two, gave them no milk, flung them away with her teeth, and would have killed them, had they been allowed to remain with her. She was as one possessed, and neither ate, nor drank, nor slept, was heavy and miserable with her milk, and in such a state of excitement that no one could remove the dead pup.

Early on the third day she was seen to take the pup in her mouth, and start across the fields towards the Tweed, striding like a race-horse—she plunged in, holding up her burden, and at the middle of the stream dropped it and swam swiftly ashore: then she stood and watched the little dark lump floating away, bobbing up and down with the current, and losing it at last far down, she made her way home, sought out the living two, devoured them with her love, carried them one by one to her lair, and gave herself up wholly to nurse them: you can fancy her mental and bodily happiness and relief when they were pulling away—and theirs.

On one occasion my brother had lent her to a woman who lived in a lonely house, and whose husband was away for a time. She was a capital watch. One day an Italian with his organ came—first begging, then demanding money—showing that he knew

she was alone, and that he meant to help himself, if
she didn't. She threatened to "lowse the dowg;"
but as this was Greek to him, he pushed on. She
had just time to set Wasp at him. It was very short
work. She had him by the throat, pulled him and his
organ down with a heavy crash, the organ giving a
ludicrous sort of cry of musical pain. Wasp thinking this was from some creature within, possibly a
whittret, left the ruffian, and set to work tooth and
nail on the box. Its master slunk off, and with
mingled fury and thankfulness watched her disem-
bowelling his only means of an honest living. The
woman good-naturedly took her off, and signed to
the miscreant to make himself and his remains scarce.
This he did with a scowl; and was found in the
evening in the village, telling a series of lies to the
watchmaker, and bribing him with a shilling to mend
his pipes—"his kist o' whussels."

JOCK

Was insane from his birth; at first an *amabilis
insania*, but ending in mischief and sudden death.
He was an English terrier, fawn coloured; his
mother's name VAMP (Vampire), and his father's
DEMON. He was more properly *daft* than mad; his
courage, muscularity, and prodigious animal spirits
making him insufferable, and never allowing one sane
feature of himself any chance. No sooner was the
street door open, than he was throttling the first dog
passing, bringing upon himself and me endless grief.
Cats he tossed up into the air, and crushed their
spines as they fell. Old ladies he upset by jumping
over their heads; old gentlemen by running between
their legs. At home, he would think nothing of leaping through the tea-things, upsetting the urn, cream,
etc., and at dinner the same sort of thing. I believe
if I could have found time to thrash him sufficiently,
and let him be a year older, we might have kept him;

but having upset an Earl when the streets were muddy, I had to part with him. He was sent to a clergyman in the island of Westray, one of the Ork-neys; and though he had a wretched voyage, and was as sick as any dog, he signalized the first moment of his arrival at the manse, by strangling an ancient monkey, or " puggy," the pet of the minister,—who was a bachelor,—and the wonder of the island. Jock henceforward took to evil courses, extracting the kidneys of the best young rams, driving whole hirsels down steep places into the sea, till at last all the guns of Westray were pointed at him, as he stood at bay under a huge rock on the shore, and blew him into space. I always regret his end, and blame myself for sparing the rod. Of

DUCHIE

I have already spoken; her oddities were endless. We had and still have a dear friend,—" Cousin Susan " she is called by many who are not her cousins—a perfect lady, and, though hopelessly deaf, as gentle and contented as was ever Griselda with the full use of her ears; quite as great a pet, in a word, of us all as Duchie was of ours. One day we found her mourning the death of a cat, a great play-fellow of the Sputchard's, and her small Grace was with us when we were condoling with her, and we saw that she looked very wistfully at Duchie. I wrote on the slate, " Would you like her?" and she through her tears said, " You know that would never do." But it did do. We left Duchie that very night, and though she paid us frequent visits, she was Cousin Susan's for life. I fear indulgence dulled her moral sense. She was an immense happi-ness to her mistress, whose silent and lonely days she made glad with her oddity and mirth. And yet the small creature, old, toothless, and blind, domi-neered over her gentle friend—threatening her some-

times if she presumed to remove the small Fury from
the inside of her own bed, into which it pleased her
to creep. Indeed, I believe it is too true, though it
was inferred only, that her mistress and friend spent
a great part of a winter night in trying to coax her
dear little ruffian out of the centre of the bed. One
day the cook asked what she would have for dinner :
" I would like a mutton chop, but then, you know,
Duchie likes minced veal better !" The faithful and
happy little creature died at a great age, of natural
decay.

But time would fail me, and I fear patience would
fail you, my reader, were I to tell you of CRAB, of
JOHN PYM, of PUCK, and of the rest. CRAB, the
Mugger's dog, grave, with deep-set, melancholy
eyes, as of a nobleman (say the Master of Ravens-
wood) in disguise, large-visaged, shaggy, indomitable, come of the pure Piper Allan's breed. This
Piper Allan, you must know, lived some two hundred years ago in Cocquet Water, piping like Homer,
from place to place, and famous not less for his dog
than for his music, his news and his songs. The Earl
of Northumberland, of his day, offered the piper a
small farm for his dog, but after deliberating for a day,
Allan said, " Na, na, ma Lord, keep yir ferum ; what
wud a piper do wi' a ferum ?" From this dog descended Davidson of Hyndlee's breed, the original
Dandie Dinmont, and Crab could count his kin up
to him. He had a great look of the Right Honourable Edward Ellice, and had much of his energy and
wecht; had there been a dog House of Commons,
Crab would have spoken as seldom, and been as great
a power in the house, as the formidable and faithful
time-out-of-mind member for Coventry.

JOHN PYM was a smaller dog than Crab, of more
fashionable blood, being a son of Mr. Somner's
famous SHEM, whose father and brother are said to
have been found dead in a drain into which the
hounds had run a fox. It had three entrances ; the

father was put in at one hole, the son at another, and speedily the fox bolted out at the third, but no appearance of the little terriers, and on digging, they were found dead, locked in each other's jaws; they had met, and it being dark, and there being no time for explanations, they had throttled each other. John was made of the same sort of stuff, and was as combative and victorious as his great name-sake, and not unlike him in some of his not so creditable qualities. He must, I think, have been related to a certain dog to whom " life was full o' sairiousness," but in John's case the same cause produced an opposite effect. John was gay and light-hearted, even when there was not " enuff of fetchin," which, however, seldom happened, there being a market every week in Melrose, and John appearing most punctually at the cross to challenge all comers, and being short legged, he inveigled every dog into an engagement by first attacking him, and then falling down on his back, in which posture he latterly fought and won all his battles.

What can I say of PUCK [1]—the thoroughbred—the simple-hearted—the purloiner of eggs warm from the hen—the flutterer of all manner of Volscians—the bandy-legged, dear, old, dilapidated buffer? I got him from my brother, and only parted with him

---

[1] In *The Dog,* by Stonehenge, an excellent book, there is a wood-cut of Puck, and " Dr. Wm. Brown's celebrated dog John Pym " is mentioned. Their pedigrees are given—here is Puck's, which shows his " strain " is of the pure azure blood—" Got by John Pym, out of Tib ; bred by Purves of Leaderfoot ; sire, Old Dandie, the famous dog of old John Stoddart of Selkirk—dam, Whin." How Homeric all this sounds ! I cannot help quoting what follows—" Sometimes a Dandie pup of a good strain may appear not to be game at an early age ; but he should not be parted with on this account, because many of them do not show their courage till nearly two years old, and then nothing can beat them : this apparent softness arising, as I suspect, *from kindness of heart* "—a suspicion, my dear " Stonehenge," which is true, and shows your own " kindness of heart," as well as sense.

because William's stock was gone. He had to the
end of life a simplicity which was quite touching.
One summer day—a dog-day—when all dogs found
straying were hauled away to the police-office, and
killed off in twenties with strychnine, I met Puck
trotting along Princes Street with a policeman, a
rope round his neck, he looking up in the fatal,
official, but kindly countenance in the most artless
and cheerful manner, wagging his tail and trotting
along. In ten minutes he would have been in the
next world; for I am one of those who believe dogs
have a next world, and why not? Puck ended his
days as the best dog in Roxburghshire. *Placide
quiescas!*

DICK

Still lives, and long may he live! As he was never
born, possibly he may never die; be it so, he will
miss us when we are gone. I could say much of
him, but agree with the lively and admirable Dr.
Jortin, when, in his dedication of his *Remarks on
Ecclesiastical History* to the then (1752) Archbishop
of Canterbury, he excuses himself for not following
the modern custom of praising his Patron, by re-
minding his Grace "that it was a custom amongst
the ancients, *not to sacrifice to heroes till after sunset.*" I defer my sacrifice till Dick's sun is set.

I think every family should have a dog : it is like
having a perpetual baby ; it is the plaything and crony
of the whole house. It keeps them all young. All
unite upon Dick. And then he tells no tales, betrays
no secrets, never sulks, asks no troublesome questions, never gets into debt, never coming down late
for breakfast, or coming in through his Chubb *too
early* to bed—is always ready for a bit of fun, lies
in wait for it, and you may, if choleric, to your relief, kick him instead of some one else, who would
not take it so meekly, and, moreover, would certainly
not, as he does, ask your pardon for being kicked.

Never put a collar on your dog—it only gets him stolen; give him only one meal a day, and let that, as Dame Dorothy, Sir Thomas Browne's wife, would say, be " rayther under." Wash him once a week, and always wash the soap out; and let him be carefully combed and brushed twice a week.

By the bye, I was wrong in saying that it was Burns who said Man is the God of the Dog—he got it from Bacon's *Essay on Atheism.*

MARJORIE FLEMING

ONE November afternoon in 1810—the year in which *Waverley* was resumed and laid aside again, to be finished off, its last two volumes in three weeks, and made immortal in 1814, and when its author, by the death of Lord Melville, narrowly escaped getting a civil appointment in India—three men, evidently lawyers, might have been seen escaping like school-boys from the Parliament House, and speeding arm-in-arm down Bank Street and the Mound, in the teeth of a surly blast of sleet.

The three friends sought the *bield* of the low wall old Edinburgh boys remember well, and sometimes miss now, as they struggle with the stout west wind.

The three were curiously unlike each other. One, " a little man of feeble make, who would be unhappy if his pony got beyond a foot pace," slight, with " small, elegant features, hectic cheek, and soft hazel eyes, the index of the quick, sensitive spirit within, as if he had the warm heart of a woman, her genuine enthusiasm, and some of her weaknesses." Another, as unlike a woman as a man can be; homely, almost common, in look and figure; his hat and his coat, and indeed his entire covering, worn to the quick, but all of the best material; what redeemed him from vulgarity and meanness, were his eyes, deep set, heavily thatched, keen, hungry, shrewd, with a slumbering glow far in, as if they could be danger-ous; a man to care nothing for at first glance, but somehow, to give a second and not-forgetting look at. The third was the biggest of the three, and though lame, nimble, and all rough and alive with power; had you met him anywhere else, you would say he was a Liddesdale store-farmer, come of gentle blood; " a stout, blunt carle," as he says of

himself, with the swing and stride and the eye of a
man of the hills—a large, sunny, out-of-door air all
about him.   On his broad and somewhat stooping
shoulders, was set that head which, with Shakspere's
and Bonaparte's, is the best known in all the world.

He was in high spirits, keeping his companions
and himself in roars of laughter, and every now and
then seizing them and stopping, that they might take
their fill of the fun; there they stood shaking with
laughter, "not an inch of their body free" from its
grip.   At George Street they parted, one to Rose
Court, behind St. Andrew's Church, one to Albany
Street, the other, our big and limping friend, to
Castle Street.

We need hardly give their names.   The first was
William Erskine, afterwards Lord Kinnedder, chased
out of the world by a calumny, killed by its foul
breath,—

> " And at the touch of wrong, without a strife,
>   Slipped in a moment out of life."

There is nothing in literature more beautiful or more
pathetic than Scott's love and sorrow for this friend
of his youth.

The   second   was   William   Clerk,—the *Darsie
Latimer of Redgauntlet;* " a man," as Scott says,
" of the most acute intellects and powerful apprehension," but of more powerful indolence, so as to leave
the world with little more than the report of what he
might have been,—a humorist as genuine, though
not quite so savagely Swiftian as his brother Lord
Eldin, neither of whom had much of that commonest
and best of all the humours, called good.

The third we all know.   What has he not done for
every one of us?   Who else ever, except Shakspere,
so diverted mankind, entertained and entertains a
world so liberally, so wholesomely?   We are fain
to say, not even Shakspere, for his is something
deeper than diversion, something higher than pleasure and yet who would care to split this hair?

Had any one watched him closely before and after the parting, what a change he would see! The bright, broad laugh, the shrewd jovial word, the man of the Parliament House and of the world; and next step, moody, the light of his eye withdrawn, as if seeing things that were invisible; his shut mouth, like a child's, so impressionable, so innocent, so sad; he was now all within, as before he was all without; hence his brooding look. As the snow blattered in his face, he muttered, "How it raves and drifts! On-ding o' snaw—ay, that's the word—on-ding—" He was now at his own door, "Castle Street, No. 39." He opened the door, and went straight to his den; that wondrous workshop, where, in one year, 1823, when he was fifty-two, he wrote *Peveril of the Peak, Quentin Durward,* and *St. Ronan's Well,* besides much else. We once took the foremost of our novelists, the greatest, we should say, since Scott, into this room, and could not but mark the solemnizing effect of sitting where the great magician sat so often and so long, and looking out upon that little shabby bit of sky and that back green, where faithful Camp lies.[1]

He sat down in his large, green morocco elbow-chair, drew himself close to his table, and glowered and gloomed at his writing apparatus, "a very handsome old box, richly carved, lined with crimson velvet, and containing ink-bottles, taper-stand, etc., in silver, the whole in such order, that it might have come from the silversmith's window half-an-hour before." He took out his paper, then starting up angrily, said, "'Go spin, you jade, go spin.' No, d— it, it won't do,—

---

[1] This favourite dog "died about January 1809, and was buried in a fine moonlight night in the little garden behind the house in Castle Street. My wife tells me she remembers the whole family in tears about the grave as her father himself smoothed the turf above Camp, with the saddest face she had ever seen. He had been engaged to dine abroad that day, but apologized, on account of the death of 'a dear old friend.' "—Lockhart's *Life of Scott.*

'My spinnin' wheel is auld and stiff,
  The rock o't wunna stand, sir,
To keep the temper-pin in tiff
  Employs ower aft my hand, sir."

I am off the fang.[1]   I can make nothing of *Waverley*
to-day; I'll awa' to Marjorie.   Come wi' me, Maida,
you thief."   The great creature rose slowly, and the
pair were off, Scott taking a *maud* (a plaid) with him.
" White as a frosted plum-cake, by jingo!" said he,
when he got to the street.   Maida gambolled and
whisked among the snow, and his master strode
across to Young Street, and through it to 1, North
Charlotte Street, to the house of his dear friend, Mrs.
William Keith of Corstorphine Hill, niece of Mrs.
Keith of Ravelston, of whom he said at her death,
eight years after, " Much tradition, and that of the
best, has died with this excellent old lady, one of the
few persons whose spirits and *cleanliness* and freshness of mind and body made old age lovely and desirable."

  Sir Walter was in that house almost every day,
and had a key, so in he and the hound went, shaking
themselves in the lobby.   " Marjorie! Marjorie!"
shouted her friend, " where are ye, my bonnie wee
croodlin doo?"   In a moment a bright, eager child
of seven was in his arms, and he was kissing her
all over.   Out came Mrs. Keith.   " Come yer ways
in, Wattie."   " No, not now.   I am going to take
Marjorie wi' me, and you may come to your tea in
Duncan Roy's sedan, and bring the bairn home in
your lap."   " Tak' Marjorie, and it *on-ding o'*
snaw!" said Mrs. Keith.   He said to himself, " On-
ding—that's odd—that is the very word."   " Hoot,
awa! look here," and he displayed the corner of his
plaid, made to hold lambs—(the true shepherd's
plaid, consisting of two breadths sewed together, and
uncut at one end, making a poke or *cul de sac*).
" Tak' yer lamb," said she, laughing at the contriv-

---

[1] Applied to a pump when it is dry, and its valve has lost
its " fang;" from the German, *fangen,* to hold.

ance, and so the Pet was first well happit up, and then put, laughing silently, into the plaid neuk, and the shepherd strode off with his lamb,—Maida gambolling through the snow, and running races in her mirth.

Didn't he face "the angry airt," and make her bield his bosom, and into his own room with her, and lock the door, and out with the warm, rosy, little wifie, who took it all with great composure! There the two remained for three or more hours, making the house ring with their laughter; you can fancy the big man's and Maidie's laugh. Having made the fire cheery, he set her down in his ample chair, and standing sheepishly before her, began to say his lesson, which happened to be—" Ziccotty, diccotty, dock, the mouse ran up the clock, the clock struck wan, down the mouse ran, ziccotty, diccotty, dock." This done repeatedly till she was pleased, she gave him his new lesson, gravely and slowly, timing it upon her small fingers,—he saying it after her,—

> " Wonery, twoery, tickery, seven ;
> Alibi, crackaby, ten, and eleven ;
> Pin, pan, musky, dan ;
> Tweedle-um, twoddle-um,
> Twenty-wan ; eerie, orie, ourie,
> You, are, out."

He pretended to great difficulty, and she rebuked him with most comical gravity, treating him as a child. He used to say that when he came to Alibi Crackaby he broke down, and Pin-Pan, Musky-Dan, Tweedle-um Twoddle-um made him roar with laughter. He said *Musky-Dan* especially was beyond endurance, bringing up an Irishman and his hat fresh from the Spice Islands and odoriferous Ind; she getting quite bitter in her displeasure at his ill behaviour and stupidness.

Then he would read ballads to her in his own glorious way, the two getting wild with excitement over *Gil Morrice* or the *Baron of Smailholm ;* and he would take her on his knee, and make her repeat Con-

stances's speeches in *King John*, till he swayed to and
fro, sobbing his fill.   Fancy the gifted little creature,
like one possessed, repeating—

> " For I am sick and capable of fears,
>   Oppressed with wrong, and therefore, full of fears;
>   A widow, husbandless, subject to fears;
>   A woman, naturally born to fears."

> " If thou that bidst me be content, wert grim,
>   Ugly and slanderous to thy mother's womb,
>   Lame, foolish, crooked, swart, prodigious—".

Or, drawing herself up " to the height of her great
argument "—

> " I will instruct my sorrows to be proud,
>   For grief is proud, and makes his owner stout.
>   Here I and sorrow sit."

Scott used to say that he was amazed at her power
over him, saying to Mrs. Keith, " She's the most
extraordinary creature I ever met with, and her
repeating of Shakspere overpowers me as nothing
else does."

Thanks to the unforgetting sister of this dear child,
who has much of the sensibility and fun of her who
has been in her small grave these fifty and more
years, we have now before us the letters and journals
of Pet Marjorie—before us lies and gleams her rich
brown hair, bright and sunny as if yesterday's, with
the words on the paper, " Cut out in her last illness,"
and two pictures of her by her beloved Isabella, whom
she worshipped; there are the faded old scraps of
paper, hoarded still, over which her warm breath and
her warm little heart had poured themselves; there
is the old water-mark, " Lingard, 1808."   The two
portraits are very like each other, but plainly done
at different times; it is a chubby, healthy face, deep-
set, brooding eyes, as eager to tell what is going on
within as to gather in all the glories from without;
quick with the wonder and the pride of life; they are
eyes that would not be soon satisfied with seeing;
eyes that would devour their object, and yet childlike

and fearless; and that is a mouth that will not be soon satisfied with love; it has a curious likeness to Scott's own, which has always appeared to us his sweetest, most mobile and speaking feature.

There she is, looking straight at us as she did at him—fearless and full of love, passionate, wild, wilful, fancy's child. One cannot look at it without thinking of Wordsworth's lines on poor Hartley Coleridge:

> " O blessed vision, happy child !
> Thou art so exquisitely wild,
> I thought of thee with many fears,
> Of what might be thy lot in future years.
> I thought of times when Pain might be thy guest,
> Lord of thy house and hospitality ;
> And Grief, uneasy lover ! ne'er at rest,
> But when she sat within the touch of thee.
> Oh, too industrious folly !
> Oh, vain and causeless melancholy !
> Nature will either end thee quite,
> Or, lengthening out thy season of delight,
> Preserve for thee by individual right,
> A young lamb's heart among the full-grown flock."

And we can imagine Scott, when holding his warm plump little playfellow in his arms, repeating that stately friend's lines :—

> " Loving she is, and tractable, though wild,
> And Innocence hath privilege in her,
> To dignify arch looks and laughing eyes,
> And feats of cunning ; and the pretty round
> Of trespasses, affected to provoke
> Mock chastisement and partnership in play.
> And, as a fagot sparkles on the hearth,
> Not less if unattended and alone,
> Than when both young and old sit gathered round,
> And take delight in its activity,
> Even so this happy creature of herself
> Is all sufficient ; solitude to her
> Is blithe society ; she fills the air
> With gladness and involuntary songs."

But we will let her disclose herself. We need hardly say that all this is true, and that these letters are as really Marjorie's as was this light brown hair;

indeed you could as easily fabricate the one as the other.

There was an old servant—Jeanie Robertson—who was forty years in her grandfather's family. Marjorie Fleming, or, as she is called in the letters, and by Sir Walter, Maidie, was the last child she kept. Jeanie's wages never exceeded £3 a year, and, when she left service, she had saved £40. She was devotedly attached to Maidie, rather despising and ill-using her sister Isabella—a beautiful and gentle child. This partiality made Maidie apt at times to domineer over Isabella. " I mention this " (writes her surviving sister) " for the purpose of telling you an instance of Maidie's generous justice. When only five years old—when walking in Raith grounds, the two children had run on before, and old Jeanie remembered they might come too near a dangerous mill-lade. She called to them to turn back. Maidie heeded her not, rushed all the faster on, and fell, and would have been lost, had her sister not pulled her back, saving her life, but tearing her clothes. Jeanie flew on Isabella to 'give it her' for spoiling her favourite's dress; Maidie rushed in between crying out, ' pay (whip) Maidjie as much as you like, and I'll not say one word; but touch Isy, and I'll roar like a bull!' Years after Maidie was resting in her grave, my mother used to take me to the place, and told the story always in the exact same words." This Jeanie must have been a character. She took great pride in exhibiting Maidie's brother William's Calvinistic acquirements when nineteen months old, to the officers of a militia regiment then quartered in Kirkcaldy. This performance was so amusing that it was often repeated, and the little theologian was presented by them with a cap and feathers. Jeanie's glory was " putting him through the carritch " (catechism) in broad Scotch, beginning at the beginning with " Wha made ye, ma bonnie man?" For the correctness of this and the three next replies Jeanie had no anxiety, but the tone changed to menace, and the closed *nieve* (fist) was shaken in the child's face as she demanded, " Of what are you made?" " DIRT " was the answer uniformly given. " Wull ye never learn to say *dust,* ye thrawn deevil?" with a cuff from the opened hand, was the as inevitable rejoinder.

Here is Maidie's first letter before she was six. The spelling unaltered, and there are no " commoes."

" MY DEAR ISA,—I now sit down to answer all your kind and beloved letters which you were so good as to write to me. This is the first time I ever wrote a letter in my Life. There are a great many Girls in the Square and they cry just like a pig when we are under the painful necessity of putting it to Death. Miss Potune a Lady of my acquaintance praises me dreadfully. I repeated something out of Dean Swift, and she said I was fit for the stage, and you may think I was primmed up with majestick Pride, but upon my word I felt myselfe turn a little birsay— birsay is a word which is a word that William composed which is as you may suppose a little enraged. This horrid fat simpliton says that my Aunt is beauti- full which is intirely impossible for that is not her nature."

What a peppery little pen we wield ! What could that have been out of the Sardonic Dean ? what other child of that age would have used " beloved " as she does ? This power of affection, this faculty of *belov-* ing, and wild hunger to be beloved, comes out more and more. She perilled her all upon it, and it may have been as well—we know, indeed, that it was far better—for her that this wealth of love was so soon withdrawn to its one only infinite Giver and Receiver. This must have been the law of her earthly life. Love was, indeed " her Lord and King ;" and it was per- haps well for her that she found so soon that her and our only Lord and King, Himself is Love.

Here are bits from her Diary at Braehead :—" The day of my existence here has been delightful and enchanting. On Saturday I expected no less than

three well made Bucks the names of whom is here
advertised. Mr. Geo. Crakey (Craigie), and Wm.
Keith and Jn. Keith—the first is the funniest of every
one of them. Mr. Crakey and walked to Crakyhall
(Craigiehall) hand in hand in Innocence and matita-
tion (meditation) sweet thinking on the kind love
which flows in our tender hearted mind which is
overflowing with majestic pleasure no one was ever
so polite to me in the hole state of my existence.
Mr. Craky you must know is a great Buck and pretty
good-looking.

"I am at Ravelston enjoying nature's fresh air.
The birds are singing sweetly—the calf doth frisk
and nature shows her glorious face."

Here is a confession:—"I confess I have been
very more like a little young divil than a creature for
when Isabella went up stairs to teach me religion and
my multiplication and to be good and all my other
lessons I stamped with my foot and threw my new hat
which she had made on the ground and was sulky
and was dreadfully passionate, but she never whiped
me but said Marjory go into another room and think
what a great crime you are committing letting your
temper git the better of you. But I went so sulkily
that the Devil got the better of me but she never never
never whips me so that I think I would be the better
of it and the next time that I behave ill I think she
should do it for she never never does it. . . . Isabella
has given me praise for checking my temper for I
was sulky even when she was kneeling an hole hour
teaching me to write."

Our poor little wifie, *she* has no doubts of the
personality of the Devil! "Yesterday I behave
extremely ill in God's most holy church for I would
never attend myself nor let Isabella attend which
was a great crime for she often, often tells me that
when to or three are geathered together God is in the
midst of them, and it was the very same Divil that
tempted Job that tempted me I am sure; but he
resisted Satan though he had boils and many many

other misfortunes which I have escaped. . . . I am now going to tell you the horible and wretched plaege (plague) that my multiplication gives me you can't conceive it the most Devilish thing is 8 times 8 and 7 times 7 it is what nature itself cant endure."

This is delicious; and what harm is there in her "Devilish"? it is strong language merely; even old Rowland Hill used to say "he grudged the Devil those rough and ready words." "I walked to that delightful place Crakyhall with a delightful young man beloved by all his friends espacially by me his loveress, but I must not talk any more about him for Isa said it is not proper for to speak of gentalmen but I will never forget him! . . . I am very very glad that satan has not given me boils and many other misfortunes—In the holy bible these words are written that the Devil goes like a roaring lyon in search of his pray but the lord lets us escape from him but we " (*pauvre petite!*) " do not strive with this awfull Spirit. . . . To-day I pronunced a word which should never come out of a lady's lips it was that I called John a Impudent Bitch. I will tell you what I think made me in so bad a humor is I got one or two of that bad bad sina (senna) tea to-day,"— a better excuse for bad humour and bad language than most.

She has been reading the Book of Esther: " It was a dreadful thing that Haman was hanged on the very gallows which he had prepared for Mordeca to hang him and his ten sons thereon and it was very wrong and cruel to hang his sons for they did not commit the crime; *but then Jesus was not then come to teach us to be merciful.*" This is wise and beautiful—has upon it the very dew of youth and of holiness. Out of the mouths of babes and sucklings He perfects His praise.

" This is Saturday and I am very glad of it because I have play half the Day and I get money too but alas I owe Isabella 4 pence for I am finned 2 pence whenever I bite my nails. Isabella is teach-

ing me to make simme colings nots of interrigations
peorids commoes, etc. . . . . As this is Sunday I will
meditate upon Senciable and Religious subjects.
First I should be very thankful I am not a begger."

This amount of meditation and thankfulness seems
to have been all she was able for.

"I am going to-morrow to a delightfull place,
Braehead by name, belonging to Mrs. Crraford,
where there is ducks cocks hens bubblyjocks 2 dogs
2 cats and swine which is delightful. I think it is
shocking to think that the dog and cat should wed
them" (this is a meditation physiological), "and
they are drowned after all. I would rather have a
man-dog than a woman-dog, because they do not bear
like women-dogs; it is a hard case—it is shocking.
I cam here to enjoy natures delightful breath it is
sweeter than a fial (phial) of rose oil."

Braehead is the farm the historical Jock Howison
asked and got from our gay James the Fifth, "the
gudeman o' Ballengiech," as a reward for the services of his flail when the King had the worst of it
at Cramond Brig with the gipsies. The farm is
unchanged in size from that time, and still in the unbroken line of the ready and victorious thrasher.
Braehead is held on the condition of the possessor
being ready to present the King with a ewer and
basin to wash his hands, Jock having done this for
his unknown king after the *splore,* and when George
the Fourth came to Edinburgh this ceremony was
performed in silver at Holyrood. It is a lovely
neuk this Braehead, preserved almost as it was 200
years ago. "Lot and his wife" mentioned by
Maidie—two quaintly cropped yew-trees—still thrive,
the burn runs as it did in her time, and sings the
same quiet tune—as much the same and as different
as *Now* and *Then.* The house full of old family
relics and pictures, the sun shining on them through
the small deep windows with their plate glass; and
there, blinking at the sun, and chattering contentedly,
is a parrot, that might, for its looks of eld, have been

in the ark, and domineered over and *deaved* the dove. Everything about the place is old and fresh.

This is beautiful :—"I am very sorry to say that I forgot God—that is to say I forgot to pray to-day and Isabella told me that I should be thankful that God did not forget me—if he did, O what become of me if I was in danger and God not friends with me—I must go to unquenchable fire and if I was tempted to sin—how could I resist it O no I will never do it again—no no—if I can help it." (Canny wee wifie!) "My religion is greatly falling off because I dont pray with so much attention when I am saying my prayers, and my charecter is lost among the Braehead people. I hope I will be religious again—but as for regaining my charecter I despare for it." (Poor little "habit and repute!")

Her temper, her passion, and her "badness" are almost daily confessed and deplored :—"I will never again trust to my own power, for I see that I cannot be good without God's assistance—I will not trust in my own selfe, and Isa's health will be quite ruined by me—it will indeed." "Isa has given me advice, which is, that when I feal Satan beginning to tempt me, that I flea him and he would flea me." "Remorse is the worst thing to bear, and I am afraid that I will fall a marter to it."

Poor dear little sinner!—Here comes the world again :—"In my travels I met with a handsome lad named Charles Balfour Esq., and from him I got ofers of marage—offers of marage, did I say? Nay plenty heard me." A fine scent for "breach of promise!"

This is abrupt and strong :—"The Divil is curced and all works. 'Tis a fine work *Newton on the profecies*. I wonder if there is another book of poems comes near the Bible. The Divil always girns at the sight of the Bible." "Miss Potune" (her "simpliton" friend) "is very fat; she pretends to be very learned. She says she saw a stone that dropt from the skies; but she is a good Christian." Here

come her views on church government :—" An Anni-
babtist is a thing I am not a member of—I am a Pis-
plekan (Episcopalian) just now, and " (Oh you little
Laodicean and Latitudinarian !) " a Prisbeteran at
Kirkcaldy !"—(*Blandula! Vagula! cœlum et animum
mutas quæ trans mare* (i.e., *trans Bodotriam*)-*curris!*)
—" my native town." " Sentiment is not what I am
acquainted with as yet, though I wish it, and should
like to practise it " (!) " I wish I had a great, great
deal of gratitude in my heart, in all my body." " There
is a new novel published, named *Self-Control* (Mrs.
Brunton's)—" a very good maxim forsooth !" This
is shocking : " Yesterday a marrade man, named Mr.
John Balfour, Esq., offered to kiss me, and offered
to marry me, though the man " (a fine directness
this !) " was espused, and his wife was present and
said he must ask her permission ; but he did not.   I
think he was ashamed and confounded before 3
gentelmen—Mr. Jobson and 2 Mr. Kings." " Mr.
Banesters' (Bannister's) " Budjet is to-night ; I hope
it will be a good one. A great many authors have
expressed themselves too sentimentally." You are
right, Marjorie. " A Mr. Burns writes a beautiful
song on Mr. Cunhaming, whose wife desarted him—
truly it is a most beautiful one." " I like to read the
Fabulous historys, about the histerys of Robin,
Dickey, flapsay, and Peccay, and it is very amusing,
for some were good birds and others bad, but Peccay
was the most dutiful and obedient to her parients."
" Thomson is a beautiful author, and Pope, but
nothing to Shakespear, of which I have a little
knolege. *Macbeth* is a pretty composition, but awful
one." " The *Newgate Calendar* is very instructive " (!) " A sailor called here to say farewell ; it
must be dreadful to leave his native country when he
might get a wife ; or perhaps me, for I love him very
much. But O I forgot, Isabella forbid me to speak
about love." This antiphlogistic regimen and lesson
is ill to learn by our Maidie, for here she sins again :
—" Love is a very papithatick thing " (it is almost

a pity to correct this into pathetic), "as well as troublesome and tiresome—but O Isabella forbid me to speak of it." Here are her reflections on a pine-apple:—"I think the price of a pine-apple is very dear: it is a whole bright goulden guinea, that might have sustained a poor family." Here is a new vernal simile:—"The hedges are sprouting like chicks from the eggs when they are newly hatched, or, as the vulgar say, *clacked*." "Doctor Swift's works are very funny; I got some of them by heart." "Moreheads sermons are I hear much praised, but I never read sermons of any kind; but I read novelettes and my Bible, and I never forget it, or my prayers." Bravo Marjorie!

She seems now, when still about six, to have broken out into song:—

"EPHIBOL (EPIGRAM OR EPITAPH—WHO KNOWS WHICH?) ON MY DEAR LOVE ISABELLA.

"Here lies sweet Isabell in bed,
    With a night-cap on her head;
    Her skin is soft, her face is fair,
    And she has very pretty hair;
    She and I in bed lies nice,
    And undisturbed by rats or mice;
    She is disgusted with Mr. Worgan,
    Though he plays upon the organ.
    Her nails are neat, her teeth are white,
    Her eyes are very, very bright;
    In a conspicuous town she lives,
    And to the poor her money gives:
    Here ends sweet Isabella's story,
    And may it be much to her glory."

Here are some bits at random:—

"Of summer I am very fond,
    And love to bathe into a pond;
    The look of sunshine dies away,
    And will not let me out to play;
    I love the morning's sun to spy
    Glittering through the casement's eye,
    The rays of light are very sweet,
    And puts away the taste of meat;
    The balmy breeze comes down from heaven,
    And makes us like for to be living."

" The casawary is an curious bird, and so is the gigantic crane, and the pelican of the wilderness, whose mouth holds a bucket of fish and water. Fighting is what ladies is not qualyfied for, they would not make a good figure in battle or in a duel. Alas ! we females are of little use to our country. The history of all the malcontents as ever was hanged is amusing."   Still harping on the Newgate Calendar !

" Braehead is extremely pleasant to me by the companie of swine, geese, cocks, &c., and they are the delight of my soul."

" I am going to tell you of a melancholy story. A young turkie of 2 or 3 months old, would you believe it, the father broke its leg, and he killed another ! I think he ought to be transported or hanged."

" Queen Street is a very gay one, and so is Princes Street, for all the lads and lasses, besides bucks and beggars, parade there."

" I should like to see a play very much, for I never saw one in all my life, and don't believe I ever shall; but I hope I can be content without going to one.   I can be quite happy without my desire being granted."

" Some days ago Isabella had a terrible fit of the toothake, and she walked with a long night-shift at dead of night like a ghost, and I thought she was one.   She prayed for nature's sweet restorer—balmy sleep—but did not get it—a ghostly figure indeed she was, enough to make a saint tremble.   It made me quiver and shake from top to toe.   Superstition is a very mean thing, and should be despised and shunned."

Here is her weakness and her strength again :—
" In the love-novels all the heroines are very desperate.   Isabella will not allow me to speak about lovers and heroins, and 'tis too refined for my taste."
" Miss Egward's (Edgeworth's) tails are very good, particularly some that are very much adapted for youth (!) as Laz Laurance and Tarelton, False Keys, &c. &c."
" Tom Jones and Grey's Elegey in a country church-

yard are both excellent, and much spoke of by both sex, particularly by the men." Are our Marjories now-a-days better or worse because they cannot read Tom Jones unharmed? More better than worse; but who among them can repeat Gray's Lines on a distant prospect of Eton College as could our Maidie?

Here is some more of her prattle :—" I went into Isabella's bed to make her smile like the Genius Demedicus " (the Venus de Medicis) " or the statute in an ancient Greece, but she fell asleep in my very face, at which my anger broke forth, so that I awoke her from a comfortable nap. All was now hushed up again, but again my anger burst forth at her biding me get up."

She begins thus loftily :—

> " Death the righteous love to see,
> But from it doth the wicked flee."

Then suddenly breaks off (as if with laughter)—

" I am sure they fly as fast as their legs can carry them !"

> " There is a thing I love to see,
> That is our monkey catch a flee."

> " I love in Isa's bed to lie,
> Oh, such a joy and luxury !
> The bottom of the bed I sleep,
> And with great care within I creep;
> Oft I embrace her feet of lillys,
> But she has goton all the pillys.
> Her neck I never can embrace,
> But I do hug her feet in place."

How childish and yet how strong and free is her use of words !—" I lay at the foot of the bed because Isabella said I disturbed her by continial fighting and kicking, but I was very dull, and continially at work reading the Arabian Nights, which I could not have done if I had slept at the top. I am reading the Mysteries of Udolpho. I am much interested in the fate of poor, poor Emily."

Here is one of her swains—

> " Very soft and white his cheeks,
>   His hair is red, and grey his breeks;
>   His tooth is like the daisy fair,
>   His only fault is in his hair."

This is a higher flight :—

> " Dedicated to Mrs. H. Crawford by the Author, M. F.

> " Three turkeys fair their last have breathed,
>   And now this world for ever leaved;
>   Their father, and their mother too,
>   They sigh and weep as well as you;
>   Indeed, the rats their bones have crunched,
>   Into eternity theire laanched.
>   A direful death indeed they had,
>   As wad put any parent mad;
>   But she was more than usual calm,
>   She did not give a single dam."

This last word is saved from all sin by its tender age, not to speak of the want of the *n*. We fear " she " is the abandoned mother, in spite of her previous sighs and tears.

" Isabella says when we pray we should pray fervently, and not rattel over a prayer—for that we are kneeling at the footstool of our Lord and Creator, who saves us from eternal damnation, and from unquestionable fire and brimston."

She has a long poem on Mary Queen of Scots :—

> " Queen Mary was much loved by all,
>   Both by the great and by the small,
>   But hark ! her soul to heaven doth rise !
>   And I suppose she has gained a prize—
>   For I do think she would not go
>   Into the *awful* place below;
>   There is a thing that I must tell,
>   Elizabeth went to fire and hell;
>   He who would teach her to be civil,
>   It must be her great friend the divil !"

She hits off Darnley well :—

> " A noble's son, a handsome lad,
>   By some queer way or other, had
>   Got quite the better of her heart,
>   With him she always talked apart;
>   Silly he was, but very fair,
>   A greater buck was not found there."

" By some queer way or other;" is not this the
general case and the mystery, young ladies and
gentlemen? Goethe's doctrine of " elective affini-
ties " discovered by our Pet Maidie.

SONNET TO A MONKEY.

" O lively, O most charming pug
　　Thy graceful air, and heavenly mug;
　　The beauties of his mind do shine,
　　And every bit is shaped and fine.
　　Your teeth are whiter than the snow,
　　Your a great buck, your a great beau;
　　Your eyes are of so nice a shape,
　　More like a Christian's than an ape;
　　Your cheek is like the rose's blume,
　　Your hair is like the raven's plume;
　　His nose's cast is of the Roman,
　　He is a very pretty woman.
　　I could not get a rhyme for Roman,
　　So was obliged to call him woman."

This last joke is good. She repeats it when writing
of James the Second being killed at Roxburgh :—

" He was killed by a cannon splinter,
　　Quite in the middle of the winter;
　　Perhaps it was not at that time,
　　But I can get no other rhyme !"

Here is one of her last letters, dated Kirkcaldy,
12th October 1811. You can see how her nature is
deepening and enriching :—" MY DEAR MOTHER,—
You will think that I entirely forget you but I assure
you that you are greatly mistaken. I think of you
always and often sigh to think of the distance between us two loving creatures of nature. We have
regular hours for all our occupations first at 7 o'clock
we go to the dancing and come home at 8 we then
read our Bible and get our repeating and then play till
ten then we get our music till 11 when we get our
writing and accounts we sew from 12 till 1 after
which I get my gramer and then work till five. At 7
we come and knit till 8 when we dont go to the
dancing. This is an exact description. I must take

a hasty farewell to her whom I love, reverence and doat on and who I hope thinks the same of
"   MARJORY FLEMING.

"*P.S.*—An old pack of cards (!) would be very exeptible."

This other is a month earlier :—" MY DEAR LITTLE MAMA,—I was truly happy to hear that you were all well.   We are surrounded with measles at present on every side, for the Herons got it, and Isabella Heron was near Death's Door, and one night her father lifted her out of bed, and she fell down as they thought lifeless. Mr. Heron said, ' That lassie's deed noo '—' I'm no deed yet.' She then threw up a big worm nine inches and a half long.   I have begun dancing, but am not very fond of it, for the boys strikes and mocks me.—I have been another night at the dancing; I like it better.   I will write to you as often as I can; but I am afraid not every week.   *I long for you with the longings of a child to embrace you—to fold you in my arms.   I respect you with all the respect due to a mother.   You dont know how I love you.   So I shall remain, your loving child* —M. FLEMING."

What rich involution of love in the words marked ! Here are some lines to her beloved Isabella, in July 1811 :—

> " There is a thing that I do want,
>   With you these beauteous walks to haunt,
>   We would be happy if you would
>   Try to come over if you could.
>   Then I would all quite happy be
>   *Now and for all eternity.*
>   My mother is so very sweet,
>   *And checks my appetite to eat;*
>   My father shows us what to do;
>   But O I'm sure that I want you.
>   I have no more of poetry;
>   O Isa do remember me,
>   And try to love your Marjory."

In a letter from " Isa " to

> " Miss Muff Maidie Marjory Fleming,
>   favored by Rare Rear-Admiral Fleming,"

she says—" I long much to see you, and talk over
all our old stories together, and to hear you read
and repeat.   I am pining for my old friend Cesario,
and poor Lear, and wicked Richard.   How is the
dear Multiplication table going on? are you still as
much attached to 9 times 9 as you used to be?"

But this dainty, bright thing is about to flee—to
come " quick to confusion."   The measles she writes
of seized her, and she died on the 19th of December
1811.   The day before her death, Sunday, she sat up
in bed, worn and thin, her eye gleaming as with
the light of a coming world, and with a tremulous,
old voice repeated the following lines by Burns—
heavy with the shadow of death, and lit with the
phantasy of the judgment-seat—the publican's prayer
in paraphrase :—

> " Why am I loth to leave this earthly scene?
>   Have I so found it full of pleasing charms?
>   Some drops of joy, with draughts of ill between,
>   Some gleam of sunshine mid renewing storms.
>   Is it departing pangs my soul alarms?
>   Or death's unlovely, dreary, dark abode?
>   For guilt, for GUILT my terrors are in arms;
>   I tremble to approach an angry God,
> And justly smart beneath his sin-avenging rod.
>
>   Fain would I say, forgive my foul offence,
>   Fain promise never more to disobey ;
>   But should my Author health again dispense,
>   Again I might forsake fair virtue's way,
>   Again in folly's path might go astray,
>   Again exalt the brute and sink the man.
>   Then how should I for heavenly mercy pray,
>   Who act so counter heavenly mercy's plan,
> Who sin so oft have mourned, yet to temptation ran?
>
>   O thou great Governor of all below,
>   If I might dare a lifted eye to thee,
>   Thy nod can make the tempest cease to blow,
>   And still the tumult of the raging sea ;

> With that controlling power assist even me
> Those headstrong furious passions to confine,
> For all unfit I feel my powers to be
> To rule their torrent in the allowed line ;
> O aid me with thy help, OMNIPOTENCE DIVINE."

It is more affecting than we care to say to read her
Mother's and Isabella Keith's letters written immediately after her death. Old and withered, tattered
and pale they are now : but when you read them,
how quick, how throbbing with life and love ! how
rich in that language of affection which only women,
and Shakspere, and Luther can use—that power of
detaining the soul over the beloved object and its
loss.

> " *K. Philip to Constance—*
> You are as fond of grief as of your child.
> *Const.*—Grief fills the room up of my absent child,
> Lies in his bed, walks up and down with me ;
> Puts on his pretty looks, repeats his words,
> Remembers me of all his gracious parts,
> Stuffs out his vacant garments with his form.
> Then I have reason to be fond of grief."

What variations cannot love play on this one string !

In her first letter to Miss Keith, Mrs. Fleming
says of her dead Maidie :—" Never did I behold so
beautiful an object. It resembled the finest wax-
work. There was in the countenance an expression
of sweetness and serenity which seemed to indicate
that the pure spirit had anticipated the joys of heaven
ere it quitted the mortal frame. To tell you what
your Maidie said of you would fill volumes ; for you
was the constant theme of her discourse, the subject
of her thoughts, and ruler of her actions. The last
time she mentioned you was a few hours before all
sense save that of suffering was suspended, when
she said to Dr. Johnstone, ' If you will let me out
at the New Year, I will be quite contented.' I asked
what made her so anxious to get out then ? ' I
want to purchase a New Year's gift for Isa Keith
with the sixpence you gave me for being patient in
the measles ; and I would like to choose it myself.'

I do not remember her speaking afterwards, except to complain of her head, till just before she expired, when she articulated, ' O, mother! mother! ' "

Do we make too much of this little child, who has been in her grave in Abbotshall Kirkyard these fifty and more years? We may of her cleverness—not of her affectionateness, her nature. What a picture the *animosa infans* gives us of herself, her vivacity, her passionateness, her precocious love-making, her passion for nature, for swine, for all living things, her reading, her turn for expression, her satire, her frankness, her little sins and rages, her great repentances! We don't wonder Walter Scott carried her off in the neuk of his plaid, and played himself with her for hours.

The year before she died, when in Edinburgh, she was at a Twelfth Night supper at Scott's, in Castle Street. The company had all come—all but Marjorie. Scott's familiars, whom we all know, were there—all were come but Marjorie; and all were dull because Scott was dull. "Where's that bairn? what can have come over her? I'll go myself and see." And he was getting up, and would have gone; when the bell rang, and in came Duncan Roy and his henchman Tougald, with the sedan chair, which was brought right into the lobby, and its top raised. And there, in its darkness and dingy old cloth, sat Maidie in white, her eyes gleaming, and Scott bending over her in ecstasy—"hung over her enamoured." " Sit ye there, my dautie, till they all see you;" and forthwith he brought them all. You can fancy the scene. And he lifted her up and marched to his seat with her on his stout shoulder, and set her down beside him; and then began the night, and such a night! Those who knew Scott best said, that night was never equalled; Maidie and he were the stars; and she gave them *Constance's* speeches and *Helvellyn,* the ballad then much in vogue—and all her *répertoire*— Scott showing her off, and being ofttimes rebuked by her for his intentional blunders.

We are indebted for the following—and our readers will not be unwilling to share our obligations —to her sister :—" Her birth was 15th January 1803 ; her death 19th December 1811.   I take this from her Bibles.[1] I believe she was a child of robust health, of much vigour of body, and beautifully formed arms, and until her last illness, never was an hour in bed. She was niece to Mrs. Keith, residing in No. 1, North Charlotte Street, who was *not* Mrs. Murray Keith, although very intimately acquainted with that old lady. My aunt was a daughter of Mr. James Rae, surgeon, and married the younger son of old Keith of Ravelstone. Corstorphine Hill belonged to my aunt's husband; and his eldest son, Sir Alexander Keith, succeeded his uncle to both Ravelstone and Dunnottar. The Keiths were not connected by relationship with the Howisons of Braehead, but my grandfather and grandmother (who was), a daughter of Cant of Thurston and Giles-Grange, were on the most intimate footing with *our* Mrs. Keith's grandfather and grandmother; and so it has been for three generations, and the friendship consummated by my cousin William Keith marrying Isabella Craufurd.

" As to my aunt and Scott, they were on a very intimate footing. He asked my aunt to be godmother to his eldest daughter Sophia Charlotte.   I had a copy of Miss Edgeworth's *Rosamund, and Harry and Lucy* for long, which was 'a gift to Marjorie from Walter Scott,' probably the first edition of that attractive series, for it wanted ' Frank,' which is always now published as part of the series, under the title of *Early Lessons*.   I regret to say these little volumes have disappeared.

" Sir Walter was no relation of Marjorie's, but of the Keiths, through the Swintons; and, like Marjorie, he stayed much at Ravelstone in his early days, with his grand-aunt Mrs. Keith ; and it was while

---

[1] " Her Bible is before me ; *a pair,* as then called ; the faded marks are just as she placed them. There is one at David's lament over Jonathan."

seeing him there as a boy, that another aunt of mine
composed, when he was about fourteen, the lines
prognosticating his future fame that Lockhart
ascribes in his Life to Mrs. Cockburn, authoress of
'The Flowers of the Forest':—

> "Go on, dear youth, the glorious path pursue
> Which bounteous Nature kindly smooths for you;
> Go bid the seeds her hands have sown arise,
> By timely culture, to their native skies;
> Go, and employ the poet's heavenly art,
> Not merely to delight, but mend the heart."

Mrs. Keir was my aunt's name, another of Dr.
Rae's daughters." We cannot better end than in
words from this same pen:—" I have to ask you to
forgive my anxiety in gathering up the fragments of
Marjorie's last days, but I have an almost sacred
feeling to all that pertains to her. You are quite
correct in stating that measles were the cause of her
death. My mother was struck by the patient quietness manifested by Marjorie during this illness, unlike her ardent, impulsive nature; but love and poetic
feeling were unquenched. When Dr. Johnstone
rewarded her submissiveness with a sixpence, the
request speedily followed that she might get out ere
New Year's day came. When asked why she was
so desirous of getting out, she immediately rejoined,
'Oh, I am so anxious to buy something with my sixpence for my dear Isa Keith.' Again, when lying
very still, her mother asked her if there was anything
she wished: 'Oh, yes! if you would just leave the
room door open a wee bit, and play "The Land o'
the Leal," and I will lie and *think,* and enjoy myself'
(this is just as stated to me by her mother and mine).
Well, the happy day came, alike to parents and child,
when Marjorie was allowed to come forth from the
nursery to the parlour. It was Sabbath evening, and
after tea. My father, who idolized this child, and
never afterwards in my hearing mentioned her name,
took her in his arms; and while walking her up and
down the room, she said, 'Father, I will repeat

something to you; what would you like?' He said,
'Just choose yourself, Maidie.' She hesitated for
a moment between the paraphrase, 'Few are thy
days and full of woe,' and the lines of Burns already
quoted, but decided on the latter, a remarkable
choice for a child. The repeating these lines seemed
to stir up the depths of feeling in her soul. She
asked to be allowed to write a poem; there was a
doubt whether it would be right to allow her, in case
of hurting her eyes. She pleaded earnestly, 'Just
this once;' the point was yielded, her slate was given
her, and with great rapidity she wrote an address of
fourteen lines, 'to her loved cousin on the author's
recovery,' her last work on earth :—

> 'Oh ! Isa, pain did visit me,
> I was at the last extremity;
> How often did I think of you,
> I wished your graceful form to view,
> To clasp you in my weak embrace,
> Indeed I thought I'd run my race :
> Good care, I'm sure, was of me taken,
> But still indeed I was much shaken,
> At last I daily strength did gain,
> And oh ! at last, away went pain;
> At length the doctor thought I might
> Stay in the parlor all the night;
> I now continue so to do,
> Farewell to Nancy and to you.'

"She went to bed apparently well, awoke in the
middle of the night with the old cry of woe to a
mother's heart, 'My head, my head !' Three days
of the dire malady, 'water in the head,' followed,
and the end came."

"Soft, silken promise, fading timelessly."

It is needless, it is impossible, to add anything to
this : the fervour, the sweetness, the flush of poetic
ecstasy, the lovely and glowing eye, the perfect
nature of that bright and warm intelligence, that
darling child,—Lady Nairne's words, and the old
tune, stealing up from the depths of the human heart,

deep calling unto deep, gentle and strong like the waves of the great sea hushing themselves to sleep in the dark ;—the words of Burns, touching the kindred chord, her last numbers " wildly sweet " traced, with thin and eager fingers, already touched by the last enemy and friend,—*moriens canit,*—and that love which is so soon to be her everlasting light, is her song's burden to the end,

> " She set as sets the morning star, which goes
> Not down behind the darkened west, nor hides
> Obscured among the tempests of the sky,
> But melts away into the light of heaven."

JEEMS THE DOORKEEPER

When my father was in Broughton Place Church, we had a doorkeeper called *Jeems*, and a formidable little man and doorkeeper he was; of unknown age and name, for he existed to us, and indeed still exists to me—though he has been in his grave these sixteen years—as *Jeems*, absolute and *per se*, no more needing a surname than did or do Abraham or Isaac, Samson or Nebuchadnezzar. We young people of the congregation believed that he was out in the '45, and had his drum shot through and quenched at Culloden; and as for any indication on his huge and grey visage, of his ever having been young, he might safely have been *Bottom* the Weaver in *A Midsummer Night's Dream*, or that excellent, ingenious, and "wisehearted" Bezaleel, the son of Uri, whom *Jeems* regarded as one of the greatest of men and of weavers, and whose "ten curtains of fine twined linen, and blue, and purple, and scarlet, each of them with fifty loops on the edge of the selvedge in the coupling, with their fifty taches of gold," he, in confidential moments, gave it to be understood were the sacred triumphs of his craft; for, as you may infer, my friend was a man of the treddles and the shuttle, as well as the more renowned grandson of Hur.

Jeems's face was so extensive, and met you so formidably and at once, that it mainly composed his whole; and such a face! Sydney Smith used to say of a certain quarrelsome man, "His very face is a breach of the peace." Had he seen our friend's, he would have said he was the imperative mood on two (very small) legs, out on business in a blue greatcoat. It was in the nose and the keen small eye that his strength lay. Such a nose of power, so undeniable, I

never saw, except in what was said to be a bust
from the antique, of Rhadamanthus, the well-known
Justice-Clerk of the Pagan Court of Session! Indeed,
when I was in the Rector's class, and watched *Jeems*
turning interlopers out of the church seats, by merely
presenting before them this tremendous organ, it
struck me that if Rhadamanthus had still been here,
and out of employment, he would have taken kindly
to *Jeems's* work,—and that possibly he was that
potentate in a U. P. disguise.

Nature having fashioned the huge face, and laid out
much material and idea upon it, had finished off the
rest of *Jeems* somewhat scrimply, as if she had run
out of means; his legs especially were of the shortest,
and, as his usual dress was a very long blue great-
coat, made for a much taller man, its tails resting
upon the ground, and its large hind buttons in a
totally preposterous position, gave him the look of
being planted, or rather after the manner of Milton's
beasts at the creation, in the act of emerging painfully
from his mother earth.

Now, you may think this was a very ludicrous old
object. If you had seen him, you would not have
said so; and not only was he a man of weight and
authority,—he was likewise a genuine, indeed a
deeply spiritual Christian, well read in his Bible, in
his own heart, and in human nature and life, knowing
both its warp and woof: more peremptory in making
himself obey his Master, than in getting himself
obeyed, and this is saying a good deal; and, like all
complete men, he had a genuine love and gift of
humour,[1] kindly and uncouth, lurking in those small,
deep-set grey eyes, shrewd and keen, which, like two
sharpest of shooters, enfiladed that massive and re-
doubtable bulwark, the nose.

[1] On one occasion a descendant of Nabal having put a
crown piece into " the plate " instead of a penny, and staring
at its white and precious face, asked to have it back, and was
refused—" In once, in for ever." " A weel, a weel," grunted
he, " I'll get credit for it in heaven." " Na, na," said *Jeems,*
" ye'll get credit only for the penny!"

One day two strangers made themselves over to *Jeems* to be furnished with seats. Motioning them to follow, he walked majestically to the farthest in corner, where he had decreed they should sit. The couple found seats near the door, and stepped into them, leaving *Jeems* to march through the passages alone, the whole congregation watching him with some relish and alarm. He gets to his destination, opens the door, and stands aside; nobody appears. He looks sharply round, and then gives a look of general wrath "at lairge." No one doubted his victory. His nose and eye fell, or seemed to fall, on the two culprits, and pulled them out instantly, hurrying them to their appointed place; *Jeems* snibbed them slowly in, and gave them a parting look they were not likely to misunderstand or forget.

At that time the crowds and the imperfect ventilation made fainting a common occurrence in Broughton Place, especially among "*thae young hizzies*," as *Jeems* called the servant girls. He generally came to me, "the young Doctor," on these occasions with a look of great relish. I had indoctrinated him in the philosophy of *syncopes*, especially as to the propriety of laying the "*hizzies*" quite flat on the floor of the lobby, with the head as low as the rest of the body; and as many of these cases were owing to what *Jeems* called "that bitter yerkin" of their boddices, he and I had much satisfaction in relieving them, and giving them a moral lesson, by cutting their stay-laces, which ran before the knife, and cracked "like a bowstring," as my coadjutor said. One day a young lady was our care. She was lying out, and slowly coming to. *Jeems*, with that huge terrific visage, came round to me with his open *gully* in his hand, whispering, "Wull oo ripp 'er up noo?" It happened not to be a case for ripping up. The gully was a great sanitary institution, and made a decided inroad upon the *yerking* system—*Jeems* having, thanks to this and Dr. Coombe, every year fewer opportunities of displaying and enjoying its powers.

He was sober in other things besides drink, could be generous on occasion, but was careful of his siller; sensitive to fierceness ("we're uncommon *zeelyous* the day," was a favourite phrase when any church matter was stirring) for the honour of his church and minister, and to his too often worthless neighbours a perpetual moral protest and lesson—a living epistle. He dwelt at the head of Big Lochend's Close in the Canongate, at the top of a long stair—ninety-six steps, as I well know—where he had dwelt, all by himself, for five-and-thirty years, and where, in the midst of all sorts of flittings and changes, not a day opened or closed without the well-known sound of *Jeems* at his prayers,—his "exercise,"—at "the Books." His clear, fearless, honest voice in psalm and chapter, and strong prayer, came sounding through that wide "*land*," like that of one crying in the wilderness.

Jeems and I got great friends; he called me John, as if he was my grandfather; and though as plain in speech as in feature, he was never rude. I owe him much in many ways. His absolute downrightness and *yaefauldness;* his energetic, unflinching fulfilment of his work; his rugged, sudden tenderness; his look of sturdy age, as the thick silver-white hair lay on his serious and weatherworn face, like moonlight on a stout old tower; his quaint Old Testament exegetics, his lonely and contented life, his simple godliness,— it was no small privilege to see much of all this.

But I must stop. I forget that you didn't know him; that he is not your *Jeems*. If it had been so, you would not soon have wearied of telling or of being told of the life and conversation of this "fell body." He was not communicative about his early life. He would sometimes speak to me about "*her*," as if I knew who and where she was, and always with a gentleness and solemnity unlike his usual gruff ways. I found out that he had been married when young, and that "she" (he never named her) and their child died on the same day,—the day of its birth.

The only indication of married life in his room, was an old and strong cradle, which he had cut down so as to rock no more, and which he made the depository of his books—a queer collection.

I have said that he had what he called, with a grave smile, *family* worship, morning and evening, never failing. He not only sang his psalm, but gave out or chanted *the line* in great style; and on seeing me one morning surprised at this, he said, " Ye see John, *oo*," meaning himself and his wife, " began that way." He had a firm, true voice, and a genuine though roughish gift of singing, and being methodical in all things, he did what I never heard of in any one else,—he had seven fixed tunes, one of which he sang on its own set day. Sabbath morning it was *French*, which he went through with great *birr*. Monday, *Scarborough*, which, he said, was like my father cantering. Tuesday, *Coleshill*, that soft exquisite air, —monotonous and melancholy, soothing and vague, like the sea. This day, Tuesday, was the day of the week on which his wife and child died, and he always sang more verses then than on any other. Wednesday was *Irish;* Thursday, *Old Hundred*; Friday, *Bangor;* and Saturday, *Blackburn*, that humdrummest of tunes, " as long, and lank, and lean, as is the ribbed sea-sand." He could not defend it, but had some secret reason for sticking to it. As to the evenings, they were just the same tunes in reversed order, only that on Tuesday night he sang *Coleshill* again, thus dropping *Blackburn* for evening work. The children could tell the day of the week by *Jeems's* tune, and would have been as much astonished at hearing *Bangor* on Monday, as at finding St. Giles's half-way down the Canongate.

I frequently breakfasted with him. He made capital porridge, and I wish I could get such buttermilk, or at least have such a relish for it, as in those days. Jeems is away—gone over to the majority; and I hope I may never forget to be grateful to the dear and queer old man. I think I see and hear him

saying his grace over our bickers with their *brats*
on, then taking his two books out of the cradle and
reading, not without a certain homely majesty, the
first verse of the 99th Psalm,

> " Th' eternal Lord doth reign as king,
>   Let all the people quake ;
> He sits between the cherubims,
>   Let th' earth be mov'd and shake ;"

then launching out into the noble depths of *Irish*.
His chapters were long, and his prayers short, very
scriptural, but by no means stereotyped, and wonderfully real, *immediate*, as if he was near Him whom
he addressed. Any one hearing the sound and not the
words, would say, " That man is speaking to some
one who is with him—who is present,"—as he often
said to me, " There's nae gude dune, John, till ye get
to *close grups*."

Now, I dare say you are marvelling—*first*, Why I
brought this grim, old Rhadamanthus, Belzaleel,
U. P. Naso of a doorkeeper up before you; and
secondly, How I am to get him down decorously in
that ancient blue greatcoat, and get at my own
proper text.

And first of the *first*. I thought it would do you
young men—the hope of the world—no harm to let
your affections go out toward this dear, old-world
specimen of homespun worth. And as to the *second*,
I am going to make it my excuse for what is to come.
One day soon after I knew him, when I thought he
was in a soft, confidential mood, I said : " *Jeems*,
what kind of weaver are you?" " *I'm in the fancical
line*, maister John," said he somewhat stiffly ; " I like
its *leecence*." So *exit Jeems—impiger, iracundus,
acer—torvus visu—placide quiescat !*

Now, my dear friends, I am in the *fancical* line as
well as *Jeems*, and in virtue of my *leecence*, I begin
my exegetical remarks on the pursuit of truth. By
the bye, I should have told Sir Henry that it was
truth, not knowledge, I was to be after. Now all

knowledge should be true, but it isn't; much of what is called knowledge is very little worth even when true, and much of the best truth is not in a strict sense knowable,—rather it is felt and believed.

Exegetical, you know, is the grand and fashionable word now-a-days for explanatory; it means bringing out of a passage all that is in it, and nothing more. For my part, being in *Jeems's* line, I am not so particular as to the nothing more. We *fancical* men are much given to make somethings of nothings; indeed, the noble Italians call imagination and poetic fancy *the little more;* its very function is to embellish and intensify the actual and the common. Now you must not laugh at me, or it, when I announce the passage from which I mean to preach upon the pursuit of truth, and the possession of wisdom :—

> " On Tintock tap there is a Mist,
> And in the Mist there is a Kist,
> And in the Kist there is a Cap ;
> Tak' up the Cap and sup the drap,
> And set the Cap on Tintock tap."

And as to what Sir Henry [1] would call the context, we are saved all trouble, there being none, the passage being self-contained, and as destitute of relations as Melchisedec.

Tintock, you all know, or should know, is a big porphyritic hill in Lanarkshire, standing alone, and dominating like a king over the Upper Ward. Then we all understand what a *mist* is ; and it is worth remembering that as it is more difficult to penetrate, to illuminate, and to see through mist than darkness, so it is easier to enlighten and overcome ignorance, than error, confusion, and mental mist. Then a *kist* is Scotch for chest, and a *cap* the same for *cup*, and *drap* for drop. Well, then, I draw out of these queer old lines—

First, That to gain real knowledge, to get it at first-hand, you must go up the Hill Difficulty—some

[1] This was read to Sir Henry W. Moncreiff's Young Men's Association, November 1862.

Tintock, something you see from afar—and you must *climb;* you must energize, as Sir William Hamilton and Dr. Chalmers said and did; you must turn your back upon the plain, and you must mainly go alone, and on your own legs. Two boys may start together on going up Tinto, and meet at the top; but the journeys are separate, each takes his own line.

Secondly, You start for your Tintock top with a given object, to get into the mist and get the drop, and you do this chiefly because you have the truth-hunting instinct; you long to know what is hidden there, for there is a wild and urgent charm in the unknown; and you want to realize for yourself what others, it may have been ages ago, tell they have found there.

Thirdly, There is no road up; no omnibus to the top of Tinto; you must zigzag it in your own way, and as I have already said, most part of it alone.

Fourthly, This climbing, this exaltation, and buckling to of the mind, of itself does you good;[1] it is capital exercise, and you find out many a thing by the way. Your lungs play freely; your mouth fills with the sweet waters of keen action; the hill tries your wind and mettle, supples and hardens your joints and limbs; quickens and rejoices, while it tests your heart.

Fifthly, You have many a fall, many a false step; you slip back, you tumble into a *moss-hagg;* you stumble over the baffling stones; you break your shins and lose your temper, and the finding of it makes you keep it better the next time; you get more patient, and yet more eager, and not unoften you come to a stand-still; run yourself up against, or to the edge of, some impossible precipice, some insoluble problem, and have to turn for your life; and you may find yourself over head in a treacherous *wellee,* whose soft inviting cushion of green has decoyed many a one before you.

[1] " In this pursuit, whether we take or whether we lose our game, the chase is certainly of service."—BURKE.

Sixthly, You are for ever mistaking the top; thinking you are at it, when, behold! there it is, as if farther off than ever, and you may have to humble yourself in a hidden valley before reascending; and so on you go, at times flinging yourself down on the elastic heather, stretched panting with your face to the sky, or gazing far away athwart the widening horizon.

Seventhly, As you get up, you may see how the world below lessens and reveals itself, comes up to you as a whole, with its just proportions and relations; how small the village you live in looks, and the house in which you were born; how the plan of the place comes out; there is the quiet churchyard, and a lamb is nibbling at that infant's grave; there, close to the little church, your mother rests till the great day; and there far off you may trace the river winding through the plain, coming like human life, from darkness to darkness,—from its source in some wild, upland solitude to its eternity, the sea. But you have rested long enough, so, up and away! take the hill once again! Every effort is a victory and joy—new skill and power and relish—takes you farther from the world below, nearer the clouds and heavens; and you may note that the more you move up towards the pure blue depths of the sky—the more lucid and the more unsearchable—the farther off, the more withdrawn into their own clear infinity do they seem. Well, then, you get to the upper story, and you find it less difficult, less steep than lower down; often so plain and level that you can run off in an ecstasy to the crowning cairn, to the sacred mist—within whose cloudy shrine rests the unknown secret; some great truth of God and of your own soul; something that is not to be gotten for gold down on the plain, but may be taken here; something that no man can give or take away; something that you must work for and learn yourself, and which, once yours, is safe beyond the chances of time.

Eighthly, You enter that luminous cloud, stooping and as a little child—as, indeed, all the best kingdoms are entered—and pressing on, you come in the shadowy light to the long-dreamt-of ark,—the chest. It is shut, it is locked; but if you are the man I take you to be, you have the key, put it gently in, steadily, and home. But what is the key? It is the love of truth; neither more nor less; no other key opens it; no false one, however cunning, can pick that lock; no assault of hammer, however stout, can force it open. But with its own key a little child may open it, often does open it, it goes so sweetly, so with a will. You lift the lid; you are all alone; the cloud is round you with a sort of tender light of its own, shutting out the outer world, filling you with an *eerie* joy, as if alone and yet not alone. You see the cup within, and in it the one crystalline, unimaginable, inestimable drop; glowing and tremulous, as if alive. You take up the cup, you sup the drop; it enters into, and becomes of the essence of yourself; and so, in humble gratitude and love, " in sober certainty of waking bliss," you gently replace the cup. It will gather again,—it is for ever gathering; no man, woman, or child ever opened that chest, and found no drop in the cup. It might not be the very drop expected; it will serve their purpose none the worse, often much the better.

And now, bending down, you shut the lid, which you hear locking itself afresh against all but the sacred key. You leave the now hallowed mist. You look out on the old familiar world again, which somehow looks both new and old. You descend, making your observations over again, throwing the light of the present on the past; and past and present set against the boundless future. You hear coming up to you the homely sounds—the sheep-dog's bark, " the cock's shrill clarion "—from the farm at the hill-foot; you hear the ring of the blacksmith's *study*, you see the smoke of his forge; your mother's grave has the long shadows of evening lying across it, the sunlight falling on the letters of her name, and on the number of her years; the lamb is asleep in the bield

of the infant's grave. Speedily you are at your own
door. You enter with wearied feet, and thankful
heart; you shut the door, and you kneel down and
pray to your Father in heaven, the Father of lights,
your reconciled Father, the God and Father of our
Lord and Saviour Jesus Christ, and our God and
Father in and through him. And as you lie down on
your own delightful bed, before you fall asleep, you
think over again your ascent of the Hill Difficulty,—
its baffling heights, its reaches of dreary moorland,
its shifting gravel, its precipices, its quagmires, its
little wells of living waters near the top, and all its
" dread magnificence;" its calm, restful summit, the
hush of silence there, the all-aloneness of the place
and hour; its peace, its sacredness, its divineness.
You see again the mist, the ark, the cup, the gleaming drop, and recalling the sight of the world below,
the earth and all its fulness, you say to yourself,—

> " These are thy glorious works, Parent of good,
>   Almighty, thine this universal frame,
>   Thus wondrous fair; Thyself how wondrous then !
>   Unspeakable, who sitt'st above these heavens."

And finding the burden too heavy even for these
glorious lines, you take refuge in the Psalms—

"Praise ye the Lord.
Praise ye the Lord from the heavens: praise him in the
    heights.
Praise him in the firmament of his power.
Praise ye him, all his angels: praise ye him, all his hosts.
Praise ye him, sun and moon: praise him, all ye stars of light.
Praise the Lord from the earth, ye dragons, and all deeps;
Fire and hail; snow and vapour; stormy wind fulfilling his
    word:
Mountains, and all hills; fruitful trees, and all cedars;
Beasts, and all cattle; creeping things, and flying fowl:
Kings of the earth, and all people; princes and all judges of
    the earth:
Both young men and maidens; old men and children:
Let them praise the name of the Lord:
For his name alone is excellent; his glory is above the earth
    and heaven.
Let everything that hath breath praise the Lord.
BLESS THE LORD, O my soul !"

I need hardly draw the moral of this, our somewhat *fancical* exercitation and exegesis. You can all make it out, such as it is. It is the toil, and the joy, and the victory in the search of truth; not the taking on trust, or learning by rote, not by heart, what other men count or call true; but the vital appropriation, the assimilation of truth to ourselves, and of ourselves to truth. All truth is of value, but one truth differs from another in weight and in brightness, in worth; and you need not me to tell you that spiritual and eternal truth, the truth as it is in Jesus, is the best. And don't think that your own hand has gotten you the victory, and that you had no unseen, and it may be unfelt and unacknowledged hand guiding you up the hill. Unless the Lord had been at and on your side, all your labour would have been in vain, and worse. No two things are more inscrutable or less uncertain than man's spontaneity and man's helplessness,—Freedom and Grace as the two poles. It is His doing that you are led to the right hill and the right road, for there are other Tintocks, with other kists, and other drops. Work out, therefore, your own knowledge with fear and trembling, for it is God that worketh in you both to will and to do, and to know of His good pleasure. There is no explaining and there is no disbelieving this.

And now, before bidding you good-bye, did you ever think of the spiritual meaning of the pillar of cloud by day, and the pillar of fire by night, as connected with our knowledge and our ignorance, our light and darkness, our gladness and our sorrow? The everyday use of this divine alternation to the wandering children of Israel, is plain enough. Darkness is best seen against light, and light against darkness; and its use, in a deeper sense of keeping for ever before them the immediate presence of God in the midst of them, is not less plain; but I sometimes think, that we who also are still in the wilderness, and coming up from our Egypt and its fleshpots, and on our way let us hope, through God's grace, to the celestial Canaan, may draw from these old-world signs and wonders, that, in the mid-day of knowledge, with daylight all about us, there is, if one could but look for it, that perpetual pillar of cloud—that sacred darkness which haunts all human knowledge, often the most at its highest noon; that " look that threatens the profane;" that something, and above all, that sense of *Some One*,—that Holy One, who inhabits eternity and its praises, who makes darkness His secret place, His pavilion round about, darkness and thick clouds of the sky.

And again, that in the deepest, thickest night of doubt, of fear, of sorrow, of despair; that then, and all the most then—if we will but look in the right *airt*, and with the seeing eye and the understanding heart—there may be seen that Pillar of fire, of light and of heat, to guide and quicken and cheer; knowledge and love, that everlasting love which we know to be the Lord's.   And how much better off are we than the chosen people; their pillars were on earth, divine in their essence, but subject doubtless to earthly perturbations and interferences; but our guiding light is in the heavens, towards which we take earnest heed that we are journeying.

> "Once on the raging seas I rode,
>   The storm was loud, the night was dark;
> The ocean yawned, and rudely blowed
>   The wind that toss'd my foundering bark.
>
> Deep horror then my vitals froze,
>   Death-struck, I ceased the tide to stem,
> When suddenly a star arose,
>   It was the Star of Bethlehem!
>
> It was my guide, my light, my all,
>   It bade my dark foreboding cease;
> And through the storm and danger's thrall
>   It led me to the port in peace.
>
> Now safely moored, my perils o'er,
>   I'll sing first in night's diadem,
> For ever and for evermore
>   The Star, the Star of Bethlehem!"

MINCHMOOR

"Sweet smells the birk, green grows, green grows the grass,
   Yellow on Yarrow's banks the gowan,
Fair hangs the apple frae the rock,
   Sweet the wave of Yarrow flowan.

Flows Yarrow sweet? as sweet, as sweet flows Tweed,
   As green its grass, its gowan yellow,
As sweet smells on its braes the birk,
   The apple frae the rock as mellow."

HAMILTON OF BANGOUR.

There is moral as well as bodily wholesomeness in a mount-tain walk, if the walker has the understanding heart, and eschews pic-nics. It is good for any man to be alone with nature and himself, or with a friend who knows when silence is more sociable than talk—

" In the wilderness alone,
There where nature worships God."

It is well to be in places where man is little and God is great —where what he sees all around him has the same look as it had a thousand years ago, and will have the same, in all like-lihood, when he has been a thousand years in his grave. It abates and rectifies a man, if he is worth the process.

" It is not favourable to religious feeling to hear only of the actions and interference of man, and to behold nothing but what human ingenuity has completed. There is an image of God's greatness impressed upon the outward face of nature fitted to make us all pious, and to breathe into our hearts a purifying and salutary fear.

*" In cities everything is man, and man alone. He seems to move and govern all, and be the Providence of cities; and there we do not render unto Cæsar the things which are Cæsar's, and unto God the things which are God's; but God is forgotten, and Cæsar is supreme—all is human policy, human foresight, human power; nothing reminds us of in-*visible dominion, and concealed omnipotence—*it is all earth, and no heaven. One cure of this is prayer and the solitary place. As the body, harassed with the noxious air of cities, seeks relief in the freedom and the purity of the fields and hills, so the mind, wearied by commerce with men, resumes its vigour in solitude, and repairs its dignity."*—From Sydney Smith's Sermon " On the effects which the tumultuous life passed in great cities produces upon the moral and religious character."—1809.

MINCHMOOR

Now that everybody is out of town, and every place in the guide-books is as well known as Princes Street or Pall-Mall, it is something to discover a hill everybody has not been to the top of, and which is not in *Black*. Such a hill is *Minchmoor*, nearly three times as high as Arthur's Seat, and lying between Tweed and Yarrow.

The best way to ascend it is from Traquair. You go up the wild old Selkirk road, which passes almost right over the summit, and by which Montrose and his cavaliers fled from Philiphaugh, where Sir Walter's mother remembered crossing, when a girl, in a coach-and-six, on her way to a ball at Peebles, several footmen marching on either side of the carriage to prop it up or drag it out of the moss *haggs;* and where, to our amazement, we learned that the Duchess of Buccleuch had lately driven her ponies. Before this we had passed the grey, old-world entrance to Traquair House, and looked down its grassy and untrod avenue to the pallid, forlorn mansion, stricken all o'er with eld, and noticed the wrought-iron gate embedded in a foot deep and more of soil, never having opened since the '45. There are the huge Bradwardine bears on each side—most grotesque supporters—with a superfluity of ferocity and canine teeth. The whole place, like the family whose it has been, seems dying out—everything subdued to settled desolation. The old race, the old religion, the gaunt old house, with its small, deep, comfortless windows, the decaying trees, the stillness about the doors, the grass overrunning everything, nature reinstating herself in her quiet way—all this makes the place look as strange and pitiful among its fellows in the vale as would the Earl who built it three hundred years ago if we met him tottering along our way in the faded dress of his youth; but it looks the Earl's house still, and has a dignity of its own.

We soon found the Minchmoor road, and took at once to the hill, the ascent being, as often is with other ascents in this world, steepest at first. Nothing could be more beautiful than the view as we ascended, and got a look of the " eye-sweet " Tweed hills, and their " silver stream." It was one of the five or six good days of this summer—in early morning, " soft " and doubtful; but the mists drawing up, and now the noble, tawny hills were dappled with gleams and shadows—

" Sunbeams upon distant hills gliding apace "—

the best sort of day for mountain scenery—that ripple of light and shadow brings out the forms and the depths of the hills far better than a cloudless sky; and the horizon is generally wider.

Before us and far away was the round flat head of Minchmoor, with a dark, rich bloom on it from the thick, short heather—the hills around being green. Near the top, on the Tweed side, its waters trotting away cheerily to the glen at Bold, is the famous *Cheese Well*—always full, never overflowing. Here every traveller—Duchess, shepherd, or houseless *mugger*—stops, rests, and is thankful; doubtless so did Montrose, poor fellow, and his young nobles and their jaded steeds, on their scurry from Lesly and his Dragoons. It is called the Cheese Well from those who rest there dropping in bits of their provisions, as votive offerings to the fairies whose especial haunt this mountain was. After our rest and drink, we left the road and made for the top. When there we were well rewarded. The great round-backed, kindly, solemn hills of Tweed, Yarrow, and Ettrick lay all about like sleeping mastiffs—too plain to be grand, too ample and beautiful to be commonplace.

There, to the north-east, is the place—*William-hope* ridge—where Sir Walter Scott bade farewell to his heroic friend Mungo Park. They had come up from *Ashestiel*, where Scott then lived, and where "Marmion" was written and its delightful epistles inspired—where he passed the happiest part of his life—leaving it, as Hogg said, "for gude an' a';" for his fatal "dreams about his cottage" were now begun. He was to have "a hundred acres, two spare bed-rooms, with dressing rooms, each of which will on a pinch have a couch-bed." We all know what the dream, and the cottage, and the hundred acres came to—the ugly Abbotsford; the over-burdened, shattered brain driven wild, and the end, death, and madness. Well, it was on that ridge that the two friends—each romantic, but in such different ways—parted never to meet again. There is the ditch Park's horse stumbled over and all but fell. "I am afraid, Mungo, that's a bad omen," said the Sheriff; to which he answered, with a bright smile on his handsome, fearless face—"*Freits* (omens) follow those who look to them." With this expression, he struck the spurs into his horse, and Scott never saw him again. He had not long been married to a lovely and much-loved woman, and had been speaking to Scott about his new African scheme, and how he meant to tell his family he had some business in Edinburgh—send them his blessing, and be off—alas! never to return! Scott used to say, when speaking of this parting, "I stood and looked back, but he did not." A more memorable place for two such men to part in would not easily be found.

Where we are standing is the spot Scott speaks of when writing to Joanna Baillie about her new tragedies—"Were it possible for me to hasten the treat I expect in such a composition with you, I would promise to read the volume *at the silence of noonday upon the top of Minchmoor*. The hour is allowed, by those skilful in demonology, *to be as full*

of witching as midnight itself; and I assure you I
have felt really oppressed with a sort of fearful loneliness when looking around the naked towering ridges
of desolate barrenness, which is all the eye takes in
from the top of such a mountain, the patches of
cultivation being hidden in the little glens, or only
appearing to make one feel how feeble and ineffectual
man has been to contend with the genius of the soil.
It is in such a scene that the unknown and gifted
author of *Albania* places the superstition which consists in hearing the noise of a chase, the baying of
the hounds, the throttling sobs of the deer, the wild
hollos of the huntsmen, and the ' hoof thick beating
on the hollow hill.' I have often repeated his verses
with some sensations of awe, in this place." The
lines—and they are noble, and must have sounded
wonderful with his voice and look—are as follows.
Can no one tell us anything more of their author?—

> " There oft is heard, at midnight, or at noon,
> Beginning faint, but rising still more loud,
> And nearer, voice of hunters, and of hounds;
> And horns, hoarse-winded, blowing far and keen!
> Forthwith the hubbub multiplies; the gale
> Labours with wilder shrieks, and rifer din
> Of hot pursuit; the broken cry of deer
> Mangled by throttling dogs; the shouts of men,
> And hoofs thick beating on the hollow hill.
> Sudden the grazing heifer in the vale
> Starts at the noise, and both the herdman's ears
> Tingle with inward dread—aghast he eyes
> The mountain's height, and all the ridges round,
> Yet not one trace of living wight discerns,
> Nor knows, o'erawed and trembling as he stands,
> To what or whom he owes his idle fear—
> To ghost, to witch, to fairy, or to fiend;
> But wonders, and no end of wondering finds."

We listened for the hunt, but could only hear the
wind sobbing from the blind " *Hopes*." [1]
     The view from the top reaches from the huge
Harestane Broadlaw—nearly as high as Ben Lomond

[1] The native word for hollows in the hills: thus, Dryhope,
Gameshope, Chapelhope, &c.

—whose top is as flat as a table, and would make a race-course of two miles, and where the clouds are still brooding, to the *Cheviot;* and from the *Maiden Paps* in Liddesdale, and that wild huddle of hills at *Moss Paul*, to *Dunse Law*, and the weird *Lammermoors*. There is *Ruberslaw*, always surly and dark. The *Dunion*, beyond which lies Jedburgh. There are the *Eildons*, with their triple heights; and you can get a glimpse of the upper woods of Abbotsford, and the top of the hill above Cauldshiels Loch, that very spot where the "wondrous potentate,"—when suffering from langour and pain, and beginning to break down under his prodigious fertility,—composed those touching lines :—

> "The sun upon the Weirdlaw Hill
>   In Ettrick's vale is sinking sweet;
> The westland wind is hushed and still;
>   The lake lies sleeping at my feet.
> Yet not the landscape to mine eye
>   Bears those bright hues that once it bore,
> Though evening, with her richest dye,
>   Flames o'er the hills of Ettrick's shore.
>
> With listless look along the plain
>   I see Tweed's silver current glide,
> And coldly mark the holy fane
>   Of Melrose rise in ruined pride.
> The quiet lake, the balmy air,
>   The hill, the stream, the tower, the tree,
> Are they still such as once they were,
>   Or is the dreary change in me?
>
> Alas! the warped and broken board,
>   How can it bear the painter's dye!
> The harp of strained and tuneless chord,
>   How to the minstrel's skill reply!
> To aching eyes each landscape lowers,
>   To feverish pulse each gale blows chill;
> And Araby or Eden's bowers
>   Were barren as this moorland hill."

There, too, is *Minto Hill*, as modest and shapely and smooth as Clytie's shoulders, and *Earlston Black Hill*, with Cowdenknowes at its foot; and there,

standing stark and upright as a warder, is the stout
old *Smailholme Tower*, seen and seeing all around.
It is quite curious how unmistakable and important
it looks at what must be twenty and more miles.   It
is now ninety years since that "lonely infant," who
has sung its awful joys, was found in a thunder-
storm, as we all know, lying on the soft grass at
the foot of the grey old Strength, clapping his hands
at each flash, and shouting, "Bonny! bonny!"

We now descended into Yarrow, and forgathered
with a shepherd who was taking his lambs over to
the great Melrose fair.   He was a fine specimen of
a border herd—young, tall, sagacious, self-contained,
and free in speech and air.   We got his heart by
praising his dog *Jed*, a very fine collie, black and
comely, gentle and keen—"Ay, she's a fell yin; she
can do a' but speak."   On asking him if the sheep
dogs needed much teaching—"Whyles ay and
whyles no; her kind (Jed's) needs nane.   She sooks
't in wi' her mither's milk."   On asking him if the
dogs were ever sold, he said—"Never, but at an
orra time.   Naebody wad sell a gude dowg, and
naebody wad buy an ill ane."   He told us with
great feeling, of the death of one of his best dogs by
poison.   It was plainly still a grief to him.   "What
was he poisoned with?"   "Strychnia," he said, as
decidedly as might Dr. Christison.   "How do you
know?"   "I opened him, puir fallow, and got him
analeezed!"

Now we are on Birkindale Brae, and are looking
down on the same scene as did

"James Boyd (the Earle of Arran, his brother was he),"

when he crossed Minchmoor on his way to deliver
James the Fifth's message to

"Yon outlaw Murray,
Surely whaur bauldly bideth he."

"Down Birkindale Brae when that he cam
He saw the feir Foreste wi' his ee."

How James Boyd fared, and what the outlaw said, and what James and his nobles said and did, and how the outlaw at last made peace with his King, and rose up " Sheriffe of Ettricke Foreste," and how the bold ruffian boasted,

> " Fair Philiphaugh is mine by right,
>   And Lewinshope still mine shall be;
> Newark, Foulshiels, and Tinnies baith
>   My bow and arrow purchased me.
>
> And I have native steads to me
>   The Newark Lee o' Hangingshaw.
> I have many steads in the Forest schaw,
>   But them by name I dinna knaw."

And how King James snubbed

> " The kene Laird of Buckscleuth,
>   A stalwart man and sterne was he."

When the Laird hinted that,

> " For a king to gang an outlaw till
>   Is beneath his state and dignitie.
> The man that wins yon forest intill
>   He lives by reif and felony."
>
> " Then out and spak the nobil King,
>   And round him cast a wilie ee.
>
> ' Now haud thy tongue, Sir Walter Scott,
>   Nor speak o' reif or felonie—
> *For, had every honest man his awin kye,*
>   *A richt puir clan thy name wud be!* ' "

(by-the-bye, why did Professor Aytoun leave out this excellent hit in his edition?)—all this and much more may you see if you take up *The Border Minstrelsy*, and read " The Sang of the Outlaw Murray," with the incomparable notes of Scott. But we are now well down the hill. There to the left, in the hollow, is *Permanscore*, where the King and the outlaw met :—

> " Bid him mete me at Permanscore,
>   And bring four in his companie;
> Five Erles sall cum wi' mysel',
>   Gude reason I sud honoured be."

And there goes our Shepherd with his long swing-ing stride. As different from his dark, wily com-panion, the Badenoch drover, as was Harry Wake-field from Robin Oig; or as the big, sunny Cheviot is from the lowering Ruberslaw; and there is *Jed* trotting meekly behind him—may she escape strych-nia, and, dying at the fireside among the children, be laid like

> " Paddy Tims—whose soul at aise is—
> With the point of his nose
> And the tips of his toes
> Turn'd up to the roots of the daisies "—

unanaleezed, save by the slow cunning of the grave. And may her master get the top price for his lambs!

Do you see to the left that little plantation on the brow of Foulshiels Hill, with the sunlight lying on its upper corner? If you were there you might find among the brackens and foxglove a little head-stone with " I. T." rudely carved on it. That is *Tibbie Tamson's grave*, known and feared all the country round.

This poor outcast was a Selkirk woman, who, under the stress of spiritual despair—that sense of perdition, which, as in Cowper's case, often haunts and overmasters the deepest and gentlest natures, making them think themselves

> " Damn'd below Judas, more abhorred than he was,"—

committed suicide; and being, with the gloomy, cruel superstition of the time, looked on by her neigh-bours as accursed of God, she was hurried into a rough white deal coffin, and carted out of the town, the people stoning it all the way till it crossed the Etterick. Here, on this wild hillside, it found its rest, being buried where three lairds' lands meet. May we trust that the light of God's reconciled coun-tenance has for all these long years been resting on that once forlorn soul, as his blessed sunshine now lies on her moorland grave! For " the mountains

shall depart, and the hills be removed; but my kindness shall not depart from thee, neither shall the
covenant of my peace be removed, saith the Lord
that hath mercy on thee."

Now, we see down into the Yarrow—there is the
famous stream twinkling in the sun. What stream
and valley was ever so be-sung! You wonder at
first why this has been, but the longer you look the
less you wonder. There is a charm about it—it is
not easy to say what. The huge sunny hills in which
it is embosomed give it a look at once gentle and
serious. They are great, and their gentleness makes
them greater. Wordsworth has the right words,
"pastoral melancholy;" and besides, the region is
"not uninformed with phantasy and looks that
threaten the profane"—the Flowers of Yarrow, the
Douglas Tragedy, the Dowie Dens, Wordsworth's
Yarrow Unvisited, Visited, and Re-Visited, and,
above all, the glamour of Sir Walter, and Park's
fatal and heroic story. Where can you find eight
more exquisite lines anywhere than Logan's, which
we all know by heart :—

> " His mother from the window looked,
>   With all the longing of a mother;
> His little sister, weeping, walked
>   The greenwood path to meet her brother.
> They sought him east, they sought him west,
>   They sought him all the forest thorough—
> They only saw the cloud of night,
>   They only heard the roar of Yarrow."

And there is *Newark Tower* among the rich woods;
and *Harehead*, that cosiest, loveliest, and hospitablest
of nests. Methinks I hear certain young voices
among the hazels; out they come on the little haugh
by the side of the deep, swirling stream, *fabulosus*
as was ever Hydaspes. There they go "running
races in their mirth," and is not that—*an me ludit
amabilis insania?*—the voice of *ma pauvre petite—
animosa infans*—the wilful, rich-eyed, delicious
Eppie?

> " Oh blessed vision, happy child,
> Thou art so exquisitely wild !"

And there is *Black Andro and Glowr owr'em* and *Foulshiels*, where Park was born and bred; and there is the deep pool in the Yarrow where Scott found him plunging one stone after another into the water, and watching anxiously the bubbles as they rose to the surface. "This," said Scott to him, "appears but an idle amusement for one who has seen so much adventure." "Not so idle, perhaps, as you suppose," answered Mungo, "this was the way I used to ascertain the depth of a river in Africa." He was then meditating his second journey, but had said so to no one.

We go down by *Broadmeadows*, now held by that Yair "Hoppringle"—who so well governed Scinde —and into the grounds of Bowhill, and passing *Philiphaugh*, see where stout David Lesly crossed in the mist at daybreak with his heavy dragoons, many of them old soldiers of Gustavus, and routed the gallant Græme; and there is *Slainmen's Lee*, where the royalists lie; and there is *Carterhaugh*, the scene of the strange wild story of *Tamlane* and Lady Janet, when

> " She prinked hersell and prinned hersell
> By the ae light of the moon,
> And she's awa' to Carterhaugh
> To speak wi' young Tamlane."

Noel Paton might paint that night, when

> " 'Twixt the hours of twelve and yin
> A north wind *tore the bent;*"

when " fair Janet " in her green mantle

> " —— heard strange elritch sounds
> Upon the wind that went."

And straightway

> " About the dead hour o' the night
> She heard the bridles ring ;

> ' Their oaten pipes blew wondrous shrill,
> The hemlock small blew clear ;
> And louder notes from hemlock large
> And bog reed, struck the ear,"

and then the fairy cavalcade swept past, while Janet,
filled with love and fear, looked out for the milk-white
steed, and " gruppit it fast," and " pu'd the rider
doon," the young Tamlane, whom, after dipping " in
a stand of milk and then in a stand of water,"

> " She wrappit ticht in her green mantle,
> And sae her true love won !"

This ended our walk. We found the carriage at
the Philiphaugh home-farm, and we drove home by
Yair and *Fernilee*, *Ashestiel* and *Elibank*, and passed
the bears as ferocious as ever, " the orange sky of
evening " glowing through their wild tusks, the old
house looking even older in the fading light. And
is not this a walk worth making? One of our number had been at the Land's End and Johnnie Groat's,
and now on Minchmoor ; and we wondered how many
other men had been at all the three, and how many
had enjoyed Minchmoor more than he.

But we must end, and how can we do it better,
and more to our readers' and our own satisfaction,
than by giving them the following unpublished lines
by Professor Shairp,[1] which, by means we do not
care to mention, are now before us?—

THE BUSH ABOON TRAQUAIR.

> Will ye gang wi' me and fare
> To the bush aboon Traquair?
> Owre the high Minchmuir we'll up and awa',
> This bonny simmer noon,
> While the sun shines fair aboon,
> And the licht sklents saftly doun on holm and ha'.

[1] No longer unpublished. The reader will find them, along
with much else that is delightful, in *Kilmahoe, a Highland
Pastoral, with other Poems.*

And what wad ye do there,
  At the bush aboon Traquair?
A lang dreich road, ye had better let it be;
  Save some auld scrunts o' birk
  I' the hill-side lirk,[1]
There's nocht i' the warld for man to see.

But the blythe lilt o' that air,
  " The Bush aboon Traquair,"
I need nae mair, it's eneuch for me;
  Owre my cradle its sweet chime
  Cam sughin' frae auld time,
Sae tide what may, I'll awa' and see.

And what saw ye there,
  At the bush aboon Traquair?
Or what did ye hear that was worth your heed?
  I heard the cushies croon
  Thro' the gowden afternoon,
And the Quair burn singing doun to the vale o' Tweed.

And birks saw I three or four,
  Wi' grey moss bearded owre,
The last that are left o' the birken shaw,
  Whar mony a simmer e'en
  Fond lovers did convene,
Thae bonny, bonny gloamins that are lang awa'.

Frae mony a but and ben,
  By muirland, holm, and glen,
They cam ane hour to spen' on the greenwood swaird;
  But lang ha'e lad an' lass
  Been lying 'neth the grass,
The green green grass o' Traquair kirkyard.

They were blest beyond compare,
  When they held their trysting there,
Amang thae greenest hills shone on by the sun;
  And then they wan a rest,
  The lownest and the best,
I' Traquair kirkyard when a' was dune.

Now the birks to dust may rot,
  Names o' luvers be forgot,
Nae lads and lasses there ony mair convene;
  But the blythe lilt o' yon air
Keeps the bush aboon Traquair,
And the luve that ance was there, aye fresh and green.

> [1] " The hills were high on ilka side,
>   And the bucht i' the *lirk o' the hill*."
>   *Ballad of Cowdenknowes.*

Have not these the true flavour of that gentle place and life,—as musical and as melancholy as their streams and glens, as fragrant as their birks and *gale?*[1] They have the unexpectedness of nature, of genius, and of true song. The " native wood-notes wild " of " the mountain nymph, sweet Liberty."

There must surely be more of this " lilting " in our minstrel's wallet; and he may be assured that such a gift of genuine Scottish feeling and verse will be welcomed if revealed. It breathes the caller, strong air of the south country hills, and is a wild " flouir o' the forest " not likely soon to be " wede awae."

" Sweet smells the birk, green grows, green grows the grass,
 Yellow on Yarrow's banks the gowan,
Fair hangs the apple frae the rock,
 Sweet the wave of Yarrow flowan.

Flows Yarrow sweet? as sweet, as sweet flows Tweed,
 As green its grass, its gowan yellow,
As sweet smells on its braes the birk,
 The apple frae the rock as mellow."

[1] The Bog-Myrtle.

THE BLACK DWARF'S BONES

. . . "*If thou wert grim,*
Lame, ugly, crooked, swart, prodigious."
KING JOHN.

THE BLACK DWARF'S BONES

THESE gnarled, stunted, useless old bones, were all that David Ritchie, the original of the Black Dwarf, had for left *femur* and *tibia*, and we have merely to look at them and add poverty, to know the

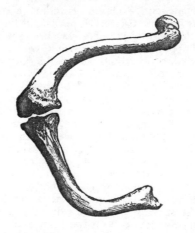

misery summed up in their possession. They seem to have been blighted and rickety. The *femur* is very short and slight, and singularly loose in texture; the *tibia* is dwarfed, but dense and stout. They were given to me many years ago by the late Andrew Ballantyne, Esq. of Woodhouse (the Wudess, as they call it on Tweedside), and their genuineness is unquestionable.

As anything must be interesting about one once so forlorn and miserable, and whom our great wizard has made immortal, I make no apology for printing the following letters from my old friend, Mr. Craig, long surgeon in Peebles, and who is now spending his evening, after a long, hard, and useful day's work, in the quiet vale of Manor, within a mile or two of "Cannie Elshie's" cottage. The picture he gives is very affecting, and should make us all thankful that we are "wiselike." There is much that is additional to Sir Walter's account, in his "Author's Edition" of the Waverley Novels.

"HALL MANOR, *Thursday, May* 20, 1858.

"MY DEAR SIR,—David Ritchie, *alias* Bowed Davie, was born at Easter Happrew, in the parish of Stobo, in the year 1741. He was brought to Woodhouse, in the parish of Manor, when very young. His father was a labourer, and occupied a cottage on that farm; his mother, Anabel Niven, was a delicate woman, severely afflicted with rheumatism, and could not take care of him when an infant. To this cause he attributed his deformity, and this, if added to imperfect clothing, and bad food, and poverty, will account for the grotesque figure which he became. He never was at school, but he could read tolerably; had many books; was fond of poetry, especially Allan Ramsay; he hated Burns. His father and mother both died early, and poor Davie became a homeless wanderer; he was two years at Broughton Mill, employed in stirring the husks of oats, which were used for drying the corn on the kiln, and required to be kept constantly in motion; he boasted, with a sort of rapture, of his doings there. From thence he went to Lyne's Mill, near his birthplace, where he continued one year at the same employment, and from thence he was sent to Edinburgh to learn brush-making, but made no progress in his education there; was annoyed by the wicked boys, or *keelies*, as he called them, and found his way back to Manor and Woodhouse. The farm now possessed by Mr. Ballantyne, was then occupied by four tenants, among whom he lived; but

his house was at Old Woodhouse, where the late
Sir James Nasmyth built him a house with two apart-
ments, and separate outer doors, one for himself
exactly his own height when standing upright in it;
and this stands as it was built, exactly four feet. A
Mr. Ritchie, the father of the late minister of Athel-
staneford, was then tenant; his wife and Davie could
not agree, and she repeatedly asked her husband to
put him away, by making the highest stone of his
house the lowest. Ritchie left, his house was pulled
down, and Davie triumphed in having the stones of
his chimney-top made a step to his door, when this
new house was built. He was not a little vindictive
at times when irritated, especially when any allusion
was made to his deformity. On one occasion, he and
some other boys were stealing pease in Mr. Gibson's
field, who then occupied Woodhouse; all the others
took *leg-bail*, but Davie's locomotion being tardy, he
was caught, shaken, and scolded by Gibson for all
the rest. This he never forgot, and vowed to be
avenged on the ' auld sinner and deevil;' and one
day when Gibson was working about his own door,
Davie crept up to the top of the house, which was low,
and threw a large stone down on his head, which
brought the old man to the ground. Davie crept
down the other side of the house, got into bed beside
his mother, and it was never known where the stone
came from, till he boasted of it long afterwards. He
only prayed that it might sink down through his
' *harn-pan* ' (his skull). His personal appearance
seems to have been almost indescribable, not bearing
any likeness to anything in this upper world. But as
near as I can learn, his forehead was very narrow
and low, sloping upwards and backward, something
of the hatchet shape; his eyes deep set, small, and
piercing; his nose straight, thin as the end of a cut
of cheese, sharp at the point, nearly touching his
fearfully projecting chin; and his mouth formed nearly
a straight line; his shoulders rather high, but his body
otherwise the size of ordinary men; his arms were

remarkably strong. With very little aid he built a high garden wall, which still stands, many of his stones of huge size; these the shepherds laid to his directions. His legs beat all power of description; they were bent in every direction, so that Mungo Park, then a surgeon at Peebles, who was called to operate on him for strangulated hernia, said he could compare them to nothing but a pair of cork-screws; but the principal turn they took was from the knee outwards, so that he rested on his inner ankles, and the lower part of his tibias. The position of the bones in the woodcut, gives some, but a very imperfect idea of this; the *thrawn* twisted limbs must have crossed each other at the knees, and looked more like roots than legs,

" And his knotted knees play'd ay knoit between."

" He had never a shoe on his feet; the parts on which he walked were rolled in rags, old stockings, etc., but the toes always bare, even in the most severe weather. His mode of progressing was as extraordinary as his shape. He carried a long pole, or " kent," like the Alpenstock, tolerably polished, with a turned top on it, on which he rested, placed it before him, he then lifted one leg, something in the manner that the oar of a boat is worked, and then the other, next advanced his staff, and repeated the operation, by diligently doing which he was able to make not very slow progress. He frequently walked to Peebles, four miles, and back again in one day. His arms had no motion at the elbow-joints, but were active enough otherwise. He was not generally ill-tempered, but furious when roused.

" ROBERT CRAIG."

" HALL MANOR, *June* 15, 1858.

" MY DEAR SIR,—I have delayed till now to finish Bowed Davie, in the hope of getting more information, and to very little purpose. His contemporaries are now so few, old, and widely scattered, that they are difficult to be got at, and when come at, their memories are failed, like their bodies. I have forgotten at what stage of his history I left off; but if I repeat, you can omit the repetitions. Sir James Nasmyth, late of Posso, took compassion on the houseless, homeless *lusus naturæ*, and had a house built for him to his own directions; the door, window, and everything to suit his diminished, grotesque form; the door four feet high, the window twelve by eighteen inches, without glass, closed by a wooden board, hung on leathern hinges, which he used to keep shut. Through it he reconnoitred all visitors, and only admitted ladies and particular favourites; he was very superstitious; ghosts, fairies, and robbers he dreaded most. I have forgotten if I mentioned how he contrived to be fed and warmed. He had a small allowance from the parish poor-box, about fifty shillings; this was eked out by an annual peregrination through the parish, when some gave him food, others money, wool, etc., which he hoarded most miserly. How he cooked his food I have not been able to learn, for his sister, who lived in the same cottage with him, was separated by a stone and lime wall, and had a separate door of the usual size, and window to match, and was never allowed to enter his dwelling; but he brought home such loads, that the shepherds had to be on the out-look for him, when on his annual eleemosynary expeditions, to carry home part of his spoil. On one occasion a servant was ordered to give him some salt, for containing which he carried a long stocking; he thought the damsel had scrimped him in quantity, and he sat and distended the stocking till it appeared less than half full, by pressing down the salt, and then called for the gudewife, showed it her, and asked if she had ordered Jenny only to give him that wee pickle saut; the maid was scolded, and the stocking filled. He spent all his evenings at the back of the Woodhouse kitchen fire, and got at least one meal every day, where he used to make the rustics gape and stare at the many ghost, fairy, and robber stories which he had either heard of or invented, and poured out with unceasing volubility, and so often, that he believed them all true.   But the Ballantyne family had no great faith in his veracity, when it suited his convenience to fib, exaggerate, or prevaricate, particularly when excited by his own lucubrations, or the waggery of his more intellectual neighbours and companions. He had a seat in the centre, which he always occupied, and a stool for his deformed feet and legs; they all rose at times, asking Davie to do likewise, and when he got upon his pins, he was shorter than when sitting, his body being of the ordinary length, and the deficiency all in his legs. On one occasion, a wag named Elder put up a log of wood opposite his loophole, made a noise, and told Davie that the robbers he dreaded so much were now at his house, and would not go away; he peeped out, and saw the log, exclaimed, ' So he is, by the Lord God and my soul; Willie Elder, gi'e me the gun, and see that she is weel charged.' Elder put in a very large supply of powder without shot, rammed it hard, got a stool, which Davie mounted, Elder handing him the gun, charging him to take time, and aim fair, for if he missed him, he would be mad at being shot at, be sure to come in, take everything in the house, cut their throats, and burn the house after. Davie tremblingly obeyed, presented the gun slowly and cautiously, drew the trigger; off went the shot, the musket rebounded, and back went Davie with a rattle on the floor. Some accomplice tumbled the log; Davie at length was encouraged to look out, and actually believed that he had shot the robber; said he had done for him now, ' that ane wad plague him nae mair at ony rate.' He took it into his head at one time that he ought to be married, and having got the consent of a haverel wench to yoke with him in the silken bonds of matrimony, went to the minister several times, and asked him to perform the ceremony. At length the minister sent him away, saying, that he could not and would not accommodate him in the matter. Davie swung himself out at the door on his kent, much crest-fallen, and in great wrath, shutting the door with a bang behind him, but opening it again, he shook his clenched fist in the parson's face, and said, ' Weel, weel, ye'll no let decent, honest folk marry; but, 'od, lad, I'se plenish your parish wi' bastards, to see what ye'll mak o' that,' and away he went. He read Hooke's *Pantheon*, and made great use of the heathen deities. He railed sadly at the taxes; some one observed that he need not grumble at them as he had none to pay. ' Hae I no'?' he replied, ' I can naither get a pickle snuff to my neb, nor a pickle tea to my mouth, but they maun tax it.' His sister and he were on very unfriendly terms. She was ill on one occasion; Miss Ballantyne asked how she was to-day. He replied, ' I dinna ken, I ha'na been in, for I hate folk that are aye gaun to dee and never do't.' In 1811 he was seized with obstruction of the bowels and consequent inflammation; blisters and various remedies were applied for three days without effect. Some one came to Mrs. Ballantyne and said that it was ' just about a' owre wi' Davie noo.' She went, and he breathed his last almost immediately. His sister, without any delay, got his keys, and went to his secret repository; Mrs. Ballantyne thought to get dead-clothes, but instead, to the amazement of all present, she threw three money-bags, one after another, into Mrs. Ballantyne's lap, telling her to count that, and that, and that. Mrs. B. was annoyed and astonished at the multitude of half-crowns and shillings, all arranged according to value. He hated sixpences, and had none, but the third contained four guineas in gold. Mrs. B. was disgusted with the woman's greed, and put them all up, saying, what would anybody think if they came in and found them counting the man's money and his breath scarcely out,—took it all home to her husband, who made out £4 2s. in gold, £10 in a bank receipt, and £7 18s. in shillings and half-crowns, in all £22. How did he get this? He had many visitors, the better class of whom gave him

half-crowns, others shillings and sixpences; the latter
he never kept, but converted them into shillings and
half-crowns whenever he got an opportunity.   I'
asked the wright how he got him into a coffin.   He
replied, ' Easily; they made it deeper than ordinary,
and wider, so as to let in his distorted legs, as it was
impossible to streek him like others.'   He often expressed a resolve to be buried on the Woodhill top,
three miles up the water from the churchyard, as he
could never ' lie amang the common trash;' however,
this was not accomplished, as his friend, Sir James
Nasmyth, who had promised to carry this wish into
effect, was on the Continent at the time.   When Sir
James returned he spoke of having his remains lifted
and buried where he had wished; but this was never
done, and the expense of a railing and plantation of
rowan-trees (mountain-ash), his favourite prophylactic
against the spells of witches and fairies, was abandoned.   The Woodhill is a romantic, green little
mount, situated at the west side of the Manor, which
washes its base on the east, and separates it from
Langhaugh heights, part of a lofty, rocky and
heathery mountain range, and on the west is the ruin
of the ancient peel-house of old Posso, long the residence of the Nasmyth family.   And now that we have
the Dwarf dead and buried, comes the history of his
resurrection in 1821.   His sister died exactly ten years
after him.   A report had been spread that he had been
lifted and taken to dissecting-rooms in Glasgow,
which at that period was the fate of many a more
seemly corpse than Davie's; and the young men—for
Manor had no sexton—who dug the sister's grave in
the vicinity of her brother's, stimulated by curiosity
to see if his body had really been carried off, and if
still there what his bones were like, lifted them up,
and carried them to Woodhouse, where they lay a
considerable time, till they were sent to Mr. Ballantyne, then in Glasgow.   Miss Ballantyne thinks the
skull was taken away with the other bones, but put
back again.   I have thus given you all the information

I can gather about the Black Dwarf that I think worth narrating. It is reported that he sometimes sold a gill, but if this is true the Ballantynes never knew it. Miss Ballantyne says that he was not ill-tempered, but on the contrary, kind, especially to children. She and her brother were very young when she went to Woodhouse, and her father objected to re-setting the farm from Sir James, on account of the fearful accounts of his horrid temper and barbarous deeds, and Sir James said if he ever troubled them that he would immediately put him away; but he was very fond of the younger ones, played with them, and amused them, though when roused and provoked by grown-up people, he raged, stormed, swore terrifically, and struck with anything that was near him, in short, he had an irritable but not a sulky, sour, misanthropic temper. The Messrs. Chambers wrote a book about him and his doings at a very early period of their literary history. Did I tell you of a female relative, Niven (whom he would never see), saying that she would come and streek him after he died? He sent word, 'that if she offered to touch his corpse he would rive the thrapple oot o' her—he would raither be streekit by Auld Clootie's ain red-het hands.'— Yours, truly obliged,

" R. C. "

This poor, vindictive, solitary, and powerful creature, was a philocalist: he had a singular love of flowers and of beautiful women. He was a sort of Paris, to whom the blushing Aphrodites of the glen used to come, and his judgment is said to have been as good, as the world generally thinks that of Œnone's handsome and faithless mate. His garden was full of the finest flowers, and it was his pleasure, when the young beauties

> " Who bore the blue sky intermixed with flame
> In their fair eyes "

came to him for their competitive examination, to scan them well, and then, without one word, present each with a flower, which was of a certain fixed and well-known value in Davie's standard *calimeter*.

I have heard that there was one kind of rose, his καλλιστεῖον, which he was known to have given only to three, and I remember seeing one of the three, when she was past seventy. Margaret Murray, or Morra, was her maiden name, and this fine old lady, whom an Oxonian would call a Double First, grave and silent, and bent with "the pains," when asked by us children, would, with some reluctance, and a curious grave smile, produce out of her Bible, Bowed Davie's withered and flattened rose; and from her looks, even then, I was inclined to affirm the decision of the connoisseur of Manor Water. One can fancy the scene in that sweet solitary valley, informed like its sister Yarrow with pastoral melancholy, with a young May, bashful and eager, presenting herself for honours, encountering from under that penthouse of eye-brows the steady gaze of the strange eldritch creature; and then his making up his mind, and proceeding to pluck his award and present it to her, " herself a fairer flower;" and then turning with a scowl, crossed with a look of tenderness, crawl into his den. Poor "gloomy Dis," slinking in alone.

They say, that when the candidate came, he surveyed her from his window, his eyes gleaming out of the darkness, and if he liked her not, he disappeared; if he would entertain her, he beckoned her into the garden.

I have often thought, that the *Brownie*, of whom the South country legends are so full, must have been some such misshapen creature, strong, willing, and forlorn, conscious of his hideous forbidding looks, and ready to purchase affection at any cost of labour, with a kindly heart, and a longing for human sympathy and intercourse. Such a being looks like the prototype of the Aiken-Drum of our infancy, and of that "drudging goblin," of whom we all know how he

"   . . . . . Sweat
To earn his cream-bowl daily set,

When in one night, ere glimpse of morn,
His shadowy flail hath thresh'd the corn,
That ten day lab'rers could not end;
Then lies him down, the lubber [1] fiend,
And stretch'd out all the chimney's length,
Basks at the fire his hairy strength,
And cropful out of doors he flings,
Ere the first cock his matin rings."

My readers will, I am sure, more than pardon me for giving them the following poem on Aiken-Drum, for the pleasure of first reading which, many years ago, I am indebted to Mr. R. Chambers's *Popular Rhymes of Scotland*, where its " extraordinary merit " is generously acknowledged.

THE BROWNIE OF BLEDNOCH.

There cam' a strange wicht to our town-en',
An' the fient a body did him ken;
He tirl'd na lang, but he glided ben
    Wi' a dreary, dreary hum.

His face did glow like the glow o' the west,
When the drumlie cloud has it half o'ercast;
Or the struggling moon when she's fair distrest,
    O, sirs! 'twas Aiken-drum.

I trow the bauldest stood aback,
Wi' a gape an' a glow'r till their lugs did crack,
As the shapeless phantom mum'ling spak,
    Hae ye wark for Aiken-drum?

O! had ye seen the bairns' fricht,
As they stared at this wild and unyirthly wicht,
As they skulkit in 'tween the dark an' the licht,
    An' graned out, Aiken-drum!

" Sauf us!" quoth Jock, " d'ye see sic een?"
Cries Kate, " There's a hole where a nose should ha' been;
An' the mouth's like a gash that a horn had ri'en;
    Wow! keep's frae Aiken-drum!"

The black dog growlin' cow'red his tail,
The lassie swarf'd, loot fa' the pail;
Rob's lingle brack as he mendit the flail,
    At the sicht o' Aiken-drum.

[1] Lob-lye-by-the-fire.

His matted head on his breast did rest,
A lang blue beard wan'ered down like a vest;
But the glare o' his e'e hath nae bard exprest,
    Nor the skimes o' Aiken-drum.

Roun' his hairy form there was naething seen,
But a philabeg o' the rashes green,
An' his knotted knees play'd ay knoit between;
    What a sicht was Aiken-drum !

On his wauchie arms three claws did meet,
As they trail'd on the grun' by his taeless feet;
E'en the auld gudeman himsel' did sweat,
    To look at Aiken-drum.

But he drew a score, himsel' did fain,
The auld wife tried, but her tongue was gane;
While the young ane closer clespit her wean,
    And turn'd frae Aiken-drum.

But the canty auld wife cam till her braith,
And she thocht the Bible micht ward aff scaith;
Be it benshee, bogle, ghaist, or wraith—
    But it fear'd na Aiken-drum.

" His presence protect us !" quoth the auld gudeman;
" What wad ye, whare won ye,—by sea or by lan'?
I conjure ye—speak—by the Beuk in my han' !"
    What a grane gae Aiken-drum !

" I lived in a lan' whare we saw nae sky,
I dwalt in a spot whare a burn rins na by;
But I'se dwall noo wi' you if ye like to try—
    Hae ye wark for Aiken-drum?

" I'll shiel a' your sheep i' the mornin' sune,[1]
I'll berry your crap by the licht o' the moon,
An' ba the bairns wi' un unkenn'd tune,
    If ye'll keep puir Aiken-drum.

" I'll loup the linn when ye canna wade,
I'll kirn the kirn, an' I'll turn the bread;
An' the wildest fillie that e'er ran rede
    I'se tame't," quoth Aiken-drum !

---

[1] On one occasion, Brownie had undertaken to gather the sheep into the bught by an early hour, and so zealously did he perform his task, that not only was there not one sheep left on the hill, but he had also collected a number of hares, which were found fairly penned along with them. Upon being congratulated on his extraordinary success, Brownie exclaimed, " Confound thae wee gray anes ! they cost me mair trouble than a' the lave o' them."

" To wear the tod frae the flock on the fell—
To gather the dew frae the heather-bell—
An' to look at my face in your clear crystal well,
     Micht gie pleasure to Aiken-drum.

" I'se seek nae guids, gear, bond, nor mark;
I use nae beddin', shoon, nor sark;
But a cogfu' o' brose 'tween the licht an' the dark,
     Is the wage o' Aiken-drum."

Quoth the wylie auld wife, " The thing speaks weel;
Our workers are scant—we hae routh o' meal;
Giff he'll do as he says—be he man, be he de'il,
     Wow! we'll try this Aiken-drum."

But the wenches skirl'd, " He's no' be here!
His eldritch look gars us swarf wi' fear;
An' the fient a ane will the house come near,
     If they think but o' Aiken-drum.

For a foul and a stalwart ghaist is he,
Despair sits brooding aboon his e'e-bree,
And unchancie to light o' a maiden's e'e,
     Is the glower o' Aiken-drum."

" Puir clipmalabors! ye hae little wit;
Is't na hallowmas noo, an' the crap out yet?"
Sae she ẛeelenc'd them wi' a stamp o' her fit,
     " Sit-yer-wa's-down, Aiken-drum."

Roun' a' that side what wark was dune,
By the streamer's gleam, or the glance o' the moon;
A word, or a wish—an' the Brownie cam sune,
     Sae helpfu' was Aiken-drum.

But he slade aye awa or the sun was up,
He ne'er could look straught on Macmillan's cup;[1]
They watch'd,—but nane saw him his brose ever sup,
     Nor a spune sought Aiken-drum.

On Blednoch banks, an' on crystal Cree,
For mony a day a toil'd wicht was he;
And the bairns they play'd harmless roun' his knee,
     Sae social was Aiken-drum.

[1] A communion cup, belonging to M'Millan, the well-known ousted minister of Balmaghie, and founder of the sect of Covenanters of his name. This cup was treasured by a zealous disciple in the parish of Kirkcowan, and long used as a test by which to ascertain the orthodoxy of suspected persons. If, on taking it into his hand, the person trembled, or gave other symptoms of agitation, he was denounced as having bowed the knee to Baal, and sacrificed at the altar of idolatry.

But a new-made wife, fu' o' rippish freaks,
Fond o' a' things feat for the five first weeks,
Laid a mouldy pair o' her ain man's breeks
    By the brose o' Aiken-drum.

Let the learn'd decide when they convene,
What spell was him an' the breeks between ;
For frae that day forth he was nae mair seen,
    An' sair miss'd was Aiken-drum.

He was heard by a herd gaun by the Thrieve,
Crying, " Lang, lang now may I greet an' grieve ;
For alas ! I hae gotten baith fee an' leave,
    O luckless Aiken-drum ! "

Awa ! ye wrangling sceptic tribe,
Wi' your pro's an' your con's wad ye decide
'Gainst the 'sponsible voice o' a hale country-side
    On the facts 'bout Aiken-drum ?

Tho' the " Brownie o' Blednoch " lang be gane,
The mark o' his feet's left on mony a stane ;
An' mony a wife an' mony a wean
    Tell the feats o' Aiken-drum.

E'en now, licht loons that jibe an' sneer
At spiritual guests an' a' sic gear,
At the Glasnock mill hae swat wi' fear,
    An' look'd roun' for Aiken-drum.

An' guidly folks hae gotten a fricht,
When the moon was set, an' the stars gaed nae licht,
At the roaring linn in the howe o' the nicht,
    Wi' sughs like Aiken-drum.

We would rather have written these lines than any amount of Aurora Leighs, Festuses, or such like, with all their mighty " somethingness," as Mr. Bailey would say. For they, are they not the " native wood-notes wild " of one of nature's darlings? Here is the indescribable, inestimable, unmistakable impress of genius. Chaucer, had he been a Galloway man, might have written it, only he would have been more garrulous, and less compact and stern. It is like Tam o' Shanter, in its living union of the comic, the pathetic, and the terrible. Shrewdness, tenderness, imagination, fancy, humour, word music, dramatic power, even wit—all are here. I have often read it aloud to children, and it is worth any one's while to do it. You will find them repeating all over the house for days such lines as take their heart and tongue.

The author of this noble ballad was William Nicholson, the Galloway poet, as he was, and is still called in his own district. He was born at Tanimaus, in the parish of Borgue, in August 1783; he died *circa* 1848, unseen, like a bird. Being extremely short-sighted, he was unfitted for being a shepherd or ploughman, and began life as a packman, like the hero of "the Excursion;" and is still remembered in that region for his humour, his music, his verse, and his ginghams; and also, alas! for his misery and his sin. After travelling the country for thirty years, he became a packless pedlar, and fell into "a way of drinking;" this led from bad to worse, and the grave closed in gloom over the ruins of a man of true genius. Mr. M'Diarmid of Dumfries prefixed a memoir of him to the Second Edition of his *Tales in Verse and Miscellaneous Poems*. These are scarcely known out of Galloway, but they are worth the knowing: none of them have the concentration and nerve of the Brownie, but they are from the same brain and heart. "The Country Lass," a long poem, is excellent; with much of Crabbe's power and compression. This, and the greater part of the volume is in the Scottish dialect, but there is a Fable—the Butterfly and Bee—the English and sense, the fine, delicate humour and turn of which might have been Cowper's; and there is a bit of rugged sarcasm called "Siller," which Burns need not have been ashamed of. Poor Nicholson, besides his turn for verse, was an exquisite musician, and sang with a powerful and sweet voice. One may imagine the delight of a lonely town-end, when Willie the packman and the piper made his appearance, with his stories, and jokes, and ballads, his songs, and reels, and "wanton wiles."

There is one story about him which has always appeared to me quite perfect. A farmer, in a remote part of Galloway, one June morning before sunrise, was awakened by music; he had been dreaming of heaven, and when he found himself awake, he still heard the strains. He looked out, and saw no one, but at the corner of a grass-field he saw his cattle, and young colts and fillies, huddled together, and looking intently down into what he knew was an old quarry. He put on his clothes, and walked across the field, everything but that strange wild melody, still and silent in this the "sweet hour of prime." As he got nearer the "beasts," the sound was louder; the colts with their long manes, and the nowt with their wondering stare, took no notice of him, straining their necks forward entranced. There, in the old quarry, the young sun "glintin" on his face, and resting on his pack, which had been his pillow, was our Wandering Willie, playing and singing like an angel—"an Orpheus; an Orpheus." What a picture! When reproved for wasting his health and time by the prosaic farmer, the poor fellow said: "Me and this quarry are lang acquant, and I've mair pleesure in pipin to thae daft cowts, than if the best leddies in the land were figurin away afore me."

OUR GIDEON GRAYS

Agricolam laudat
Sub galli cantum consultor ubi ostia pulsat.

"I would rather go back to Africa than practise again at Peebles."—MUNGO PARK.

OUR GIDEON GRAYS[1]

It might perhaps have been better, if our hard-headed, hard-hitting, clever, and not over mansuete friend " *Fuge Medicos* " had never allowed those " wild and stormy writings " of his to come into print, and it might perhaps also have been as well, had we told him so at once; but as we are inclined to be optimists when a thing is past, we think more good than evil has come out of his assault and its repulse. " F. M." (we cannot be always giving at full length his uncouth Hoffmannism) has, in fact, in his second letter, which is much the better, answered his first, and turned his back considerably upon himself, by abating some of his most offensive charges; and our country doctors in their replies have shown that they have sense as well as spirit, and can write like gentlemen, while they of the town have cordially and to good purpose spoken up for their hard-working country brethren.

We are not now going to adjudicate upon the strictly professional points raised by " F. M.," whether, for instance, bleeding is ever anything but mischievous; whether the constitution, or type of disease, changes or not; whether Dr. Samuel Dickson of " the Fallacies " is an impudent quack or the Newton of medicine; whether Dr. Wilkinson is an amiable and bewildered Swedenborgian, with much

[1] The following short paper from the *Scotsman* was occasioned by a correspondence in that newspaper, in which doctors in general, and country doctors in particular, were attacked and defended. It is reprinted here as a record of the amazing facts brought out by Dr. Alison's Association. In the attack by " Fuge Medicos," consisting of two long letters, there was much ability with not much fairness, and not a little misapplied energy of language, and sharpness of invective.

imagination, little logic, and less knowledge, and a wonderful power of beautiful writing, or the herald of a new gospel of health. We may have our own opinions on these subjects, but their discussion lies out of our beat; they are strictly professional in their essence, and ought to remain so in their treatment. We are by no means inclined to deny that there are ignorant and dangerous practitioners in the country, as well as in the city. What we have to say against " F. M." and in favour of the class he has attacked is, that no man should bring such charges against any large body of men, without offering such an amount and kind of proof of their truth, as, it is not too much to say, it is impossible for any mere amateur to produce, even though that amateur were as full of will and energy as " F. M.;" and unless he can do so, he stands convicted of something very like what he himself calls "reckless, maleficent stupidity." It is true, " F. M." speaks of "ignorant country doctors;" but his general charges against the profession have little meaning, and his Latin motto still less, if ignorance be not predicated of country doctors in general. One, or even half a dozen worthless, mischievous country doctors, is too small an induction of particulars, to warrant " F. M." in inferring the same qualities of some 500 or more unknown men. But we are not content with proving the negative: we speak not without long, intimate, and extensive knowledge of the men who have the charge of the lives of our country population, when we assert, that not only are they as a class fully equal to other rural professional men in intelligence, humanity, and skill, and in all that constitutes what we call worth, but that, take them all in all, they are the best educated, the most useful, the most enlightened, as they certainly are the worst paid and hardest-worked country doctors in Christendom. Gideon Gray, in Scott's story of the Surgeon's Daughter, is a faithful type of this sturdy, warmhearted, useful class of men, " under whose rough

coat and blunt exterior," as he truly says, "you
find professional skill and enthusiasm, intelligence,
humanity, courage, and science."

Moreover, they have many primary mental qualities
in which their more favoured brethren of the ctiy are
necessarily behind them—self-reliance, presence of
mind, simplicity and readiness of resource, and a certain homely sagacity. These virtues of the mind
are, from the nature of things, more likely to be fully
brought out, where a man must be self-contained and
everything to himself; he cannot be calling in another
to consult with him in every anxious case, or indulge
himself in the luxury of that safety which has wag-
gishly been expounded as attaching more to the multitude of counsellors than to the subject of their
counsel. Were this a fitting place, we could relate
many instances of this sagacity, decision, and tact,
as shown by men never known beyond their own
country-side, which, if displayed in more public life,
would have made their possessors take their place
among our public great men.

Such men as old Reid of Peebles, Meldrum of
Kincardine, Darling of Dunse, Johnston of Stirling,
Clarkson (the original of Gideon Gray) and Anderson of Selkirk, Robert Stevenson of Gilmerton,
Kirkwood of Auchterarder, and many as good—these
were not likely to be the representatives of a class
who are guilty of "assaults upon life," "who are
let loose upon some unhappy rural district, to send
vigorous men and women to their graves," who "in
youth have been reckless and cruel, given to hanging sparrows and cats, and fit for no humane profession," &c. &c. Now, is there either good sense,
good feeling, or good breeding, in using these un-
measured terms against an entire class of men? As-
suming—as from the subtlety and hairsplitting
character of his arguments, and the sharpness and
safety of his epithets, we are entitled to do—that
"F. M." belongs to another of the learned profes-
sions, we ask, What would he say if a "*Fuge Juridi-*

cos " were to rise up, who considered that the true
reading in Scripture should be, " The devil was a
lawyer from the beginning," " asserting that all
country lawyers in Scotland were curses to the community, that it would be well if the Lord Advocate
" would try half a dozen every year," for devouring
widows' houses and other local villanies ; and, moreover, what would he think of the brains and the
modesty of an M.D. making an assault upon the legal
profession on purely professional questions, and settling *ab extra*, and off-hand and for ever, matters
which the wisest heads *ab intra* have left still in doubt ?
The cases are strictly parallel ; and it is one of the
worst signs of our times, this public intermeddling
of everybody, from the *Times* down to " F. M.,"
with every science, profession, and trade. Sydney
Smith might now say of the public, what he said of
the Master of Trinity, " Science is his *forte*, omniscience is his *foible*." Every profession, and every
man in it, knows something more and better than any
non-professional man can, and it is the part of a
wise man to stick to his trade. He is more likely to
excel in it, and to honour and wonder at the skill
of others. For it is a beautiful law of our nature
that we must wonder at everything which we see well
done, and yet do not know how it is done, or at any
rate know we could not do it. Look at any art, at
boot-closing, at a saddler at his work, at basket-
making, at our women with their nimble and exact
fingers—somebody is constantly doing something
which everybody cannot do, and therefore everybody
admires. We are afraid " F. M." does not know
many things he could not do.

We repeat that our Gideon Grays are, as a class,
worthy and intelligent, skilful and safe, doing much
more good than evil.[1] They deserve well of, and live
in the hearts of the people, and work day and night
for less than anybody but themselves and their wives
are likely ever to know, for they are most of them

[1] Note, page 169.

unknown to the Income-tax collectors. They are like
the rest of us, we hope, soberer, better read, more
enlightened, than they were fifty years ago; they
study and trust Nature more, and conquer her by
submission; they bleed and blister less, and are more
up to the doctrine that prevention is the best of all
cures. They have participated in the general acknowledgment among the community, thanks to the
two Combes and others, and to the spirit of the age,
of those divine laws of health which He who made
us implanted in us, and the study and obedience of
which is a fulfilling of His word. We can only hope
that our clever and pancratic friend " F. M.," if on
his autumn holidays in Teviotdale or Lochaber, he
has his shoulder or his lower jaw dislocated, or has
a fit of colic or a hernia, or any of those ills which
even his robust self is heir to, may have sense left
him to send for Gideon Gray, and to trust him, and,
making a slight alteration on his Hoffmannism, may
be led to cry lustily out, in worse Latin and with
better sense—"*Fuge pro Medico*"—Run for the
Doctor !

As already said, all of us who have been much in
the country know the hard life of its doctors—how
much they do, and for how little they do it; but we
dare say our readers are not prepared for the following account of their unremunerated labour among
paupers : —

In 1846, a voluntary association of medical men
was formed in Edinburgh, with the public-hearted Dr.
Alison as chairman. Its object was to express their
sympathy with their brethren in the remote country districts of Scotland, in regard to their unremunerated
attendance on paupers, and to collect accurate information on this subject. The results of their benevolent exertions may be found in the Appendix to the
First Report of the Board of Supervision. It is probably very little known beyond those officially concerned; we therefore give some of its astounding and
lamentable revelations. The queries referred to the

state and claims of the medical practitioners in the rural districts of Scotland, in relation to their attendance upon the permanent or occasional parochial poor. Out of 325 returns, 94 had received *some* remuneration for attendance and outlay. In one of these instances, the remuneration *consisted of three shillings for twelve years' attendance on seventy constant, and thirteen occasional paupers;* a fine question in decimals—what would each visit come to? But worse remains. One man attended 400 paupers for eight years, and never received one farthing for his skill, his time, or his drugs. Another has the same story to tell of 350, some of them thirty miles off; he moderately calculates his direct loss, from these calls on his time and purse, at £70 a year. Out of 253 who report, 208 state that, besides attending for nothing, they had to give on occasions food, wine, and clothes, and had to pay tolls, &c. 136 of the returns contain a more or less definite estimate, in money value, of their unrequited labours; the sum-total given in by them amounts to *thirty-four thousand four hundred and fifty-seven pounds in ten years! being at the rate of £238 for each!* They seem to have calculated the amount of medical attendance, outlay, and drugs, for each pauper annually, at the very moderate average of four shillings.

Is there any other country on the face of the earth where such a state of matters can be found? Such active charity, such an amount of public good, is not likely to have been achieved by men whose lives were little else than the development of a juvenile mania for hanging sparrows and cats. We believe we are below the mark when we say, that over head, the country doctors of Scotland do one-third of their work for nothing, and this in cases where the receiver of their attendance would scorn to leave his shoes or his church seats unpaid.

We are glad to see that " F. M." reads Sir William Hamilton. We doubt not he does more than read him, and we trust that he will imitate him in some things besides his energy, his learning, and his hardihood of thought. As to his and other wise men's pleasantries about doctors and their drugs, we all know what they mean, and what they are worth; they are the bitter-sweet joking human nature must have at those with whom it has close dealings —its priests, its lawyers, its doctors, its wives and husbands; the very existence of such expressions proves the opposite; it is one of the luxuries of disrespect. But in " F. M.'s " hands these ancient and harmless jokes are used as deadly solemnities upon which arguments are founded.

To part pleasantly with him, nevertheless, we give him three good old jokes :—The Visigoths abandoned an unsuccessful surgeon to the family of his deceased patient, " *ut quod de eo facere voluerint, habeant potestatem.*" Montaigne, who is great upon doctors, used to beseech his friends, that if he felt ill they would let him *get a little stronger* before sending for the doctor ! Louis the Fourteenth, who, of course, was a slave to his physicians, asked his friend Molière what he did with his doctor. " Oh, Sire," said he, " when I am ill I send for him. He comes, we have a chat, and enjoy ourselves. He prescribes. I don't take it—and I am cured !"

We end with four quotations, which our strongheaded friend " F. M.," we are sure, will cordially relish :—

> " In Juvene Theologo conscientiæ detrimentum,
> In Juvene Legistâ bursæ decrementum,
> In Juvene Medico cæmeterii incrementum."

" To imagine Nature incapable to cure diseases, is blasphemy; because that would be imputing imperfection to the Deity, who has made a great provision for the preservation of animal life."—SYDENHAM.

" When I consider the degree of patience and attention that is required to follow Nature in her slow manner of proceeding, I am no longer surprised that men of lively parts should be always repeating, ' *con-traria adhibenda.*' But Hippocrates says :—' *Con-traria paulatim adhibere oportet, et interquiescere. Periculosius censeo incidere in medicum, qui nesciat quiescere, quam qui nesciat contraria adhibere, nam qui nescit quiescere, nescit occasiones contraria adhi-bendi; quare nescit contraria adhibere. Qui nescit contraria adhibere, tamen, si prudens est, scit quies-cere, atque si prodesse non potest, tamen non obest. Præstantissimus vero est medicus eruditus pariter ac prudens, qui novit festinare lente; pro ipsius morbi urgentia, auxiliis instare, atque in occasione uti maxime opportunis, alioque quiescere.*' "—GRANT ON FEVERS, page 311.

" Philosophi qui vitæ rationem doceant, vitiis eripiant—ærumnus, metus, angustias, anxietates, tristitias, impotentias expugnent tranquillitati, hila-ritati αὐταρκεία vindicent."—STAHL.

I don't know who " QUIS " was, but the Hudi-brastics are vigorous :—

THE COUNTRY SURGEON.

Luckless is he, whom hard fates urge on
To practise as a country surgeon—
To ride regardless of all weather,
Through frost, and snow, and hail together—
To smile and bow when sick and tired
Consider'd as a servant hired.
At every quarter of the compass,
A surly patient makes a rumpus,
Because he is not seen the first,
(For each man thinks his case the worst).
And oft at two points diametric,
Called to a business obstetric.
There lies a man with broken limb,
A lady here with nervous whim,
Who, at the acme of her fever,
Calls him a savage if he leave her.
For days and nights in some lone cottage
Condemn'd to live on crusts and pottage,
To kick his heels, and spin his brains,
Waiting, forsooth, for labour's pains;
And that job over, happy he,
If he squeeze out a guinea fee.

Now comes the night, with toil opprest,
He seeks his bed in hope of rest ;
Vain hope, his slumbers are no more,
Loud sounds the knocker at the door,
A farmer's wife, at ten miles' distance,
Shouting, calls out for his assistance :
Fretting and fuming in the dark,
He in the tinder strikes a spark,
And, as he yawning heaves his breeches,
Envies his neighbour blest with riches.

QUIS.

Edin. Ann. Register, 1817.

NOTE—p. 164

I have to thank his son, Dr. Henry Anderson, who now reigns in his stead, for the following notes of an ordinary day's work of his father, whose sister was Mungo Park's wife. Selkirk is the " Middlemas " of Sir Walter.

" Dr. Anderson practised in Selkirk for forty-five years, and never refused to go to any case, however poor, or however deep in his debt, and however far off. One wife in Selkirk said to her neighbours, as he passed up the street, ' There goes my honest doctor, that brought a' my ten bairns into the world, and ne'er got a rap for ane o' them.'

" His methodical habits, and perfect arrangement of his time, enabled him to overtake his very wide practice, and to forget no one. He rose generally at six every morning, often sooner, and saw his severe cases in the town early, thus enabling him to start for his long journeys ; and he generally took a stage to breakfast of fifteen or twenty miles.

" One morning he left home at six o'clock, and after being three miles up the Yarrow, met a poor barefoot woman, who had walked from St. Mary's loch to have two teeth extracted. Out of his pocket with his ' key ' (she, of course, shouting ' Murder ! murder ! mercy !') ; down sat the good woman ; the teeth were out at once, and the doctor rode on his journey, to breakfast at Eldinhope, fourteen miles up, calling on all his patients in Yarrow as he rode along. After breakfast, by Dryhope, and along St. Mary's Loch, to the famed Tibby's, whose son was badly, up to the head of the Loch of the Lows, and over the high hills into Ettrick, and riding up the Tima to Delgliesh, and back down the Ettrick, landed at ' Gideon's o' the Singlie ' to dinner ; and just when making a tumbler of toddy, a boy was brought into the kitchen, with a finger torn off in a thrashing-mill. The doctor left after another tumbler, and still making calls about Ettrickbridge, &c., reached home about eight, after riding fifty miles; not to rest, however, for various messages await his return; all are visited, get medicines from him, for there were no laboratories in his days, then home to prepare all the various prescriptions for those he had seen during the long day. He had just finished this when off he was called to a midwifery case, far up Ale Water.

"To show how pointed to time he was, one day he had to go to Buccleugh, eighteen miles up the Ettrick, and having to ride down the moors by Ashkirk, and then to go on to St. Boswell's to see old Raeburn, he wished a change of horse at Riddell—fixed one o'clock, and one of his sons met him at a point of the road at the very hour, though he had ridden forty miles through hills hardly passable.

"I have seen him return from the head of Yarrow half frozen, and not an hour in bed till he had to rise and ride back the same road, and all without a murmur.

"It was all on horseback in his day, as there was only one gig in the county; and his district extended west up the valleys of Ettrick and Yarrow above twenty miles; south in Ale Water seven to ten miles; the same distance east; and north about fourteen miles by Tweedside, and banks of the Gala and Caddon. His early rising enabled him also to get through his other work, for he made up all his books at that time, had accounts ready, wrote all his business letters, of which he had not a few.

"In coming home late in the night from his long journeys, he often slept on horseback for miles together. In fine, he was the hardest-worked man in the shire; always cheerful, and always ready to join in any cheerful and harmless amusement, as well as every good work; *but he killed himself by it,* bringing on premature decay."

He was many years Provost of the Burgh, took his full share of business, was the personal adviser of his patients, and had more curatorships than any one else in the county. What a pattern of active beneficence, bringing up three sons to his profession, giving his family a first-rate education, and never getting anything for the half of his everyday's work! We can fancy we see the handsome, swarthy, ruddy old man coming jogging (his normal pace) on his well-known mare down the Yarrow by Black Andro (a wooded hill), and past Foulshiels (Mungo Park's birthplace), after being all night up the glen with some "crying wife," and the cottagers at Glower-ower-'im, blessing him as he passed *sound asleep,* or possibly wakening him out of his dreams, to come up and "lance" the bairn's eye-tooth.

Think of a man like this—a valuable, an invaluable public servant, the king of health in his own region—having to start in a winter's night "on-ding o' snaw" for the head of Ettrick, to preside over a primiparous herd's wife, at the back of Boodsbeck, who was as normal and independent as her cows, or her husband's two score of cheviots; to have to put his faithful and well-bred mare (for he knew the value of blood) into the byre, the door of which was secured by an old harrow, or possibly in the course of the obstetric transaction by a snow-drift; to have to sit idle amid the discomforts of a shepherd's hut for hours, no books, except perhaps a ten-year-old *Belfast Almanac,* or the *Fourfold State* (an admirable book), or a volume of ballads, all of which he knew by heart, —when all that was needed, was " Mrs. Jaup," or indeed any neighbour wife, or her mother. True, our doctor made the best of it, heard all the clavers of the country, took an interest in all their interests, and was as much at home by the side of the ingle, with its bit of " licht " or cannel coal, as he would be next day at Bowhill with the Duchess. But what a waste of time, of health! what a waste of an admirable man! and, then, with impatient young men, what an inlet to mischievous interference, to fatal curtailing of attendance!

"WITH BRAINS, SIR."

" Multi multa sciunt, pauci multum."

" It is one thing to wish to have Truth on our side, and another thing to wish to be on the side of Truth."—WHATELY.

"'Αταλαίπωρος τοῖς πολλοῖς ἡ ζήτησις τῆς ἀληθείας, καὶ ἐπὶ τὰ ἕτοιμα μᾶλλον τρέπονται."—THUCYDIDES.

" The most perfect philosophy of the natural *kind, only staves off our* IGNORANCE *a little longer ; as, perhaps, the most perfect philosophy of the* moral *or* metaphysical *kind, serves only to discover larger portions of it."*—DAVID HUME.

"WITH BRAINS, SIR"

PRAY, Mr. Opie, may I ask what you mix your colours with?" said a brisk dilettante student to the great painter. "With *Brains*, Sir," was the gruff reply—and the right one. It did not give much of what we call information; it did not expound the principles and rules of the art; but, if the inquirer had the commodity referred to, it would awaken him; it would set him a-going, a-thinking, and a-painting to good purpose. If he had not the wherewithal, as was likely enough, the less he had to do with colours and their mixture the better. Many other artists, when asked such a question, would have either set about detailing the mechanical composition of such and such colours, in such and such proportions, rubbed up so and so; or perhaps they would (and so much the better, but not the best) have shown him how they laid them on; but even this would leave him at the critical point. Opie preferred going to the quick and the heart of the matter: "With *Brains*, Sir."

Sir Joshua Reynolds was taken by a friend to see a picture. He was anxious to admire it, and he looked it over with a keen and careful but favourable eye. "Capital composition; correct drawing; the colour, tone, chiaroscuro excellent; but—but—it wants, hang it, it wants—*That!*" snapping his fingers; and, wanting "that," though it had everything else, it was worth nothing.

Again, Etty was appointed teacher of the students of the Royal Academy, having been preceded by a clever, talkative, scientific expounder of æsthetics, who delighted to tell the young men *how* everything was done, how to copy this, and how to express that. A student came up to the new master, "How should I do this, Sir?" "Suppose you try." Another,

"What does this mean, Mr. Etty?" "Suppose you
look." "But I have looked." "Suppose you look
again." And they did try, and they did look, and
looked again; and they saw and achieved what they
never could have done, had the how or the what (supposing this possible, which it is not in its full and
highest meaning) been told them, or done for them;
in the one case, sight and action were immediate,
exact, intense, and secure; in the other mediate,
feeble, and lost as soon as gained. But what are
"*Brains*"? what did Opie mean? and what is Sir
Joshua's "*That*"? What is included in it? and what
is the use, or the need of trying and trying, of missing
often before you hit, when you can be told at once and
be done with it; or of looking when you may be
shown? Everything in medicine and in painting—
practical arts—as means to ends, let their scientific
enlargement be ever so rapid and immense, depends
upon the right answers to these questions.

First of all, "brains," in the painter, are not diligence, knowledge, skill, sensibility, a strong will, or
a high aim,—he may have all these, and never paint
anything so truly good or effective as the rugged
woodcut we must all remember, of Apollyon bestriding
the whole breadth of the way, and Christian girding
at him like a man, in the old sixpenny *Pilgrim's
Progress;* and a young medical student may have
zeal, knowledge, ingenuity, attention, a good eye and
a steady hand—he may be an accomplished anatomist,
stethoscopist, histologist, and analyst; and yet, with
all this, and all the lectures, and all the books, and
all the sayings, and all the preparations, drawings,
tables, and other helps of his teachers, crowded into
his memory or his notebooks, he may be beaten in
treating a whitlow or a colic, by the nurse in the wards
where he was clerk, or by the old country doctor who
brought him into the world, and who listens with such
humble wonder to his young friend's account, on his
coming home after each session, of all he had seen
and done,—of all the last astonishing discoveries and

operations of the day. What the painter wants, in addition to, and as the complement of, the other elements, is *genius and sense;* what the doctor needs to crown and give worth and safety to his accomplishments, is *sense and genius:* in the first case, more of this, than of that; in the second, more of that, than of this. These are the " *Brains* " and the " *That.*"

And what is genius? and what is sense? Genius is a peculiar native aptitude, or tendency, to any one calling or pursuit over all others. A man may have a genius for governing, for killing, or for curing the greatest number of men, and in the best possible manner : a man may have a genius for the fiddle, or his mission may be for the tight-rope, or the Jew's harp; or it may be a natural turn for seeking, and finding, and teaching truth, and for doing the greatest possible good to mankind; or it may be a turn equally natural for seeking, and finding, and teaching a lie, and doing the *maximum* of mischief. It was as natural, as inevitable, for Wilkie to develop himself into a painter, and such a painter as we know him to have been, as it is for an acorn when planted to grow up into an oak, a specific *quercus robur*. But *genius*, and nothing else, is not enough, even for a painter : he must likewise have *sense;* and what is sense? *Sense* drives, or ought to drive, the coach ; sense regulates, combines, restrains, commands, all the rest—even the genius ; and sense implies exactness and soundness, power and promptitude of mind.

Then for the young doctor, he must have as his main, his master faculty, SENSE—Brains—*voûs*, justness of mind, because his subject-matter is one in which principle works, rather than impulse, as in painting; the understanding has first to do with it, however much it is worthy of the full exercise of the feelings, and the affections. But all will not do, if GENIUS is not there,—a real turn for the profession. It may not be a liking for it—some of the best of its practitioners never really liked it, at least liked other things better; but there must be a fitness of faculty of body and mind for its full, constant, exact pursuit. This sense and this genius, such a special therapeutic gift, had Hippocrates, Sydenham, Pott, Pinel, John Hunter, Delpech, Dupuytren, Kellie, Cheyne, Baillie, and Abercrombie. We might, to pursue the subject, pick out painters who had much genius and little or no sense, and *vice versâ;* and physicians and surgeons, who had sense without genius, and genius without sense, and some perhaps who had neither, and yet were noticeable, and, in their own sideways, useful men.

But our great object will be gained if we have given our young readers (and these remarks are addressed exclusively to students) any idea of what we mean, if we have made them think, and look inwards. The noble and sacred science you have entered on is large, difficult, and deep, beyond most others; it is every day becoming larger, deeper, and in many senses more difficult, more complicated and involved. It requires *more than the average* intellect, energy, attention, patience, and courage, and that singular but imperial quality, at once a gift and an acquirement, *presence of mind—ἀγχινοία*, or nearness of the *νοῦς*, as the subtile Greeks called it—than almost any other department of human thought and action, except perhaps that of ruling men. Therefore it is, that we hold it to be of paramount importance that the parents, teachers, and friends of youths intended for medicine, and above all, that those who examine them on their entering on their studies, should at least (we might safely go much further) satisfy themselves as far as they can, that they are not below *par* in intelligence; they may be deficient and unapt, *quâ medici*, and yet, if taken in time, may make excellent men in other useful and honourable callings.

But suppose we have got the requisite amount and specific kind of capacity, how are we to fill it with its means; how are we to make it effectual for its end? On this point we say nothing, except that the fear now-a-days, is rather that the mind gets too much of too many things, than too little or too few. But this means of turning knowledge to action, making it what Bacon meant when he said it was power, invigorating the thinking substance—giving tone, and you may call it muscle and nerve, blood and bone, to the mind—a firm gripe, and a keen and sure eye : *that*, we think, is far too little considered or cared for at present, as if the mere act of filling in everything for ever into a poor lad's brain, would give him the ability to make anything of it, and above all, the power to appropriate the small portions of true nutriment, and reject the dregs.

One comfort we have, that in the main, and in the last resort, there is really very little that *can* be done for any man by another. Begin with the sense and the genius—the keen appetite and the good digestion —and, amid all obstacles and hardships, the work goes on merrily and well; without these, we all know what a laborious affair, and a dismal, it is to make an incapable youth apply. Did any of you ever set yourselves to keep up artificial respiration, or to trudge about for a whole night with a narcotized victim of opium, or transfuse blood (your own perhaps) into a poor, fainting exanimate wretch? If so, you will have some idea of the heartless attempt, and its generally vain and miserable result, to make a dull student apprehend—a debauched, interested, knowing, or active in anything beyond the base of his brain —a weak, etiolated intellect hearty, and worth anything; and yet how many such are dragged through their dreary *curricula*, and by some miraculous process of cramming, and equally miraculous power of turning their insides out, get through their examinations : and then—what then? providentially, in most cases, they find their level; the broad daylight of the world—its shrewd and keen eye, its strong instinct of what can, and what cannot serve *its* purpose—puts all, except the poor object himself, to rights; happy is it for him if he turns to some new and more congenial pursuit in time.

But it may be asked, how are the brains to be
strengthened, the sense quickened, the genius
awakened, the affections raised—the whole man
turned to the best account for the cure of his fellow-
men? How are you, when physics and physiology
are increasing so marvellously, and when the burden
of knowledge, the quantity of transferable information, of registered facts, of current names—and such
names !—is so infinite : how are you to enable a
student to take all in, bear up under all, and use it
as not abusing it, or being abused by it? You must
invigorate the containing and sustaining mind, you
must strengthen him from within, as well as fill him
from without; you must discipline, nourish, edify, re-
lieve, and refresh his entire nature; and how? We
have no time to go at large into this, but we will
indicate what we mean :—encourage languages, especially French and German, at the early part of their
studies; encourage not merely the book knowledge,
but the personal pursuit of natural history, of field
botany, of geology, of zoology; give the young, fresh,
unforgetting eye, exercise and free scope upon the
infinite diversity and combination of natural colours,
forms, substances, surfaces, weights, and sizes—
everything, in a word, that will educate their eye or ear,
their touch, taste, and smell, their sense of muscular
resistance; encourage them by prizes, to make skele-
tons, preparations, and collections of any natural
objects; and, above all, try and get hold of their affections, and make them put their hearts into their work.
Let them, if possible, have the advantage of a regulated *tutorial*, as well as the ordinary professional
system. Let there be no excess in the number of
clases and frequency of lectures. Let them be drilled
in composition; by this we mean the writing and
spelling of correct, plain English (a matter not of
every-day occurrence, and not on the increase),—let
them be directed to the best books of the old masters
in medicine, and *examined in them,*—let them be
encouraged in the use of a wholesome and manly

literature. We do not mean popular, or even modern literature—such as Emerson, Bulwer, or Alison, or the trash of inferior periodicals or novels—fashion, vanity, and the spirit of the age, will attract them readily enough to all these; we refer to the treasures of our elder and better authors. If our young medical student would take our advice, and for an hour or two twice a week take up a volume of Shakspere, Cervantes, Milton, Dryden, Pope, Cowper, Montaigne, Addison, Defoe, Goldsmith, Fielding, Scott, Charles Lamb, Macaulay, Jeffrey, Sydney Smith, Helps, Thackeray, &c., not to mention authors on deeper and more sacred subjects—they would have happier and healthier minds, and make none the worse doctors. If they, by good fortune—for the tide has set in strong against the *literæ humaniores*—have come off with some Greek or Latin, we would supplicate for an ode of Horace, a couple of pages of Cicero or of Pliny once a month, and a page of Xenophon. French and German should be mastered either before or during the first years of study. They will never afterwards be acquired so easily or so thoroughly, and the want of them may be bitterly felt when too late.

But one main help, we are persuaded, is to be found in studying, and by this we do not mean the mere reading, but the digging into and through, the energizing upon, and mastering such books as we have mentioned at the close of this paper. These are not, of course, the only works we would recommend to those who wish to understand thoroughly, and to make up their minds, on these great subjects as wholes; but we all know too well that our Art is long, broad, and deep,—and Time, opportunity, and our little hour, brief and uncertain, therefore, we would recommend those books as a sort of game of the mind, a mental exercise—like cricket, a gymnastic, a clearing of the eyes of their mind as with euphrasy, a strengthening their power over particulars, a getting fresh, strong views of worn out, old things, and, above all, a learning the right use of their reason, and

by knowing their own ignorance and weakness, finding true knowledge and strength.   Taking up a book
like Arnauld, and reading a chapter of his lively
manly sense, is like throwing your manuals, and
scalpels, and microscopes, and natural (most unnatural) orders out of your hand and head, and taking
a game with the Grange Club, or a run to the top of
Arthur Seat.   Exertion quickens your pulse, expands
your lungs, makes your blood warmer and redder, fills
your mouth with the pure waters of relish, strengthens
and supples your legs; and though on your way to the
top you may encounter rocks, and baffling *débris,* and
gusts of fierce winds rushing out upon you from
behind corners, just as you will find in Arnauld, and
all truly serious and honest books of the kind, difficulties and puzzles, winds of doctrine, and deceitful
mists; still you are rewarded at the top by the wide
view.   You see, as from a tower, the end of all.   You
look into the perfections and relations of things.   You
see the clouds, the bright lights, and the everlasting
hills on the far horizon.   You come down the hill a
happier, a better, and a hungrier man, and of a better
mind.   But, as we said, you must eat the book, you
must crush it, and cut it with your teeth and swallow
it; just as you must walk up, and not be carried up the
hill, much less imagine you are there, or look upon a
picture of what you would see were you up, however
accurately or artistically done; no—you yourself must
do both.

   Philosophy—the love and the possession of wisdom
—is divided into two things, science or knowledge;
and a habit, or power of mind.   He who has got the
first is not truly wise unless his mind has reduced and
assimilated it, as Dr. Prout would have said, unless he
appropriates and can use it for his need.

   The prime qualifications of a physician may be
summed up in the words *Capax, Perspicax, Sagax,
Efficax.   Capax*—there must be room to receive, and
arrange, and keep knowledge; *Perspicax*—senses and
perceptions, keen, accurate, and immediate, to bring

in materials from all sensible things; *Sagax*—a central power of knowing what is what, and what it is worth, of choosing and rejecting, of judging; and finally, *Efficax*—the will and the way—the power to turn all the other three—capacity, perspicacity, sagacity, to account, in the performance of the thing in hand, and thus rendering back to the outer world, in a new and useful form, what you have received from it. These are the intellectual qualities which make up the physician, without any one of which he would be *mancus*, and would not deserve the name of a complete artsman, any more than proteine would be itself if any one of its four elements were amissing.

We have left ourselves no room to speak of the books we have named at the end of this paper. We recommend them all to our young readers. Arnauld's excellent and entertaining *Art of Thinking*—the once famous *Port-Royal Logic*—is, if only one be taken, probably the best. Thomson's little book is admirable, and is specially suited for a medical student, as its illustrations are drawn with great intelligence and exactness from chemistry and physiology. We know nothing more perfect than the analysis, at page 348, of Sir H. Davy's beautiful experiments to account for the traces of an alkali, found when decomposing water by galvanism. It is quite exquisite, the hunt after and the unearthing of " *the residual cause.*" This book has the great advantage of a clear, lively, and strong style. We can only give some short extracts.

INDUCTION AND DEDUCTION

" We may define the inductive method as the process of discovering laws and rules from facts, and causes from effects; and the deductive, as the method of deriving facts from laws, and effects from their causes."

There is a valuable paragraph on anticipation and its uses—there is a power and desire of the mind to project itself from the known into the unknown, in the expectation of finding what it is in search of.

"This power of divination, this sagacity, which is the mother of all science, we may call anticipation. The intellect, with a dog-like instinct, will not hunt until it has found the scent. It must have some presage of the result before it will turn its energies to its attainment. The system of anatomy which has immortalized the name of Oken, is the consequence of a *flash of anticipation*, which glanced through his mind when he picked up, in a chance walk, the skull of a deer, bleached by the weather, and exclaimed— '*It is a vertebral column!*'"

"The man of science possesses principles—the man of art, not the less nobly gifted, is possessed and carried away by them. The principles which art *involves*, science *evolves*. The truths on which the success of art depends lurk in the artist's mind in an undeveloped state, guiding his hand, stimulating his invention, balancing his judgment, but not appearing in regular propositions." "An art (that of medicine for instance) will of course admit into its limits, everything (*and nothing else*) which can conduce to the performances of *its own proper work;* it recognizes no other principles of selection."

"He who reads a book on logic, probably thinks no better when he rises up than when he sat down, but if any of the principles there unfolded cleave to his memory, and he afterwards, perhaps unconsciously, shapes and corrects his thoughts by them, no doubt the whole powers of his reasoning receive benefit. In a word, every art, from reasoning to riding and rowing, is learned by assiduous practice, and if principles do any good, it is proportioned to the readiness with which they can be converted into rules, and the patient constancy with which they are applied in all our attempts at excellence."

"*A man can teach names to another man, but he cannot plant in another's mind that far higher gift— the power of naming.*"

"*Language is not only the vehicle of thought, it is a great and efficient instrument in thinking.*"

"The whole of every *science* may be made the subject of teaching. Not so with *art;* much of it is not teachable."

Coleridge's profound and brilliant, but unequal, and often somewhat nebulous *Essay on Method*, is worth reading over, were it only as an exercitation, and to impress on the mind the meaning and value of *method*. Method is the road by which you reach, or hope to reach, a certain end; it is a process. It is the best direction for the search after truth. System, again, which is often confounded with it, is a mapping out, a circumscription of knowledge, either already gained, or theoretically laid down as probable. Aristotle had a system which did much good, but also much mischief. Bacon was chiefly occupied in preparing and pointing out the way—the only way—of procuring knowledge. He left to others to systematize the knowledge after it was got; but the pride and indolence of the human spirit led it constantly to build systems on imperfect knowledge. It has the trick of filling up out of its own fancy what it has not the diligence, the humility, and the honesty, to seek in nature; whose servant, and articulate voice, it ought to be.

Descartes' little tract on Method is like everything the lively and deep-souled Breton did, full of original and bright thought.

Sir John Herschel's volume needs no praise. We know no work of the sort, fuller of the best moral worth, as well as the highest philosophy. We fear it is more talked of than read.

We would recommend the article in the *Quarterly Review* as first-rate, and written with great eloquence and grace.

SYDNEY SMITH's *Sketches of Lectures on Moral Philosophy*. Second Edition.
SEDGWICK's *Discourse on the Studies at Cambridge, with a Preface and Appendix*. Sixth Edition.

We have put these two worthies here, not because
we had forgotten them,—much less because we think
less of them than the others, especially Sydney.   But
because we bring them in at the end of our small
entertainment, as we hand round a liqueur—be it
Curaçoa, Kimmel, or old Glenlivet—after dinner, and
end with the heterogeneous plum-pudding—that most
English of realized ideas.   Sydney Smith's book is one
of rare excellence, and well worthy of the study of
men and women, though perhaps not transcendental
enough for our modern philosophers, male and female.
It is really astonishing how much of the best of everything, from patriotism to nonsense, is to be found in
this volume of sketches.   You may read it through,
if your sides can bear such an accumulation of laughter, with great benefit; and if you open it anywhere,
you can't read three sentences without coming across
some, it may be common thought, and often original
enough, better expressed and *put* than you ever before
saw it.   The lectures on the Affections, the Passions
and Desires, and on Study, we would have everybody
to read and enjoy.

Sedgwick is a different, and, as a whole, an inferior
man; but a *man* every inch of him, and an Englishman
too, in his thoughts, and in his fine mother wit and
tongue.   He has, in the midst of all his confusion and
passionateness, the true instinct of philosophy—the
true venatic sense of objective truth.   We know
nothing better in the main, than his demolition of
what is untrue, and his reduction of what is absurd,
and his taking the wind out of what is tympanitic, in
the notorious *Vestiges;* we don't say he always does
justice to what is really good in it; his mission is to
execute justice *upon it*, and that he does.   His remarks
on Oken and Owen, and his quotations from Dr.
Clarke's admirable paper on the *Development of the
Fœtus*, in the *Cambridge Philosophical Transactions*,
we would recommend to our medical friends.   The very
confusion of Sedgwick is the free outcome of a deep
and racy nature; it puts us in mind of what happened,

when an Englishman was looking with astonishment
and disgust at a Scotchman eating a singed sheep's
head, and was asked by the eater what he thought of
that dish? "*Dish*, Sir, do you call that a dish?"
"Dish or no dish," rejoined the Caledonian, "there's
a deal o' fine confused feedin' aboot it, let me tell
you."

We conclude these rambling remarks with a quotation from Arnauld, the friend of Pascal, and the intrepid antagonist of the Vatican and the Grand
Monarque; one of the noblest, freest, most untiring
and honest intellects, our world has ever seen. "Why
don't you rest sometimes?" said his friend Nicole to
him. "Rest! why should I rest here? haven't I an
eternity to rest in?" The following sentence from his
Port-Royal Logic, so well introduced and translated
by Mr. Baynes, contains the gist of all we have been
trying to say. It should be engraven on the tablets
of every young student's heart—for the heart has to
do with study as well as the head.

"There is nothing more desirable than *good sense
and justness of mind*,—all other qualities of mind are
of limited use, but exactness of judgment is of general
utility in every part and in all employments of life.

"*We are too apt to employ reason merely as an
instrument for acquiring the sciences, whereas we
ought to avail ourselves of the sciences, as an instrument for perfecting our reason;* justness of mind being
infinitely more important than all the speculative
knowledge which we can obtain by means of sciences
the most solid. This ought to lead wise men to make
their sciences *the exercise and not the occupation of
their mental powers*. Men are not born to employ all
their time in measuring lines, in considering the various movements of matter : their minds are too great,
and their life too short, their time too precious, to be
so engrossed ; but they are born to be just, equitable,
and prudent, in all their thoughts, their actions, their
business ; to these things they ought specially to train
and discipline themselves."

So, young friends, bring *Brains* to your work, and mix everything with them, and them with everything. *Arma virumque*, tools and a man to use them. Stir up, direct, and give free scope to Sir Joshua's "*that*," and try again and again; and look, *oculo intento, acie acerrimâ*. Looking is a voluntary act,—it is the man within coming to the window; seeing is a state,—passive and receptive, and, at the best, little more than registrative.

Since writing the above, we have read with great satisfaction Dr. Forbes' Lecture delivered before the Chichester Literary Society and Mechanics' Institute, and published at their request. Its subject is, Happiness in its relation to Work and Knowledge. It is worthy of its author, and is, we think, more largely and finely imbued with his personal character, than any one other of his works that we have met with. We could not wish a fitter present for a young man starting on the game of life. It is a wise, cheerful, manly, warm-hearted discourse on the words of Bacon,—"He that is wise, let him pursue some desire or other : for he that doeth not affect some one thing in chief, unto him all things are distasteful and tedious." We will not spoil this little volume by giving any account of it. Let our readers get it, and read it. The extracts from his Thesis, *De Mentis Exercitatione et Felicitate exinde derivandâ*, are very curious—showing the native vigour and bent of his mind, and indicating also, at once the identity and the growth of his thoughts during the lapse of thirty-three years.

We give the last paragraph, the sense and the filial affection of which are alike admirable. Having mentioned to his hearers that they saw in himself a living illustration of the truth of his position, that happiness is a necessary result of knowledge and work, he thus concludes :—

"If you would further desire to know to what besides I am chiefly indebted for so enviable a lot, I would say :—1st, Because I had the good fortune to come into the world with a healthful frame, and with a sanguine temperament. 2nd, Because I had no patrimony, and was therefore obliged to trust to my own exertions for a livelihood. 3rd, Because I was born in a land where instruction is greatly prized and readily accessible. 4th, Because I was brought up to a profession which not only compelled mental exercise, but supplied for its use materials of the most delightful and varied kind. *And lastly and principally, because the good man to whom I owe my existence, had the foresight to know what would be best for his children. He had the wisdom, and the courage, and the exceeding love, to bestow all that could be spared of his worldly means, to purchase for his sons, that which is beyond price,* EDUCATION; well judging that the means so expended, if hoarded for future use, would be, if not valueless, certainly evanescent, while the precious treasure for which they were exchanged, a cultivated and instructed mind, would not only last through life, but might be the fruitful source of treasures far more precious than itself. So equipped he sent them forth into the world to fight Life's battle, leaving the issue in the hand of God; confident, however, that though they might fail to achieve renown or to conquer Fortune, they possessed *that* which, if rightly used, could win for them the yet higher prize of HAPPINESS."

Since this was written, many good books have appeared, but we would select three, which all young men should read and get—Hartley Coleridge's *Lives of Northern Worthies*, Thackeray's *Letters of Brown the Elder*, and *Tom Brown's School-days*,—in spirit and in expression, we don't know any better models for manly courage, good sense, and feeling, and they are as well written as they are thought.

There are the works of another man, one of the greatest, not only of our, but of any time, to which we cannot too earnestly draw our young readers. We mean the philosophical writings of Sir William

Hamilton. We know no more invigorating, quickening, rectifying kind of exercise, than reading with a will, anything he has written upon permanently important subjects. There is a greatness and simplicity, a closeness of thought, a glance keen and wide, a play of the entire nature, and a truthfulness and downrightness, with an amount, and accuracy, and vivification of learning, such as we know of in no one other writer, ancient or modern—not even Leibnitz; and we know no writings which so wholesomely at once exalt and humble the reader, make him feel what is in him, and what he can and may, as well as what he cannot, and need never hope to know. In this respect, Hamilton is as grand as Pascal, and more simple; he exemplifies everywhere his own sublime adaptation of Scripture—unless a man become a little child, he cannot enter into the kingdom; he enters the temple stooping, but he presses on, intrepid and alone, to the inmost *adytum*, worshipping the more the nearer he gets to the inaccessible shrine, whose veil no mortal hand has ever rent in twain. And we name after him, the thoughtful, candid, impressive little volume of his pupil, his friend, and his successor, Professor Fraser.

The following passage from Sir William Hamilton's *Dissertations*, besides its wise thought, sounds in the ear like the pathetic and majestic sadness of a symphony by Beethoven :—

" There are two sorts of ignorance : we philosophize to escape ignorance, and the consummation of our philosophy is ignorance; we start from the one, we repose in the other ; they are the goals from which, and to which, we tend ; and the pursuit of knowledge is but a course between two ignorances, as human life is itself only a travelling from grave to grave.

Τίς βίος ;—'Εκ τύμβοιο θορών, ἐπὶ τύμβον ὁδεύω.

The highest reach of human science is the scientific recognition of human ignorance; ' Qui nescit ignorare ignorat scire.' This ' learned ignorance ' is the rational conviction by the human mind of its in-

ability to transcend certain limits; it is the knowledge
of ourselves,—the science of man.   This is accomplished by a demonstration of the disproportion between what is to be known, and our faculties of
knowing,—the disproportion, to wit, between the
infinite and the finite.   In fact, the recognition of
human ignorance, is not only the one highest, but the
one true, knowledge; and its first-fruit, as has been
said, is humility.   Simple nescience is not proud; consummated science is positively humble.   For this
knowledge it is not, which 'puffeth up;' but its
opposite, the conceit of false knowledge,—the conceit,
in truth, as the apostle notices, of an ignorance of the
very nature of knowledge :—

> " Nam nesciens quid scire sit,
>   Te scire cuncta jactitas. "

"But as our knowledge stands to Ignorance, so
stands it also to Doubt.   Doubt is the beginning and
the end of our efforts to know; for as it is true,—' Alte
dubitat qui altius credit,' so it is likewise true,—
' Quo magis quærimus magis dubitamus.'

"The grand result of human wisdom, is thus only
a consciousness that what we know is as nothing to
what we know not, (' Quantum est quod nescimus !')
—an articulate confession, in fact, by our natural
reason, of the truth declared in revelation, that ' *now*
we see through a glass, darkly.' "

His pupil writes in the same spirit and to the same
end :   " A discovery, by means of reflection and
mental experiment, of the *limits* of knowledge, is the
highest and most universally applicable discovery of
all; it is the one through which our intellectual life
most strikingly blends with the moral and practical
part of human nature.   Progress in knowledge is
often paradoxically indicated by a diminution in the
apparent bulk of what we know.   Whatever helps to
work off the dregs of false opinion, and to purify the
intellectual mass—whatever deepens our conviction
of our infinite ignorance—really adds to, although it

sometimes seems to diminish, the rational possessions of man. This is the highest kind of merit that is claimed for Philosophy, by its earliest as well as by its latest representatives. It is by this standard that Socrates and Kant measure the chief results of their toil."

BOOKS REFERRED TO

1. Arnauld's Port-Royal Logic; translated by T. S. Baynes. —2. Thomson's Outlines of the Necessary Laws of Thought. —3. Descartes on the Method of Rightly Conducting the Reason, and Seeking Truth in the Sciences.—4. Coleridge's Essay on Method.—5. Whately's Logic and Rhetoric; new and cheap edition.—6. Mill's Logic; new and cheap edition. —7. Dugald Stewart's Outlines.—8. Sir John Herschel's Preliminary Dissertation.—9. Quarterly Review, vol. lxviii; Article upon Whewell's Philosophy of Inductive Sciences.— 10. Isaac Taylor's Elements of Thought.—11. Sir William Hamilton's edition of Reid; Dissertations; and Lectures.— 12. Professor Fraser's Rational Philosophy.

HER LAST HALF-CROWN

Once I had friends—though now by all forsaken;
Once I had parents—they are now in heaven.
I had a home once——

Worn out with anguish, sin, and cold, and hunger,
Down sunk the outcast, death had seized her senses.
There did the stranger find her in the morning—
*   God had released her.*

SOUTHEY.

HER LAST HALF-CROWN

Hugh Miller, the geologist, journalist, and man of genius, was sitting in his newspaper office late one dreary winter night. The clerks had all left, and he was preparing to go, when a quick rap came to the door. He said "Come in," and, looking towards the entrance, saw a little ragged child all wet with sleet. "Are ye Hugh Miller?" "Yes." "Mary Duff wants ye." "What does she want?" "She's deein." Some misty recollection of the name made him at once set out, and with his well-known plaid and stick, he was soon striding after the child, who trotted through the now deserted High Street, into the Canongate. By the time he got to the Old Playhouse Close, Hugh had revived his memory of Mary Duff; a lively girl who had been bred up beside him in Cromarty. The last time he had seen her was at a brother mason's marriage, where Mary was "best maid," and he "best man." He seemed still to see her bright young careless face, her tidy shortgown, and her dark eyes, and to hear her bantering, merry tongue.

Down the close went the ragged little woman, and up an outside stair, Hugh keeping near her with difficulty; in the passage she held out her hand and touched him; taking it in his great palm, he felt that she wanted a thumb. Finding her way like a cat through the darkness, she opened a door, and saying "That's her!" vanished. By the light of a dying fire he saw lying in the corner of the large empty room something like a woman's clothes, and on drawing nearer became aware of a thin pale face and two dark eyes looking keenly but helplessly up at him. The eyes were plainly Mary Duff's, though he could recognize no other feature. She wept silently, gazing steadily at him. "Are you Mary Duff?" "It's a' that's o' me, Hugh." She then tried to speak to him, something plainly of great urgency, but she couldn't, and seeing that she was very ill, and was making herself worse, he put half-a-crown into her feverish hand, and said he would call again in the morning. He could get no information about her from the neighbours: they were surly or asleep.

When he returned next morning, the little girl met him at the stair-head, and said, "She's deid." He went in, and found that it was true; there she lay, the fire out, her face placid, and the likeness to her maiden self restored. Hugh thought he would have known her now, even with those bright black eyes closed as they were, *in æternum*.

Seeking out a neighbour, he said he would like to bury Mary Duff, and arranged for the funeral with an undertaker in the close. Little seemed to be known of the poor outcast, except that she was a "licht," or, as Solomon would have said, a "strange woman." "Did she drink?" "Whiles."

On the day of the funeral one or two residents in the close accompanied him to the Canongate Churchyard. He observed a decent looking little old woman watching them, and following at a distance, though the day was wet and bitter. After the grave was filled, and he had taken off his hat, as the men finished their business by putting on and slapping the sod, he saw this old woman remaining. She came up and, courtesying, said, "Ye wad ken that lass, Sir?" "Yes; I knew her when she was young." The woman then burst into tears, and told Hugh that she "keepit a bit shop at the Closemooth, and Mary dealt wi' me, and aye paid reglar, and I was feared she was dead, for she had been a month awin' me half-a-crown:" and then with a look and voice of awe, she told him how on the night he was sent for, and immediately after he had left, she had been awakened by some one in her room; and by her bright fire—for she was a *bein,*

well-to-do body—she had seen the wasted dying creature, who came forward and said, " Wasn't it half-a-
crown?"   " Yes."   " There it is," and putting it
under the bolster, vanished !

Alas for Mary Duff ! her career had been a sad one
since the day when she had stood side by side with
Hugh at the wedding of their friends.   Her father
died not long after, and her mother supplanted her
in the affections of the man to whom she had given
her heart.   The shock was overwhelming, and made
home intolerable.   Mary fled from it blighted and
embittered, and after a life of shame and sorrow,
crept into the corner of her wretched garret, to die
deserted and alone; giving evidence in her latest
act that honesty had survived amid the wreck of
nearly every other virtue.

" My thoughts are not your thoughts, neither are
your ways my ways, saith the Lord.   For as the
heavens are higher than the earth, so are my ways
higher than your ways, and my thoughts than your
thoughts."

QUEEN MARY'S CHILD-GARDEN

If any one wants a pleasure that is sure to please, one over which he needn't growl the sardonic beatitude of the great Dean, let him, when the Mercury is at " Fair," take the nine A.M. train to the North and a return ticket for Callander, and when he arrives at Stirling, let him ask the most obliging and knowing of station-masters to telegraph to " the Dreadnought " for a carriage to be in waiting. When passing Dunblane Cathedral, let him resolve to write to the *Scotsman*, advising the removal of a couple of shabby trees which obstruct the view of that beautiful triple end window which Mr. Ruskin and everybody else admires, and by the time he has written this letter in his mind, and turned the sentences to it, he will find himself at Callander and the carriage all ready. Giving the order for the *Port of Monteith*, he will rattle through this hard-featured, and to our eye comfortless village, lying ugly amid so much grandeur and beauty, and let him stop on the crown of the bridge, and fill his eyes with the perfection of the view up the Pass of Leny—the Teith lying diffuse and asleep, as if its heart were in the Highlands and it were loath to go, the noble Ben Ledi imaged in its broad stream. Then let him make his way across a bit of pleasant moorland—flushed with maiden-hair and white with cotton grass, and fragrant with the *Orchis conopsia*, well deserving its epithet *odoratissima*.

He will see from the turn of the hillside the Blair of Drummond waving with corn and shadowed with rich woods, where eighty years ago there was a black peat-moss; and far off, on the horizon, Damyat

and the Touch Fells; and at his side the little loch
of Ruskie, in which he may see five Highland cattle,
three tawny brown and two brindled, standing in the
still water—themselves as still, all except their
switching tails and winking ears—the perfect images
of quiet enjoyment. By this time he will have come
in sight of the Lake of Monteith, set in its woods,
with its magical shadows and soft gleams. There
is a loveliness, a gentleness and peace about it more
like "lone St. Mary's Lake," or Derwent Water,
than of any of its sister lochs. It is lovely rather
than beautiful, and is a sort of gentle prelude, in the
minor key, to the coming glories and intenser charms
of Loch Ard and the true Highlands beyond.

You are now at the Port, and have passed the
secluded and cheerful manse, and the parish kirk
with its graves, close to the lake, and the proud aisle
of the Grahams of Gartmore washed by its waves.
Across the road is the modest little inn, a Fisher's
Tryst. On the unruffled water lie several islets,
plump with rich foliage, brooding like great birds of
calm. You somehow think of them as on, not in the
lake, or like clouds lying in a nether sky—" like
ships waiting for the wind." You get a coble, and
a *yauld* old Celt, its master, and are rowed across to
Inchmahome, the Isle of Rest. Here you find on
landing huge Spanish chestnuts, one lying dead,
others standing stark and peeled, like gigantic antlers,
and others flourishing in their *viridis senectus*, and
in a thicket of wood you see the remains of a monas-
tery of great beauty, the design and workmanship
exquisite. You wander through the ruins, overgrown
with ferns and Spanish filberts, and old fruit trees,
and at the corner of the old monkish garden you
come upon one of the strangest and most touching
sights you ever saw—an oval space of about 18 feet
by 12, with the remains of a double row of boxwood
all round, the plants of box being about fourteen feet
high, and eight or nine inches in diameter, healthy,
but plainly of great age.

What is this? it is called in the guide-books Queen

Mary's Bower; but besides its being plainly not in the least a bower, what could the little Queen, then five years old, and "fancy free," do with a bower? It is plainly, as was, we believe, first suggested by our keen-sighted and diagnostic Professor of Clinical Surgery,[1] *the Child-Queen's Garden*, with her little walk, and its rows of boxwood, left to themselves for three hundred years. Yes, without doubt, "here is that first garden of her simpleness." Fancy the little, lovely royal child, with her four Marys, her playfellows, her child maids of honour, with their little hands and feet, and their innocent and happy eyes, pattering about that garden all that time ago, laughing, and running, and gardening as only children do and can. As is well known, Mary was placed by her mother in this Isle of Rest before sailing from the Clyde for France. There is something "that tirls the heartstrings a' to the life" in standing and looking on this unmistakable living relic of that strange and pathetic old time. Were we Mr. Tennyson, we would write an Idyll of that child Queen, in that garden of hers, eating her bread and honey—getting her teaching from the holy men, the monks of old, and running off in wild mirth to her garden and her flowers, all unconscious of the black, lowering thunder-cloud on Ben Lomond's shoulder.

> "Oh, blessed vision! happy child!
> Thou art so exquisitely wild;
> I think of thee with many fears
> Of what may be thy lot in future years.
> I thought of times when Pain might be thy guest,
> Lord of thy house and hospitality.
> And Grief, uneasy lover! never rest
> But when she sat within the touch of thee.
> What hast thou to do with sorrow,
> Or the injuries of to-morrow?"

[1] The same seeing eye and understanding mind, when they were eighteen years of age, discovered and published the Solvent of Caoutchouc, for which a patent was taken out afterwards by the famous Mackintosh. If the young discoverer had secured the patent, he might have made a fortune as large as his present reputation—I don't suppose he much regrets that he didn't.

You have ample time to linger there amid

"The gleams, the shadows, and the peace profound,"

and get your mind informed with quietness and
beauty, and fed with thoughts of other years, and of
her whose story, like Helen of Troy's, will continue
to move the hearts of men as long as the grey hills
stand round about that gentle lake, and are mirrored
at evening in its depths. You may do and enjoy all
this, and be in Princes Street by nine P.M.; and we
wish we were as sure of many things as of your
saying, "Yes, this *is* a pleasure that has pleased,
and will please again; this was something expected
which did not disappoint."

———

There is another garden of Queen Mary's, which
may still be seen, and which has been left to itself like
that in the Isle of Rest. It is in the grounds at
Chatsworth, and is moated, walled round, and raised
about fifteen feet above the park. Here the Queen,
when a prisoner under the charge of "Old Bess of
Hardwake," was allowed to walk without any guard.
How different the two! and how different she who
took her pleasure in them!

Lines written on the steps of a small moated garden at
Chatsworth, called

"QUEEN MARY'S BOWER.

"The moated bower is wild and drear,
    And sad the dark yew's shade;
The flowers which bloom in silence here,
    In silence also fade.

"The woodbine and the light wild rose
    Float o'er the broken wall;
And here the mournful nightshade blows,
    To note the garden's fall.

"Where once a princess wept her woes,
    The bird of night complains;
And sighing trees the tale disclose
    They learnt from Mary's strains.

"A. H."

ΑΓΧΙΝΟΙΑ: or, NEARNESS OF THE Νοῦς

" Depend upon it a lucky guess is never merely luck—there is always some Talent in it."—MISS AUSTEN, *in Emma.*

DR. CHALMERS used to say that in the dynamics of human affairs, two qualities were essential to greatness—Power and Promptitude. One man might have both, another power without promptitude, another promptitude without power. We must all feel the common sense of this, and can readily see how it applies to a general in the field, to a pilot in a storm, to a sportsman, to a fencer, to a debater. It is the same with an operating surgeon at all times, and may be at any time with the practitioner of the art of healing. He must be ready for what are called emergencies—cases which rise up at your feet, and must be dealt with on the instant,—he must have power and promptitude.

It is a curious condition of mind that this requires: it is like sleeping with your pistol under your pillow, and it on full cock; a moment lost and all may be lost. There is the very nick of time. This is what we mean by presence of mind; by a man having such a subject at his finger ends; that part of the mind lying nearest the outer world, and having to act on it through the bodily organs, through the will—the outposts must be always awake. It is of course, so to speak, only a portion of the mind that is thus needed and thus available; if the whole mind were for ever at the advanced posts, it would soon lose itself in this endeavour to keep it. Now, though the thing needed to be done may be simple enough, what goes to the doing of it, and to the being at once ready and able to do it, involves much: the wedge would not be a wedge, or do a wedge's work, without the width

behind as well as the edge in front. Your men of
promptitude without genius or power, including
knowledge and will, are those who present the wedge
the wrong way. Thus your extremely prompt people
are often doing the wrong thing, which is almost
always worse than nothing. Our vague friend who
bit " Yarrow's " tail instead of " the Chicken's,"
was full of promptitude; as was also that other man,
probably a relative, who barred the door with a
boiled carrot : each knew what was needed—the
biting the tail, the barring the door; both erred as
to the means—the one by want of presence of mind,
the other by lack of mind itself. We must have just
enough of the right knowledge and no more; we must
have the habit of using this; we must have self-
reliance, and the consentaneousness of the entire
mind; and what our hand finds to do, we must do
with our might as well as with it. Therefore it is
that this master act of the man, under some sudden
and great unexpected crisis, is in a great measure
performed unconsciously as to its mental means. The
man is so *totus in illo*, that there is no bit of the mind
left to watch and record the acts of the rest; therefore men, when they have done some signal feat of
presence of mind, if asked how they did it, generally
don't very well know—they just did it : it was, in
fact, done and then thought of, not thought of and
then done, in which case it would likely never have
been done. Not that the act was uncaused by mind;
it is one of the highest powers of mind thus to act;
but it is done, if I may use the phrase, by an acquired
instinct. You will find all this in that wonderful old
Greek who was Alexander the Great's and the old
world's school-master, and ours if we were wise,—
whose truthfulness and clear insight one wonders at
the longer he lives. He seems to have seen the human
mind as a bird or an engineer does the earth—he
knew the plan of it. We now-a-days see it as one
sees a country, athwart and in perspective, and from
the side; he saw it from above and from below. There

are therefore no shadows, no foreshortenings, no clear-obscure, indeed no disturbing medium; it is as if he examined every thing *in vacuo*. I refer my readers to what he says on Ἀγχινοία and Εὐστοχία.[1]

[1] As I am now, to my sorrow and shame, too much of a mediate Grecian, I give a Balliol friend's note on these two words :—" What you have called ' presence of mind ' and ' happy guessing ' may, I think, be identified respectively with Aristotle's ἀγχινοία and εὐστοχία. The latter of these, εὐστοχία, Aristotle mentions incidentally when treating of εὐβουλία, or good deliberation. *Eth. Nic.* bk. vi. ch. 9. Good deliberation, he says, is not εὐστοχία, for the former is a slow process, whereas the latter is not guided by reason, and is rapid. In the same passage he tells us that ἀγχινοία is a sort of εὐστοχία. But he speaks of ἀγχινοία more fully in *Ana. Post.* i. 34 :—Ἀγχινοία is a sort of happy guessing at the intermediate, when there is not time for consideration : as when a man, seeing that the bright side of the moon is always turned towards the sun, comprehends that her light is borrowed from the sun ; or concludes, from seeing one conversing with a capitalist that he wants to borrow money ; or infers that people are friends from the fact of their having common enemies.' And then he goes on to make these simple observations confused and perplexing by reducing them to his logical formula.

" The derivation of the words will confirm this view. Εὐστοχία is a hitting the *mark* successfully, a reaching to the end, the rapid and, as it were, intuitive perception of the truth. This is what Whewell means by saying, ' all induction is a happy conjecture.' But when Aristotle says that this faculty is not guided by reason (ἄνευ τε γὰρ λόγου), he does not mean to imply that it grows up altogether independent of reason, any more than Whewell means to say that all the discoveries in the inductive sciences have been made by men taking ' shots ' at them, as boys at school do at hard passages in their Latin lessons. On the contrary, no faculty is so absolutely the child of reason as this faculty of happy guessing. It only attains to perfection after the reason has been long and painfully trained in the sphere in which the guesses are to be made. What Aristotle does mean is, that when it has attained perfection, we are not conscious of the share which reason has in its operation—it is so rapid that by no analysis can we detect the presence of reason in its action. Sir Isaac Newton seeing the apple fall, and thence ' guessing ' at the law of gravitation, is a good instance of εὐστοχία.

" Ἀγχινοία, on the other hand, is a *nearness of mind* ; not a reaching to the end, but an apprehension of the best means ; not a perception of the truth, but a perception of how the truth

My object in what I have now written and am going to write, is to impress upon medical students the value of power and promptitude in combination, for their professional purposes; the uses to them of nearness of the Νοῦς and of happy guessing; and how you may see the sense, and neatness, and pith of that excellent thinker, as well as best of all story-tellers, Miss Austin, when she says in *Emma*, "Depend upon it, a lucky guess is never merely luck, there is always some talent in it." Talent here denoting intelligence and will in action. In all sciences except those called exact, this happy guessing plays a large part, and in none more than in medicine, which is truly a tentative art, founded upon likelihood, and is therefore what we call contingent. Instead of this view of the healing art discouraging us from making our ultimate principles as precise, as we should make our observations, it should urge us the more to this; for, depend upon it, that guess as we may often have to do, he will guess best, most happily for himself and his patient, who has the greatest amount of true knowledge, and the most serviceable amount of what we may call mental cash, ready money, and ready weapons.

We must not only have wisdom, which is knowledge assimilated and made our own, but we must, as the Lancashire men say and do, *have wit to use it*. We may carry a nugget of gold in our pocket, or a £100 bank-note, but unless we can get it *changed*, it is of little use, and we must moreover have the coin of the country we are in. This want of presence of mind, and having your wits about you, is as fatal to a surgeon as to a general.

is to be supported. It is sometimes translated ' sagacity,' but readiness or presence of mind is better, as sagacity rather involves the idea of consideration. In matters purely intellectual it is ready wit. It is a sort of shorter or more limited εὐστοχία. It is more of a natural gift than εὐστοχία, because the latter is a far higher and nobler faculty, and therefore more dependent for its perfection on cultivation, as all our highest faculties are. Εὐστοχία is more akin to genius, ἀγχινοία to practical common sense."

That wise little man, Dr. Henry Marshall, little in body but not little in mind, in brain, and in worth, used to give an instance of this. A young, well-educated surgeon, attached to a regiment quartered at Musselburgh, went out professionally with two officers who were in search of "satisfaction." One fell shot in the thigh, and in half-an-hour after he was found dead, the surgeon kneeling pale and grim over him, with his two thumbs sunk in his thigh *below* the wound, the grass steeped in blood. If he had put them two inches higher, or extemporized a tourniquet with his sash and the pistol's ramrod and a stone, he might have saved his friend's life and his own—for he shot himself that night.

Here is another. Robbie Watson, whom I now see walking mildly about the streets—having taken to coal—was driver of the Dumfries coach by Biggar. One day he had changed horses, and was starting down a steep hill, with an acute turn at the foot, when he found his wheelers, two new horses, utterly ignorant of backing. They got furious, and we outside got alarmed. Robbie made an attempt to pull up, and then with an odd smile took his whip, gathered up his reins, and lashed the entire four into a gallop. If we had not seen his face we would have thought him a maniac; he kept them well together, and shot down like an arrow, as far as we could see to certain destruction. Right in front at the turn was a stout gate into a field, shut; he drove them straight at that, and through we went, the gate broken into shivers, and we finding ourselves safe, and the very horses enjoying the joke. I remember we emptied our pockets into Robbie's hat, which he had taken off to wipe his head. Now, in a few seconds all this must have passed through his head— "that horse is not a wheeler, nor that one either; we'll come to mischief; there's the gate; yes, I'll do it." And he did it; but then he had to do it with his might; he had to make it impossible for his four horses to do anything but toss the gate before them.

Here is another case. Dr. Reid of Peebles, long famous in the end of last and beginning of this century, as the Doctor of Tweeddale; a man of great force of character, and a true Philip, a lover of horses, saw one Fair day a black horse, entire, thoroughbred. The groom asked a low price, and would answer no questions. At the close of the fair the doctor bought him, amid the derision of his friends. Next morning he rode him up Tweed, came home after a long round, and had never been better carried. This went on for some weeks; the fine creature was without a fault. One Sunday morning, he was posting up by Neidpath at a great pace, the country people trooping into the town to church. Opposite the fine old castle, the thoroughbred stood stock still, and it needed all the doctor's horsemanship to counteract the law of projectiles; he did, and sat still, and not only gave no sign of urging the horse, but rather intimated that it was his particular desire that he should stop. He sat there a full hour, his friends making an excellent joke of it, and he declining, of course, all interference. At the end of the hour, the Black Duke, as he was called, turned one ear forward, then another, looked aside, shook himself, and moved on, his master intimating that this was exactly what he wished; and from that day till his death, some fifteen years after, never did these two friends allude to this little circumstance, and it was never repeated; though it turned out that he had killed his two men previously. The doctor must have, when he got him, said to himself, " if he is not stolen there is a reason for his paltry price," and he would go over all the possibilities. So that when he stood still, he would say, " Ah, this is it;" but then he saw this at once, and lost no time, and did nothing. Had he given the horse one dig with his spurs, or one cut with his whip, or an impatient jerk with his bit, the case would have failed. When a colt it had been brutally used, and being nervous, it lost its judgment, poor thing, and lost its presence of mind.

One more instance of nearness of the Noûs. A lady was in front of her lawn with her children, when a mad dog made his appearance, pursued by the peasants. What did she do? What would you have done? Shut your eyes and think. She went straight to the dog, received its head in her thick stuff gown, between her knees, and muffling it up, held it with all her might till the men came up. No one was hurt. Of course, she fainted after it was all right.

We all know (but why should we not know again?) the story of the Grecian mother who saw her child sporting on the edge of the bridge. She knew that a cry would startle it over into the raging stream— she came gently near, and opening her bosom allured the little scapegrace.

I once saw a great surgeon, after settling a particular procedure as to a life-and-death operation, as a general settles his order of battle. He began his work, and at the second cut altered the entire conduct of the operation. No one not in the secret could have told this : not a moment's pause, not a quiver of the face, not a look of doubt. This is the same master power in man, which makes the difference between Sir John Moore and Sir John Cope.

Mrs. Major Robertson, a woman of slight make, great beauty, and remarkable energy, courage, and sense (she told me the story herself), on going up to her bedroom at night—there being no one in the house but a servant girl, in the ground floor—saw a portion of a man's foot projecting from under the bed. She gave no cry of alarm, but shut the door as usual, set down her candle, and began as if to undress, when she said aloud to herself, with an impatient tone and gesture, " I've forgotten that key again, I declare;" and leaving the candle burning, and the door open, she went down stairs, got the watchman, and secured the proprietor of the foot, which had not moved an inch. How many women or men could have done, or rather been all this !

DR. CHALMERS'S POST-HUMOUS WORKS

WHEN, towards the close of some long summer day, we come suddenly, and, as we think, before his time, upon the broad sun, "sinking down in his tranquillity" into the unclouded west, we cannot keep our eyes from the great spectacle,—and when he is gone the shadow of him haunts our sight: we see everywhere,—upon the spotless heaven, upon the distant mountains, upon the fields, and upon the road at our feet,—that dim, strange changeful image; and if our eyes shut, to recover themselves, we still find in them, like a dying flame, or like a gleam in a dark place, the unmistakable phantom of the mighty orb that has set,—and were we to sit down, as we have often done, and try to record by pencil or by pen, our impression of that supreme hour, still would IT be there. We must have patience with our eye, it will not let the impression go,—that spot on which the radiant disc was impressed, is insensible to all other outward things, for a time: its best relief is, to let the eye wander vaguely over earth and sky, and repose itself on the mild shadowy distance.

So it is when a great and good and beloved man departs, sets—it may be suddenly—and to us who know not the times and the seasons, *too soon*. We gaze eagerly at his last hours, and when he is gone, never to rise again on our sight, we see his image wherever we go, and in whatsoever we are engaged, and if we try to record by words our wonder, our sorrow, and our affection, we cannot see to do it, for the "idea of his life" is for ever coming into our "study of imagination"—into all our thoughts, and we can do little else than let our mind, in a wise passiveness, hush itself to rest.

The sun returns—he knows his rising—

> "To-morrow he repairs his drooping head,
> And tricks his beams, and with new spangled ore
> Flames in the forehead of the morning sky;"

but man lieth down, and riseth not again till the heavens are no more. Never again will he whose "Meditations" are now before us, lift up the light of his countenance upon us.

We need not say we look upon him, as a great man, as a good man, as a beloved man,—*quis desiderio sit pudor tam cari capitis?* We cannot now go very curiously to work, to scrutinize the composition of his character,—we cannot take that large, free, genial nature to pieces, and weigh this and measure that, and sum up and pronounce; we are too near as yet to him, and to his loss, he is too dear to us to be so handled. "His death," to use the pathetic words of Hartley Coleridge, "is a recent sorrow; his image still lives in eyes that weep for him." The prevailing feeling is,—He is gone—"*abiit ad plures*—he has gone over to the majority, he has joined the famous nations of the dead."

It is no small loss to the world, when one of its master spirits—one of its great lights—a king among the nations—leaves it. A sun is extinguished; a great attractive, regulating power is withdrawn. For though it be a common, it is also a natural thought, to compare a great man to the sun; it is in many respects significant. Like the sun, he rules his day, and he is "for a sign and for seasons, and for days and for years;" he enlightens, quickens, attracts, and leads after him his host—his generation.

To pursue our image. When the sun sets to us, he rises elsewhere—he goes on rejoicing, like a strong man, running his race. So does a great man: when he leaves us and our concerns—he rises elsewhere; and we may reasonably suppose that one who has in

this world played a great part in its greatest histories
—who has through a long life been pre-eminent for
promoting the good of men and the glory of God—
will be looked upon with keen interest, when he joins
the company of the immortals. They must have
heard of his fame; they may in their ways have seen
and helped him already.

Every one must have trembled when reading that
passage in Isaiah, in which Hell is described as moved
to meet Lucifer at his coming: there is not in human
language anything more sublime in conception, more
exquisite in expression; it has on it the light of the
terrible crystal. But may we not reverse the scene?
May we not imagine, when a great and good man—a
son of the morning—enters on his rest, that Heaven
would move itself to meet him at his coming? That
it would stir up its dead, even all the chief ones of the
earth, and that the kings of the nations would arise
each one from his throne to welcome their brother?
that those who saw him would " narrowly consider
him," and say, " is this he who moved nations, enlightened and bettered his fellows, and whom the
great Taskmaster welcomes with ' Well done !' "

We cannot help following him, whose loss we now
mourn, into that region, and figuring to ourselves
his great, childlike spirit, when that unspeakable scene
bursts upon his view, when, as by some inward, instant
sense, he is conscious of God—of the immediate
presence of the All-seeing Unseen; when he beholds
" His honourable, true, and only Son," face to face,
enshrined in " that glorious form, that light unsuffer-
able, and that far-beaming blaze of majesty," that
brightness of His glory, that express image of His
person; when he is admitted into the goodly fellowship of the apostles—the glorious company of the
prophets—the noble army of martyrs—the general
assembly of just men—and beholds with his loving
eyes the myriads of " little ones," outnumbering their
elders as the dust of stars with which the galaxy is
filled exceeds in multitude the hosts of heaven.

What a change! death the gate of life—a second birth, in the twinkling of an eye: this moment, weak, fearful, in the amazement of death; the next, strong, joyful,—at rest,—all things new! To adopt his own words: all his life, up to the last, " knocking at a door not yet opened, with an earnest indefinite longing,—his very soul breaking for the longing,—drinking of water, and thirsting again "—and then—suddenly and at once—a door opened into heaven, and the Master heard saying, 'Come in, and come up hither!'' drinking of the river of life, clear as crystal, of which if a man drink he will never thirst,—being filled with all the fulness of God!

Dr. Chalmers was a ruler among men: this we know historically; this every man who came within his range felt at once. He was like Agamemnon, a native ἄναξ ἀνδρῶν, and with all his homeliness of feature and deportment, and his perfect simplicity of expression, there was about him " that divinity that doth hedge a king." You felt a power, in him, and going from him, drawing you to him in spite of yourself. He was in this respect a *solar* man, he drew after him his own firmament of planets. They, like all free agents, had their centrifugal forces acting ever towards an independent, solitary course, but the centripetal also was there, and they moved with and around their imperial sun,—gracefully or not, willingly or not, as the case might be, but there was no breaking loose: they again, in their own spheres of power, might have their attendant moons, but all were bound to the great massive luminary in the midst.

There is to us a continual mystery in this power of one man over another. We find it acting everywhere, with the simplicity, the ceaselessness, the energy of gravitation; and we may be permitted to speak of this influence as obeying similar conditions; it is proportioned to *bulk*—for we hold to the notion of a bigness in souls as well as bodies—one soul differing from another in quantity and momentum as

well as in quality and force, and its intensity increases
by nearness. There is much in what Jonathan Edwards
says of one spiritual essence having more being than
another, and in Dr. Chalmers's question, " Is he a
man of *wecht?*"

But when we meet a *solar* man, of ample nature—
soul, body, and spirit; when we find him from his
earliest years moving among his fellows like a king,
moving them whether they will or not—this feeling
of mystery is deepened; and though we would not,
like some men (who should know better), worship the
creature and convert the hero into a god, we do feel
more than in other cases the truth, that it is the inspiration of the Almighty which has given to that man
understanding, and that all power, all energy, all
light, come to him, from the First and the Last—the
Living One. God comes to be regarded by us, in
this instance, as He ought always to be, " the final
centre of repose "—the source of all being, of all life
—the *Terminus ad quem* and the *Terminus a quo*.
And assuredly, as in the firmament that simple law
of gravitation reigns supreme—making it indeed a
kosmos—majestic, orderly, comely in its going—
ruling, and binding not the less the fiery and nomadic
comets, than the gentle, punctual moons—so certainly, and to us moral creatures to a degree transcen-
dently more important, does the whole intelligent
universe move around and move towards and in the
Father of Lights.

It would be well if the world would, among the
many other uses they make of its great men, make
more of this,—that they are manifestors of God—
revealers of His will—vessels of His omnipotence—
and are among the very chiefest of His ways and
works.

As we have before said, there is a perpetual wonder
in this power of one man over his fellows, especially
when we meet with it in a great man. You see its
operations constantly in history, and through it the
Great Ruler has worked out many of His greatest

and strangest acts. But however we may understand
the accessory conditions by which the one man rules
the many, and controls, and fashions them to his
purposes, and transforms them into his likeness—
multiplying as it were himself—there remains at the
bottom of it all a mystery—a reaction between body
and soul that we cannot explain. Generally, however, we find accompanying its manifestation, a
capacious understanding—a strong will—an emo-
tional nature quick, powerful, urgent, undeniable,
in perpetual communication with the energetic will
and the large resolute intellect—and a strong, hearty
capable body; a countenance and person expressive
of this combination—the mind finding its way at once
and in full force to the face, to the gesture, to every
act of the body. He must have what is called a
" presence;" not that he must be great in size, beautiful, or strong; but he must be expressive and impressive—his outward man must communicate to the
beholder at once and without fail, something of indwelling power, and he must be and act as *one*.
You may in your mind analyze him into his several
parts; but practically he acts in everything with his
whole soul and his whole self; whatsoever his hand
finds to do, he does it with his might. Luther, Moses,
David, Mahomet, Cromwell—all verified these conditions.

And so did Dr. Chalmers. There was something
about his whole air and manner, that disposed you
at the very first to make way where he went—he held
you before you were aware. That this depended
fully as much upon the activity and the quantity—if
we may so express ourselves—of his affections, upon
that combined action of mind and body which we call
temperament, and upon a straightforward, urgent
will, as upon what is called the pure intellect, will be
generally allowed; but with all this, he could not have
been and done, what he was and did, had he not had
an understanding, in vigour and in capacity, worthy
of its great and ardent companions. It was large,

and free, mobile, and intense, rather than penetrative, judicial, clear, or fine,—so that in one sense he was more a man to make others *act* than *think*; but his own actings had always their origin in some fixed, central, inevitable *proposition*, as he would call it, and he began his onset with stating plainly, and with lucid calmness, what he held to be a great seminal truth; from this he passed at once, not into exposition, but into illustration and enforcement—into, if we may make a word, overwhelming insistance. Something was to be done, rather than explained.

There was no separating his thoughts and expressions from his person, and looks, and voice. How perfectly we can at this moment recall him! Thundering, flaming, lightening in the pulpit; teaching, indoctrinating, drawing after him the students in his lecture-room; sitting among other public men, the most unconscious, the most king-like of them all, with that broad leonine countenance, that beaming, liberal smile; or on the way out to his home, in his old-fashioned great-coat, with his throat muffled up, his big walking-stick moved outwards in an arc, its point fixed, its head circumferential, a sort of companion, and playmate, with which doubtless, he demolished legions of imaginary foes, errors, and stupidities in men and things, in Church and State. His great look, large chest, large head, his amplitude every way; his broad, simple, childlike, inturned feet; his short, hurried impatient step; his erect, royal air; his look of general goodwill; his kindling up into a warm but vague benignity when one he did not recognize spoke to him; the addition, for it was not a change, of keen speciality to his hearty recognition; the twinkle of his eyes; the immediately saying something very personal to set all to rights, and then the sending you off with some thought, some feeling, some remembrance, making your heart burn within you; his voice indescribable; his eye— that most peculiar feature—not vacant, but *asleep*— innocent, mild, and large; and his soul, its great

inhabitant, not always at his window; but then, when
he did awake, how close to you was that burning
vehement soul! how it penetrated and overcame you!
how mild, and affectionate, and genial its expression
at his own fireside!

Of his portraits worth mentioning, there are Watson Gordon's, Duncan's—the Calotypes of Mr. Hill
—Kenneth M'Leay's miniatures—the Daguerreotype,
and Steell's bust. These are all good, and all give
bits of him, some nearly the whole, but not one of
them that τι θερμόν, that *fiery particle*—that inspired
look—that " diviner mind "—the *poco più*, or little
more. Watson Gordon's is too much of the mere
clergyman—is a pleasant likeness, and has the
shape of his mouth, and the setting of his feet very
good. Duncan's is a work of genius, and is the
giant looking up, awakening, but not awakened—it
is a very fine picture. Mr. Hill's Calotypes we like
better than all the rest; because what in them is true,
is absolutely so, and they have some delicate renderings which are all but beyond the power of any human
artist; for though man's art is mighty, nature's is
mightier. The one of the Doctor sitting with his
grandson " *Tommy*," is to us the best; we have the
true grandeur of his form—his bulk. M'Leay's is
admirable—spirited—and has that look of shrewdness and vivacity and immediateness which he had
when he was observing and speaking keenly; it is,
moreover, a fine, manly bit of art. M'Leay is the
Raeburn of miniature painters—he does a great deal
with little. The Daguerreotype is, in its own way,
excellent; it gives the externality of the man to perfection, but it is Dr. Chalmers at a stand-still—his
mind and feelings " pulled up " for the second that
it was taken. Steell's is a noble bust—has a stern
heroic expression and pathetic beauty about it, and
from wanting colour and shadow and the eyes, it
relies upon a certain simplicity and grandeur;—in
this it completely succeeds—the mouth is handled
with extraordinary subtlety and sweetness, and the

hair hangs over that huge brow like a glorious cloud.
We think this head of Dr. Chalmers the artist's
greatest bust.

In reference to the assertion we have made as to
bulk forming one primary element of a powerful
mind, Dr. Chalmers used to say, when a man of
activity and public mark was mentioned, " Has he
wecht? he has promptitude—has he power? he has
power—has he promptitude? and, moreover, has he
a discerning spirit?"

These are great practical, universal truths. How
few even of our greatest men have had all these three
faculties large—fine, sound, and in " perfect diapason." Your men of promptitude, without power or
judgment, are common and are useful. But they are
apt to run wild, to get needlessly brisk, unpleasantly
incessant. A weasel is good or bad as the case may
be,—good against vermin—bad to meddle with;—
but inspired weasels, weasels on a mission, are terrible
indeed, mischievous and fell, and swiftness making
up for want of momentum by inveteracy; " fierce
as wild bulls, *untamable as flies.*" Of such men we
have now-a-days too many. Men are too much in the
way of supposing that *doing* is *being;* that theology
and excogitation, and fierce dogmatic assertion of
what they consider truth, is godliness; that obedience
is merely an occasional great act, and not a series of
acts, issuing from a state, like the stream of water
from its well.

> " Action is transitory—a step—a blow,
>   The motion of a muscle—this way or that;
>   'Tis done—and in the after vacancy,
>   We wonder at ourselves like men betrayed.
>   Suffering " (*obedience*, or *being* as opposed to *doing*)—
>   " Suffering is permanent,———
>   And has the nature of infinity."

Dr. Chalmers was a man of genius—he had his
own way of thinking, and saying, and doing, and
looking everything. Men have vexed themselves in
vain to define what genius is; like every ultimate

term we may describe it by giving its effects, we can
hardly succeed in reaching its essence. Fortunately,
though we know not what are its elements, we know
it when we meet it; and in him, in every movement
of his mind, in every gesture, we had its unmistakable
tokens. Two of the ordinary accompaniments of
genius—Enthusiasm and Simplicity—he had in rare
measure.

He was an *enthusiast* in its true and good sense;
he was " entheat," as if full of God, as the old poets
called it. It was this ardour, this superabounding
life, this immediateness of thought and action, idea
and emotion, setting the whole man agoing at once—
that gave a power and a charm to everything he did.
To adopt the old division of the Hebrew Doctors, as
given by Nathaniel Culverwel, in his *Light of Nature*:
In man we have—1st, πνεῦμα ζωοποιοῦν, *the sensitive
soul*, that which lies nearest the body—the very
blossom and flower of life; 2nd, τὸν νοῦν, *animam
rationis*, sparkling and glittering with intellectuals,
crowned with light; and 3rd, τὸν θυμόν, *impetum
animi, motum mentis*, the vigour and energy of the
soul—its temper—the mover of the other two—the
first being, as they said, resident *in hepate*—the
second *in cerebro*—the third *in corde*, where it pre-
sides over the issues of life, commands the circulation, and animates and sets the blood a-moving. The
first and second are informative, explicative, they
" take in and do "—the other " gives out." Now in
Dr. Chalmers the great ingredient was the ὁ θυμός as
indicating *vis animæ et vitæ*,—and in close fellowship
with it, and ready for its service, was a large, capacious ὁ νοῦς, and an energetic, sensuous, rapid τὸ
πνεῦμα. Hence his energy, his contagious enthusiasm—this it was which gave the peculiar character
to his religion, to his politics, to his *personnel;* everything he did was done heartily—if he desired heavenly
blessings he " panted " for them—" his soul broke
for the longing." To give again the words of the
spiritual and subtle Culverwel, " Religion (and

indeed everything else) was no matter of indifferency to him. It was θερμὸν τι πρᾶγμα, a certain fiery thing, as Aristotle calls love; it required and it got, the very flower and vigour of the spirit—the strength and sinews of the soul—the prime and top of the affections —this is that grace, that panting grace—we know the name of it and that's all—'tis called zeal—a flaming edge of the affection—the ruddy complexion of the soul." Closely connected with this temperament, and with a certain keen sensation of truth, rather than a perception of it, if we may so express ourselves, an intense consciousness of objective reality,—was his simple animating faith. He had faith in God—faith in human nature—faith, if we may say so, in his own instincts—in his ideas of men and things—*in himself;* and the result was, that unhesitating bearing up and steering right onward— " never bating one jot of heart or hope " so characteristic of him. He had " the *substance* of things hoped for." He had " the *evidence* of things not seen."

By his *simplicity* we do not mean the simplicity of the head—of that he had none; he was eminently shrewd and knowing—more so than many thought; but we refer to that quality of the heart and of the life, expressed by the words, " in simplicity a child." In his own words, from his Daily Readings,—

" When a child is filled with any strong emotion by a surprising event or intelligence, it *runs* to discharge it on others, impatient of their sympathy; and it marks, I fancy, the simplicity and greater naturalness of this period (Jacob's), that the grown-up men and women *ran* to meet each other, giving way to their first impulses—even as children do."

His emotions were as lively as a child's, and he ran to discharge them. There was in all his ways a certain beautiful unconsciousness of self—an outgoing of the whole nature that we see in children, who are by learned men said to be long ignorant of the Ego—blessed in many respects in their ignorance! This same Ego, as it now exists, being perhaps part of " the fruit of that forbidden tree ;" that mere knowledge of *good* as well as of *evil*, which our great mother bought for us at such a price. In this meaning of the word, Dr. Chalmers, considering the size of his understanding—his personal eminence—his dealings with the world—his large sympathies—his scientific knowledge of mind and matter—his relish for the practical details, and for the spirit of public business—was quite singular for his simplicity ; and taking this view of it, there was much that was plain and natural in his manner of thinking and acting, which otherwise was obscure, and liable to be misunderstood. We cannot better explain what we mean than by giving a passage from Fénélon, which D'Alembert, in his *Eloge*, quotes as characteristic of that " sweet-souled " prelate. We give the passage entire, as it seems to us to contain a very beautiful, and by no means commonplace truth :—

" Fénelon," says D'Alembert, " a caractérisé lui-même en peu de mots cette simplicité qui se rendoit si cher à tous les cœurs, ' La simplicité est la droiture d'une âme qui s'interdit tout retour sur elle et sur ses actions—cette vertu est différente de la sincérité, et la surpasse. On voit beaucoup de gens qui sont sincères sans être simples—Ils ne veulent passer que pour ce qu'ils sont, mais ils craignent sans cesse de passer pour ce qu'ils ne sont pas. L'homme simple n'affecte ni la vertu, ni la vérité même ; il n'est jamais occupé de lui, il semble d'avoir perdu ce *moi* dont on est si jaloux.' "

What delicacy and justness of expression ! how true and clear ! how little we see now-a-days, among grown-up men, of this straightness of the soul—of this losing or never finding " *ce moi !*" There is more than is perhaps generally thought in this. Man in a state of perfection, would no sooner think of asking himself—am I right? am I appearing to be what inwardly I am? than the eye asks itself—do I see? or a child says to itself—do I love my mother? We have lost this instinctive sense ; we have set one portion of ourselves aside to watch the rest ; we must keep up appearances and our consistency ; we must respect —that is, look back upon—ourselves, and be respected, if possible; we must, by hook or by crook, be respectable.

Dr. Chalmers would have made a sorry Balaam; he was made of different stuff, and for other purposes. Your " respectable " men are ever doing their best to keep their status, to maintain their position. He never troubled himself about his status; indeed, we would say *status* was not the word for him. He had a *sedes* on which he sat, and from which he spoke; he had an *imperium*, to and fro which he roamed as he listed : but a *status* was as little in his way as in that of a Mauritanian lion. Your merely " sincere " men are always thinking of what they said yesterday, and what they may say to-morrow, at the very moment when they should be putting their whole self into to-day. Full of his idea, possessed by it, moved altogether by its power,—believing, he spoke, and without stint or fear, often *apparently* contradicting his former self—careless about everything, but speaking fully his mind. One other reason for his apparent inconsistencies was, if one may so express it, the spaciousness of his nature. He had room in that capacious head, and affection in that great, hospitable heart, for relishing and taking in the whole range of human thought and feeling. He was several men in one. Multitudinous but not multiplex, in him odd and apparently incongruous notions dwelt peaceably together. The lion lay down with the lamb. Voluntaryism and an endowment—both were best.

He was *childlike* in his simplicity : though in understanding a man, he was himself in many things a child. Coleridge says, every man should include all his former selves in his present, as a tree has its former years' growths inside its last; so Dr. Chalmers bore along with him his childhood, his youth, his early and full manhood into his mature old age. This gave himself, we doubt not, infinite delight—multiplied his joys, strengthened and sweetened his whole nature, and kept his heart young and tender, it enabled him to sympathize, to have a fellow-feeling

with all, of whatever age. Those who best knew
him, who were most habitually with him, know how
beautifully this point of his character shone out in
daily hourly life. We well remember long ago
loving him before we had seen him—from our having
been told, that being out one Saturday at a friend's
house near the Pentlands, he collected all the children
and small people—the *other* bairns, as he called them
—and with no one else of his own growth, took the
lead to the nearest hill-top,—how he made each take
the biggest and roundest stone he could find, and
carry,—how he panted up the hill himself with one
of enormous size,—how he kept up their hearts, and
made them shout with glee, with the light of his
countenance, and with all his pleasant and strange
ways and words,—how having got the breathless
little men and women to the top of the hill, he, hot
and scant of breath—looked round on the world and
upon them with his broad benignant smile like the
ἀνήριθμον κυμάτων γέλασμα—the unnumbered laughter
of the sea,—how he set off his own huge "fellow,"
—how he watched him setting out on his race, slowly,
stupidly, vaguely at first, almost as if he might die
before he began to live, then suddenly giving a spring
and off like a shot—bounding, tearing, αὖτις ἔπειτα
πέδονδε κυλίνδετο λᾶας ἀναιδής, *vires acquirens eundo;*
how the great and good man was *totus in illo;* how he
spoke to, upbraided him, cheered him, gloried in
him, all but prayed for him,—how he joked philosophy to his wondering and ecstatic crew, when he
(the stone) disappeared among some brackens—telling
them they had the evidence of their senses that he
was in, they might even know he was there by his
effects, by the moving brackens, himself unseen;
how plain it became that he had gone in, when he
actually came out!—how he ran up the opposite side
a bit, and then fell back, and lazily expired at the
bottom,—how to their astonishment, but not displeasure—for he "set them off so well," and "was
so funny"—he took from each his cherished stone,

and set it off himself ! showing them how they all ran
alike, yet differently ; how he went on, " making," as
he said, " an induction of particulars," till he came
to the Benjamin of the flock, a *wee wee* man, who
had brought up a stone bigger than his own big head ;
then how he let him, *unicus omnium*, set off his own,
and how wonderfully IT ran ! what miraculous leaps !
what escapes from impossible places ! and how it ran
up the other side farther than any, and by some
felicity remained there.

He was an orator in its specific and highest sense.
We need not prove this to those who have heard him ;
we cannot to those who have not.   It was a living
man sending living, burning words into the minds
and hearts of men before him, radiating his intense
fervour upon them all ; but there was no reproducing
the entire effect when alone and cool ; some one of the
elements was gone.   We say nothing of this part of
his character, because upon this all are agreed.   His
eloquence rose like a tide, a sea, setting in, bearing
down upon you, lifting up all its waves—" deep calling unto deep ;" there was no doing anything but
giving yourself up for the time to its will.   Do our
readers remember Horace's description of Pindar?

> " Monte decurrens velut amnis, imbres
>   Quem super notas aluere ripas,
> Fervet, immensusque ruit profundo
>   Pindarus ore :
>
> ——' per audaces nova dithyrambos
> Verba devolvit, numerisque fertur
>   Lege solutis.' "

This is to our mind singularly characteristic of our
perfervid Scotsman.   If we may indulge our conceit,
we would paraphrase it thus.   His eloquence was like
a flooded Scottish river,—it had its origin in some
exalted region—in some mountain-truth—some high,
immutable reality ; it did not rise in a plain, and
quietly drain its waters to the sea,—it came sheer

down from above.   He laid hold of some simple truth
—the love of God, the Divine method of justification,
the unchangeableness of human nature, the supremacy
of conscience, the honourableness of all men; and
having got this vividly before his mind, on he moved
—the river rose at once, drawing everything into its
course—

> " All thoughts, all passions, all desires,—
> Whatever stirs this mortal frame,"

things outward and things inward, interests immediate and remote—God and eternity—men, miserable
and immortal—this world and the next—clear light
and unsearchable mystery—the word and the works
of God—everything contributed to swell the volume
and add to the onward and widening flood.   His river
did not flow like Denham's Thames,—

> " Though deep yet clear, though gentle yet not dull;
> Strong without rage, without o'erflowing full."

There was strength, but there was likewise rage;
a fine frenzy—not unoften due mainly to its rapidity
and to its being raised suddenly by his affections;
there was some confusion in the stream of his
thoughts, some overflowing of the banks, some tur-
bulence, and a certain noble immensity; but its origin
was clear and calm, above the region of clouds and
storms.   If you saw *it;* if you took up and admitted
his proposition, his starting idea, then all else moved
on; but once set agoing, once on his way, there was
no pausing to inquire, why or how—*fervet—ruit—
fertur*, he boils—he rushes—he is borne along; and
so are all who hear him.

To go on with our figure—There was no possibility
of sailing up his stream.   You must go with him, or
you must go ashore.   This was a great peculiarity
with him, and puzzled many people.   You could argue
with him, and get him to entertain your ideas on any
purely abstract or simple proposition,—at least for a

time; but once let him get down among practicals,
among applications of principles, into the regions of
the affections and active powers, and such was the
fervour and impetuosity of his nature, that he could
not stay leisurely to discuss, he could not then entertain the opposite; it was hurried off, and made light
of, and disregarded, like a floating thing before a
cataract.

To play a little more with our conceit—The greatest
man is he who is both born and made—who is at once
poetical and scientific—who has genius and talent—
each supporting the other.   So with rivers.   Your
mighty world's river rises in high and lonely places,
among the everlasting hills; amidst clouds, or inaccessible clearness.   On he moves, gathering to himself all waters; refreshing, cheering all lands.   Here
a cataract, there a rapid; now lingering in some
corner of beauty, as if loath to go.   Now shallow and
wide, rippling and laughing in his glee; now deep,
silent, and slow; now narrow and rapid and deep, and
not to be meddled with.   Now in the open country;
not so clear, for other waters have come in upon him,
and he is becoming useful, no longer turbulent,—
travelling more contentedly; now he is navigable,
craft of all kinds coming and going upon his surface
for ever; and then, as if by some gentle and great
necessity, " deep and smooth, passing with a still foot
and a sober face," he pays his last tribute to " the
Fiscus, the great Exchequer, the sea "—running out
fresh, by reason of his power and volume, into the
main for many a league.

Your   mere   genius,   who   has   instincts,   and   is
poetical and not scientific, who grows from within—
he is like our mountain river, clear, wilful, odd;
running round corners; disappearing it may be under
ground, coming up again quite unexpectedly and
strong, as if fed from some unseen spring, deep down
in darkness; rising in flood without warning, and
coming down like a lion; often all but dry; never to
be trusted to for driving mills; must at least be

tamed and led off to the mill; and going down at full pace, and without stop or stay, into the sea.

Your man of talent, of acquirements, of science—who is made,—who is not so much educed as edified; who, instead of acquiring his *vires, eundo* gets his *vires eundi,* from acquirement, and grows from without; who serves his brethren and is useful; he rises often no one knows where or cares; has perhaps no proper fountain at all, but is the result of the gathered rain water in the higher flats; he is never quite clear, never brisk, never dangerous; always from the first useful, and goes pleasantly in harness; turns mills; washes rags—makes them into paper; carries down all manner of dye-stuffs and feculence; and turns a bread-mill to as good purpose as any clearer stream; is docile, and has, as he reaches the sea, in his dealings with the world, a river trust, who look after his and their own interests, and dredge him, and deepen him, and manage him, and turn him off into docks, and he is in the sea before he or you know it.

Though we do not reckon the *imagination* of Dr. Chalmers among his master faculties, it was powerful, effective, magnificent. It did not move him, he took it up as he went along; its was not that imperial, penetrating, transmuting function that we find it in Dante, in Jeremy Taylor, in Milton, or in Burke; he used it to emblazon his great central truths, to hang clouds of glory on the skirts of his illustration; but it was too passionate, too material, too encumbered with images, too involved in the general *mêlée* of the soul, to do its work as a master. It was not in him, as Thomas Fuller calls it, " that inward sense of the soul, its most boundless and restless faculty; for while the understanding and the will are kept as it were *in liberâ custodiâ* to their objects of *verum et bonum,* it is free from all engagements—digs without spade, flies without wings, builds without charges, in a moment striding from the centre to the circumference of the world by a kind of omnipotency, creating and

annihilating things in an instant—restless, ever working, never wearied." We may say, indeed, that men
of his temperament are not generally endowed with
this power in largest measure; in one sense they can
do without it, in another they want the conditions
on which its highest exercise depends.   Plato and
Milton, Shakspere and Dante, and Wordsworth, had
imaginations tranquil, sedate, cool, originative, penetrative, intense, which dwelt in the " highest heaven
of invention."   Hence it was that Chalmers could
personify or paint a passion; he could give it in one
of its actions; he could not, or rather he never did
impassionate, create, and vivify a person—a very
different thing from personifying a passion—all the
difference, as Henry Taylor says, between Byron
and Shakspere.

In his impetuosity, we find the rationale of much
that is peculiar in the style of Dr. Chalmers.   As a
spoken style it was thoroughly effective.[1]   He seized

---

[1] We have not noticed his iterativeness, his reiterativeness,
because it flowed naturally from his primary qualities.   In
speaking it was effective, and to us pleasing, because there
was some new modulation, some addition in the manner, just
as the sea never sets up one wave exactly like the last or the
next.   But in his books it did somewhere encumber his
thoughts, and the reader's progress and profit.   It did not
arise, as in many lesser men, from his having said his say—
from his having no more in him; much less did it arise from
conceit, either of his idea or of his way of stating it; but
from the intensity with which the sensation of the idea—if
we may use the expression—made its first mark on his mind.
Truth to him never seemed to lose its first freshness, its
edge, its flavour; and Divine truth, we know, had come to
him so suddenly, so fully, at mid-day, when he was in the
very prime of his knowledge and his power and quickness—
had so possessed his entire nature, as if, like him who was
journeying to Damascus, a Great Light had shone round
about him—that whenever he reproduced that condition, ne
began afresh, and with his whole utterance, to proclaim it.
He could not but speak the things he had seen and felt, and
heard and believed; and he did it much in the same way,
and in the same words, for the thoughts and affections and
posture of his soul were the same.   Like all men of vivid
perceptions and keen sensibility, his mind and his body con-

the nearest weapons, and smote down whatever he hit. But from this very vehemence, this haste, there was in his general style a want of correctness, of selectness, of nicety, of that curious felicity which makes thought immortal, and enshrines it in imperishable crystal. In the language of the affections he was singularly happy; but, in a formal statement, rapid argumentation and analysis, he was often as we might think, uncouth, and imperfect, and incorrect: chiefly owing to his temperament, to his fiery, impatient, swelling spirit, this gave his orations their fine audacity—this brought out hot from the furnace, his new words—this made his numbers run wild— *lege solutis.* We are sure this view will be found confirmed by these *Daily Readings*, when he wrote little, and had not time to get heated, and when the nature of the work, the hour at which it was done, and his solitariness, made his thoughts flow at their " own sweet will;" they are often quite as classical in expression, as they are deep and lucid in thought— reflecting heaven with its clouds and stars, and letting us see deep down into its own secret depths : this is to us one great charm of these volumes. Here he is broad and calm; in his great public performances by mouth and pen, he soon passed from the lucid into the luminous.

What, for instance, can be finer in expression than

tinued under impressions, both material and spiritual, after the objects were gone. A curious instance of this occurs to us. Some years ago, he roamed up and down through the woods near Auchindinny, with two boys as companions. It was the first burst of summer, and the trees were more than usually enriched with leaves. He wandered about delighted, silent, looking at the leaves, " thick and numberless." As the three went on, they came suddenly upon a high brick wall, newly built, for peach trees, not yet planted. Dr. Chalmers halted, and looking steadfastly at the wall, exclaimed most earnestly, " What foliage ! what foliage !" The boys looked at one another, and said nothing ; but on getting home, expressed their astonishment at this very puzzling phenomenon. What a difference ! leaves and parallelograms ; a forest and a brick wall !

this? " It is well to be conversant with great elements—life and death, reason and madness." " God
forgets not His own purposes, though He executes
them in His own way, and maintains His own pace,
which he hastens not and shortens not to meet our
impatience." " I find it easier to apprehend the greatness of the Deity than any of his moral perfections,
or his sacredness;" and this—

> " One cannot but feel an interest in Ishmael, figuring him
> to be a noble of nature—one of those heroes of the wilder-
> ness who lived on the produce of his bow, and whose spirit
> was nursed and exercised among the wild adventures of the
> life he led. And it does soften our conception of him whose
> hand was against every man, and every man's hand against
> him, when we read of his mother's influence over him, in
> the deference of Ishmael to whom we read another example
> of the respect yielded to females even in that so-called bar-
> barous period of the world. There was a civilization, the
> immediate effect of religion, in these days, from which men
> fell away as the world grew older."

That he had a keen relish for material and moral
beauty and grandeur we all know; what follows
shows that he had also the true ear for beautiful
words, as at once pleasant to the ear and suggestive
of some higher feelings :—" I have often felt, in
reading Milton and Thomson, a strong poetical effect
in the bare enumeration of different countries, and
this strongly enhanced by the statement of some
common and prevailing emotion, which passed from
one to another." This is set forth with great beauty
and power in verses 14th and 15th of Exodus xv.,—
" The people shall hear and be afraid—sorrow shall
take hold of the inhabitants of Palestina. Then the
dukes of Edom shall be amazed—the mighty men of
Moab, trembling shall take hold of them—the inhabitants of Canaan shall melt away." Any one who
has a tolerable ear and any sensibility, must remember the sensation of delight in the mere sound—like
the colours of a butterfly's wing, or the shapeless
glories of evening clouds, to the eye—in reading aloud
such passages as these : " Heshbon shall cry and

Elealeh—their voice shall be heard to Jabez—for by the way of Luhith with weeping shall they go it up —for in the way of Horonaim they shall raise a cry. God came from Teman, the Holy One from Mount Paran. Is not Calno as Carchemish? is not Hamath as Arpad? is not Samaria as Damascus? He is gone to Aiath, he is passed to Migron; at Michmash he hath laid up his carriages: Ramath is afraid; Gibeah of Saul is fled—Lift up thy voice, O daughter of Gallim: cause it to be heard unto Laish, O poor Anathoth. Madmenah is removed; the inhabitants of Gebim gather themselves to flee. The fields of Heshbon languish—the vine of Sibmah—I will water thee with my tears, O Heshbon and Elealeh." Any one may prove to himself that much of the effect and beauty of these passages depends on these names; put others in their room, and try them.

We remember well our first hearing Dr. Chalmers. We were in a moorland district in Tweeddale, rejoicing in the country, after nine months of the High School. We heard that the famous preacher was to be at a neighbouring parish church, and off we set, a cartful of irrepressible youngsters. "Calm was all nature as a resting wheel." The crows, instead of making wing, were impudent and sat still; the carthorses were standing, knowing the day, at the field-gates, gossiping and gazing, idle and happy; the moor was stretching away in the pale sun-light—vast, dim, melancholy, like a sea; everywhere were to be seen the gathering people, "sprinklings of blithe company;" the country-side seemed moving to one centre. As we entered the kirk we saw a notorious character, a drover, who had much of the brutal look of what he worked in, with the knowing eye of a man of the city, a sort of big Peter Bell—

> " He had a hardness in his eye,
> He had a hardness in his cheek."

He was our terror, and we not only wondered, but were afraid when we saw *him* going in. The kirk

was as full as it could hold. How different in looks
to a brisk town congregation! There was a fine
leisureliness and vague stare; all the dignity and
vacancy of animals; eyebrows raised and mouths
open, as is the habit with those who speak little and
look much, and at far-off objects. The minister comes
in, homely in his dress and gait, but having a great
look about him, like a mountain among hills. The
High School boys thought him like a "big one of ourselves," he looks vaguely round upon his audience,
as if he saw in it *one great object, not many.* We
shall never forget his smile! its general benignity;—
how he let the light of his countenance fall on us!
He read a few verses quietly; then prayed briefly,
solemnly, with his eyes wide open all the time, but
not seeing. Then he gave out his text; we forget it,
but its subject was "Death reigns." He stated
slowly, calmly, the simple meaning of the words;
what death was, and how and why it reigned; then
suddenly he started, and looked like a man who had
seen some great sight, and was breathless to declare
it; he told us how death reigned—everywhere, at all
times, in all places; how we all knew it, how we
would yet know more of it. The drover, who had sat
down in the table-seat opposite, was gazing up in a
state of stupid excitement; he seemed restless, but
never kept his eye from the speaker. The tide set in
—everything added to its power, deep called to deep,
imagery and illustration poured in; and every now
and then the theme,—the simple, terrible statement,
was repeated in some lucid interval. After overwhelming us with proofs of the reign of Death, and
transferring to us his intense urgency and emotion;
and after shrieking, as if in despair, these words,
"Death is a tremendous necessity,"—he suddenly
looked beyond us as if into some distant region, and
cried out, "Behold a mightier!—who is this? He
cometh from Edom, with dyed garments from Bozrah,
glorious in his apparel, speaking in righteousness,

travelling in the greatness of his strength, mighty to save." Then, in a few plain sentences, he stated the truth as to sin entering, and death by sin, and death passing upon all. Then he took fire once more, and enforced, with redoubled energy and richness, the freeness, the simplicity, the security, the sufficiency of the great method of justification. How astonished and impressed we all were! He was at the full thunder of his power; the whole man was in an agony of earnestness. The drover was weeping like a child, the tears running down his ruddy, coarse cheeks—his face opened out and smoothed like an infant's; his whole body stirred with emotion. We all had insensibly been drawn out of our seats, and were converging towards the wonderful speaker. And when he sat down, after warning each one of us to remember who it was, and what it was, that followed death on his pale horse,[1] and how alone we could escape—we all sunk back into our seats. How beautiful to our eyes did the thunderer look—exhausted—but sweet and pure! How he poured out his soul before his God in giving thanks for sending the Abolisher of Death! Then, a short psalm, and all was ended.

We went home quieter than we came; we did not recount the foals with their long legs, and roguish eyes, and their sedate mothers; we did not speculate upon whose dog *that* was, and whether *that* was a crow or a man in the dim moor,—we thought of other things. That voice, that face; those great, simple, living thoughts; those floods of resistless eloquence; that piercing, shattering voice,—"that tremendous necessity."

Were we desirous of giving to one who had never seen or heard Dr. Chalmers an idea of what manner of man he was—what he was as a whole, in the full round of his notions, tastes, affections, and powers—we would put this book into their hands, and ask

---

[1] "And I looked, and behold a pale horse; and his name that sat on him was Death, and Hell followed with him."—Rev. vi. 8.

them to read it slowly, bit by bit, as he wrote it. In it he puts down simply, and at once, what passes through his mind as he reads; there is no making of himself feel and think—no getting into a frame of mind; he was not given to frames of mind; he preferred states to forms—substances to circumstances. There is something of everything in it—his relish for abstract thought—his love of taking soundings in deep places and finding no bottom—his knack of starting subtle questions, which he did not care to run to earth—his penetrating, regulating godliness—his delight in nature—his turn for politics, general economical, and ecclesiastical—his picturesque eye—his humanity—his courtesy—his warm-heartedness—his impetuosity—his sympathy with all the wants, pleasures, and sorrows of his kind—his delight in the law of God, and his simple, devout, manly treatment of it—his acknowledgment of difficulties—his turn for the sciences of quantity and number, and indeed for natural science and art generally—his shrewdness—his worldly wisdom—his genius; all these come out—you gather them like fruit, here a little, and there a little. He goes over the Bible, not as a philosopher, or a theologian, or a historian, or a geologist, or a jurist, or a naturalist, or a statist, or a politician—picking out all that he wants, and a great deal more than he has any business with, and leaving everything else as barren to his reader as it has been to himself; but he looks abroad upon his Father's *word*—as he used so pleasantly to do on his *world*—as a man, and as a Christian; he submits himself to its influences, and lets his mind go out fully and naturally in its utterances. It is this which gives to this work all the charm of multitude in unity, of variety in harmony; and that sort of unexpectedness and ease of movement which we see everywhere in nature and in natural men.

Our readers will find in these delightful Bible Readings not a museum of antiquities, and curiosities, and laborious trifles; nor of scientific specimens, analysed to the last degree, all standing in order, labelled and useless. They will not find in it an armoury of weapons for fighting with and destroying their neighbours. They will get less of the physic of controversy than of the diet of holy living. They will find much of what Lord Bacon desired, when he said, " We want short, sound, and judicious notes upon Scripture, without running into commonplaces, pursuing controversies, or reducing those notes to artificial method, but leaving them quite loose and native. For certainly, as those wines which flow from the first treading of the grape are sweeter and better than those forced out by the press, which gives them the roughness of the husk and the stone, so are those doctrines best and sweetest which flow from a gentle crush of the Scriptures, and are not wrung into controversies and commonplaces." They will find it as a large pleasant garden; no great system; not trim, but beautiful, and in which there are things pleasant to the eye as well as good for food—flowers and fruits, and a few good esculent, wholesome roots. There are Honesty, Thrift, Eye-bright (Euphrasy that cleanses the sight), Heart's-ease. The good seed in abundance, and the strange mystical Passion-flower; and in the midst, and seen everywhere, if we but look for it, the Tree of Life, with its twelve manner of fruits—the very leaves of which are for the healing of the nations. And, perchance, when they take their walk through it at evening time, or at " the sweet hour of prime," they may see a happy, wise, beaming old man at his work there—they may hear his well-known voice; and if they have their spiritual senses exercised as they ought, they will not fail to see by his side, " one like unto the Son of Man."

LETTER TO JOHN CAIRNS, D.D.

" I praised the dead which are already dead, more than the living which are yet alive."

23, RUTLAND STREET, 15th August, 1860.

MY DEAR FRIEND,—When, at the urgent request of his trustees and family, and in accordance with what I believe was his own wish, you undertook my father's Memoir, it was in a measure on the understanding that I would furnish you with some domestic and personal details. This I hoped to have done, but was unable.

Though convinced more than ever how little my hand is needed, I will now endeavour to fulfil my promise. Before doing so, however, you must permit me to express our deep gratitude to you for this crowning proof of your regard for him

" Without whose life we had not been ;"

to whom for many years you habitually wrote as " My father," and one of whose best blessings, when he was " such an one as Paul the aged," was to know that you were to him " mine own son in the gospel."

With regard to the manner in which you have done this last kindness to the dead, I can say nothing more expressive of our feelings, and, I am sure, nothing more gratifying to you, than that the record you have given of my father's life, and of the series of great public questions in which he took part, is done in the way which would have been most pleasing to himself —that which, with his passionate love of truth and liberty, his relish for concentrated, just thought and expression, and his love of being loved, he would have most desired, in any one speaking of him after he was gone. He would, I doubt not, say, as one said to a great painter, on looking at his portrait, " It is

237

certainly like, but it is much better-looking;" and you might well reply as did the painter, " It is the truth, told lovingly "—and all the more true that it is so told.   You have, indeed, been enabled to speak the truth, or as the Greek has it, ἀληθεύειν ἐν ἀγάπῃ—to truth it in love.

I have over and over again sat down to try and do what I promised and wished—to give some faint expression of my father's life; not of what he did or said or wrote—not even of what he was as a man of God and a public teacher; but what he was in his essential nature—what he would have been had he been anything else than what he was, or had lived a thousand years ago.

Sometimes I have this so vividly in my mind that I think I have only to sit down and write it off, and do it to the quick.   " The idea of his life," what he was as a whole, what was his self, all his days, would, —to go on with words which not time or custom can ever wither or make stale,—

> " Sweetly creep
> Into my study of imagination ;
> And every lovely organ of his life
> Would come apparelled in more precious habit—
> More moving delicate, and full of life,
> Into the eye and prospect of my soul,
> Than when he lived indeed,"

as if the sacredness of death and the bloom of eternity were on it; or as you may have seen in an untroubled lake, the heaven reflected with its clouds, brighter, purer, more exquisite than itself; but when you try to put this into words, to detain yourself over it, it is by this very act disturbed, broken and bedimmed, and soon vanishes away, as would the imaged heavens in the lake, if a pebble were cast into it, or a breath of wind stirred its face.   The very anxiety to transfer it, as it looked out of the clear darkness of the past, makes the image grow dim and disappear.

Every one whose thoughts are not seldom with the dead, must have felt both these conditions; how, in certain passive, tranquil states, there comes up into the darkened chamber of the mind, its " chamber of imagery "—uncalled, as if it blossomed out of space, exact, absolute, consummate, vivid, speaking, not darkly as in a glass, but face to face, and " moving delicate "—this " idea of his life;" and then how an effort to prolong and perpetuate and record all this, troubles the vision and kills it ! It is as if one should try to paint in a mirror the reflection of a dear and unseen face; the coarse, uncertain passionate handling and colour, ineffectual and hopeless, shut out the very thing itself.

I will therefore give this up as in vain, and try by some fragmentary sketches, scenes, and anecdotes, to let you know in some measure what manner of man my father was. Anecdotes, if true and alive, are always valuable; the man in the concrete, the *totus quis* comes out in them; and I know you too well to think that you will consider as trivial or out of place anything in which his real nature displayed itself, and your own sense of humour as a master and central power of the human soul, playing about the very essence of the man, will do more than forgive anything of this kind which may crop out here and there, like the smile of wild-flowers in grass, or by the wayside.

My first recollection of my father, my first impression, not only of his character, but of his eyes and face and presence, strange as it may seem, dates from my fifth year. Doubtless I had looked at him often enough before that, and had my own childish thoughts about him; but this was the time when I got my fixed, compact idea of him, and the first look of him which I felt could never be forgotten. I saw him, as it were, by a flash of lightning, sudden and complete. A child begins by seeing bits of everything; it knows in part—here a little, there a little; it makes up its wholes out of its own littles, and is long of reaching the fulness of a whole; and in this we are children all our lives in much. Children are long of seeing, or at least of looking at what is above them; they like the ground, and its flowers and stones, its " red sodgers " and lady-birds, and all its queer things; their world is about three feet high, and they are more often stooping than gazing up. I know I was past ten before I saw, or cared to see, the ceilings of the rooms in the manse at Biggar.

On the morning of the 28th May, 1816, my eldest sister Janet and I were sleeping in the kitchen-bed with Tibbie Meek,[1] our only servant. We were all three awakened by a cry of pain—sharp, insufferable, as if one were stung. Years after we two confided to each other, sitting by the burnside, that we thought that " great cry " which arose at midnight in Egypt must have been like it. We all knew whose voice it was, and, in our night-clothes, we ran into the passage, and into the little parlour to the left hand, in which was a closet-bed. We found my father standing before us, erect, his hands clenched in his black hair, his eyes full of misery and amazement, his face white as that of the dead. He frightened us. He saw this, or else his intense will had mastered his agony, for, taking his hands from his head, he said, slowly and gently, " Let us give thanks," and turned to a little sofa in the room; there lay our mother, dead.[2] She had long been ailing. I remember her sitting in a shawl,—an Indian one with little dark green spots on a light ground,—and watching her growing pale with what I afterwards knew must

[1] A year ago, I found an elderly countrywoman, a widow, waiting for me. Rising up, she said, " D'ye mind me?" I looked at her, but could get nothing from her face; but the voice remained in my ear, as if coming from " the fields of sleep," and I said by a sort of instinct, " Tibbie Meek !" I had not seen her or heard her voice for more than forty years. She had come to get some medical advice. Voices are often like the smells of flowers and leaves, the tastes of wild fruits—they touch and awaken memory in a strange way. " Tibbie " is now living at Thankerton.

[2] This sofa, which was henceforward sacred to the house, he had always beside him. He used to tell us he set her down upon it when he brought her home to the manse.

have been strong pain.   She had, being feverish,
slipped out of bed, and " grandmother," her mother,
seeing her " change come," had called my father, and
they two saw her open her blue, kind, and true eyes,
" comfortable " to us all " as the day "—I remember
them better than those of any one I saw yesterday—
and, with one faint look of recognition to him, close
them till the time of the restitution of all things.

" She had another morn than ours."

Then were seen in full action his keen, passionate
nature, his sense of mental pain, and his supreme
will, instant and unsparing, making himself and his
terrified household give thanks in the midst of such
a desolation,—and for it.   Her warfare was accomplished, her iniquities were pardoned ; she had already
received from her Lord's hand double for all her
sins : this was his supreme and over-mastering
thought, and he gave it utterance.

No man was happier in his wives.   My mother
was modest, calm, thrifty, reasonable, tender, happy-
hearted.   She was his student-love, and is even now
remembered in that pastoral region, for " her sweet
gentleness and wifelike government."   Her death and
his sorrow and loss, settled down deep into the heart
of the countryside.   He was so young and bright, so
full of fire, so unlike any one else, so devoted to his
work, so chivalrous in his look and manner, so fearless, and yet so sensitive and self-contained.   She was
so wise, good and gentle, gracious and frank.

His subtlety of affection, and his almost cruel self-
command, were shown on the day of the funeral.   It
was to Symington, four miles off,—a quiet little
churchyard, lying in the shadow of Tinto ; a place
where she herself had wished to be laid.   The funeral
was chiefly on horseback.   We, the family, were in
coaches.   I had been since the death in a sort of
stupid musing and wonder, not making out what it
all meant.   I knew my mother was said to be dead.
I saw she was still, and laid out, and then shut up,

and didn't move; but I did not know that when she was carried out in that long black box, and we all went with her, she alone was never to return.

When we got to the village all the people were at their doors. One woman, the blacksmith Thomas Spence's wife, had a nursing baby in her arms, and he leapt up and crowed with joy at the strange sight, the crowding horsemen, the coaches, and the nodding plumes of the hearse. This was my brother William, then nine months old, and Margaret Spence was his foster-mother. Those with me were overcome at this sight; he of all the world whose, in some ways, was the greatest loss, the least conscious, turning it to his own childish glee.

We got to the churchyard and stood round the open grave. My dear old grandfather was asked by my father to pray; he did. I don't remember his words; I believe he, through his tears and sobs, repeated the Divine words, " All flesh is grass, and all the glory of man as the flower of the grass; the grass withereth, and the flower thereof falleth away, but the word of the Lord endureth for ever;" adding, in his homely and pathetic way, that the flower would again bloom, never again to fade; that what was now sown in dishonour and weakness, would be raised in glory and power, like unto His own glorious body. Then to my surprise and alarm, the coffin, resting on its bearers, was placed over that dark hole, and I watched with curious eye the unrolling of those neat black bunches of cords, which I have often enough seen since. My father took the one at the head, and also another much smaller springing from the same point as his, which he had caused to be put there, and unrolling it, put it into my hand. I twisted it firmly round my fingers, and awaited the result; the burial men with their real ropes lowered the coffin, and when it rested at the bottom, it was too far down for me to see it—the grave was made very deep, as he used afterwards to tell us, that it might hold us all—my father first and abruptly let his cord drop, followed by the rest. This

was too much. I now saw what was meant, and held
on and fixed my fist and feet, and I believe my father
had some difficulty in forcing open my small fingers;
he let the little black cord drop, and I remember, in
my misery and anger, seeing its open end disappearing in the gloom.

My mother's death was the second epoch in my
father's life; it marked a change at once and for life;
and for a man so self-reliant, so poised upon a centre
of his own, it is wonderful the extent of change it
made. He went home, preached her funeral sermon,
every one in the church in tears, himself outwardly
unmoved.[1] But from that time dates an entire,
though always deepening, alteration in his manner
of preaching, because an entire change in his way of
dealing with God's Word. Not that his abiding
religious views and convictions were then originated
or even altered—I doubt not that from a child he
not only knew the Holy Scriptures, but was " wise
unto salvation "—but it strengthened and clarified,
quickened and gave permanent direction to, his sense
of God as revealed in His Word. He took as it were
to subsoil ploughing; he got a new and adamantine
point to the instrument with which he bored, and
with a fresh power—with his whole might, he sunk
it right down into the living rock, to the virgin gold.
His entire nature had got a shock, and his blood was
drawn inwards, his surface was chilled; but fuel was
heaped all the more on the inner fires, and his zeal,
that τι θερμὸν πρᾶγμα, burned with a new ardour;
indeed had he not found an outlet for his pent-up
energy, his brain must have given way, and his
faculties have either consumed themselves in wild,
wasteful splendour and combustion, or dwindled into
lethargy.[2]

The manse became silent; we lived and slept and

[1] I have been told that *once* in the course of the sermon his
voice trembled, and many feared he was about to break down.

[2] There is a story illustrative of this altered manner and
matter of preaching. He had been preaching when very
young, at Galashiels, and one wife said to her " neebor,"

played under the shadow of that death, and we saw,
or rather felt, that he was another father than before.
No more happy laughter from the two in the parlour,
as he was reading Larry, the Irish postboy's letter
in Miss Edgeworth's tale, or the last Waverley
novel; no more visitings in a cart with her, he riding
beside us on his white thorough-bred pony, to Kil-
bucho, or Rachan Mill, or Kirklawhill. He went
among his people as usual when they were ill; he
preached better than ever—they were sometimes
frightened to think how wonderfully he preached;
but the sunshine was over—the glad and careless
look, the joy of young life and mutual love. He was
little with us, and, as I said, the house was still,
except when he was *mandating* his sermons for Sabbath. This he always did, not only *vivâ voce*, but
with as much energy and loudness as in the pulpit;
we felt his voice was sharper, and rang keen through
the house.

What we lost, the congregation and the world
gained. He gave himself wholly to his work. As
you have yourself said, he changed his entire system
and fashion of preaching; from being elegant, rhetor-
ical, and ambitious, he became concentrated, urgent,
moving (being himself moved), keen, searching, un-
swerving, authoritative to fierceness, full of the
terrors of the Lord, if he could but persuade men.
The truth of the words of God had shone out upon
him with an immediateness and infinity of meaning
and power, which made them, though the same words
he had looked on from childhood, other and greater
and deeper words. He then left the ordinary commentators, and men who write about meanings and
flutter around the circumference and corners; he was
bent on the centre, on touching with his own fingers,
on seeing with his own eyes, the pearl of great price.

"Jean, what think ye o' the lad?" "*It's maist o't tinsel
wark,*" said Jean, neither relishing nor appreciating his fine
sentiments and figures. After my mother's death, he
preached in the same place, and Jean, running to her friend,
took the first word, "*It's a' gowd noo.*"

Then it was that he began to dig into the depths, into the primary and auriferous rock of Scripture, and take nothing at another's hand : then he took up with the word " apprehend;" he had laid hold of the truth, —there it was, with its evidence, in his hand; and every one who knew him must remember well how, in speaking with earnestness of the meaning of a passage, he, in his ardent, hesitating way, looked into the palm of his hand as if he actually saw there the truth he was going to utter.   This word *apprehend* played a large part in his lectures, as the thing itself did in his processes of investigation, or, if I might make a word, *indigation*.   Comprehension, he said, was for few; apprehension was for every man who had hands and a head to rule them, and an eye to direct them.   Out of this arose one of his deficiencies.   He *could* go largely into the generalities of a subject, and relished greatly others doing it, so that they did do it really and well; but he was averse to abstract and wide reasonings.   Principles he rejoiced in : he worked with them as with his choicest weapons; they were the polished stones for his sling, against the Goliaths of presumption, error, and tyranny in thought or in polity, civil or ecclesiastical; but he somehow divined a principle, or got at it naked and alone, rather than deduced it and brought it to a point from an immensity of particulars, and then rendered it back so as to bind them into one *cosmos*. One of my young friends now dead, who afterwards went to India, used to come and hear him in Broughton Place with me, and this word *apprehend* caught him, and as he had a great love for my father, in writing home to me, he never forgot to ask how " grand old Apprehend " was.

From this time dates my father's possession and use of the German Exegetics.   After my mother's death I slept with him; his bed was in his study, a small room,[1] with a very small grate; and I remember

[1] On a low chest of drawers in this room there lay for many years my mother's parasol, by his orders—I dare say, for long, the only one in Biggar.

well his getting those fat, shapeless, spongy German
books, as if one would sink in them, and be bogged
in their bibulous, unsized paper; and watching him
as he impatiently cut them up, and dived into them
in his rapid, eclectic way, tasting them, and dropping
for my play such a lot of soft, large, curled bits from
the paper-cutter, leaving the edges all shaggy.   He
never came to bed when I was awake, which was not
to be wondered at; but I can remember often awaking
far on in the night or morning, and seeing that keen,
beautiful, intense face bending over these Rosen-
müllers,and Ernestis, and Storrs, and Kuinoels—the
fire out, and the grey dawn peering through the window; and when he heard me move, he would speak to
me in the foolish words of endearment my mother was
wont to use, and come to bed, and take me, warm as
I was, into his cold bosom.

Vitringa in Jesaiam I especially remember, a noble
folio. Even then, with that eagerness to communicate
what he had himself found, of which you must often
have been made the subject, he went and told it.   He
would try to make me, small man as I was, " apprehend " what he and Vitringa between them had made
out of the fifty-third chapter of his favourite prophet,
the princely Isaiah.[1]   Even then, so far as I can recall,

---

[1] His reading aloud of everything from John Gilpin to
John Howe was a fine and high art, or rather gift. Henderson could not have given

> " The dinner waits, and we are tired;"
> Says Gilpin, " So am I,"

better; and to hear him sounding to the depths and cadences
of the Living Temple, " bearing on its front this doleful
inscription, ' Here God once dwelt,' " was like listening to
the recitative of Handel. But Isaiah was his masterpiece;
and I remember quite well his startling us all when reading
at family worship, " His name shall be called Wonderful,
Counsellor, the mighty God," by a peremptory, explosive
sharpness, as of thunder overhead, at the words " the mighty
God," similar to the rendering now given to Handel's music,
and doubtless so meant by him; and then closing with " the
Prince of Peace," soft and low. No man who wishes to feel
Isaiah, as well as understand him, should be ignorant of
Handel's " Messiah." His prelude to " Comfort ye "—its
simple theme, cheerful and infinite as the ripple of the un-

he never took notes of what he read. He did not need this, his intellectual force and clearness were so great; he was so *totus in illo*, whatever it was, that he recorded by a secret of its own, his mind's results and victories and *memoranda*, as he went on; he did not even mark his books, at least very seldom; he marked his mind.

He was thus every year preaching with more and more power, because with more and more knowledge and " pureness;" and, as you say, there were probably nowhere in Britain such lectures delivered at that time to such an audience, consisting of country people, sound, devout, well-read in their Bibles and in the native divinity, but quite unused to persistent, deep, critical thought.

Much of this—most of it—was entirely his own, self-originated and self-sustained, and done for its own sake,

> " All too happy in the pleasure
> Of his own exceeding treasure."

But he often said, with deep feeling, that one thing put him always on his mettle, the knowledge that " yonder in that corner, under the gallery, sat, Sabbath after Sabbath, a man who knew his Greek Testament better than I did."

This was his brother-in-law, and one of his elders, Mr. Robert Johnston, married to his sister Violet, a merchant and portioner in Biggar, a remarkable man, of whom it is difficult to say to strangers what is true, without being accused of exaggeration. A shop-

---

searchable sea—gives a deeper meaning to the words. One of my father's great delights in his dying months was reading the lives of Handel and of Michael Angelo, then newly out. He felt that the author of " He was despised," and " He shall feed his flock," and those other wonderful airs, was a man of profound religious feeling, of which they were the utterance; and he rejoiced over the warlike airs and choruses of " Judas Maccabæus." You have recorded his estimate of the religious nature of him of the *terribile via;* he said it was a relief to his mind to know that such a mighty genius walked humbly with his God.

keeper in that remote little town, he not only inter-
meddled fearlessly with all knowledge, but mastered
more than many practised and University men do in
their own lines. Mathematics, astronomy, and especially what may be called *selenology*, or the doctrine
of the moon, and the higher geometry and physics;
Hebrew, Sanscrit, Greek, and Latin, to the veriest
rigours of prosody and metre; Spanish and Italian,
German, French, and any odd language that came in
his way; all these he knew more or less thoroughly,
and acquired them in the most leisurely, easy, cool
sort of way, as if he grazed and browsed perpetually
in the field of letters, rather than made formal meals,
or gathered for any ulterior purpose, his fruits, his
roots, and his nuts—he especially liked mental nuts—
much less bought them from any one.

With all this, his knowledge of human, and especially of Biggar human nature, the ins and outs of its
little secret ongoings, the entire gossip of the place,
was like a woman's; moreover, every personage great
or small, heroic or comic, in Homer—whose poems he
made it a matter of conscience to read once every four
years—Plautus, Suetonius, Plutarch, Tacitus, and
Lucian, down through Boccaccio and Don Quixote,
which he knew by heart and from the living Spanish,
to Joseph Andrews, the Spectator, Goldsmith and
Swift, Miss Austen, Miss Edgeworth, and Miss
Ferrier, Galt and Sir Walter,—he was as familiar
with, as with David Crockat the nailer, or the parish
minister, the town-drummer, the mole-catcher, or the
poaching weaver, who had the night before leistered
a prime kipper at Rachan Mill, by the flare of a tarry
wisp, or brought home his surreptitious grey hen or
maukin from the wilds of Dunsyre or the dreary
Lang Whang.[1]

This singular man came to the manse every Friday
evening for many years, and he and my father dis-
cussed everything and everybody;—beginning with

---

[1] With the practices of this last worthy, when carried on
moderately, and for the sport's sake, he had a special sympathy.

tough, strong head work—a bout at wrestling, be it Cæsar's Bridge, the Epistles of Phalaris, the import of μέν and δέ, the Catholic question, or the great roots of Christian faith; ending with the latest joke in the town or the *West Raw*, the last effusion by Affleck, tailor and poet, the last blunder of Æsop the apothecary, and the last repartee of the village fool, with the week's Edinburgh and Glasgow news by their respective carriers; the whole little life, sad and humorous—who had been born, and who was dying or dead, married or about to be, for the past eight days.[1]

This amused, and, in the true sense, diverted my father, and gratified his curiosity, which was great, and his love of men, as well as for man. He was shy, and unwilling to ask what he longed to know, liking better to have it given him without the asking; and no one could do this better than " Uncle Johnston."

You may readily understand what a thorough exercise and diversion of an intellectual and social kind this was, for they were neither of them men to shirk from close gripes, or trifle and flourish with their weapons; they laid on and spared not. And then my uncle had generally some special nut of his own to crack, some thesis to fling down and offer battle on, some " particle " to energize upon; for though quiet and calm, he was thoroughly combative, and enjoyed seeing his friend's blood up, and hearing his emphatic and bright speech, and watching his flashing eye. Then he never spared him; criticised and sometimes quizzed— for he had great humour—his style, as well as debated and weighed his apprehendings and

---

[1] I believe this was the true though secret source of much of my father's knowledge of the minute personal history of every one in his region, which,—to his people, knowing his reserved manner and his devotion to his studies, and his so rarely meeting them or speaking to them except from the pulpit, or at a diet of visitation, was a perpetual wonder, and of which he made great use in his dealings with his afflicted or erring " members."

exegeses, shaking them heartily to test their strength. He was so thoroughly independent of all authority, except that of reason and truth, and his own humour; so ready to detect what was weak, extravagant, or unfair; so full of relish for intellectual power and accuracy, and so attached to and proud of my father, and bent on his making the best of himself, that this trial was never relaxed. His firm and close-grained mind was a sort of whetstone on which my father sharpened his wits at this weekly " setting."

The very difference of their mental tempers and complexions drew them together—the one impatient, nervous, earnest, instant, swift, vehement, regardless of exertion, bent on his goal, like a thorough-bred racer, pressing to the mark; the other leisurely to slowness and provokingness, with a constitution which could stand a great deal of ease, unimpassioned, still, clear, untroubled by likings or dislikings, dwelling and working in thought and speculation and observation as ends in themselves, and as their own rewards :[1] the one hunting for a principle or a " divine method;" the other sapping or shelling from a distance, and for his pleasure, a position, or gaining a point, or setting a rule, or verifying a problem, or getting axiomatic and proverbial.

In appearance they were as curiously unlike; my uncle short and round to rotundity, homely and florid

[1] He was curiously destitute of all literary ambition or show; like the *cactus* in the desert, always plump, always taking in the dew of heaven, and caring little to give it out. He wrote many papers in the *Repository* and *Monitor*, an acute and clever tract on the Voluntary controversy, entitled *Calm Answers to Angry Questions,* and was the author of a capital bit of literary banter—a Congratulatory Letter to the Minister of Liberton, who had come down upon my father in a pamphlet, for his sermon on " There remaineth much land to be possessed." It is a mixture of Swift and Arbuthnot. I remember one of the flowers he culls from him he is congratulating, in which my father is characterized as one of those " shallow, sallow souls that would swallow the bait, without perceiving the cloven foot!" But a man like this never is best in a book; he is always greater than his work.

in feature. I used to think Socrates must have been like him in visage as well as in much of his mind. He was careless in his dress, his hands in his pockets as a rule, and strenuous only in smoking or in sleep; with a large, full skull, a humorous twinkle in his cold, blue eye, a soft, low voice, expressing every kind of thought in the same, sometimes plaguily *douce* tone; a great power of quiet and telling sarcasm, large capacity of listening to and of enjoying other men's talk, however small.

My father—tall, slim, agile, quick in his movements, graceful, neat to nicety in his dress, with much in his air of what is called style, with a face almost too beautiful for a man's, had not his eyes commanded it and all who looked at it, and his close, firm mouth been ready to say what the fiery spirit might bid; his eyes, when at rest, expressing—more than almost any other's I ever saw—sorrow and tender love, a desire to give and to get sympathy, and a sort of gentle, deep sadness, as if that was their permanent state, and gladness their momentary act; but when awakened, full of fire, peremptory, and not to be trifled with; and his smile, and flash of gaiety and fun, something no one could forget; his hair in early life a dead black; his eyebrows of exquisite curve, narrow and intense; his voice deep when unmoved and calm; keen and sharp to piercing fierceness when vehement and roused—in the pulpit, at times a shout, at times a pathetic wail; his utterance hesitating, emphatic, explosive, powerful,—each sentence shot straight and home; his hesitation arising from his crowd of impatient ideas, and his resolute will that they should come in their order, and some of them not come at all, only the best, and his settled determination that each thought should be dressed in the very and only word which he stammered on till it came,—it was generally worth his pains and ours.

Uncle Johnston, again, flowed on like Cæsar's *Arar*, *incredibili lenitate*, or like linseed out of a poke. You can easily fancy the spiritual and bodily contrast of

252 Letter to John Cairns, D.D.

these men, and can fancy too, the kind of engagements they would have with their own proper weapons
on these Friday evenings, in the old manse dining-
room, my father showing uncle out into the darkness
of the back-road, and uncle, doubtless, lighting his
black and ruminative pipe.

If my uncle brought up nuts to crack, my father
was sure to have some difficulties to consult about, or
some passages to read, something that made him put
his whole energy forth; and when he did so, I never
heard such reading. To hear him read the story of
Joseph, or passages in David's history, and Psalms
6th, 11th, and 15th, or the 52nd, 53rd, 54th, 55th,
63rd, 64th, and 40th chapters of Isaiah, or the Sermon
on the Mount, or the Journey to Emmaus, or our
Saviour's prayer in John, or Paul's speech on Mars'
Hill, or the first three chapters of Hebrews and the
latter part of the 11th, or Job, or the Apocalypse; or,
to pass from those divine themes—Jeremy Taylor, or
George Herbert, Sir Walter Raleigh, or Milton's
prose, such as the passage beginning "Come forth
out of thy royal chambers, O thou Prince of all the
kings of the earth!" and "Truth, indeed, came once
into the world with her divine Master," or Charles
Wesley's Hymns, or, most loved of all, Cowper, from
the rapt "Come thou, and, added to thy many
crowns," or "O that those lips had language!" to
the Jackdaw, and his incomparable Letters; or Gray's
Poems, Burns's "Tam O'Shanter," or Sir Walter's
"Eve of St. John," [1] and "The Grey Brother."

---

[1] Well do I remember when driving him from Melrose to
Kelso, long ago, we came near Sandyknowe, that grim tower
of Smailholm, standing erect like a warder turned to stone,
defying time and change, his bursting into that noble
ballad—

> "The Baron of Smaylho'me rose with day,
>   He spurred his courser on,
> Without stop or stay, down the rocky way,
>   That leads to Brotherstone;"

and pointing out the "Watchfold height," "the eiry Beacon
Hill," and "Brotherstone."

But I beg your pardon : Time has run back with me, and fetched that blessed past, and awakened its echoes. I hear his voice; I feel his eye; I see his whole nature given up to what he is reading, and making its very soul speak.

Such a man then as I have sketched, or washed faintly in, as the painters say, was that person who sat in the corner under the gallery every Sabbath-day, and who knew his Greek Testament better than his minister. He is dead too, a few months ago, dying surrounded with his cherished hoard of books of all sizes, times, and tongues—tatterdemalion many; all however drawn up in an order of his own; all thoroughly mastered and known; among them David Hume's copy of Shaftesbury's *Characteristics*, with his autograph, which he had picked up at some stall.

I have said that my mother's death was the second epoch in my father's life. I should perhaps have said the third; the first being his mother's long illness and death, and the second his going to Elie, and beginning the battle of life at fifteen. There must have been something very delicate and close and exquisite in the relation between the ailing, silent, beautiful and pensive mother, and that dark-eyed, dark-haired, bright and silent son; a sort of communion it is not easy to express. You can think of him at eleven slowly writing out that small book of promises in a distinct and minute hand, quite as like his mature hand, as the shy, lustrous-eyed boy was to his after self in his manly years, and sitting by the bedside while the rest were out and shouting, playing at hide-and-seek round the little church, with the winds from Ben-lomond or the wild uplands of Ayrshire blowing through their hair. He played seldom, but when he did run out, he jumped higher and farther, and ran faster than any of them. His peculiar beauty must have come from his mother. He used at rare times, and with a sort of shudder, to tell of her when a lovely girl of fifteen, having been seen by a gentleman of rank, in Cheapside, hand in hand with an evil woman, who was decoying her to ruin, on pretence of showing her the way home; and how he stopped his carriage, and taking in the unconscious girl, drove her to her uncle's door.   But you have said all this better than I can.

His time with his mother, and the necessary confinement and bodily depression caused by it, I doubt not deepened his native thoughtful turn, and his tendency to meditative melancholy, as a condition under which he viewed all things, and quickened and intensified his sense of the suffering of this world, and of the profound seriousness and mystery in the midst of which we live and die.

The second epoch was that of his leaving home with his guinea, the last he ever got from any one but himself and his going among utter strangers to be master of a school one half of the scholars of which were bigger and older than himself, and all rough colts—wilful and unbroken.   This was his first fronting of the world.   Besides supporting himself, this knit the sinews of his mind, and made him rely on himself in action as well as in thought.   He sometimes, but not often, spoke of this, never lightly, though he laughed at some of his predicaments.   He could not forget the rude shock.   Generally those familiar revelations were at supper, on the Sabbath evening, when, his work over, he enjoyed and lingered over his meal.

From his young and slight, almost girlish look, and his refined, quiet manners, the boys of the school were inclined to annoy and bully him.   He saw this, and felt it was now or never,—nothing between.   So he took his line.   The biggest boy, much older and stronger, was the rudest, and infected the rest.   The " *wee maister* " ordered him, in that peremptory voice we all remember, to stand up and hold out his hand, being not at all sure but the big fellow might knock him down on the word.   To the astonishment of the school, and to the big rebel's too, he obeyed and was punished on the instant, and to the full; out went the hand, down came the "*taws*," and bit like fire. From that moment he ruled them by his eye, the *taws* vanished.

There was an incident at this time of his life which I should perhaps not tell, and yet I don't know why I shouldn't, it so perfectly illustrates his character in many ways. He had come home during the vacation of his school to Langrig, and was about to go back; he had been renewing his intercourse with his old teacher and friend whom you mention, from whom he used to say he learned to like Shakspere, and who seems to have been a man of genuine literary tastes. He went down to bid him good-bye, and doubtless they got on their old book loves, and would be spouting their pet pieces. The old dominie said, "John, my man, if you are walking into Edinburgh, I'll convoy you a bit." "John" was too happy, so next morning they set off, keeping up a constant fire of quotation and eager talk. They got past Mid-Calder to near East, when my father insisted on his friend returning, and also on going back a bit with him; on looking at the old man, he thought he was tired, so on reaching the well-known Kippen's Inn, he stopped and insisted on giving him some refreshment. Instead of ordering bread and cheese and a bottle of ale, he, doubtless full of Shakspere, and great upon sack and canary, ordered *a bottle of wine!* Of this, you may be sure, the dominie, as he most needed it, had the greater share, and doubtless it warmed the cockles of his old heart. "John" making him finish the bottle, and drink the health of "Gentle Will," saw him off, and went in to pay the reckoning. What did he know of the price of wine! It took exactly every penny he had; I doubt not, most boys, knowing that the landlord knew them, would have either paid a part, or asked him to score it up. This was not his way; he was too proud and shy and honest for such an expedient. By this time, what with discussing Shakspere, and witnessing his master's leisurely emptying of that bottle, and releasing the

"Dear prisoned spirits of the impassioned grape,"

he found he must run for it to Edinburgh, or rather Leith, fourteen miles; this he did, and was at the pier just in time to jump into the Elie pinnace, which was already off. He often wondered what he would have done if he had been that one moment late. You can easily pick out the qualities this story unfolds.

His nature, capable as it was of great, persistent, and indeed dogged labour, was, from the predominance of the nervous system in his organization, excitable, and therefore needed and relished excitement —the more intense the better. He found this in his keen political tastes, in imaginative literature, and in fiction. In the highest kinds of poetry he enjoyed the sweet pain of tears; and he all his life had a steady liking, even a hunger, for a good novel. This refreshed, lightened, and diverted his mind from the strain of his incessant exegesis. He used always to say that Sir Walter and Goldsmith, and even Fielding, Miss Edgeworth, Miss Austen, and Miss Ferrier, were true benefactors to the race, by giving such genuine, such secure and innocent pleasure; and he often repeated with admiration Lord Jeffrey's words on Scott, inscribed on his monument. He had no turn for gardening or for fishing or any field sports or games; his sensitive nature recoiled from the idea of pain, and above all, needless pain. He used to say the lower creation had groans enough, and needed no more burdens; indeed, he was fierce to some measure of unfairness against such of his brethren—Dr. Wardlaw, for instance [1]—as resembled the apostles in fishing for other things besides men.

But the exercise and the excitement he most of all others delighted in, was riding; and had he been a country gentleman and not a clergyman, I don't think he could have resisted fox-hunting. With the exception of that great genius in more than horsemanship, Andrew Ducrow, I never saw a man sit a horse as he did. He seemed inspired, gay, erect, full of the joy

[1] After a tight discussion between these two attached friends, Dr. Wardlaw said, "Well, I can't answer you, but fish I must and shall."

of life, fearless and secure. I have heard a farmer friend say if he had not been a preacher of the gospel he would have been a cavalry officer, and would have fought as he preached.

He was known all over the Upper Ward and down Tweeddale for his riding. " There goes the minister," as he rode past at a swift canter. He had generally well-bred horses, or as I would now call them, ponies; if he had not, his sufferings from a dull, hardmouthed, heavy-hearted and footed, plebeian horse were almost comic. On his grey mare, or his little blood bay horse, to see him setting off and indulging it and himself in some alarming gambols, and in the midst of his difficulties, partly of his own making, taking off his hat or kissing his hand to a lady, made one think of " young Harry with his beaver up." He used to tell with much relish, how, one fine summer Sabbath evening, after preaching in the open air for a collection, in some village near, and having put the money, chiefly halfpence, into his handkerchief, and that into his hat, he was taking a smart gallop home across the moor, happy and relieved, when three ladies—I think, the Miss Bertrams of Kersewell—came suddenly upon him; off went the hat, down bent the head, and over him streamed the cherished collection, the ladies busy among the wild grass and heather picking it up, and he full of droll confusion and laughter.

The grey mare he had for many years. I can remember her small head and large eyes; her neat, compact body, round as a barrel; her finely flea-bitten skin, and her thorough-bred legs. I have no doubt she had Arabian blood. My father's pride in her was quite curious. Many a wild ride to and from the Presbytery at Lanark, and across flooded and shifting fords, he had on her. She was as sweet-tempered and enduring, as she was swift and sure; and her powers of running were appreciated and applied in a way which he was both angry and amused to discover. You know what riding the *bruse* means. At a country

wedding the young men have a race to the bride-
groom's home, and he who wins brings out a bottle
and glass and drinks the young wife's health. I wish
Burns had described a *bruse;* all sorts of steeds,
wild, unkempt lads as well as colts, old broken-down
thoroughbreds that did wonders when *soopled*, huge,
grave cart horses devouring the road with their
shaggy hoofs, wilful ponies, &c.   You can imagine
the wild hurry-skurry and fun, the comic situations
and upsets over a rough road, up and down places
one would be giddy to look at.

Well, the young farmers were in the habit of
coming to my father, and asking the loan of the mare
to go and see a friend, &c., &c., praising knowingly
the fine points and virtues of his darling.   Having
through life, with all his firmness of nature, an ab-
horrence of saying " No " to any one, the interview
generally ended with, " Well, Robert, you may have
her, but take care of her, and don't ride her fast." In
an hour or two Robert was riding the *bruse*, and
flying away from the crowd, Grey first, and the rest
nowhere, and might be seen turning the corner of the
farm-house with the victorious bottle in his uplifted
hand, the motley pack panting vainly up the hill.
This went on for long, and the grey was famous,
almost notorious, all over the Upper Ward; sometimes if she appeared, no one would start, and she
trotted the course.   Partly from his own personal
abstraction from outward country life, and partly
from Uncle Johnston's sense of waggery keeping him
from telling his friend of the grey's last exploit at
Hartree Mill, or her leaping over the " best man " at
Thriepland, my father was the last to hear of this
equivocal glory of " the minister's *meer*."   Indeed,
it was whispered she had once won a whip at Lanark
races.   They still tell of his feats on this fine creature,
one of which he himself never alluded to without a
feeling of shame.   He had an engagement to preach
somewhere beyond the Clyde on a Sabbath evening,
and his excellent and attached friend and elder, Mr.

Kello of Lindsay-lands, accompanied him on his big plough horse. It was to be in the open air, on the river side. When they got to the Clyde they found it in full flood, heavy and sudden rains at the head of the water having brought it down in a wild *spate*. On the opposite side were the gathered people and the tent. Before Mr. Kello knew where he was, there was his minister on the mare swimming across, and carried down in a long diagonal, the people looking on in terror. He landed, shook himself, and preached with his usual fervour. As I have said, he never liked to speak of this bit of hardihood, and he never repeated it; but it was like the man—there were the people, that was what he would be at, and though timid for anticipated danger as any woman, *in* it he was without fear.

One more illustration of his character in connection with his riding. On coming to Edinburgh he gave up this kind of exercise; he had no occasion for it, and he had enough, and more than enough of excitement in the public questions in which he found himself involved, and in the miscellaneous activities of a popular town minister. I was then a young doctor—it must have been about 1840—and had a patient, Mrs. James Robertson, eldest daughter of Mr. Pirie, the predecessor of Dr. Dick in what was then Shuttle Street congregation, Glasgow. She was one of my father's earliest and dearest friends,—a mother in the Burgher Israel, she and her cordial husband "given to hospitality," especially to "the Prophets." She was hopelessly ill at Juniper Green, near Edinburgh. Mr. George Stone, then living at Muirhouse, one of my father's congregation in Broughton Place, a man of equal originality and worth, and devoted to his minister, knowing my love of riding, offered me his blood-chestnut to ride out and make my visit. My father said, " John, if you are going, I would like to ride out with you;" he wished to see his dying friend. " You ride !" said Mr. Stone, who was a very Yorkshireman in the matter of horses. " Let him try," said I. The upshot was, that Mr. Stone sent the chestnut for me, and a sedate pony—called, if I forget not, Goliath—for his minister, with all sorts of injunctions to me to keep him off the thoroughbred, and on Goliath.

My father had not been on a horse for nearly twenty years. He mounted and rode off. He soon got teased with the short, pattering steps of Goliath, and looked wistfully up at me, and longingly to the tall chestnut, stepping once for Goliath's twice, like the Don striding beside Sancho. I saw what he was after, and when past the toll he said in a mild sort of way, " John, did you promise *absolutely* I was not to ride your horse?" " No, father, certainly not. Mr. Stone, I dare say, wished me to do so, but I didn't." " Well then, I think we'll change; this beast shakes me." So we changed. I remember how noble he looked; how at home : his white hair and his dark eyes, his erect, easy, accustomed seat. He soon let his eager horse slip gently away. It was first *evasit*, he was off, Goliath and I jogging on behind; then *erupit*, and in a twinkling—*evanuit*. I saw them last flashing through the arch under the Canal, his white hair flying. I was uneasy, though from his riding I knew he was as yet in command, so I put Goliath to his best, and having passed through Slateford, I asked a stonebreaker if he saw a gentleman on a chestnut horse. " Has he white hair?" " Yes." " And een like a gled's?" " Yes." " Weel then, he's fleein' up the road like the wund; he'll be at Little Vantage " (about nine miles off) " in nae time if he haud on." I never once sighted him, but on coming into Juniper Green there was his steaming chestnut at the gate, neighing cheerily to Goliath. I went in, he was at the bedside of his friend, and in the midst of prayer; his words as I entered were, " When thou passest through the waters I will be with thee, and through the rivers, they shall not overflow thee;" and he was not the least instant in prayer that his blood was up with his ride. He never again saw Mrs. Robertson, or as she was called when they were young, Sibbie (Sibella) Pirie. On coming out he said nothing, but took the chestnut, mounted her, and we came home quietly. His heart was opened; he spoke of old times and old friends; he stopped at the exquisite view at Hailes into the valley, and up the Pentlands beyond, the smoke of Kate's Mill rising in the still and shadowy air, and broke out into Cowper's words: Yes,

> " HE sets the bright procession on its way,
> And marshals all the order of the year ;
> And ere one flowery season fades and dies,
> Designs the blooming wonders of the next."

Then as we came slowly in, the moon shone behind Craiglockhart hill among the old Scotch firs; he pulled up again, and gave me Collins' Ode to Evening, beginning—

> " If aught of oaten stop, or pastoral song,
> May hope, chaste Eve, to soothe thy modest ear,
> Thy springs, and dying gales;"

repeating over and over some of the lines, as

> " Thy modest ear,
> Thy springs, and dying gales."

> " —And marks o'er all
> Thy dewy fingers draw
> The gradual dusky veil."

And when she looked out on us clear and full, " Yes—

> " The moon takes up the wondrous tale,
> And nightly to the listening earth
> Repeats the story of her birth."

As we passed through Slateford, he spoke of Dr. Belfrage, his great-hearted friend, of his obligations to him, and of his son, my friend, both lying together in Colinton churchyard; and of Dr. Dick, who was minister before him, of the Coventrys, and of Stitchel and Sprouston, of his mother, and of himself,—his doubts of his own sincerity in religion, his sense of sin, of God—reverting often to his dying friend. Such a thing only occurred to me with him once or twice all my life; and then when we were home, he was silent, shut up, self-contained as before.   He was himself conscious of this habit of reticence, and what may be called *selfism* to us, his children, and lamented it.   I remember his saying in a sort of mournful joke, " I have a well of love; I know it; but it is a *well*, and a *draw*-well, to your sorrow and mine, and it seldom overflows, but," looking with that strange power of tenderness as if he put his voice and his heart into his eyes, " you may always come hither to draw;" he used to say he might take to himself Wordsworth's lines,—

> " I am not one who much or oft delights
>   To season my fireside with personal talk."

And changing " though " into " if :"

> " A well of love it may be deep,
>   I trust it is, and never dry ;
> What matter, though its waters sleep
>   In silence and obscurity?"

The expression of his affection was more like the shock of a Leyden jar, than the continuous current of a galvanic circle.

There was, as I have said, a permanent chill given by my mother's death, to what may be called the outer surface of his nature, and we at home felt it much.   The blood was thrown in upon the centre, and went forth in energetic and victorious work, in searching the Scriptures and saving souls; but his social faculty never recovered that shock! it was blighted; he was always desiring to be alone and at his work.   A stranger who saw him for a short time, bright, animated, full of earnest and cordial talk, pleasing and being pleased, the life of the company, was apt to think how delightful he must always be, —and so he was; but these times of bright talk were like angels' visits; and he smiled with peculiar be-nignity on his retiring guest, as if blessing him not the less for leaving him to himself.   I question if there ever lived a man so much in the midst of men, and in the midst of his own children,[1] in whom the silences, as Mr. Carlyle would say, were so predominant. Every Sabbath he spoke out of the abundance of his heart, his whole mind; he was then communicative and frank enough: all the week, before and after, he would not unwillingly have never opened his mouth. Of many people we may say that their mouth is always open except when it is shut; of him that his mouth was always shut except when it was opened. Every one must have been struck with the seeming inconsistency of his occasional brilliant, happy, energetic talk, and his habitual silentness—his difficulty in getting anything to say. But, as I have already said, what we lost, the world and the church gained.

When travelling he was always in high spirits and full of anecdote and fun. Indeed I knew more of his inner history in this *one* way, than during years of living with him. I recollect his taking me with him to Glasgow when I must have been about fourteen; we breakfasted in The Ram's Horn Tavern, and I felt a new respect for him at his commanding the waiters. He talked a great deal during our short tour, and often have I desired to recall the many things he told me of his early life, and of his own religious crises, my mother's death, his fear of his own death, and all this intermingled with the drollest stories of his boy and student life.

We went to Paisley and dined, I well remember, we two alone, and, as I thought, magnificently, in a great apartment in The Saracen's Head, at the end of which was the county ball-room. We had come across from Dunoon and landed in a small boat at the Water Neb along with Mrs. Dr. Hall, a character Sir Walter or Galt would have made immortal. My father with characteristic ardour took an oar, for the first time in his life, and I believe for the last, to help the old boatman on the Cart, and wishing to do something decided, missed the water,

[1] He gave us all the education we got at Biggar.

and went back head over heels to the immense enjoy-ment of Mrs. Hall, who said, " Less pith, and mair to the purpose, my man." She didn't let the joke die out.

Another time—it was when his second marriage was fixed on, to our great happiness and his—I had just taken my degree of M.D., and he took Isabella, William, and myself to Moffat. By a curious felicity we got into Miss Geddes' lodgings, where the village circulating library was kept, the whole of which we aver he read in ten days. I never saw him so happy, so open and full of mirth, reading to us, and reciting the poetry of his youth. On these rare but delightful occasions he was fond of exhibiting, when asked, his powers of rapid speaking, in which he might have rivalled old Matthews or his son. His favourite feat was repeating " Says I to my Lord, quo' I—what for will ye no grund ma barleymeal mouter-free, says I to my Lord, quo' I, says I, I says." He was brilliant upon the final, " I says." Another *chef-d'œuvre* was, " On Tintock tap there is a mist, and in the mist there is a kist (a chest), and in the kist there is a cap (a wooden bowl), and in the cap there is a drap, tak' up the cap, and sup the drap, and set the cap on Tintock tap." This he could say, if I mistake not, five times without drawing breath. It was a favourite passage this, and he often threatened to treat it exegetically; laughing heartily when I said, in that case, he would not have great trouble with the *context*, which in others cost him a good deal.

His manners to ladies, and indeed to all women, was that of a courtly gentleman; they could be roman-tic in their *empressement* and devotion, and I used to think Sir Philip Sydney, or Ariosto's knights and the Paladins of old, must have looked and moved as he did. He had great pleasure in the company of high-bred, refined, thoughtful women; and he had a pecu-liar sympathy with the sufferings, the necessary mournfulness of women, and with all in their lot con-nected with the fruit of that forbidden tree—their loneliness, the sorrows of their time, and their pangs in travail, their peculiar relation to their children. I think I hear him reading the words, " Can a woman forget her sucking child, that she should not have compassion on the son of her womb? Yea " (as if it was the next thing to impossible), " she may forget, yet will not I forget thee." Indeed, to a man who saw so little of, and said so little to his own children, perhaps it may be *because* of all this, his sympathy for mothers under loss of children, his real suffering for their suffering, not only endeared him to them as their minister, their consoler, and gave him opportunities of dropping in divine and saving truth and comfort, when the heart was full and soft, tender, and at his mercy, but it brought out in his only loss of this kind, the mingled depth, tenderness, and also the peremptoriness of his nature.

In the case of the death of little Maggie—a child the very image of himself in face, lovely and pensive, and yet ready for any fun, with a keenness of affection that perilled everything on being loved, who must cling to some one and be clasped, made for a garden, for the first garden, not for the rough world, the child of his old age—this peculiar meeting of opposites was very marked. She was stricken with sudden illness, malignant sore-throat; her mother was gone, and so she was to my father as a flower he had the sole keeping of; and his joy in her wild mirth, his watching her childish moods of sadness, as if a shadow came over her young heaven, were themselves something to watch. Her delicate life made no struggle with disease; it as it were declined to stay on such conditions. She therefore sunk at once and without much pain, her soul quick and unclouded, and her little forefinger playing to the last with my father's silvery curls, her eyes trying in vain to brighten his :—

> " Thou wert a dew-drop which the morn brings forth,
> Not fitted to be trailed along the soiling earth;
> But at the touch of wrong, without a strife,
> Slips in a moment out of life."

His distress, his anguish at this stroke, was not only intense, it was in its essence permanent; he went mourning and looking for her all his days; but after she was dead, that resolved will compacted him in an instant. It was on a Sabbath morning she died, and he was all day at church, not many yards from where lay her little corpse alone in the house. His colleague preached in the forenoon, and in the afternoon he took his turn, saying before beginning his discourse :—
"It has pleased the Father of Lights to darken one of the lights of my dwelling—had the child lived I would have remained with her, but now I have thought it right to arise and come into the house of the Lord and worship."   Such violence to one part of his nature by that in it which was supreme, injured him : it was like pulling up on the instant an express train; the whole inner organization is minutely, though it may be invisibly hurt; its molecular constitution damaged by the cruel stress and strain.   Such things are not right; they are a cruelty and injustice and injury from the soul to the body, its faithful slave, and they bring down, as in his case they too truly did, their own certain and specific retribution. A man who did not feel keenly might have preached; a man whose whole nature was torn, shattered, and astonished as his was, had in a high sense *no right* so to use himself; and when too late he opened his eyes to this. It was part of our old Scottish severe unsparing character—calm to coldness outside, burning to fierceness, tender to agony within.

I was saying how much my father enjoyed women's company. He liked to look on them, and watch them, listening [1] to their keen, unconnected, and unreason-

---

[1] One day my mother, and her only sister, Agnes—married to James Aitken of Cullands, a man before his class and his time, for long the only Whig and Seceder laird in Peeblesshire, and with whom my father shared the *Edinburgh Review* from its beginning—the two sisters who were, the one to the other, as Martha was to Mary, sat talking of their household doings; my aunt was great upon some things she could do; my father looked up from his book, and said, "There is one thing, Mrs. Aitken, you cannot do—you cannot turn the heel

ing, but not unreasonable talk. Men's argument, or rather arguing, and above all debating, he disliked. He had no turn for it. He was not combative, much less contentious. He was, however, warlike. Anything that he could destroy, any falsehood or injustice, he made for, not to discuss, but to expose and kill. He could not fence with his mind much less with his tongue, and had no love for the exploits of a nimble dialectic. He had no readiness either in thought or word for this; his way was slowly to *think out* a subject, to get it well " bottomed," as Locke would say; he was not careful as to recording the steps he took in their order, but the spirit of his mind was logical, as must be that of all minds who seek and find truth, for logic is nothing else than the arithmetic of thought; having therefore *thought it out*, he proceeded to put it into formal expression. This he did so as never again to undo it. His mind seemed to want the wheels by which this is done, *vestigia nulla retrorsum*, and having stereotyped it, he was never weary of it; it never lost its life and freshness to him, and he delivered it as emphatically thirty years after it had been cast, as the first hour of its existence.

I have said he was no swordsman, but he was a heavy shot; he fired off his ball, compact, weighty, the *maximum* of substance in the *minimum* of bulk; he put in double charge, pointed the muzzle, and fired, with what force and sharpness we all remember. If it hit, good; if not, all he could do was to load again, with the same ball, and in the same direction. You must come to him to be shot, at least you must stand still, for he had a want of mobility of mind in great questions. He could not stalk about the field like a sharp-shooter; his was a great sixty-eight pounder, and it was not much of a swivel. Thus it was that he rather dropped into the minds of others his authoritative assertions, and left them to breed

of a stocking;" and he was right, he had noticed her make over this " kittle " turn to her mother.

conviction. If they gave them entrance and cherished them, they would soon find how full of primary truth they were, and how well they would serve them, as they had served him. With all this heavy artillery, somewhat slow and cumbrous, on great questions, he had no want, when he was speaking off-hand, of quick, *snell* remark, often witty and full of spirit, and often too unexpected, like lightning—flashing, smiting and gone. In Church Courts this was very marked. On small ordinary matters, a word from him would settle a long discussion. He would, after lively, easy talk with his next neighbour, set *him* up to make a speech, which was conclusive. But on great questions he must move forward his great gun with much solemnity and effort, partly from his desire to say as much of the truth at once as he could, partly from the natural concentration and rapidity of his mind in action, as distinguished from his slowness when *incubating*, or in the process of thought,—and partly from a sort of self-consciousness—I might almost call it a compound of pride and nervous diffidence—which seldom left him. He desired to say it so that it might never need to be said again or otherwise by himself, or any one else.

This strong personality, along with a prevailing love to be alone, and dwell with thoughts rather than with thinkers, pervaded his entire character. His religion was deeply personal,[1] not only as affecting himself, but as due to a personal God, and presented through the sacrifice and intercession of the God-man; and it was perhaps owing to his "conversation" being so habitually in heaven—his social and affectionate desires filling themselves continually from "all the fulness of God," through living faith and love—that he the less felt the need of giving and receiving human affection. I never knew any man who lived more truly under the power, and sometimes

[1] In his own words, "A personal Deity is the soul of Natural Religion; a personal Saviour—the real living Christ —is the soul of Revealed Religion."

under the shadow of the world to come. This world had to him little reality except as leading to the next; little interest, except as a time of probation and sentence. A child brought to him to be baptized was in his mind, and in his words, " a young immortal to be educated for eternity;" a birth was the beginning of what was never to end; sin—his own and that of the race—was to him, as it must be to all men who can think, the great mystery, as it is the main curse of time. The idea of it—of its exceeding sinfulness—haunted and oppressed him. He used to say of John Foster, that this deep and intense, but sometimes narrow and grim thinker, had, in his study of the disease of the race, been, as it were, fascinated by its awful spell, so as almost to forget the remedy. This was not the case with himself. As you know, no man held more firmly to the objective reality of his religion —that it was founded upon fact. It was not the polestar he lost sight of, or the compass he mistrusted; it was the sea-worthiness of the vessel. His constitutional deficiency of hope, his sensibility to sin, made him not unfrequently stand in doubt of himself, of his sincerity and safety before God, and sometimes made existence—the being obliged to continue to be—a doubtful privilege.

When oppressed with this feeling,—" the burden and the mystery of all this unintelligible world," the hurry of mankind out of this brief world into the unchangeable and endless next,—I have heard him, with deep feeling, repeat Andrew Marvell's strong lines :—

> " But at my back I always hear
> Time's wingèd chariots hurrying near;
> And yonder all before me lie
> Deserts of vast eternity."

His living so much on books, and his strong personal attachment to men, as distinct from his adhesion to their principles and views, made him, as it were, live and commune with the dead—made him intimate, not merely with their thoughts, and the public events of their lives, but with themselves—Augustine, Milton, Luther, Melanchthon, George Herbert, Baxter, Howe, Owen, Leighton, Barrow, Bunyan, Philip and Matthew Henry, Doddridge, Defoe, Marvel, Locke, Berkeley, Halliburton, Cowper, Gray, Johnson, Gibbon, and David Hume,[1] Jortin, Boston, Bengel, Neander, &c., not to speak of the apostles, and above all, his chief friend the author of the Epistle to the Romans, whom he looked on as the greatest of men, —with all these he had personal relations as men, he cordialized with them.   He had thought much more about them—would have had more to say to them had they met, than about or to any but a very few living men.[2]   He delighted to possess books which

[1] David Hume's *Treatise on Human Nature* he knew thoroughly, and read it carefully during his last illness.   He used to say it not only was a miracle of intellectual and literary power for a man of twenty-eight, but contained the essence of all that was best on the philosophy of mind; " It's all there, if you will think it out."

[2] This tendency was curiously seen in his love of portraits, especially of men whose works he had and liked.   He often put portraits into his books, and he seemed to enjoy this way of realizing their authors; and in exhibitions of pictures he was more taken up with what is usually and justly the most tiresome departments, the portraits, than with all else.   He was not learned in engravings, and made no attempt at collecting them, so that the following list of portraits in his rooms shows his liking for the men much more than for the art which delineated them.   Of course they by no means include all his friends, ancient and modern, but they all *were* his friends :—

Robert Hall — Dr. Carey — Melanchthon — Calvin — Pollok — Erasmus (very like " Uncle Ebenezer ") — John Knox — Dr. Waugh—John Milton (three all framed)—Dr. Dick—Dr. Hall—Luther (two)—Dr. Heugh—Dr. Mitchell—Dr. Balmer— Dr. Henderson—Dr. Wardlaw—Shakspere (a small oil painting which he had since ever I remember)—Dugald Stewart— Dr. Innes—Dr. Smith, Biggar—the two Erskines and Mr. Fisher—Dr. John Taylor of Toronto—Dr. Chalmers—Mr. William Ellis—Rev. James Elles—J. B. Patterson—Vinet— Archibald M'Lean—Dr. John Erskine—Tholuck—John Pym— Gesenius—Professor Finlayson—Richard Baxter—Dr. Lawson —Dr. Peddie (two, and a copy of Joseph's noble bust) ; and they were thus all about him for no other reason than that he liked to look at and think of them through their countenances.

any of them might have held in their hands, on which they had written their names. He had a number of these, some very curious; among others, that wild soldier, man of fashion and wit among the reformers, Ulric von Hütten's autograph on Erasmus' beautiful folio Greek Testament, and John Howe's (spelt How) on the first edition of Milton's Speech on Unlicensed Printing.[1] He began collecting books when he was twelve, and he was collecting up to his last hours.

[1] In a copy of Baxter's *Life and Times,* which he picked up at Maurice Ogle's shop in Glasgow, which had belonged to Anna, Countess of Argyll, besides her autograph, there is a most affecting and interesting note in that venerable lady's handwriting. It occurs on the page where Baxter brings a charge of want of veracity against her eldest and name-daughter, who was perverted to Popery. They are in a hand tremulous with age and feeling :—" I can say wt truth I neuer in all my lyff did hear hir ly, and what she said, if it was not trew, it was by others sugested to hir, as yt she wold embak on Wednesday. She belived she wold, bot thy took hir, alles! from me who never did sie her mor. The minester of Cuper, Mr. John Magill, did sie hir at Paris in the convent. Said she was a knowing and vertuous person, and hed retined the living principels of our relidgon, which made him say it was good to grund young persons weel in ther relidgion, as she was one it appired weel grunded."

The following is Lord Lindsay's letter, on seeing this re-markable marginal note :—

EDINBURGH, DOUGLAS' HOTEL,
26th December, 1856.

MY DEAR SIR,—I owe you my sincerest thanks for your kindness in favouring me with a sight of the volume of Baxter's Life, which formerly belonged to my ancestrix, Anna, Countess of Argyll. The MS. note inserted by her in it respecting her daughter is extremely interesting. I had always been under the impression that the daughter had died very shortly after her removal to France, but the contrary appears from Lady Argyll's memorandum. That memorandum throws also a pleasing light on the later life of Lady Anna, and forcibly illustrates the undying love and tenderness of the aged mother, who must have been very old when she penned it, the book having been printed as late as 1696.

I am extremely obliged to you for communicating to me this new and interesting information.—Believe me, my dear Sir, your much obliged and faithful servant,

LINDSAY.

JOHN BROWN, ESQ., M.D.

He cared least for merely fine books, though he enjoyed, no one more so, fine type, good binding, and all the niceties of the book-fancier. What he liked were such books as were directly useful in his work, and such as he liked to live in the midst of; such, also, as illustrated any great philosophical, historical, or ecclesiastical epoch. His collection of Greek Testaments was, considering his means, of great extent and value, and he had a quite singular series of books, pamphlets, and documents, referring not merely to his own body—the Secession, with all its subdivisions and reunions—but to Nonconformity and Dissent everywhere, and, indeed, to human liberty, civil and religious, in every form,—for this, after the great truths, duties, and expectations of his faith, was the one master passion of his life—liberty in its greatest sense, the largest extent of individual and public spontaneity consistent with virtue and safety. He was in this as intense, persistent in his devotion, as Sydney, Locke, or old Hollis. For instance, his admiration of Lord Macaulay as a writer and a man of letters, an orator and a statesman, great as it was, was as nothing to his gratitude to him for having placed permanently on record, beyond all risk of obscuration or doubt, the doctrine of 1688—the right and power of the English people to be their own law-givers, and to appoint their own magistrates, of whom the sovereign is the chief.

His conviction of the sole right of God to be Lord of the conscience, and his sense of his own absolute religious independence of every one but his Maker, were the two elements in building up his beliefs on all church matters; they were twin beliefs. Hence the simplicity and thoroughness of his principles. Sitting in the centre, he commanded the circumference. But I am straying out of my parish into yours. I only add to what you have said, that the longer he lived, the more did he insist upon it being not less true and not less important, that the Church must not intermeddle with the State, than that the State must not intermeddle with the Church. He used to say, "Go down into the world, with all its complications and confusions, with this double-edged weapon, and you can cut all the composite knots of Church and State." The element of God and of eternity predominates in the religious more than in the civil affairs of men, and thus far transcends them; but the principle of mutual independence is equally applicable to each. All that statesmen, as such, have to do with religion, is to be themselves under its power; all that Christians, as such, have to do with the State, is to be good citizens.

The fourth epoch of his personal life I would date from his second marriage. As I said before, no man was ever happier in his wives. They had much alike in nature,—only one could see the Divine wisdom of his first wife being his first, and his second his second; each did best in her own place and time. His marriage with Miss Crum was a source of great happiness and good not only to himself, but to us his first children. She had been intimately known to us for many years, and was endeared to us long before we saw her, by her having been, as a child and girl, a great favourite of our own mother. The families of my grandfather Nimmo, and of the Crums, Ewings, and Maclaes, were very intimate. I have heard my father tell, that being out at Thornliebank with my mother, he asked her to take a walk with him to the Rouken, a romantic waterfall and glen up the burn. My mother thought they might take "Miss Margaret" with them, and so save appearances, and with Miss Crum, then a child of ten, holding my father's hand, away the three went!

So you may see that no one could be nearer to being our mother; and she was curiously ingenious, and completely successful in gaining our affection and regard. I have, as a boy, a peculiarly pleasant remembrance of her, having been at Thornliebank when about fourteen, and getting that impression of her gentle, kind, wise, calm, and happy nature—her entire lovableness—which it was our privilege to see ministering so much to my father's comfort. That fortnight in 1824 or 1825 is still to me like the memory of some happy dream; the old library, the big chair in which I huddled myself up for hours with the New Arabian Nights, and all the old-fashioned and unforgotten books I found there, the ample old garden, the wonders of machinery and skill going on in "the works," the large water-wheel going its stately rounds in the midst of its own darkness, the petrifactions I excavated in the bed of the burn, *ammonites*, &c., and brought home to my museum (!) the hospitable lady of the house, my hereditary friend, dignified, anxious and kind; and above all, her only daughter who made me a sort of pet, and was always contriving some unexpected pleasure,—all this feels to me even now like something out of a book.

My father's union with Miss Crum was not only one of the best blessings of his life,—it made him more of a blessing to others, than it is likely he would otherwise have been. By her cheerful, gracious ways, her love for society as distinguished from company, her gift of making every one happy and at ease when with her, and her tender compassion for all suffering, she in a measure won my father from himself and his books, to his own great good, and to the delight and benefit of us all. It was like sunshine and a glad sound in the house. She succeeded in what is called "drawing out" the inveterate solitary. Moreover, she encouraged and enabled him to give up a moiety of his ministerial labours, and thus to devote himself to the great work of his later years, the preparing for and giving to the press the results of his life's study of God's Word. We owe entirely to her that immense *armamentarium libertatis*, the third edition of his treatise on Civil Obedience.

One other source of great happiness to my father by this marriage was the intercourse he had with the family at Thornliebank, deepened and endeared as this was by her unexpected and irreparable loss. But

on this I must not enlarge, nor on that death itself,
the last thing in the world he ever feared—leaving
him once more, after a brief happiness, and when he
had still more reason to hope that he would have
" grown old with her, leaning on her faithful bosom."
The urn was again empty—and the only word was
vale! he was once more *viduus*, bereft.

> " God gives us love; something to love
>   He lends us; but, when love is grown
> To ripeness, that on which it throve
>   Falls off, and love is left alone.
> This is the curse of time "—

But still

> " 'Tis better to have loved and lost,
>   Than never to have loved at all."

It was no easy matter to get him from home and
away from his books. But once off, he always enjoyed himself,—especially in his visits to Thornliebank, Busby, Crofthead, Biggar, and Melrose. He
was very fond of preaching on these occasions, and
his services were always peculiarly impressive. He
spoke more slowly and with less vehemence than in
his own pulpit, and, as I often told him, with all the
more effect. When driving about Biggar, or in the
neighbourhood of Langrig, he was full of the past,
showing how keenly, with all his outward reserve, he
had observed and felt. He had a quite peculiar interest in his three flocks, keeping his eye on all their
members, through long years of absence.

His love for his people and for his " body " was
a special love; and his knowledge of the Secession,
through all its many divisions and unions,—his knowledge, not only of its public history, with its immense
controversial and occasional literature, but of the lives
and peculiarities of its ministers,—was of the most
minute and curious kind. He loved all mankind, and
specially such as were of " the household of faith;"
and he longed for the time when, as there was one
Shepherd, there would be but one sheepfold; but he

gloried in being not only a Seceder, but a Burgher; and he often said, that take them all in all, he knew no body of professing Christians in any country or in any time, worthier of all honour than that which was founded by the Four Brethren, not only as God-fearing, God-serving men, but as members of civil society; men who on every occasion were found on the side of liberty and order, truth and justice. He used to say he believed there was hardly a Tory in the Synod, and that no one but He whose service is perfect freedom, knew the public good done, and the public evil averted, by the lives and the principles, and when need was, by the votes of such men, all of whom were in the working classes, or in the lower half of the middle. The great Whig leaders knew this, and could always depend on the Seceders.

There is no worthy portrait of my father in his prime. I believe no man was ever more victimized in the way of being asked to " sit;" indeed, it was probably from so many of them being of this kind, that the opportunity of securing a really good one was lost. The best—the one portrait of his habitual expression—is Mr. Harvey's, done for Mr. Crum of Busby : it was taken when he was failing, but it is an excellent likeness as well as a noble picture; such a picture as one would buy without knowing anything of the subject. So true it is, that imaginative painters, men gifted and accustomed to render their own ideal conceptions in form and colour, grasp and impress on their canvas the features of real men more to the quick, more faithfully as to the central qualities of the man, than professed portrait painters.

Steell's bust is beautiful, but it is wanting in expression. Slater's, though rude, is better. Angus Fletcher's has much of his air, but is too much like a Grecian God. There is a miniature by Mrs. Robertson of London, belonging to my sister, Mrs. Young, which I always liked, though more like a gay, brilliant French Abbé, than the Seceder minister of Rose Street, as he then was. It gives, however, more of

his exquisite brightness and spirit, the dancing light
in his dark eyes, and his smile, when pleased and
desiring to please, than any other.   I have a drawing
by Mr. Harvey, done from my father for his picture
of the Minister's Visit, which I value very much, as
giving the force and depth, the *momentum*, so to
speak, of his serious look.   He is sitting in a cottar's
house, reading the Bible to an old bed-ridden woman,
the farm servants gathered round to get his word.

Mungo Burton painted a good portrait which my
brother William has; from his being drawn in a
black neckcloth, and standing, he looks as he sometimes did, more like a member of Parliament than a
clergyman.   The print from this is good and very
scarce.   Of Photographs, I like D. O. Hill's best,
in which he is represented as shaking hands with the
(invisible) Free Church—it is full of his earnest,
cordial power; that by Tunny, from which the beautiful engraving by Lumb Stocks in this Memoir was
taken, is very like what he was about a year and a
half before his death.   All the other portraits, as far
as I can remember, are worthless and worse, missing
entirely the true expression.   He was very difficult
to take, partly because he was so full of what may
be called spiritual beauty, evanescent, ever changing,
and requiring the highest kind of genius to fix it;
and partly from his own fault, for he thought it was
necessary to be lively, or rather to try to be so to his
volunteering artist, and the consequence was, his
giving them, as his habitual expression, one which
was rare, and in this particular case more made than
born.

The time when I would have liked his look to have
been perpetuated, was that of all others the least
likely, or indeed possible;—it was, when after ad-
ministering the Sacrament to his people, and having
solemnized every one, and been himself profoundly
moved by that Divine, everlasting memorial, he left
the elders' seat and returned to the pulpit, and after
giving out the psalm, sat down wearied and satisfied,

filled with devout gratitude to his Master—his face pale, and his dark eyes looking out upon us all, his whole countenance radiant and subdued. Any likeness of him in this state, more like that of the protomartyr, when his face was as that of an angel, than anything I ever beheld, would have made one feel what it is so impossible otherwise to convey,—the mingled sweetness, dignity, and beauty of his face. When it was winter, and the church darkening, and the lights at the pulpit were lighted so as to fall upon his face and throw the rest of the vast assemblage into deeper shadow, the effect of his countenance was something never to forget.

He was more a man of power than of genius in the ordinary sense. His imagination was not a primary power; it was not originative, though in a quite uncommon degree receptive, having the capacity of realizing the imaginations of others, and through them bodying forth the unseen. When exalted and urged by the understanding, and heated by the affections, it burst out with great force, but always as servant, not master. But if he had no one faculty that might be, to use the loose words of common speech, original, he was so as a whole,—such a man as stood alone. No one ever mistook his look, or would, had they been blind, have mistaken his voice or words, for those of any one else, or any one else's for his.

His mental characteristics, if I may venture on such ground, were clearness and vigour, intensity, fervour,[1] concentration, penetration, and persever-

---

[1] This earnestness of nature pervaded all his exercises. A man of great capacity and culture, with a head like Benjamin Franklin's, an avowed unbeliever in Christianity, came every Sunday afternoon, for many years, to hear him. I remember his look well, as if interested, but not impressed. He was often asked by his friends why he went when he didn't believe one word of what he heard. " Neither I do, but I like to hear and see a man earnest once a week, about anything." It is related of David Hume, that having heard my grandfather preach, he said, " That's the man for me, he means what he says, he speaks as if Jesus Christ was at his elbow."

ance,—more of depth than width.[1] The moral conditions under which he lived were the love, the pur-

---

[1] The following note from the pen to which we owe " St. Paul's Thorn in the Flesh " is admirable, both for its reference to my father, and its own beauty and truth.

" One instance of his imperfect discernment of associations of thought that were not of a purely logical character was afforded, we used to think, by the decided and almost contemptuous manner in which he always rejected the theory of what is called the double interpretation of prophecy. This, of course, is not the place to discuss whether he was absolutely right or wrong in his opinion. The subject, however, is one of somewhat curious interest, and it has also a strictly literary as well as a theological aspect, and what we have to say about it shall relate exclusively to the former. When Dr. Brown then said, as he was accustomed in his strong way to do, that ' if prophecy was capable of two senses, it was impossible it could have any sense at all,' it is plain, we think, that he forgot the specific character of prophetic literature, viz., its being in the highest degree poetic. Now every one knows that poetry of a very elevated cast almost invariably possesses great breadth, variety, we may say multiplicity of meaning. Its very excellence consists in its being capable of two, three, or many meanings and applications. Take, for example, these familiar lines in the ' Midsummer Night's Dream : '—

> ' Ah me ! for aught that ever I could read,
> Could ever hear by tale or history,
> The course of true love never did run smooth :
> But either it was different in blood,
> Or else misgraffed in respect of years,
> Or else it stood upon the choice of friends ;
> Or if there were a sympathy in choice,
> War, death, or sickness did lay siege to it,
> Making it momentary as a sound,
> Swift as a shadow, short as any dream,
> Brief as the lightning in the collied night,
> That in a spleen unfolds both heaven and earth,
> And ere a man hath time to say " Behold ! "
> The jaws of darkness do devour it up ;
> So quick bright things come to confusion.'

We remember once quoting these lines to a lady, and being rather taken aback by her remark, ' They are very beautiful, but I don't think they are true.' We really had forgot for the moment the straightforward, matter-of-fact sense of which they are capable, and were not adverting to the possibility of their being understood to mean that—nothing but love-crosses are going, and that no tolerable amount of comfort or happiness is to be found in the life matrimonial, or in any of the approaches towards it. Every intelligent student of Shakspere's, however, will at once feel that the poet's mind

suit, and the practice of truth in everything; strength and depth, rather than external warmth of affection; fidelity to principles and to friends. He used often to speak of the moral obligations laid upon every man to *think truly*, as well as to speak and act truly, and said that much intellectual demoralization and ruin resulted from neglecting this. He was absolutely tolerant of all difference of opinion, so that it was sincere; and this was all the more remarkable from his being the opposite of an indifferentist, being very strong in his own convictions, holding them keenly, even passionately, while, from the structure of his mind, he was somehow deficient in comprehending, much less of sympathizing with the opinions of men who greatly differed from him. This made his homage to entire freedom of thought all the more genuine and rare. In the region of theological thought he was scientific, systematic, and authoritative, rather than philosophical and speculative. He held so strongly that the Christian religion was mainly a religion of facts, that he perhaps allowed too little to its also being a philosophy that was ready to meet, out of its own essence and its ever unfolding powers, any new form of unbelief, disbelief, or misbelief, and must front itself to them as they moved up.

With devotional feeling—with everything that

speedily passes away from the idea with which he starts, and becomes merged into a far wider theme, viz., in the disenchantment to which all lofty imaginations are liable, the disappointment to which all extravagant earthly hopes and wishes are doomed. This, in fact, is distinctly expressed in the last line, and in this sense alone can the words be regarded as at all touching or impressive. Sudden expansions and transitions of thought, then, are nothing more than what is common to all poetry; and when we find the Hebrew bards, in their prophetic songs, mingling in the closest conjunction the anticipations of the glories of Solomon's reign, or the happy prospects of a return from Babylon, with the higher glory and happiness of Messiah's advent, such transitions of thought are in perfect accordance with the ordinary laws of poetry, and ought not to perplex even the most unimaginative student of the Bible."

showed reverence and godly fear—he cordialized wherever and in whomsoever it was found,—Pagan, or Christian, Romanist or Protestant, bond or free; and while he disliked, and had indeed a positive antipathy to intellectual mysticism, he had a great knowledge of and relish for such writers as Dr. Henry More, Culverwel, Scougall, Madame Guyon, whom (besides their other qualities) I may perhaps be allowed to call affectionate mystics, and for such poets as Herbert and Vaughan, whose poetry was pious, and their piety poetic. As I have said, he was perhaps too impatient of all obscure thinking, from not considering that on certain subjects, necessarily in their substance, and on the skirts of all subjects, obscurity and vagueness, difficulty and uncertainty, are inherent, and must therefore appear in their treatment. Men who rejoiced in making clear things obscure, and plain things the reverse, he could not abide, and spoke with some contempt of those who were original merely from their standing on their heads, and tall from walking upon stilts. As you have truly said, his character mellowed and toned down in his later years, without in any way losing its own individuality, and its clear, vigorous, unflinching perception of and addiction to principles.

His affectionate ways with his students were often very curious : he contrived to get at their hearts, and find out all their family and local specialities, in a sort of short-hand way, and he never forgot them in after life; and watching him with them at tea, speaking his mind freely and often jocularly upon all sorts of subjects, one got a glimpse of that union of opposites which made him so much what he was—he gave out far more liberally to them the riches of his learning and the deep thoughts of his heart, than he ever did among his full-grown brethren. It was like the flush of an Arctic summer, blossoming all over, out of and into the stillness, the loneliness, and the chill rigour of winter. Though authoritative in his class without any effort, he was indulgent to everything but conceit, slovenliness of mind and body, irreverence, and above all handling the Word of God deceitfully. On one occasion a student having delivered in the Hall a discourse tinged with Arminianism, he said, "That may be the gospel according to Dr. Macknight, or the gospel according to Dr. Taylor of Norwich, but it is not the gospel according to the Apostle Paul; and if I thought the sentiments expressed were his own, if I had not thought he has taken his thoughts from commentators without carefully considering them, I would think it my duty to him and to the church to make him no longer a student of divinity here." He was often unconsciously severe, from his saying exactly what he felt. On a student's ending his discourse, his only criticism was, "the strongest characteristic of this discourse is weakness," and feeling that this was really all he had to say, he ended. A young gentleman on very good terms with himself, stood up to pray with his hands in his pockets, and among other things he put up a petition he might "be delivered from the fear of man, which bringeth a snare;" my father's only remark was that there was part of his prayer which seemed to be granted before it was asked. But he was always unwilling to criticise prayer, feeling it to be too sacred, and as it were beyond his province, except to deliver the true principles of all prayer, which he used to say were admirably given in the *Shorter Catechism*—"Prayer is an offering up of the desires of the heart to God, for things agreeable to His will, in the name of Christ; with confession of our sins, and thankful acknowledgment of His mercies."

For the "heroic" old man of Haddington my father had a peculiar reverence, as indeed we all have —as well we may. He was our king, the founder of our dynasty; we dated from him, and he was "hedged" accordingly by a certain sacredness or "divinity." I well remember with what surprise and pride I found myself asked by a blacksmith's wife in a remote hamlet among the hop gardens of Kent, if I was "the son of the Self-interpreting Bible." I possess, as an heirloom, the New Testament which my father fondly regarded as the one his grandfather, when a herd laddie, got from the Professor who heard him ask for it, and promised him it if he could read a verse; and he has in his beautiful small hand written in it what follows :—" He (John Brown of Haddington) had now acquired so much of Greek as encouraged him to hope that he might at length be prepared to reap the richest of all rewards which classical learning could confer on him, the capacity of reading in the original tongue the blessed New Testament of our Lord and Saviour. Full of this hope, he became anxious to possess a copy of the invaluable volume. One night, having committed the charge of his sheep to a companion, he set out on a midnight journey to St. Andrews, a distance of twenty-four miles. He reached his destination in the morning, and went to the bookseller's shop asking for a copy of the Greek New Testament. The master of the shop, surprised at such a request from a shepherd boy, was disposed to make game of him. Some of the professors coming into the shop questioned the lad about his employment and studies. After hearing his tale, one of them desired the bookseller to bring the volume. He did so, and drawing it down, said, ' Boy, read this, and you shall have it for nothing.' The boy did so, acquitted himself to the admiration of his judges, and carried off his Testament, and when the evening arrived, was studying it in the midst of his flock on the braes of Abernethy."—*Memoir of Rev. John Brown of Haddington*, by Rev. J. B. Patterson.

" There is reason to believe *this* is the New Testament referred to. The name on the opposite page was written on the fly-leaf. It is obviously the writing of a boy, and bears a resemblance to Mr. Brown's handwriting in mature life. It is imperfect, wanting a great part of the Gospel of Matthew. The autograph at the end is that of his son, Thomas, when a youth at college, afterwards Rev. Dr. Thomas Brown of Dalkeith.—J. B."

I doubt not my father regarded this little worn old book, the sword of the Spirit which his ancestor so nobly won, and wore, and warred with, with not less honest veneration and pride than does his dear friend James Douglas of Cavers the Percy pennon borne away at Otterbourne. When I read, in Uncle William's admirable Life of his father, his own simple story of his early life—his loss of father and mother before he was eleven, his discovering (as true a *discovery* as Dr. Young's of the characters of the Rosetta stone, or Rawlinson's of the cuneiform letters) the Greek characters, his defence of himself against the astonishing and base charge of getting his learning from the devil (that shrewd personage would not have employed him on the Greek Testament), his eager, indomitable study, his running miles to and back again to hear a sermon after folding his sheep at noon, his keeping his family creditably on never more than 50l., and for long on 40l. a year, giving largely in charity, and never wanting, as he said, "lying money"—when I think of all this, I feel what a strong, independent, manly nature he must have had. We all know his saintly character, his devotion to learning, and to the work of preaching and teaching; but he seems to have been, like most complete men, full of humour and keen wit. Some of his *snell* sayings are still remembered. A lad of an excitable temperament waited on him, and informed him he wished to be a preacher of the gospel. My great-grandfather, finding him as weak in intellect as he was strong in conceit, advised him to continue in his present vocation. The young man said, "But I wish to preach and glorify God." "My young friend, a man may glorify God making broom besoms; stick to your trade, and glorify God by your walk and conversation."

The late Dr. Husband of Dunfermline called on

him when he was preparing to set out for Gifford, and was beginning to ask him some questions as to the place grace held in the Divine economy. "Come away wi' me, and I'll expound that; but when I'm speaking, look you after my feet." They got upon a rough bit of common, and the eager and full-minded old man was in the midst of his unfolding the Divine scheme, and his student was drinking in his words, and forgetting *his* part of the bargain. His master stumbled and fell, and getting up, somewhat sharply said, "James, the grace o' God can do much, but it canna gi'e a man common sense;" which is as good theology as sense.

A scoffing blacksmith seeing him jogging up to a house near the smithy on his pony, which was halting, said to him, "Mr. Brown, ye're in the Scripture line the day—'the legs o' the lame are not equal.'" "So is a parable in the mouth of a fool."

On his coming to Haddington, there was one man who held out against his "call." Mr. Brown meeting him when they could not avoid each other, the non-content said, "Ye see, sir, I canna say what I dinna think, and I think ye're ower young and inexperienced for this charge." "So I think too, David, *but it would never do for you and me to gang in the face o' the hale congregation!*"

The following is a singular illustration of the prevailing dark and severe tone of the religious teaching of that time, and also of its strength :—A poor old woman, of great worth and excellent understanding, in whose conversation Mr. Brown took much pleasure, was on her death-bed. Wishing to try her faith, he said to her, "Janet, what would you say if, after all He has done for you, God should let you drop into hell?" "E'en's (even as) He likes; if He does, *He'll lose mair than I'll do.*" There is something not less than sublime in this reply.

Than my grandfather and "Uncle Ebenezer," no two brothers could be more different in nature or more united in affection. My grandfather was a man of great natural good sense, well read and well know-ledged, easy but not indolent, never overflowing but never empty, homely but dignified, and fuller of love to all sentient creatures than any other human being I ever knew.   I had, when a boy of ten, two rabbits, Oscar and Livia : why so named is a secret I have lost ; perhaps it was an Ossianic union of the Roman with the Gael.   Oscar was a broad-nosed, manly, rather *brusque* husband, who used to snort when angry, and bite too; Livia was a thin-faced, meek, and I fear, deceitfullish wife, who could smile, and then bite.   One evening I had lifted both these worthies, by the ears of course, and was taking them from their clover to their beds, when my grandfather, who had been walking out in the cool of the evening, met me.   I had just kissed the two creatures, out of mingled love to them, and pleasure at having caught them without much trouble.   He took me by the chin, and kissed me, and then *Oscar and Livia!*   Wonder-ful man, I thought, and still think ! doubtless he had seen me in my private fondness, and wished to please me.

He was for ever doing good in his quiet yet earnest way.   Not only on Sunday when he preached solid gospel sermons, full of quaint familiar expressions, such as I fear few of my readers could take up, full of solemn, affectionate appeals, full of his own sim-plicity and love, the Monday also found him ready with his everyday gospel.   If he met a drover from Lochaber who had crossed the Campsie Hills, and was making across Carnwath Moor to the Calstane Slap, and thence into England by the drove-road, he accosted him with a friendly smile,—gave him a reasonable tract, and dropped into him some words of Divine truth.   He was thus *continually* doing good.   Go where he might, he had his message to every one; to a servant lass, to a poor wanderer on the bleak streets, to gentle and simple—he flowed for ever *pleno rivo*.

Uncle Ebenezer, on the other hand, flowed *per*

saltum; he was always good and saintly, but he was great once a week; six days he brooded over his message, was silent, withdrawn, self-involved; on the Sabbath, that downcast, almost timid man, who shunned men, the instant he was in the pulpit, stood up a son of thunder. Such a voice! such a piercing eye! such an inevitable forefinger, held out trembling with the terrors of the Lord; such a power of asking questions and letting them fall deep into the hearts of his hearers, and then answering them himself, with an "ah, sirs!" that thrilled and quivered from him to them.

I remember him astonishing us all with a sudden burst. It was a sermon upon the apparent *plus* of evil in this world, and he had driven himself and us all to despair—so much sin, so much misery—when, taking advantage of the chapter he had read, the account of the uproar at Ephesus in the Theatre, he said, "Ah, sirs! what if some of the men who, for 'about the space of two hours,' cried out, 'Great is Diana of the Ephesians,' have for the space of eighteen hundred years and more been crying day and night, 'Great and marvellous are thy works, Lord God Almighty; just and true are all thy ways, thou King of saints; who shall not fear thee, O Lord, and glorify thy name? for thou only art holy.'"

You have doubtless heard of the story of Lord Brougham going to hear him. It is very characteristic, and as I had it from Mrs. Cuninghame, who was present, I may be allowed to tell it. Brougham and Denman were on a visit to James Stuart of Dunearn, about the time of the Queen's trial. They had asked Stuart where they should go to church; he said he would take them to a Seceder minister at Inverkeithing. They went, and as Mr. Stuart had described the saintly old man, Brougham said he would like to be introduced to him, and arriving before service time, Mr. Stuart called, and left a message that some gentlemen wished to see him. The answer was that "Maister" Brown saw nobody before divine worship. He then sent in Brougham and Denman's names. " Mr. Brown's compliments to Mr. Stuart, and he sees nobody before sermon," and in a few minutes out came the stooping shy old man, and passed them, unconscious of their presence. They sat in the front gallery, and he preached a faithful sermon, full of fire and of native force. They came away greatly moved, and each wrote to Lord Jeffrey to lose not a week in coming to hear the greatest natural orator they had ever heard. Jeffrey came next Sunday, and often after declared he never heard such words, such a sacred, untaught gift of speech. Nothing was more beautiful than my father's admiration and emotion when listening to his uncle's rapt passages, or than his childlike faith in my father's exegetical prowess. He used to have a list of difficult passages ready for " my nephew," and the moment the oracle gave a decision, the old man asked him to repeat it, and then took a permanent note of it, and would assuredly preach it some day with his own proper unction and power. One story of him I must give; my father, who heard it not long before his own death, was delighted with it, and for some days repeated it to every one. Uncle Ebenezer, with all his mildness and general complaisance, was, like most of the Browns, *tenax propositi*, firm to obstinacy. He had established a week-day sermon at the North Ferry, about two miles from his own town, Inverkeithing. It was, I think, on the Tuesdays. It was winter, and a wild, drifting, and dangerous day; his daughters—his wife was dead—besought him not to go; he smiled vaguely, but continued getting into his big-coat. Nothing would stay him, and away he and the pony stumbled through the dumb and blinding snow. He was half-way on his journey, and had got into the sermon he was going to preach, and was utterly insensible to the outward storm: his pony getting his feet *balled,* staggered about, and at last upset his master and himself into the ditch at the roadside. The feeble, heedless, rapt old man might have perished there, had not some carters, bringing up whisky casks from the Ferry, seen the catastrophe, and rushed up, raising him, and *dichtin'* him, with much commiseration and blunt speech—" Puir auld man, what brocht ye here in sic a day?" There they were, a rough crew, surrounding the saintly man, some putting on his hat, sorting and cheering him, and others knocking the balls off the pony's feet, and stuffing them with grease. He was most polite and grateful, and one of these cordial ruffians having pierced a cask, brought him a horn of whisky, and said, " Tak that, it'll hearten ye." He took the horn, and bowing to them, said," Sirs, let us give thanks !" and there, by the road-side, in the drift and storm, with these wild fellows, he asked a blessing on it, and for his kind deliverers, and took a tasting of the horn. The men cried like children. They lifted him on his pony, one going with him, and when the rest arrived in Inverkeithing, they repeated the story to everybody, and broke down in tears whenever they came to the blessing. " And to think o' askin' a blessin' on a tass o' whisky !" Next Presbytery day, after the ordinary business was over, he rose up —he seldom spoke—and said, " Moderator, I have something personal to myself to say. I have often said, that real kindness belongs only to true Christians, but "—and then he told the story of these men ; " but more true kindness I never experienced than from these lads. They may have had the grace of God, I don't know ; but I never mean again to be so *positive* in speaking of this matter."

When he was on a missionary tour in the north, he one morning met a band of Highland shearers on their way to the harvest ; he asked them to stop and hear the word of God. They said they could not, as they had their wages to work for. He offered them what they said they would lose ; to this they agreed, and he paid them, and closing his eyes engaged in prayer ; when he had ended, he looked up, and his congregation had vanished ! His shrewd brother

Thomas, to whom he complained of this faithlessness, said, " Eben, the next time ye pay folk to hear you preach, keep your eyes open, and pay them when you are done." I remember, on another occasion, in Bristo Church, with an immense audience, he had been going over the Scripture accounts of great sinners repenting and turning to God, repeating their names, from Manasseh onwards. He seemed to have closed the record, when, fixing his eyes on the end of the central passage, he called out abruptly, " I see a man !" Every one looked to that point—" I see a man of Tarsus; and he says, Make mention of me !" It must not be supposed that the discourses of " Uncle Ebenezer," with these abrupt appeals and sudden starts, were unwritten or extempore; they were carefully composed and written out,—only these flashes of thought and passion came on him suddenly when writing, and were therefore quite natural when delivered—they came on him again.

The Rev. John Belfrage, M.D., had more power over my father's actions and his relations to the world, than any other of his friends : over his thoughts and convictions proper, not much,—few living men had, and even among the mighty dead, he called no man master. He used to say that the three master intellects devoted to the study of divine truth since the apostles, were Augustine, Calvin, and Jonathan Edwards; but that even they were only *primi inter pares*,—this by the bye.

On all that concerned his outward life as a public teacher, as a father, and as a member of society, he consulted Dr. Belfrage, and was swayed greatly by his judgment, as, for instance, the choice of a profession for myself, his second marriage, &c. He knew him to be his true friend, and not only wise and honest, but pre-eminently a man of affairs, *capax rerum*. Dr. Belfrage was a great man *in posse*, if ever I saw one,—" a village Hampden." Greatness was of his essence ; nothing paltry, nothing second-ary, nothing untrue. Large in body, large and handsome in face, lofty in manner to his equals or superiors;[1] homely, familiar, cordial with the young and the poor,—I never met with a more truly royal nature—more native and endued to rule, guide, and benefit mankind. He was for ever scheming for the good of others, and chiefly in the way of helping them to help themselves. From a curious want of ambition—his desire for advancement was for that of his friends, not for his own, and here he was ambitious and zealous enough,—from non-concentration of his faculties in early life, and from an affection of the heart which ultimately killed him—it was too big for his body, and, under the relentless hydrostatic law, at last shattered the tabernacle it moved, like a steam-engine too powerful for the vessel it finds itself in,—his mental heart also was too big for his happiness,—from these causes, along with a love for gardening, which was a passion, and an inherited competency, which took away what John Hunter calls " the stimulus of necessity," you may understand how this remarkable man—instead of being a Prime Minister, a Lord Chancellor, or a Dr. Gregory, a George Stephenson, or likeliest of all, a John Howard, without some of his weaknesses, lived and died minister of the small congregation of Slateford, near Edinburgh. It is also true that he was a physician, and an energetic and successful one, and got rid of some of his love of doing good to and managing human beings in this way; he was also an oracle in his district, to whom many had the wisdom to go to take as well as ask advice, and who was never weary of entering into the most minute details, and taking endless pains, being like Dr. Chalmers a strong believer in " the power of littles." It would be out of

[1] On one occasion, Mr. Hall of Kelso, an excellent but very odd man, in whom the *ego* was very strong, and who, if he had been a Spaniard, would, to adopt Coleridge's story, have taken off or touched his hat whenever he spoke of himself, met Dr. Belfrage in the lobby of the Synod, and drawing himself up as he passed, he muttered, " high and michty!" " There's a pair of us, Mr. Hall."

place, though it would be not uninteresting, to tell how this great resident power—this strong will and authority, this capacious, clear, and beneficent intellect—dwelt in its petty sphere, like an oak in a flower-pot; but I cannot help recalling that signal act of friendship and of power in the matter of my father's translation from Rose Street to Broughton Place, to which you have referred.

It was one of the turning-points of my father's history. Dr. Belfrage, though seldom a speaker in the public courts of his Church, was always watchful of the interests of the people and of his friends. On the Rose Street question he had from the beginning formed a strong opinion. My father had made his statement, indicating his leaning, but leaving himself absolutely in the hands of the Synod. There was some speaking, all on one side, and for a time the Synod seemed to incline to be absolute, and refuse the call of Broughton Place. The house was everywhere crowded, and breathless with interest, my father sitting motionless, anxious, and pale, prepared to submit without a word, but retaining his own mind; everything looked like a unanimous decision for Rose Street, when Dr. Belfrage rose up and came forward into the " passage," and with his first sentence and look, took possession of the house. He stated, with clear and simple argument, the truth and reason of the case; and then having fixed himself there, he took up the personal interests and feelings of his friend, and putting before them what they were about to do in sending back my father, closed with a burst of indignant appeal—" I ask you now, not as Christians, I ask you as gentlemen, are you prepared to do this?" Every one felt it was settled, and so it was. My father never forgot this great act of his friend.

This remarkable man, inferior to my father in learning, in intensity, in compactness and in power of—so to speak—*focussing* himself,—admiring his keen eloquence, his devotedness to his sacred art, rejoicing in his fame, jealous of his honour—was, by reason of his own massive understanding, his warm and great heart, and his instinctive knowledge of men, my father's most valued friend, for he knew best and most of what my father knew least; and on his death, my father said he felt himself thus far unprotected and unsafe. He died at Rothesay of hypertrophy of the heart. I had the sad privilege of being with him to the last; and any nobler spectacle of tender, generous affection, high courage, child-like submission to the Supreme Will, and of magnanimity in its true sense, I do not again expect to see. On the morning of his death he said to me, " John, come and tell me honestly how this is to end; tell me the last symptoms in their sequence." I knew the man, and was honest, and told him all I knew. " Is there any chance of stupor or delirium?" " I think not. Death (to take Bichat's division) will begin at the heart itself, and you will die conscious." " I am glad of that. It was Samuel Johnson, wasn't it, who wished not to die unconscious, that he might enter the eternal world with his mind unclouded; but you know, John, that was physiological nonsense. We leave the brain, and all this ruined body, behind; but I would like to be in my senses when I take my last look of this wonderful world," looking across the still sea towards the Argyleshire hills, lying in the light of sunrise, " and of my friends—of you," fixing his eyes on a faithful friend and myself. And it was so; in less than an hour he was dead, sitting erect in his chair—his disease had for weeks prevented him from lying down, —all the dignity, simplicity, and benignity of its master resting upon, and, as it were, supporting that " ruin," which he had left.

I cannot end this tribute to my father's friend and mine, and my own dear and earliest friend's father, without recording one of the most extraordinary instances of the power of will, under the pressure of affection, I ever witnessed or heard of. Dr. Belfrage was twice married. His second wife was a woman of great sweetness and delicacy, not only of mind, but, to his sorrow, of constitution. She died, after less than a year of singular and unbroken happiness. There was no portrait of her. He resolved there should be one; and though utterly ignorant of drawing, he determined to do it himself. No one else could have such a perfect image of her in his mind, and he resolved to realize this image. He got the materials for miniature painting, and, I think, eight prepared ivory plates. He then shut himself up from every one, and from everything, for fourteen days, and came out of his room, wasted and feeble, with one of the plates (the others he had used and burnt), on which was a portrait, full of subtle likeness, and drawn and coloured in a way no one could have dreamt of having had such an artist. I have seen it; and though I never saw the original, I felt that it must be like, as indeed every one who knew her said it was. I do not, as I said before, know anything more remarkable in the history of human sorrow and resolve.

I remember well that Dr. Belfrage was the first man I ever heard speak of Free-trade in religion and in education. It was during the first election after the Reform Bill, when Sir John Dalrymple, afterwards Lord Stair, was canvassing the county of Mid-Lothian. They were walking in the Doctor's garden, Sir John anxious and gracious. Dr. Belfrage, like, I believe, every other minister in his body, was a thorough-going Liberal, what was then called a Whig; but partly from his natural sense of humour and relish of power, and partly, I believe, for my benefit, he was putting the Baronet through his facings with some strictness, opening upon him startling views, and ending by asking him, "Are you, Sir John, for free-trade in corn, free-trade in education, free-trade in religion? I am." Sir John said, "Well, doctor, I have heard of free-trade in corn, but never in the other two." "You'll hear of them before ten years are gone, Sir John, or I'm mistaken."

I have said thus much of this to me memorable

man, not only because he was my father's closest and most powerful personal friend, but because by his word he probably changed the whole future course of his life. Devotion to his friends was one of the chief ends of his life, not caring much for, and having in the affection of his heart a warning against the perils and excitement of distinction and energetic public work, he set himself far more strenuously than for any selfish object, to promote the triumphs of those whom his acquired instinct—for he knew a man as a shepherd knows a sheep, or "*Caveat Emptor*" a horse—picked out as deserving them. He rests in Colinton churchyard,

> "Where all that mighty heart is lying still,"—

his only child William Henry buried beside him. I the more readily pay this tribute to Dr. Belfrage, that I owe to him the best blessing of my professional and one of the best of my personal life—the being apprenticed to Mr. Syme. This was his doing. With that sense of the capacities and capabilities of other men, which was one of his gifts, he predicted the career of this remarkable man. He used to say, "Give him life, let him live, and I know what and where he will be thirty years hence;" and this long before our greatest clinical teacher and wisest surgeon, had made the public and the profession feel and acknowledge the full weight of his worth.

Another life-long and ever strengthening friendship was that with James Henderson, D.D., Galashiels, who survived my father only a few days. This remarkable man, and exquisite preacher, whose intellect and worth had for nearly fifty years glowed with a pure, steady, and ever-growing warmth and lustre in his own region, died during the night, and probably asleep, when, like Moses, no one but his Maker was with him. He had for years laboured under that form of disease of the heart called *angina pectoris* (Dr. Arnold's disease), and for more than twenty years lived as it were on the edge of instant death;

but during his later years his health had improved, though he had always to "walk softly," like one whose next step might be into eternity. This bodily sense of peril gave to his noble and leonine face a look of suffering and of seriousness, and of what, in his case, we may truly call godly fear, which all must remember. He used to say he carried his grave beside him. He came in to my father's funeral, and took part in the services. He was much affected, and we fear the long walk through the city to the burial-place was too much for him; he returned home, preached a sermon on his old and dear friend's death of surpassing beauty. The text was, "For to me to live is Christ, and to die is gain." It was, as it were, his own funeral sermon too, and there was, besides its fervour, depth, and heavenly-mindedness, a something in it that made his old hearers afraid—as if it were to be the last crush of the grapes. In a letter to me soon after the funeral, he said :—" His removal is another *memento* to me that my own course is drawing near to its end. Nearly all of my contemporaries and of the friends of my youth are now gone before me. Well! I may say, in the words of your friend Vaughan—

'They are all gone to that world of light,
    And I alone sit lingering here ;
  Their very memory's calm and bright,
    And my sad thoughts doth cheer.'"

The evening before his death he was slightly unwell, and next morning, not coming down as usual, was called, but did not answer; and on going in, was found in the posture of sleep, quite dead : at some unknown hour of the night *abiit ad plures*—he had gone over to the majority, and joined the famous nations of the dead. *Tu vero felix non vitæ tantum claritate, sed etiam opportunitate mortis !* dying with his lamp burning, his passport made out for his journey ; death an instant act, not a prolonged process of months, as with his friend.

I have called Dr. Henderson a remarkable man, and an exquisite preacher; he was both, in the strict senses of the words. He had the largest brain I ever saw or measured. His hat had to be made for him; and his head was great in the nobler regions; the anterior and upper were full, indeed immense. If the base of his brain and his physical organization, especially his circulating system, had been in proportion, he would have been a man of formidable power, but his defective throb of the heart, and a certain lentitude of temperament, made this impossible; and his enormous organ of thought and feeling, being thus shut from the outlet of active energy, became intensely *meditative,* more this than even reflective. The consequence was, in all his thoughts an exquisiteness and finish, a crystalline lustre, purity, and concentration; but it was the exquisiteness of a great nature. If the first edge was fine, it was the sharp end of a wedge, the broad end of which you never reached, but might infer. This gave *momentum* to everything he said. He was in the true sense what Chalmers used to call a "man of *wecht.*" His mind acted by its sheer absolute power; it seldom made an effort; it was the hydraulic pressure, harmless, manageable, but irresistible; not the perilous compression of steam. Therefore it was that he was untroubled and calm, though rich; clear, though deep; though gentle, never dull; "strong without rage, without o'erflowing full." Indeed this element of water furnishes the best figure of his mind and its expression. His language was like the stream of his own Tweed; it was a translucent medium, only it brightened everything seen through it, as wetting a pebble brings out its lines and colour. That lovely, and by him much-loved river was curiously like him, or he like it, gentle, great, strong, with a prevailing mild seriousness all along its course, but clear and quiet; sometimes, as at old Melrose, turning upon itself, reflecting, losing itself in beauty, and careless to go, deep and inscrutable, but stealing away cheerily down to

Lessudden, all the clearer of its rest; and then again at the Trows, showing unmistakably its power in removing obstructions and taking its own way, and chafing nobly with the rocks, sometimes, too, like him, its silver stream rising into sudden flood, and rolling irresistibly on its way.[1]

We question if as many carefully thought and worded, and rapidly and by no means laboriously written sermons, were composed anywhere else in Britain during his fifty years—every Sunday two new ones; the composition faultless—such as Cicero or Addison would have made them, had they been U. P. ministers; only there was always in them more soul than body, more of the spirit than of the letter. What a contrast to the much turbid, hot, hasty, perilous stuff of our day and preachers! The original power and *size* of Dr. Henderson's mind, his roominess for all thoughts, and his still reserve, his lentitude, made, as we have said, his expressions clear and quiet, to a degree that a coarse and careless man, spoiled by the violence and noise of other pulpit men, might think insipid. But let him go over the words slowly, and he would not say this again; and let him see and feel the solemnizing, commanding power of that large, square, leonine countenance, the broad massive frame, as of a compressed Hercules, and the living,

[1] Such an occasional paroxysm of eloquence is thus described by Dr. Cairns :—" At certain irregular intervals, when the loftier themes of the gospel ministry were to be handled, his manner underwent a transformation which was startling, and even electrical. He became rapt and excited as with new inspiration; his utterance grew thick and rapid; his voice trembled and faltered with emotion; his eye gleamed with a wild unearthly lustre, in which his countenance shared; and his whole frame heaved to and fro, as if each glowing thought and vivid figure that followed in quick succession were only a fragment of some greater revelation which he panted to overtake. The writer of this notice has witnessed nothing similar in any preacher, and numbers the effects of a passage which he once heard upon the scenes and exercises of the heavenly world among his most thrilling recollections of sacred oratory."—*Memoir prefixed to posthumous volume of Discourses.*

pure, melodious voice, powerful, but not by reason of loudness, dropping out from his compressed lips the words of truth, and he would not say this again. His voice had a singular pathos in it; and those who remember his often-called-for sermon on " The Bright and the Morning Star," can reproduce in their mind its tones and refrain. The thoughts of such men—so rare, so apt to be unvisited and unvalued—often bring into my mind a spring of pure water I once saw near the top of Cairngorm; always the same, cool in summer, keeping its few plants alive and happy with its warm breath in winter, floods and droughts never making its pulse change; and all this because it came from the interior heights, and was distilled by nature's own cunning, and had taken its time—was indeed a well of living water. And with Dr. Henderson this of the mountain holds curiously; he was retired, but not concealed; and he was of the primary formation, he had no *organic remains* of other men in him; he liked and fed on all manner of literature; knew poetry well; but it was all outside of him; his thoughts were essentially his own.

He was peculiarly a preacher for preachers, as Spenser is a poet for poets. They felt he was a master. He published, after the entreaties of years, a volume of sermons which has long been out of print, and which he would never prepare for a second edition; he had much too little of the love of fame, and though not destitute of self-reliance and self-value, and resolved and unchangeable to obstinacy, he was not in the least degree vain.

But you will think I am writing more about my father's friends and myself than about him. In a certain sense we may know a man by his friends; a man chooses his friends from harmony, not from sameness, just as we would rather sing in parts than all sing the air. One man fits into the mind of another not by meeting his points, but by dovetailing; each finds in the other what he in a double sense wants. This was true of my father's friends. Dr.

Balmer was like him in much more than perhaps any,—in love of books and lonely study, in his general views of divine truth, and in their metaphysical and literary likings, but they differed deeply. Dr. Balmer was serene and just rather than subtle and profound; his was the still, translucent stream,—my father's the rapid, and it might be deep; on the one you could safely sail, the other hurried you on, and yet never were two men, during a long life of intimate intercourse, more cordial.

I must close the list; one only and the best—the most endeared of them all—Dr. Heugh. He was, in mental constitution and temper, perhaps more unlike my father than any of the others I have mentioned. His was essentially a practical understanding; he was a man of action, a man for men more than for man, the curious reverse in this of my father. He delighted in public life, had a native turn for affairs, for all that society needs and demands,—clear-headed, ready, intrepid, adroit; with a fine temper, but keen and honest, with an argument and a question and a joke for every one; not disputatious, but delighting in a brisk argument, fonder of wrestling than of fencing, but ready for action; not much of a long shot, always keeping his eye on the immediate, the possible, the attainable, but in all this guided by genuine principle, and the finest honour and exactest truth. He excelled in the conduct of public business, saw his way clear, made other men see theirs, was for ever getting the Synod out of difficulties and confusions, by some clear, tidy, conclusive " motion;" and then his speaking, so easy and bright and pithy, manly and gentlemanly, grave when it should be, never when it should not—mobile, fearless, rapid, brilliant as Saladin—his silent, pensive, impassioned and emphatic friend was more like the lion-hearted Richard, with his heavy mace; he might miss, but let him hit, and there needed no repetition. Each admired the other; indeed Dr. Heugh's love of my father was quite romantic; and though they were opposed on several great public questions, such as the Apocrypha controversy, the Atonement question at its commencement; and though they were both of them too keen and too honest to mince matters or be mealy-mouthed, they never misunderstood each other, never had a shadow of estrangement, so that our Paul and Barnabas, though their contentions were sometimes sharp enough, never "departed asunder;" indeed they loved each other the longer the more.

Take him all in all, as a friend, as a gentleman, as a Christian, as a citizen, I never knew a man so thoroughly delightful as Dr. Heugh. Others had more of this or more of that, but there was a symmetry, a compactness, a sweetness, a true *delightfulness* about him I can remember in no one else. No man, with so much temptation to be heady and highminded, sarcastic, and managing, from his overflowing wit and talent, was ever more natural, more honest, or more considerate, indeed tender-hearted. He was full of animal spirits and of fun, and one of the best wits and jokers I ever knew; and such an asker of questions, of posers! We children had a pleasing dread of that nimble, sharp, exact man, who made us explain and name everything. Of Scotch stories he had as many original ones as would make a second volume for Dean Ramsay. How well I remember the very corner of the room in Biggar manse, forty years ago, when from him I got the first shock and relish of humour; became conscious of mental tickling; of a word being made to carry double, and being all the lighter of it. It is an old story now, but it was new then: a big, perspiring countryman rushed into the Black Bull coach-office, and holding the door, shouted, "Are yir insides a' oot?" This was my first tasting of the flavour of a joke.

Had Dr. Heugh, instead of being the admirable clergyman he was, devoted himself to public civil life, and gone into Parliament, he would have taken a high place as a debater, a practical statesman and patriot. He had many of the best qualities of Canning, and our own Premier, with purer and higher qualities than either. There is no one our church should be more proud of than this beloved and excellent man, the holiness and humility, the jealous, godly fear in whose nature was not known fully even to his friends, till he was gone, when his private daily self-searchings and prostrations before his Master and Judge were for the first time made known. There are few characters, *both sides* of which are so unsullied, so pure, and without reproach.

I am back at Biggar at the old sacramental times; I see and hear my grandfather, or Mr. Horne of Braehead, Mr. Leckie of Peebles, Mr. Harper of Lanark, as inveterate in argument as he was warm in heart, Mr. Comrie of Penicuik, with his keen, Voltaire-like face, and much of that unhappy and unique man's wit, and sense, and perfection of expression, without his darker and baser qualities. I can hear their hearty talk, can see them coming and going between the meeting-house and the *Tent* on the side of the burn, and then the Monday dinner, and the cheerful talk, and the many clerical stories and pleasantries, and their going home on their hardy little horses, Mr. Comrie leaving his curl-papers till the next solemnity, and leaving also some joke of his own, clear and compact as a diamond, and as cutting.

I am in Rose Street on the monthly lecture, the church crammed, passages and pulpit stairs. Exact to a minute, James Chalmers—the old soldier and beadle, slim, meek, but incorruptible by proffered half-crowns from ladies who thus tried to get in before the doors opened—appears, and all the people in that long pew rise up, and he, followed by his minister, erect and engrossed, walks in along the seat, and they struggle up to the pulpit. We all know what he is to speak of; he looks troubled even to distress;—it is the matter of Uriah the Hittite. He gives out the opening verses of the 51st Psalm, and offering up a short and abrupt prayer, which every one takes to

himself, announces his miserable and dreadful subject, *fencing* it, as it were, in a low, penetrating
voice, daring any one of us to think an evil thought;
there was little need at that time of the warning,—
he infused his own intense, pure spirit, into us all.

He then told the story without note or comment,
only personating each actor in the tragedy with extraordinary effect, above all, the manly, loyal, simple-
hearted soldier. I can recall the shudder of that multitude as of one man when he read, "And it came to
pass in the morning, that David wrote a letter to
Joab, and sent it by the hand of Uriah. And he wrote
in the letter, saying, Set ye Uriah in the forefront of
the hottest battle, and retire ye from him, that he may
be smitten and die." And then, after a long and
utter silence, his exclaiming, "Is this the man according to God's own heart? Yes, it is; we must
believe that both are true." Then came Nathan.
"There were two men in one city; the one rich, and
the other poor. The rich man had exceeding many
flocks and herds; but the poor man had nothing, save
one little ewe lamb"—and all that exquisite, that
divine fable—ending, like a thunder-clap, with "Thou
art the man!" Then came the retribution, so awfully
exact and thorough,—the misery of the child's death;
that brief tragedy of the brother and sister, more
terrible than anything in Æschylus, in Dante, or in
Ford; then the rebellion of Absalom, with its hideous
dishonour, and his death, and the king covering his
face, and crying in a loud voice, "O my son Absalom!
O Absalom! my son! my son!"—and David's psalm,
"Have mercy upon me, O God, according to Thy
loving-kindness; according unto the multitude of Thy
tender mercies blot out my transgressions,"—then
closing with "Yes; 'when lust hath conceived, it
bringeth forth sin: and sin, when it is finished,
bringeth forth death. Do not err,' do not stray, do
not transgress ($\mu\grave{\eta}$ $\pi\lambda\alpha\nu\hat{\alpha}\sigma\theta\epsilon$),[1] 'my beloved brethren,'

---

[1] James i. 15, 16. It is plain that "do not err" should
have been in verse 15th.

it is first ' earthly, then sensual, then devilish;' "
he shut the book, and sent us all away terrified,
shaken, and humbled, like himself.

I would fain say a few words on my father's last
illness, or rather what led to it, and I wish you and
others in the ministry would take to heart, as matter
of immediate religious duty, much of what I am
going to say. My father was a seven months' child,
and lay, I believe, for a fortnight in black wool, un-
dressed, doing little but breathe and sleep, not capable
of being fed. He continued all his life slight in make,
and not robust in health, though lively, and capable
of great single efforts. His attendance upon his
mother must have saddened his body as well as his
mind, and made him willing and able to endure, in
spite of his keen and ardent spirit, the sedentary life
he in the main led. He was always a very small
eater, and nice in his tastes, easily put off from his
food by any notion. He therefore started on the full
work of life with a finer and more delicate mechanism
than a man's ought to be, indeed, in these respects
he was much liker a woman; and being very soon
" placed," he had little travelling, and little of that
tossing about the world, which in the transition from
youth to manhood, hardens the frame as well as
supples it. Though delicate, he was almost never ill.
I do not remember, till near the close of his life, his
ever being in bed a day.

From his nervous system, and his brain predomin-
ating steadily over the rest of his body, he was
habitually excessive in his professional work. As to
quantity, as to quality, as to manner and expression,
he flung away his life without stint every Sabbath-
day, his sermons being laboriously prepared, loudly
mandated, and at great expense of body and mind,
and then delivered with the utmost vehemence and
rapidity. He was quite unconscious of the state he
worked himself into, and of the loud piercing voice
in which he often spoke. This I frequently warned
him about, as being, I knew, injurious to himself,

and often painful to his hearers, and his answer always was, that he was utterly unaware of it; and thus it continued to the close, and very sad it was to me who knew the peril, and saw the coming end, to listen to his noble, rich, persuasive, imperative appeals, and to know that the surplus of power, if retained, would, by God's blessing, retain him, while the effect on his people would, I am sure, not have lost, but in some respects have gained, for much of the discourse which was shouted and sometimes screamed at the full pitch of his keen voice, was of a kind to be better rendered in his deep, quiet, settled tones. This, and the great length of his public services, I knew he himself felt, when too late, had injured him, and many a smile he had at my proposal to have a secret sub-congregational string from him to me in the back seat, to be authoritatively twitched when I knew he had done enough; but this string was never pulled, even in his mind.

He went on in this expensive life, sleeping very little, and always lightly, eating little, never walking except of necessity; little in company, when he would have eaten more and been, by the power of social relish, made likelier to get the full good out of his food; never diverting his mind by any change but that of one book or subject for another; and every time that any strong affliction came on him, as when made twice a widower, or at his daughter's death, or from such an outrage upon his entire nature and feelings as the Libel, then his delicate machinery was shaken and damaged, not merely by the first shock, but even more by that unrelenting self-command by which he terrified his body into instant submission. Thus it was, and thus it ever must be, if the laws of our bodily constitution, laid down by Him who knows our frame, and from whom our substance is not hid, are set at nought, knowingly or not—if knowingly, the act is so much the more spiritually bad—but if not, it is still punished with the same unerring nicety, the same commensurate meting out of the penalty, and paying "in full tale," as makes the sun to know his time, and splits an erring planet into fragments, driving it into space "with hideous ruin and combustion." It is a pitiful and a sad thing to say, but if my father had not been a prodigal in a true but very different meaning, if he had not spent his substance, the portion of goods that fell to him, the capital of life given him by God, in what we must believe to have been needless and therefore preventable excess of effort, we might have had him still with us, shining more and more, and he and they who were with him would have been spared those two years of the valley of the shadow, with its sharp and steady pain, its fallings away of life, its longing for the grave, its sleepless nights and days of weariness and languor, the full expression of which you will find nowhere but in the Psalms and in Job.

I have said that though delicate he was never ill: this was all the worse for him, for, odd as it may seem, many a man's life is lengthened by a sharp illness; and this in several ways. In the first place, he is laid up, out of the reach of all external mischief and exertion, he is like a ship put in dock for repairs; time is gained. A brisk fever clarifies the entire man: if it is beaten and does not beat, it is like cleaning a chimney by setting it on fire; it is perilous but thorough. Then the effort to throw off the disease often quickens and purifies and corroborates the central powers of life; the flame burns more clearly; there is a cleanness, so to speak, about all the wheels of life. Moreover, it is a warning, and makes a man meditate on his bed, and resolve to pull up; and it warns his friends, and likewise, if he is a clergyman, his people, who if their minister is always with them, never once think he can be ever anything but as able as he is.

Such a pause, such a breathing-time my father never got during that part of his life and labours when it would have availed most, and he was an old man in years, before he was a regular patient of any

doctor. He was during life subject to sudden head-
aches, affecting his memory and eyesight, and even
his speech; these attacks were, according to the
thoughtless phrase of the day, called bilious; that is,
he was sick, and was relieved by a blue pill and smart
medicine. Their true seat was in the brain; the liver
suffered because the brain was ill, and sent no nervous
energy to it, or poisoned what it did send. The
sharp racking pain in the forehead was the cry of
suffering from the anterior lobes, driven by their
master to distraction, and turning on him wild with
weakness and fear and anger. It was well they did
cry out; in some brains (large ones) they would have
gone on dumb to sudden and utter ruin, as in
apoplexy or palsy; but he did not know, and no one
told him their true meaning, and he set about seeking for the outward cause in some article of food, in
some recent and quite inadequate cause.

He used, with a sort of odd shame and distress,
to ask me why it was that he was subjected to so
much suffering from what he called the lower and
ignoble regions of his body; and I used to explain to
him that he had made them suffer by long years of
neglect, and that they were now having their revenge,
and in their own way. I have often found, that the
more the nervous centres are employed in those offices
of thought and feeling the most removed from material
objects,—the more the nervous energy of the entire
nature is concentrated, engrossed, and used up in
such offices,—so much the more, and therefore, are
those organs of the body which preside over that
organic life, common to ourselves and the lowest
worm, defrauded of their necessary nervous food,—
and being in the organic and not in the animal department, and having no voice to tell their wants or
wrongs, till they wake up and annoy their neighbours
who have a voice, that is, who are sensitive to pain,
they may have been long ill before they come into the
sphere of consciousness. This is the true reason—
along with want of purity and change of air, want of

exercise,[1] want of shifting the work of the body— why clergymen, men of letters, and all men of intense mental application, are so liable to be affected with indigestion, constipation, lumbago, and lowness of spirits, *melancholia*—black bile. The brain may not give way for long, because for a time the law of exercise strengthens it; it is fed high, gets the best of everything, of blood and nervous pabulum, and then men have a joy in the victorious work of their brain, and it has a joy of its own, too, which deludes and misleads.

All this happened to my father. He had no formal disease when he died—no structural change; his sleep and his digestion would have been quite sufficient for life even up to the last; the mechanism was entire, but the motive power was gone—it was expended. The silver cord was not so much loosed as relaxed. The golden bowl, the pitcher at the fountain, the wheel at the cistern, were not so much broken as emptied and stayed. The clock had run down before its time, and there was no one but He who first wound it up and set it who could wind it up again; and this He does not do, because it is His law—an express injunction from Him—that, having measured out to his creatures each his measure of life, and left him to the freedom of his own will and the regulation of his reason, He also leaves him to reap as he sows.

Thus it was that my father's illness was not so much a disease as a long death; life ebbing away, consciousness left entire, the certain issue never out of sight. This, to a man of my father's organization —with a keen relish for life, and its highest pleasures and energies, sensitive to impatience, and then oversensitive of his own impatience; cut to the heart with the long watching and suffering of those he

---

[1] "The youth Story is in all respects healthy, and even robust; he died of overwork, or rather, as I understand, of a two years' almost total want of exercise, which it was impossible to induce him to take."—*Arnold's Report to the Committee of Council on Education,* 1860.

loved, who, after all, could do so little for him; with
a nervous system easily sunk, and by its strong play
upon his mind darkening and saddening his most
central beliefs, shaking his most solid principles, tearing and terrifying his tenderest affections : his mind
free and clear, ready for action if it had the power,
eager to be in its place in the work of the world and
of its Master, to have to spend two long years in this
ever-descending road—here was a combination of
positive and negative suffering not to be thought of
even now, when it is all sunk under that "far more
exceeding and eternal weight of glory."

He often spoke to me freely about his health, went into
it with the fearlessness, exactness, and persistency of
his nature; and I never witnessed, or hope to witness,
anything more affecting than when, after it had been
dawning upon him, he apprehended the true secret of
his death. He was deeply humbled, felt that he had
done wrong to himself, to his people, to us all, to his
faithful and long-suffering Master; and he often said,
with a dying energy lighting up his eye, and nerving
his voice and gesture, that if it pleased God to let him
again speak in his old place, he would not only proclaim again, and, he hoped, more simply and more
fully, the everlasting gospel to lost man, but proclaim
also the gospel of God to the body, the religious and
Christian duty and privilege of living in obedience
to the divine laws of health. He was delighted when
I read to him, and turned to this purpose that wonderful passage of St. Paul—" For the body is not one
member, but many. If the whole body were an eye,
where were the hearing? if the whole were hearing,
where were the smelling? But now hath God set the
members every one of them in the body, as it hath
pleased Him. And the eye cannot say unto the hand,
I have no need of thee; nor again the head to the
feet, I have no need of you. Nay, much more those
members of the body, which seem to be more feeble,
are necessary;" summing it all up in words with life
and death in them—" That there should be no schism

in the body; but that the members should have the same care one for another. And whether one member suffer, all the members suffer with it; or one member be honoured, all the members rejoice with it."

The lesson from all this is, Attend to your bodies, study their structure, functions, and laws. This does not at all mean that you need be an anatomist, or go deep into physiology, or the doctrines of prevention and cure. Not only has each organism a resident doctor, placed there by Him who can thus heal all our diseases; but this doctor, if watched and waited on, informs any man or woman of ordinary sense what things to do, and what things not to do. And I would have you, who, I fear, not unfrequently sin in the same way, and all our ardent, self-sacrificing young ministers, to reflect whether, after destroying themselves and dying young, they have lost or gained. It is said that God raises up others in our place. God gives you no title to say this. Men—such men as I have in my mind—are valuable to God in proportion to the time they are here. They are the older, the better, the riper and richer, and more enriching. Nothing will make up for this absolute loss of life. For there is something which every man who is a good workman is gaining every year just because he is older, and this nothing can replace. Let a man remain on his ground, say a country parish, during half a century or more—let him be every year getting fuller and sweeter in the knowledge of God and man, in utterance and in power—can the power of that man for good over all his time, and especially towards its close, be equalled by that of three or four young, and, it may be, admirable men, who have been succeeding each other's untimely death, during the same space of time? It is against all spiritual, as well as all simple arithmetic, to say so.

You have spoken of my father's prayers. They were of two kinds: the one, formal, careful, systematic, and almost stereotyped, remarkable for fulness and compression of thought; sometimes too

manifestly the result of study, and sometimes not
purely prayer, but more of the nature of a devotional
and even argumentative address; the other, as in the
family, short, simple, and varied.   He used to tell
of his master, Dr. Lawson, reproving him, in his
honest but fatherly way, as they were walking home
from the Hall.   My father had in his prayer the
words, " that through death He might destroy him
that had the power of death,—that is, the devil." The
old man, leaning on his favourite pupil, said, " John,
my man, you need not have said ' *that is the devil;*'
you might have been sure that *He* knew whom you
meant."   My father, in theory, held that a mixture of
formal, fixed prayer, in fact, a liturgy, along with
extempore prayer, was the right thing.   As you
observe, many of his passages in prayer, all who were
in the habit of hearing him could anticipate, such as
" the enlightening, enlivening, sanctifying, and comforting influences of the good Spirit," and many
others. One in especial you must remember; it was
only used on very solemn occasions, and curiously
unfolds his mental peculiarities; it closed his prayer—
" And now, unto Thee, O Father, Son, and Holy
Ghost, the one Jehovah and our God, we would—as
is most meet—with the church on earth and the
church in heaven, ascribe all honour and glory, dominion and majesty, as it was in the beginning, is
now, and ever shall be, world without end.   Amen."
Nothing could be liker him than the interjection, " as
is most meet."   Sometimes his abrupt, short state-
ments in the Synod were very striking.   On one occasion, Mr. James Morison having stated his views as
to prayer very strongly, denying that a sinner *can*
pray, my father, turning to the Moderator, said—
" Sir, let a man feel himself to be a sinner, and, for
anything the universe of creatures can do for him,
hopelessly lost,—let him feel this, sir, and let him
get a glimpse of the Saviour, and all the eloquence
and argument of Mr. Morison will not keep that
man from crying out, ' God be merciful to me, a

sinner.' That, sir, is prayer—that is acceptable prayer.''

There must be, I fear, now and then an apparent discrepancy between you and me, especially as to the degree of mental depression which at times overshadowed my father's nature. *You* will understand this, and I hope our readers will make allowance for it. Some of it is owing to my constitutional tendency to overstate, and much of it to my having had perhaps more frequent, and even more private, insights into this part of his life. But such inconsistency as that I speak of—the co-existence of a clear, firm faith, a habitual sense of God and of His infinite mercy, the living a life of faith, as if it was in his organic and inner life, more than in his sensational and outward—is quite compatible with that tendency to distrust himself, that bodily darkness and mournfulness, which at times came over him. Any one who knows '' what a piece of work is man,'' how composite, how varying, how inconsistent human nature is, that each of us are

> '' Some several men, all in an hour,''

—will not need to be told to expect, or how to harmonize these differences of mood. You see this in that wonderful man, the apostle Paul, the true typical fulness, the *humanness*, so to speak, of whose nature comes out in such expressions of opposites as these— '' By honour and dishonour, by evil report and good report : as deceivers, and yet true ; as unknown, and yet well known ; as dying, and, behold, we live ; as chastened, and not killed ; as sorrowful, yet alway rejoicing ; as poor, yet making many rich ; as having nothing, and yet possessing all things.''

I cannot, and after your impressive and exact history of his last days, I need not say anything of the close of those long years of suffering, active and passive, and that slow ebbing of life ; the body, without help or hope, feeling its doom steadily though slowly drawing on ; the mind mourning for its suffering friend, companion, and servant, mourning also, some-times, that it must be "unclothed," and take its flight all alone into the infinite unknown; dying daily, not in the heat of fever, or in the insensibility or lethargy of paralytic disease, but having the mind calm and clear, and the body conscious of its own decay,—dying, as it were, in cold blood. One thing I must add. That morning when you were obliged to leave, and when "cold obstruction's apathy" had already begun its reign—when he knew us, and that was all, and when he followed us with his dying and loving eyes, but could not speak—the end came; and then, as through life, his will asserted itself supreme in death. With that love of order and decency which was a law of his life, he deliberately composed him-self, placing his body at rest, as if setting his house in order before leaving it, and then closed his eyes and mouth, so that his last look—the look his body carried to the grave and faced dissolution in—was that of sweet, dignified self-possession.

I have made this letter much too long, and have said many things in it I never intended saying, and omitted much I had hoped to be able to say. But I must end.

Yours ever affectionately,

J. BROWN.

'MYSTIFICATIONS'[1]

" Health to the auld wife, and weel mat she be,
That busks her fause rock wi' the lint o' the lee (lie),
Whirling her spindle and twisting the twine,
Wynds aye the richt pirn into the richt line."

THOSE who knew the best of Edinburgh society eight-and-thirty years ago—and when was there ever a better than that best?—must remember the person-ations of an old Scottish gentlewoman by Miss Stir-ling Graham, one of which, when Lord Jeffrey was victimized, was famous enough to find its way into *Blackwood*, but in an incorrect form.

Miss Graham's friends have for years urged her to print for them her notes of these pleasant records of the harmless and heart-easing mirth of bygone times; to this she has at last assented, and the result is this entertaining, curious, and beautiful little quarto, in which her friends will recognize the strong under-standing and goodness, the wit and invention, and fine *pawky* humour of the much-loved and warm-hearted representative of Viscount Dundee—the ter-rible Clavers.[2] They will recall that blithe and winning face, sagacious and sincere, that kindly, cheery voice, that rich and quiet laugh, that mingled sense and

[1] Edinburgh : printed privately, 1859.
[2] Miss Graham's genealogy in connexion with Claverhouse —the same who was killed at Killiecrankie—is as follows :— John Graham of Claverhouse married the Honourable Jean Cochrane, daughter of William Lord Cochrane, eldest son of the first Earl of Dundonald. Their only son, an infant, died December 1689. David Graham, his brother, fought at Killiecrankie, and was outlawed in 1690—died without issue—when the representation of the family devolved on his cousin, David Graham of Duntrune. Alexander Graham of Duntrune died 1782 ; and on the demise of his last surviving son, Alexander, in 1804, the property was inherited equally by his four surviving sisters, Anne, Amelia, Clementina, and Alison. Amelia, who married Patrick Stirling, Esq., of Pittendreich, was her mother. Clementina married Captain Gavin Drummond of Keltie ; their only child was Clementina Countess of Airlie, and mother of the present Earl.

sensibility, which all met, and still, to our happiness, meet in her, who, with all her gifts and keen perception of the odd, and power of embodying it, never gratified her consciousness of these powers, or ever played

" Her quips and cranks and wanton wiles,"

so as to give pain to any human being.

The title of this memorial is *Mystifications*, and in the opening letter to her dear kinswoman and lifelong friend, Mrs. Gillies, widow of Lord Gillies, she thus tells her story :—

DUNTRUNE, *April* 1859.

MY DEAREST MRS. GILLIES,
    To you and the friends who have partaken in these " Mystifications," I dedicate this little volume, trusting that, after a silence of forty years, its echoes may awaken many agreeable memorials of a society that has nearly passed away.

I have been asked if I had no remorse in ridiculing singularities of character, or practising deceptions ;— certainly not.

There was no personal ridicule or mimicry of any living creature, but merely the personation or type of a bygone class, that had survived the fashion of its day.

It was altogether a fanciful existence, developing itself according to circumstances, or for the amusement of a select party, among whom the announcement of a stranger lady, an original, led to no suspicion of deception. No one ever took offence: indeed it generally elicited the finest individual traits of sympathy in the minds of the dupes, especially in the case of Mr. Jeffrey, whose sweet-tempered kindly nature manifested itself throughout the whole of the tiresome interview with the law-loving Lady Pitlyal.

No one enjoyed her eccentricities more than he did, or more readily devised the arrangement of a similar scene for the amusement of our mutual friends.

The cleverest people were the easiest mystified, and

when once the deception took place, it mattered not how arrant the nonsense or how exaggerated the costume. Indeed, children and dogs were the only detectives.

I often felt so identified with the character, so charmed with the pleasure manifested by my audience, that it became painful to lay aside the veil, and descend again into the humdrum realities of my own self.

These personations never lost me a friend; on the contrary, they originated friendships that cease only with life.

The Lady Pitlyal's course is run; she bequeaths to you these reminiscences of beloved friends and pleasant meetings.

And that the blessing of God may descend on " each and all of you," is the fervent prayer of her kins-woman and executrix,

CLEMENTINA STIRLING GRAHAM.

I now beg to " convey," as Pistol delicately calls it, or as we on our side the Border would say, to " lift," enough of this unique volume to make my readers hunger for the whole.

MRS. RAMSAY SPELDIN

Another evening Miss Guthrie requested me to introduce my old lady to Captain Alexander Lindsay, a son of the late Laird of Kinblethmont, and brother to the present Mr. Lindsay Carnegie, and Mr. Sand-ford, the late Sir Daniel Sandford.

She came as a Mrs. Ramsay Speldin, an old sweet-heart of the laird's, and was welcomed by Mrs. Guthrie as a friend of the family. The young people hailed her as a perfectly delightful old lady, and an original of the pure Scottish character, and to the laird she was endeared by a thousand pleasing recollections.

He placed her beside himself on the sofa, and they

talked of the days gone by—before the green parks of Craigie were redeemed from the muir of Gotterston, and ere there was a tree planted between the auld house of Craigie and the Castle of Claypotts.

She spoke of the " gude auld times, when the laird of Fintry widna gie his youngest dochter to Abercairney, but tell'd him to tak them as God had gien them to him, or want."

" And do you mind," she continued, " the grand ploys we had at the Middleton ; and hoo Mrs. Scott of Gilhorn used to grind lilts out o' an auld kist to wauken her visitors i' the mornin'.

" And some o' them didna like it sair, tho' nane o' them had courage to tell her sae, but Anny Graham o' Duntrune.

" ' Lord forgie ye,' said Mrs. Scott, ' ye'll no gae to heaven, if ye dinna like music ;' but Anny was never at a loss for an answer, and she said, ' Mrs. Scott— heaven's no the place I tak it to be, if there be auld wives in 't playing on hand-organs.' "

Many a story did Mrs. Ramsay tell. The party drew their chairs close to the sofa, and many a joke she related, till the room rung again with the merriment, and the laird, in ecstasy, caught her round the waist, exclaiming " Oh ! ye are a cantie wifie."

The strangers seemed to think so too ; they absolutely hung upon her, and she danced reels, first with the one, and then with the other, till the entrance of a servant with the newspapers produced a seasonable calm.

They lay, however, untouched upon the table till Mrs. Ramsay requested some one to read over the claims that were putting in for the King's coronation, and see if there was any mention of hers.

" What is your claim?" said Mr. Sandford.

" To pyke the King's teeth," was the reply.

" You will think it very singular," said Mr. Guthrie, " that I never heard of it before ; will you tell us how it originated?"

" It was in the time of James the First," said she,

" that monarch cam to pay a visit to the monks of Arbroath, and they brought him to Ferryden to eat a fish dinner at the house o' ane o' my forefathers. The family name, ye ken, was Speldin, and the dried fish was ca'd after them.

" The king was well satisfied wi' a' thing that was done to honour him.   He was a very polished prince, and when he had eaten his dinner he turned round to the lady and sought a preen to pyke his teeth.

" And the lady, she took a fish bane and wipit it, and gae it to the king; and after he had cleaned his teeth wi' it, he said, ' *They 're weel pykit.*'

" ' And henceforth,' continued he, ' the Speldins of Ferryden shall pyke the king's teeth at the coronation.   And it shall be done wi' a fish bone, and a pearl out o' the Southesk on the end of it.   And their crest shall be a lion's head wi' the teeth displayed, and the motto shall be *weel pykit.*' "

Mr. Sandford read over the claims, but there was no notice given of the Speldins.

" We maun just hae patience," said Mrs. Ramsay, " and nae doubt it will appear in the next newspaper."

Some one inquired who was the present representative?

" It's me," replied Mrs. Ramsay Speldin; " and I mean to perform the office mysel'.   The estate wad hae been mine too, had it existed; but Neptune, ye ken, is an ill neighbour, and the sea has washed it a' awa but a sand bunker or twa, and the house I bide in at Ferryden."

At supper every one was eager to have a seat near Mrs. Ramsay Speldin.   She had a universal acquaintance, and she even knew Mr. Sandford's mother, when he told her that her name was Catherine Douglas.   Mr. Sandford had in his own mind composed a letter to Sir Walter Scott, which was to have been written and despatched on the morrow, giving an account of this fine specimen of the true Scottish character whom he had met in the county of Angus.

We meant to carry on the deception next morning, but the laird was too happy for concealment. Before the door closed on the good-night of the ladies, he had disclosed the secret, and before we reached the top of the stairs, the gentlemen were scampering at our heels like a pack of hounds in full cry.

Here are at random some extracts from the others :—

Mr. Jeffrey now inquired what the people in her part of the country thought of the trial of the Queen. She could not tell him, but she would say what she herself had remarked on siclike proceedings : " Tak' a wreath of snaw, let it be never so white, and wash it through clean water, it will no come out so pure as it gaed in, far less the dirty dubs the poor Queen has been drawn through."

Mr. Russell inquired if she possessed any relics of Prince Charles from the time he used to spin with the lasses :—

" Yes," she said, " I have a *flech* that loupit aff him upon my aunty, the Lady Brax, when she was helping him on wi' his short-gown; my aunty rowed it up in a sheet of white paper, and she keepit it in the tea canister, and she ca'd it aye the King's Flech; and the laird, honest man, when he wanted a cup of gude tea, sought aye a cup of the *Prince's mixture*." This produced peals of laughter, and her ladyship laughed as heartily as any of them. When somewhat composed again, she looked across the table to Mr. Clerk, and offered to let him see it. " It is now set on the pivot of my watch, and a' the warks gae round the *flech* in place of turning on a diamond."

Lord Gillies thought this flight would certainly betray her, and remarked to Mr. Clerk that the flea must be painted on the watch, but Mr. Clerk said he had known of relics being kept of the Prince quite as extraordinary as a flea ; that Mr. Murray of Simprim has a pocket-handkerchief in which Prince Charles had blown his nose.

The Lady Pitlyal said her daughter did not value

these things, and that she was resolved to leave it as a legacy to the Antiquarian Society.

Holmehead was rather amused with her originality, though he had not forgotten the attack. He said he would try if she was a real Jacobite, and he called out, " Madam, I am going to propose a toast for ye !

" May the Scotch Thistle choke the Hanoverian Horse."

" I wish I binna among the Whigs," she said.

" And whare wad ye be sae weel?" retorted he.

" They murdered Dundee's son at Glasgow."

" There was nae great skaith," he replied; " but ye maun drink my toast in a glass of this cauld punch, if ye be a true Jacobite."

" Aweel, aweel," said the Lady Pitlyal; " as my auld friend Lady Christian Bruce was wont to say, ' The best way to get the better of temptation is just to yield to it;'" and as she nodded to the toast and emptied the glass, Holmehead swore exultingly— " *Faith, she's true !*"

Supper passed over, and the carriages were announced. The Lady Pitlyal took her leave with Mrs. Gillies.

Next day the town rang with the heiress of Pitlyal. Mr. W. Clerk said he had never met with such an extraordinary old lady, " for not only is she amusing herself, but my brother John is like to expire, when I relate her stories at second-hand."

He talked of nothing else for a week after, but the heiress, and the flea, and the rent-roll, and the old turreted house of Pitlyal, till at last his friends thought it would be right to undeceive him; but that was not so easily done, for when the Lord Chief-Commissioner Adam hinted that it might be Miss Stirling, he said that was impossible, for Miss Stirling was sitting by the old lady the whole of the evening.

Here is a bit of Sir Walter—

Turning to Sir Walter, " I am sure you had our

laird in your e'e when you drew the character of Monkbarns."

"No," replied Sir Walter, "but I had in my eye a very old and respected friend of my own, and one with whom, I dare say you, Mrs. Arbuthnott, were acquainted—the late Mr. George Constable of Wallace, near Dundee."

"I kenned him weel," said Mrs. Arbuthnott, "and his twa sisters that lived wi' him, Jean and Christian, and I've been in the blue-chamber of his *Hospitium;* but I think," she continued, "our laird is the likest to Monkbarns o' the twa. He's at the Antiquarian Society the night, presenting a great curiosity that was found in a quarry of mica slate in the hill at the back of Balwylie. He's sair taken up about it, and puzzled to think what substance it may be; but James Dalgetty, wha's never at a loss either for the name or the nature of onything under the sun, says it's just Noah's auld wig that blew aff yon time he put his head out of the window of the ark to look after his corbie messenger."

James Dalgetty and his opinion gave subject of much merriment to the company, but Doctor Coventry thought there was nothing so very ludicrous in the remark, for in that kind of slate there are frequently substances found resembling hairs.

Lord Gillies presented Doctor Coventry to Mrs. Arbuthnott, as the well-known professor of agriculture, and they entered on a conversation respecting soils. She described those of Balwylie, and the particular properties of the *Surroch Park*, which James Dalgetty curses every time it's spoken about, and says, "it greets a' winter, and girns a' simmer."

The doctor rubbed his hands with delight, and said that was the most perfect description of cold wet land he had ever heard of; and Sir Walter expressed a wish to cultivate the acquaintance of James Dalgetty, and extorted a promise from Mrs. Arbuthnott that she would visit Abbotsford, and bring James with her. "I have a James Dalgetty of my own," continued Sir Walter, "that governs me just as yours does you."

Lady Ann and Mr. Wharton Duff and their daughter were announced, and introduced to Mrs. Arbuthnott.

At ten, Sir Walter and Miss Scott took leave, with a promise that they should visit each other, and bending down to the ear of Mrs. Arbuthnott, Sir Walter addressed her in these words: "Awa! awa! the deil's ower grit wi' you."

And now are we not all the better for this pleasantry? so womanly, so genial, so rich, and so without a sting,—such a true diversion, with none of the sin of effort or of mere cleverness; and how it takes us into the midst of the strong-brained and strong-hearted men and women of that time! what an atmosphere of sense and good breeding and kindliness! And then the Scotch! cropping out everywhere as blithe and expressive and unexpected as a gowan or sweetbriar rose, with an occasional thistle, sturdy, erect, and bristling with *Nemo me*. Besides the deeper and general interest of these *Mystifications*, in their giving, as far as I know, a unique specimen of true personation—distinct from acting—I think it a national good to let our youngsters read, and, as it were, hear the language which our gentry and judges and men of letters spoke not long ago, and into which such books as Dean Ramsay's and this are breathing the breath of its old life. Was there ever anything better or so good, said of a stiff clay, than that it "girns (grins) a' simmer, and greets (weeps) a' winter"?

'OH, I'M WAT, WAT!'

The father of the Rev. Mr. Steven of Largs, was the son of a farmer, who lived next farm to Mossgiel. When a boy of eight, he found " Robbie," who was a great friend of his, and of all the children, engaged digging a large trench in a field, Gilbert, his brother, with him. The boy pausing on the edge of the trench, and looking down upon Burns, said " Robbie, what's that ye're doin'?" " Howkin' a muckle hole, Tammie." " What for?" " To bury the Deil in, Tammie!" (one can fancy how those eyes would glow.) " A'but, Robbie," said the logical Tammie, " hoo 're ye to get him in?" " Ay," said Burns, " that's it, hoo are we to get him in!" and went off into shouts of laughter; and every now and then during that summer day shouts would come from that hole, as the idea came over him. If one could only have daguerreotyped his day's fancies!

'OH, I'M WAT, WAT!'

"WHAT is love, Mary?" said Seventeen to Thirteen, who was busy with her English lessons.

"Love! what do you mean, John?"

"I mean, what's love?"

"Love's just love, I suppose."

(Yes, Mary, you are right to keep by the concrete; analysis kills love as well as other things. I once asked a useful-information young lady what her mother was. "Oh, mamma's a *biped!*" I turned in dismay to her younger sister, and said, "What do you say?" "Oh, my mother's just my mother.")

"But what part of speech is it?"

"It's a substantive or a verb." (Young Horne Tooke didn't ask her if it was an active or passive, an irregular or defective verb; an inceptive, as *calesco*, I grow warm, or *dulcesco*, I grow sweet; a frequentative or a desiderative, as *nupturio*, I desire to marry.)

"I think it is a verb," said John, who was deep in other diversions, besides those of Purley; "and I think it must have been originally *the Perfect of Live*, like thrive throve, strive strove."

"Capital, John!" suddenly growled Uncle Old-buck, who was supposed to be asleep in his arm-chair by the fireside, and who snubbed and supported the entire household. "It was that originally, and it will be our own faults, children, if it is not that at last, as well as, ay, and more than at first. What does Richardson say, John? read him out." John reads—

327

LOVE, *v. s.*	To prefer, to desire, as an
-LESS.	object of possession or enjoy-
-LY, *ad. av.*	ment ; to delight in, to be
-LILY.	pleased or gratified with, to
-LINESS.	take pleasure or gratification
-ER.	in, delight in.
-ING.	*Love*, the *s* is app. emph. to
-INGLY.	the passion between the sexes.
-INGNESS.	*Lover* is, by old writers, app.
-ABLE.[1]	as *friend*—by male to male.
-SOME.[2]	*Love* is much used—pref.
ERED.[3]	[1] *Wiclif.* [2] *Chaucer.* [3] *Shak.*

Love-locks,—locks (of hair) to set off the beauty ; the loveliness.

A. S. *Luf-ian*; D. *Lie-ven*; Ger. *-ben*, amare, diligere. Wach. derives from *lieb*, bonum, because every one desires that which is good : *lieb*, it is more probable, is from *lieb-en*, grateful, and therefore *good*. It may at least admit a conjecture that A. S. *Luf-ian*, to love, has a reason for its application similar to that of L. *Di-ligere* (*legere*, to gather), to take up or out (of a number), to choose, sc. one in preference to another, to prefer ; and that it is formed upon A. S. *Hlif-ian*, to lift or take up, to pick up, to select, to prefer. Be- Over- Un-

Uncle impatiently.—" Stuff ; ' grateful !' ' pick up !' stuff ! These word-mongers know nothing about it. Live, love ; that is it, the perfect of live." [1]

After this, Uncle sent the cousins to their beds. Mary's mother was in hers, never to rise from it again. She was a widow, and Mary was her husband's niece. The house quiet, Uncle sat down in his chair, put his feet on the fender, and watched the dying fire ; it had a rich central glow, but no flame, and no smoke, it was flashing up fitfully, and bit by bit falling in. He fell asleep watching it, and when he slept, he dreamed. He was young ; he was seventeen ; he was prowling about the head of North St. David Street, keeping his eye on a certain door,—

---

[1] They are strange beings, these lexicographers. Richardson, for instance, under the word SNAIL, gives this quotation from Beaumont and Fletcher's *Wit at Several Weapons,*

" Oh, Master Pompey ! how is't, man ?
Clown—SNAILS, I'm almost starved with love and cold, and one thing or other."

Any one else knows of course that it is " 's nails "—the contraction of the old oath or interjection—*God's nails.*

we call them common stairs in Scotland. He was
waiting for Mr. White's famous English class for
girls coming out. Presently out rushed four or five
girls, wild and laughing; then came one, bounding
like a roe:

> " Such eyes were in her head,
> And so much grace and power!"

She was surrounded by the rest, and away they
went laughing, she making them always laugh the
more. Seventeen followed at a safe distance, studying
her small, firm, downright heel. The girls dropped
off one by one, and she was away home by herself,
swift and reserved. He, impostor as he was, disappeared through Jamaica Street, to reappear and meet
her, walking as if on urgent business, and getting a
cordial and careless nod. This beautiful girl of
thirteen was afterwards the mother of our Mary, and
died in giving her birth. She was Uncle Oldbuck's
first and only sweetheart; and here was he, the only
help our young Horne Tooke, and his mother and
Mary had. Uncle awoke, the fire dead, and the room
cold. He found himself repeating Lady John Scott's
lines—

> " When thou art near me,
>   Sorrow seems to fly,
> And then I think, as well I may,
> That on this earth there is no one
>   More blest than I.
>
> But when thou leav'st me,
>   Doubts and fears arise,
> And darkness reigns,
>   Where all before was light.
>
> The sunshine of my soul
>   Is in those eyes,
> And when they leave me
>   All the world is night.
>
> But when thou art near me,
>   Sorrow seems to fly,
> And then I feel, as well I may,
> That on this earth there dwells not one
>   So blest as I." [1]

[1] Can the gifted author of these lines and of their music
not be prevailed on to give them and others to the world, as
well as to her friends?

Then taking down *Chambers's Scottish Songs*, he read aloud :—

> " O I'm wat, wat,
>   O I'm wat and weary;
>   Yet fain wad I rise and rin,
>   If I thocht I would meet my dearie.
>   Aye waukin', O !
>   Waukin' aye, and weary;
>   Sleep, I can get nane
>   For thinkin' o' my dearie.
>
> Simmer's a pleasant time,
>   Flowers o' every colour;
> The winter rins ower the heugh,
>   And I long for my true lover.
>
> When I sleep I dream,
>   When I wauk I'm eerie,
> Sleep I can get nane,
>   For thinkin' o' my dearie.
>
> Lanely nicht comes on,
>   A' the lave are sleepin';
> I think on my true love,
>   And blear my e'en wi' greetin'.
>
> Feather beds are saft—
>   Pentit rooms are bonnie ;
> But ae kiss o' my dear love
>   Better 's far than ony.
>
> O for Friday nicht !—
>   Friday at the gloamin';
> O for Friday nicht—
>   Friday's lang o' comin' !"

This love-song, which Mr. Chambers gives from recitation, is, thinks Uncle to himself, all but perfect; Burns, who in almost every instance, not only adorned, but transformed and purified whatever of the old he touched, breathing into it his own tenderness and strength, fails here, as may be seen in reading his version.

> " Oh, spring's a pleasant time !
>   Flowers o' every colour—
>   *The sweet bird builds her nest,*
>   And I lang for my lover.
>   Aye wakin', oh !
>   Wakin' aye and *wearie;*
>   Sleep I can get nane,
>   For thinkin' o' my dearie !

When I sleep I dream,
  When I wauk I'm eerie,
Rest I canna get,
  For thinkin' o' my dearie.
Aye wakin', oh!
  Wakin' aye and weary;
Come, come, blissful dream,
  Bring me to my dearie.

Darksome nicht comes doun—
  A' the lave are sleepin';
I think on my kind lad,
  And blin' my een wi' greetin'.
Aye wakin', oh!
  Wakin' aye and wearie;
Hope is sweet, but ne'er
  Sae sweet as my dearie!"

How weak these italics! No one can doubt which of these is the better. The old song is perfect in the procession, and in the simple beauty of its thoughts and words. A ploughman or shepherd—for I hold that it is a man's song—comes in " wat, wat " after a hard day's work among the furrows, or on the hill. The *watness* of wat, wat, is as much wetter than wet as a Scotch mist is more of a mist than an English one; and he is not only wat, wat, but "weary," longing for a dry skin and a warm bed and rest; but no sooner said and felt, than, by the law of contrast, he thinks on " Mysie " or " Ailie," his Genevieve; and then " all thoughts, all passions, all delights," begin to stir him, and " fain wad I rise and rin (what a swiftness beyond run is " rin "!) Love now makes him a poet; the true imaginative power enters and takes possession of him. By this time his clothes are off, and he is snug in bed; not a wink can he sleep; that " fain " is domineering over him,—and he breaks out into what is as genuine passion and poetry, as anything from Sappho to Tennyson—abrupt, vivid, heedless of syntax. " Simmer's a pleasant time." Would any of our greatest geniuses, being limited to one word, have done better than take " pleasant "? and then the fine vagueness of " time !" " Flowers o' every colour;" he gets a glimpse of

"herself a fairer flower," and is off in pursuit.
"The water rins ower the heugh" (a steep precipice);
flinging itself wildly, passionately over, and so do I
long for my true lover. Nothing can be simpler and
finer than

> "When I sleep, I dream;
>   When I wauk, I'm eerie."

"Lanely nicht;" how much richer and touching than
"darksome." "Feather beds are saft;" "paintit
rooms are bonnie;" I would infer from this, that his
"dearie," his "true love," was a lass up at "the
big house"—a dapper Abigail possibly—at Sir
William's at the Castle, and then we have the final
paroxysm upon Friday nicht—Friday at the gloamin'!
O for Friday nicht!—Friday's lang o' comin'!—it
being very like Thursday before daybreak, when
this affectionate *ululatus* ended in repose.

Now, is not this rude ditty, made very likely by
some clumsy, big-headed Galloway herd, full of the
real stuff of love? He does not go off upon her eye-
brows, or even her eyes; he does not sit down, and in
a genteel way announce that "love in thine eyes for
ever sits," &c. &c., or that her feet look out from
under her petticoats like little mice : he is far past
that; he is not making love, he is in it. This is one
and a chief charm of Burns' love-songs, which are
certainly of all love-songs except those wild snatches
left to us by her who flung herself from the Leucadian
rock, the most in earnest, the tenderest, the "most
moving delicate and full of life." Burns makes you
feel the reality and the depth, the truth of his passion :
it is not her eyelashes or her nose, or her dimple, or
even

> "A mole cinque-spotted, like the crimson drops
>   I' the bottom of a cowslip,"

that are "winging the fervour of his love;" not even
her soul; it is herself. This concentration and earnestness, this *perfervor* of our Scottish love poetry,
seems to me to contrast curiously with the light,

trifling philandering of the English; indeed, as far as
I remember, we have almost no love-songs in English,
of the same class as this one, or those of Burns.
They are mostly either of the genteel, or of the
nautical (some of these capital), or of the comic
school. Do you know the most perfect, the finest
love song in our or in any language; the love being
affectionate more than passionate, love in possession
not in pursuit?

> " Oh, wert thou in the cauld blast
>   On yonder lea, on yonder lea,
> My plaidie to the angry airt,
>   I'd shelter thee, I'd shelter thee :
> Or did Misfortune's bitter storms
>   Around thee blaw, around thee blaw,
> Thy bield should be my bosom,
>   To share it a', to share it a'.
>
> Or were I in the wildest waste,
>   Sae black and bare, sae black and bare,
> The desert were a paradise,
>   If thou wert there, if thou wert there :
> Or were I monarch o' the globe,
>   Wi' thee to reign, wi' thee to reign,
> The brightest jewel in my crown
>   Wad be my queen, wad be my queen."

The following is Mr. Chambers' account of the
origin of this song :—Jessy Lewars had a call one
morning from Burns. He offered, if she would play
him any tune of which she was fond, and for which
she desired new verses, that he would do his best to
gratify her wish. She sat down at the piano, and
played over and over the air of an old song, beginning
with the words—

> " The robin cam' to the wren's nest,
>   And keekit in, and keekit in :
> ' O weel's me on your auld pow !
>   Wad ye be in, wad ye be in?
> Ye'se ne'er get leave to lie without,
>   And I within, and I within,
> As lang's I hae an auld clout,
>   To row ye in, to row ye in.' "

Uncle now took his candle, and slunk off to bed,

slipping up noiselessly that he might not disturb the thin sleep of the sufferer, saying in to himself—" I'd shelter thee, I'd shelter thee;" " If thou wert there, if thou wert there;" and though the morning was at the window, he was up by eight, making breakfast for John and Mary.

Love never faileth; but whether there be prophecies, they shall fail; whether there be tongues, they shall cease; whether there be knowledge, it shall vanish away; but love is of God, and cannot fail.

ARTHUR H. HALLAM

" Præsens *imperfectum,—perfectum, plusquam perfectum*
Futurum."—Grotius.

> " The idea of thy life shall sweetly creep
> Into my study of imagination;
> And every lovely organ of thy life
> Shall come apparelled in more precious habit—
> More moving delicate, and full of life,
> Into the eye and prospect of my soul,
> Than when thou lived'st indeed."—
>
> Much Ado about Nothing.

ARTHUR H. HALLAM

In the chancel of Clevedon Church, Somersetshire, rest the mortal remains of Arthur Henry Hallam, eldest son of our great philosophic historian and critic, —and the friend to whom "*In Memoriam*" is sacred. This place was selected by his father, not only from the connection of kindred, being the burial-place of his maternal grandfather, Sir Abraham Elton, but likewise "on account of its still and sequestered situation, on a lone hill that overhangs the Bristol Channel." That lone hill, with its humble old church, its outlook over the waste of waters, where "the stately ships go on," was, we doubt not, in Tennyson's mind, when the poem, "Break, break, break," which contains the burden of that volume in which are enshrined so much of the deepest affection, poetry, philosophy, and godliness, rose into his "study of imagination"—"into the eye and prospect of his soul." [1]

[1] The passage from Shakspere prefixed to this paper, contains probably as much as can be said of the mental, not less than the affectionate conditions, under which such a record as *In Memoriam* is produced, and may give us more insight into the imaginative faculty's mode of working, than all our philosophizing and analysis. It seems to let out with the fulness, simplicity, and unconsciousness of a child—"Fancy's Child" —the secret mechanism or procession of the greatest creative mind our race has produced. In itself, it has no recondite meaning, it answers fully its own sweet purpose. We are not believers, like some folks, in the omniscience of even Shakspeare. But like many things that he and other wise men and many simple children say, it has a germ of universal meaning, which it is quite lawful to bring out of it, and which may be enjoyed to the full without any wrong to its own original beauty and fitness. A dew-drop is not the less beautiful that it illustrates in its structure the law of gravitation which holds the world together, and by which "the most ancient heavens are fresh and strong." This is the passage.

" Break, break, break,
      On thy cold grey stones, O sea !
And I would that my tongue could utter
      The thoughts that arise in me.

O well for the fisherman's boy
      That he shouts with his sister at play !
O well for the sailor lad
      That he sings in his boat on the bay !

And the stately ships go on
      To their haven under the hill !
But O for the touch of a vanish'd hand,
      And the sound of a voice that is still !

Break, break, break,
      At the foot of thy crags, O sea !
But the tender grace of a day that is dead
      Will never come back to me."

The Friar speaking of Claudio, hearing that Hero " died upon
his word," says,—

> "The idea of her life shall sweetly creep
> Into his study of imagination ;
> And every lovely organ of her life
> Shall come apparelled in more precious habit—
> More moving delicate, and full of life,
> Into the eye and prospect of his soul,
> Than when she lived indeed."

We have here expressed in plain language the imaginative
memory of the beloved dead, rising upon the past, like moonlight upon midnight,—

> " The gleam, the shadow, and the peace supreme."

This is its simple meaning—the statement of a truth, the
utterance of personal feeling. But observe its hidden abstract
significance—it is the revelation of what goes on in the
depths of the soul, when the dead elements of what once was,
are laid before the imagination, and so breathed upon as to
be quickened into a new and higher life. We have first the
Idea of her Life—all he remembered and felt of her, gathered
into one vague shadowy image, not any one look, or action,
or time—then the idea of her life *creeps*—is in before he is
aware, and SWEETLY creeps,—it might have been softly or
gently, but it is the addition of affection to all this, and bringing in another sense—and now it is in his *study of imagination*
—what a place ! fit for such a visitor. Then out comes the
Idea, more particular, more questionable, but still ideal,
spiritual,—*every lovely organ of her life*—then the clothing
upon, the mortal putting on its immortal, spiritual body—
*shall come apparelled in more precious habit, more moving
delicate*—this is the transfiguring, the putting on strength, the
poco più—the little more which makes immortal,—*more full
of life,* and all this submitted to—*the eye and prospect of the
soul.*

Out of these few simple words, deep and melancholy, and sounding as the sea, as out of a well of the living waters of love, flows forth all *In Memoriam*, as a stream flows out of its spring—all is here. "I would that my tongue could utter the thoughts that arise in me,"—"the touch of the vanished hand— the sound of the voice that is still,"—the body and soul of his friend. Rising as it were out of the midst of the gloom of the valley of the shadow of death,

> "The mountain infant to the sun comes forth
> Like human life from darkness;"

and how its waters flow on! carrying life, beauty, magnificence,—shadows and happy lights, depths of blackness, depths clear as the very body of heaven. How it deepens as it goes, involving larger interests, wider views, "thoughts that wander through eternity," greater affections, but still retaining its pure living waters, its unforgotten burden of love and sorrow. How it visits every region! "the long unlovely street," pleasant villages and farms, "the placid ocean-plains," waste howling wildernesses, grim woods, *nemorumque noctem*, informed with spiritual fears, where may be seen, if shapes they may be called—

> "Fear and trembling Hope,
> Silence and Foresight; Death the Skeleton,
> And Time the Shadow;"

now within hearing of the Minster clock, now of the College bells, and the vague hum of the mighty city. And over head through all its course the heaven with its clouds, its sun, moon, and stars; but always, and in all places, declaring its source; and even when laying its burden of manifold and faithful affection at the feet of the Almighty Father, still remembering whence it came,

> "That friend of mine who lives in God,
> That God which ever lives and loves;
> One God, one law, one element,
> And one far-off divine event,
> To which the whole creation moves."

It is to that chancel, and to the day, 3rd January, 1834, that he refers in poem XVIII. of *In Memoriam*.

> " 'Tis well, 'tis something, we may stand
>   Where he in English earth is laid,
>   And from his ashes may be made
> The violet of his native land.
>
> 'Tis little; but it looks in truth
>   As if the quiet bones were blest
>   Among familiar names to rest,
> And in the places of his youth."

And again in XIX. :

> " The Danube to the Severn gave
>   The darken'd heart that beat no more;
>   They laid him by the pleasant shore,
> And in the hearing of the wave.
>
> There twice a day the Severn fills,
>   The salt sea-water passes by,
>   And hushes half the babbling Wye,
> And makes a silence in the hills."

Here, too, it is, LXVI. :

> When on my bed the moonlight falls,
>   I know that in thy place of rest,
>   By that broad water of the west;
> There comes a glory on the walls:
>
> Thy marble bright in dark appears,
>   As slowly steals a silver flame
>   Along the letters of thy name,
> And o'er the number of thy years."

This young man, whose memory his friend has consecrated in the hearts of all who can be touched by such love and beauty, was in no wise unworthy of all this. It is not for us to say, for it was not given to us the sad privilege to know, all that a father's heart buried with his son in that grave, all " the hopes of unaccomplished years;" nor can we feel in its fulness all that is meant by

> " Such
> A friendship as had mastered Time;
> Which masters Time indeed, and is
>   Eternal, separate from fears.
>   The all-assuming months and years
> Can take no part away from this."

But this we may say, we know of nothing in all literature to compare with the volume from which these
lines are taken, since David lamented with this
lamentation : " The beauty of Israel is slain.   Ye
mountains of Gilboa, let there be no dew, neither rain
upon you.   I am distressed for thee, my brother
Jonathan : very pleasant hast thou been unto me;
thy love for me was wonderful."   We cannot, as some
have done, compare it with Shakspere's Sonnets,
or with *Lycidas*.   In spite of the amazing genius and
tenderness, the never-wearying, all-involving reiter-
ation of passionate attachment, the idolatry of admiring love, the rapturous devotedness, displayed in
these sonnets, we cannot but agree with Mr. Hallam
in thinking, " that there is a tendency now, especially
among young men of poetical tempers, to exaggerate
the beauties of these remarkable productions;" and
though we would hardly say with him, " that it is
impossible not to wish that Shakspere had never
written them," giving us, as they do, and as perhaps
nothing else could do, such proof of a power of
loving, of an amount of *attendrissement*, which is not
less wonderful than the bodying forth of that myriad-
mind, which gave us Hamlet, and Lear, Cordelia,
and Puck, and all the rest, and indeed explaining to
us how he could give us all these ;—while we hardly
go so far, we agree with his other wise words :—
" There is a weakness and folly in all misplaced and
excessive affection;" which in Shakspere's case is
the more distressing, when we consider that " Mr.
W. H., the only begetter of these ensuing sonnets,"
was, in all likelihood, William Herbert, Earl of
Pembroke, a man of noble and gallant character, but
always of licentious life.

As for *Lycidas*, we must confess that the poetry—
and we all know how consummate it is—and not the
affection, seems uppermost in Milton's mind, as it
is in ours.   The other element, though quick and
true, has no glory through reason of the excellency
of that which invests it.   But there is no such draw-

back in *In Memoriam*. The purity, the temperate
but fervent goodness, the firmness and depth of
nature, the impassioned logic, the large, sensitive,
and liberal heart, the reverence and godly fear, of

> "That friend of mine who lives in God,"

which from these Remains we know to have dwelt
in that young soul, give to *In Memoriam* the character of exactest portraiture. There is no excessive or
misplaced affection here; it is all founded in fact:
while everywhere and throughout it all, affection—
a love that is wonderful—meets us first and leaves us
last, giving form and substance and grace, and the
breath of life and love, to everything that the poet's
thick-coming fancies so exquisitely frame. We can
recall few poems approaching to it in this quality of
sustained affection. The only English poems we can
think of as of the same order, are Cowper's lines on
seeing his mother's portrait:—

> "O that those lips had language!"

Burns' "To Mary in Heaven;" and two pieces of
Vaughan—one beginning

> "O thou who know'st for whom I mourn;"

and the other—

> "They are all gone into the world of light."

But our object now is, not so much to illustrate Mr.
Tennyson's verses, as to introduce to our readers,
what we ourselves have got so much delight, and
we trust, profit from—*The Remains, in Verse and
Prose, of Arthur Henry Hallam*, 1834; privately
printed. We had for many years been searching
for this volume, but in vain; a sentence quoted
by Henry Taylor struck us, and our desire was
quickened by reading *In Memoriam*. We do not
remember when we have been more impressed than
by these Remains of this young man, especially when
taken along with his friend's Memorial; and instead

of trying to tell our readers what this impression is, we have preferred giving them as copious extracts as our space allows, that they may judge and enjoy for themselves. The italics are our own. We can promise them few finer, deeper, and better pleasures than reading, and detaining their minds over these two books together, filling their hearts with the fulness of their truth and tenderness. They will see how accurate as well as how affectionate and " of imagination all compact " Tennyson is, and how worthy of all that he has said of him, that friend was. The likeness is drawn *ad vivum*,

> " When to the sessions of sweet silent thought
> He summons up remembrance of things past."

" The idea of his Life " has been sown a natural body, and has been raised a spiritual body, but the identity is unhurt; the countenance shines and the raiment is white and glistering, but it is the same face and form.

The Memoir is by Mr. Hallam. We give it entire, not knowing anywhere a nobler or more touching record of a father's love and sorrow.

" Arthur Henry Hallam was born in Bedford Place,[1] London, on the 1st of February, 1811. Very few years had elapsed before his parents observed strong indications of his future character, in a peculiar clearness of perception, a facility of acquiring knowledge, and, above all, in an undeviating sweetness of disposition, and adherence to his sense of what was right and becoming. As he advanced to another stage of childhood, it was rendered still more manifest that he would be distinguished from ordinary persons, by an increasing thoughtfulness, and a fondness for a class of books, which in general are

---

[1] " Dark house, by which once more I stand
Here in the long unlovely street;
Doors, where my heart was wont to beat
So quickly, waiting for a hand."
In Memoriam.

so little intelligible to boys of his age, that they excite in them no kind of interest.

" In the summer of 1818 he spent some months with his parents in Germany and Switzerland, and became familiar with the French language, which he had already learned to read with facility. He had gone through the elements of Latin before this time; but that language having been laid aside during his tour, it was found upon his return that, a variety of new scenes having effaced it from his memory, it was necessary to begin again with the first rudiments. He was nearly eight years old at this time; and in little more than twelve months he could read Latin with tolerable facility. In this period his mind was developing itself more rapidly than before; he now felt a keen relish for dramatic poetry, and wrote several tragedies, if we may so call them, either in prose or verse, with a more precocious display of talents than the Editor remembers to have met with in any other individual. The natural pride, however, of his parents, did not blind them to the uncertainty that belongs to all premature efforts of the mind; and they so carefully avoided everything like a boastful display of blossoms which, in many cases, have withered away in barren luxuriance, that the circumstance of these compositions was hardly ever mentioned out of their own family.

" In the spring of 1820, Arthur was placed under the Rev. W. Carmalt, at Putney, where he remained nearly two years. After leaving this school, he went abroad again for some months; and in October 1822, became the pupil of the Rev. E. C. Hawtrey, an Assistant Master of Eton College. At Eton he continued till the summer of 1827. He was now become a good though not perhaps a first-rate scholar in the Latin and Greek languages. The loss of time, relatively to this object, in travelling, but far more his increasing avidity for a different kind of knowledge, and the strong bent of his mind to subjects which exercise other faculties than such as the acquirement

of languages calls into play, will sufficiently account
for what might seem a comparative deficiency in
classical learning. It can only, however, be reckoned
one, comparatively to his other attainments, and to
his remarkable facility in mastering the modern languages. The Editor has thought it not improper to
print in the following pages an Eton exercise, which,
as written before the age of fourteen, though not
free from metrical and other errors, appears, perhaps
to a partial judgment, far above the level of such
compositions. It is remarkable that he should have
selected the story of Ugolino, from a poet with whom,
and with whose language, he was then but very
slightly acquainted, but who was afterwards to
become, more perhaps than any other, the master-
mover of his spirit. It may be added, that great
judgment and taste are perceptible in this translation, which is by no means a literal one; and in which
the phraseology of Sophocles is not ill substituted, in
some passages, for that of Dante.

" The Latin poetry of an Etonian is generally
reckoned at that School the chief test of his literary
talent. That of Arthur was good without being excellent; he never wanted depth of thought, or truth
of feeling; but it is only in a few rare instances, if
altogether in any, that an original mind has been
known to utter itself freely and vigorously, without
sacrifice of purity, in a language the capacities of
which are so imperfectly understood; and in his productions there was not the thorough conformity to
an ancient model which is required for perfect
elegance in Latin verse. He took no great pleasure
in this sort of composition; and perhaps never returned to it of his own accord.

" In the latter part of his residence at Eton, he
was led away more and more by the predominant bias
of his mind, from the exclusive study of ancient literature. The poets of England, especially the older
dramatists, came with greater attraction over his
spirit. He loved Fletcher, and some of Fletcher's

contemporaries, for their energy of language and intenseness of feeling; but it was in Shakspere alone that he found the fulness of soul which seemed to slake the thirst of his own rapidly expanding genius from an inexhaustible fountain of thought and emotion.   He knew Shakspere thoroughly; and indeed his acquaintance with the earlier poetry of this country was very extensive.   Among the modern poets, Byron was at this time, far above the rest, and almost exclusively, his favourite; a preference which, in later years, he transferred altogether to Wordsworth and Shelley.

" He became, when about fifteen years old, a member of the debating society established among the elder boys, in which he took great interest; and this served to confirm the bias of his intellect towards the moral and political philosophy of modern times.   It was probably, however, of important utility in giving him that command of his own language which he possessed, as the following Essays will show, in a very superior degree, and in exercising those powers of argumentative discussion, which now displayed themselves as eminently characteristic of his mind. It was a necessary consequence that he declined still more from the usual paths of study, and abated perhaps somewhat of his regard for the writers of antiquity.   It must not be understood, nevertheless, as most of those who read these pages will be aware, that he ever lost his sensibility to those ever-living effusions of genius which the ancient languages preserve.   He loved Æschylus and Sophocles (to Euripides he hardly did justice), Lucretius and Virgil; if he did not seem so much drawn towards Homer as might at first be expected, this may probably be accounted for by his increasing taste for philosophical poetry.

" In the early part of 1827, Arthur took a part in the Eton Miscellany, a periodical publication, in which some of his friends in the debating society were concerned.   He wrote in this, besides a few papers in prose, a little poem on a story connected with the Lake of Killarney. It has not been thought by the Editor advisable, upon the whole, to reprint these lines; though, in his opinion, they bear very striking marks of superior powers. This was almost the first poetry that Arthur had written, except the childish tragedies above mentioned. No one was ever less inclined to the trick of versifying. Poetry with him was not an amusement, but the natural and almost necessary language of genuine emotion; and it was not till the discipline of serious reflection, and the approach of manhood, gave a reality and intenseness to such emotions, that he learned the capacities of his own genius. That he was a poet by nature, these remains will sufficiently prove; but certainly he was far removed from being a versifier by nature; nor was he probably able to perform, what he scarce ever attempted, to write easily and elegantly on an ordinary subject. The lines on the story of Pygmalion, are so far an exception, that they arose out of a momentary amusement of society; but he could not avoid, even in these, his own grave tone of poetry.

" Upon leaving Eton in the summer of 1827, he accompanied his parents to the Continent, and passed eight months in Italy. This introduction to new scenes of nature and art, and to new sources of intellectual delight, at the very period of transition from boyhood to youth, sealed no doubt the peculiar character of his mind, and taught him, too soon for his peace, to sound those depths of thought and feeling, from which, after this time, all that he wrote was derived. He had, when he passed the Alps, only a moderate acquaintance with the Italian language; but during his residence in the country he came to speak it with perfect fluency, and with a pure Sienese pronunciation. In its study he was much assisted by his friend and instructor, the Abbate Pifferi, who encouraged him to his first attempts at versification. The few sonnets, which are now printed, were, it is to be remembered, written by a foreigner, hardly seventeen years old, and after a very short stay in Italy. The Editor might not, probably, have suffered them to appear, even in this private manner, upon his own judgment. But he knew that the greatest living writer of Italy, to whom they were shown some time since at Milan, by the author's excellent friend, Mr. Richard Milnes, has expressed himself in terms of high approbation.

" The growing intimacy of Arthur with Italian poetry led him naturally to that of Dante. No poet was so congenial to the character of his own reflective mind; in none other could he so abundantly find that disdain of flowery redundance, that perpetual reference of the sensible to the ideal, that aspiration for somewhat better and less fleeting than earthly things, to which his inmost soul responded. Like all genuine worshippers of the great Florentine poet, he rated the *Inferno* below the two later portions of the *Divina Commedia;* there was nothing even to revolt his taste, but rather much to attract it, in the scholastic theology and mystic visions of the *Paradiso.* Petrarch he greatly admired, though with less idolatry than Dante; and the sonnets here printed will show to all competent judges how fully he had imbibed the spirit, without servile centonism, of the best writers in that style of composition who flourished in the 16th century.

" But poetry was not an absorbing passion at this time in his mind. His eyes were fixed on the best pictures with silent intense delight. He had a deep and just perception of what was beautiful in this art, at least in its higher schools; for he did not pay much regard, or perhaps quite do justice, to the masters of the 17th century. To technical criticism he made no sort of pretension; painting was to him but the visible language of emotion; and where it did not aim at exciting it, or employed inadequate means, his admiration would be withheld. Hence he highly prized the ancient paintings, both Italian and German, of the age which preceded the full development of art. But he was almost as enthusiastic an admirer of the Venetian, as of the Tuscan and Roman schools; considering these masters as reaching the same end by the different agencies of form and colour. This predilection for the sensitive beauties of painting is somewhat analogous to his fondness for harmony of verse, on which he laid more stress than poets so thoughtful are apt to do. In one of the last days of his life, he lingered long among the fine Venetian pictures of the Imperial Gallery at Vienna.

" He returned to England in June 1828; and, in the following October went down to reside at Cambridge; having been entered on the boards of Trinity College before his departure to the Continent. He was the pupil of the Rev. William Whewell. In some respects, as soon became manifest, he was not formed to obtain great academical reputation. An acquaintance with the learned languages, considerable at the school where he was educated, but not improved, to say the least, by the intermission of a year, during which his mind had been so occupied by other pursuits, that he had thought little of antiquity even in Rome itself, though abundantly sufficient for the gratification of taste and the acquisition of knowledge, was sure to prove inadequate to the searching scrutiny of modern examinations. He soon, therefore, saw reason to renounce all competition of this kind; nor did he ever so much as attempt any Greek or Latin composition during his stay at Cambridge. In truth, he was very indifferent to success of this kind; and conscious as he must have been of a high reputation among his contemporaries, he could not think that he stood in need of any University distinctions. The Editor became by degrees almost equally indifferent to what he perceived to be so uncongenial to Arthur's mind. It was however to be regretted, that he never paid the least attention to mathematical studies. That he should not prosecute them with the diligence usual at Cambridge, was of course to be expected; yet his clearness and acumen would certainly have enabled him to master the principles of geometrical reasoning; nor, in fact, did he so much find a difficulty in apprehending demonstrations, as a want of interest, and a consequent inability to retain them in his memory. A little more practice in the strict logic of geometry, a little more familiarity with the physical laws of the universe, and the phenomena to which they relate, would possibly have repressed the tendency to vague and mystical speculations which he was too fond of indulging. In the philosophy of the human mind, he was in no danger of the materializing theories of some ancient and modern schools; but in shunning this extreme, he might sometimes forget that, in the honest pursuit of truth, we can shut our eyes to no real phenomena, and that the physiology of man must always enter into any valid scheme of his psychology.

" The comparative inferiority which he might show in the usual trials of knowledge, sprung in a great measure from the want of a prompt and accurate memory. It was the faculty wherein he shone the least, according to ordinary observation; though his very extensive reach of literature, and his rapidity in acquiring languages, sufficed to prove that it was capable of being largely exercised. He could remember anything, as a friend observed to the Editor, that was associated with an idea. But he seemed, at least after he reached manhood, to want almost wholly the power, so common with inferior understandings, of retaining with regularity and exactness, a number of unimportant uninteresting particulars. It would have been nearly impossible to make him recollect for three days the date of the battle of Marathon, or the names in order of the Athenian months. Nor could he repeat poetry, much as he loved it, with the correctness often found in young men. It is not improbable, that a more steady discipline in early life would have strengthened this faculty, or that he might have supplied its deficiency by some technical devices; but where the higher powers of intellect were so extraordinarily manifested, it would have been preposterous to complain of what may perhaps have been a necessary consequence of their amplitude, or at least a natural result of their exercise.

" But another reason may be given for his deficiency in those unremitting labours which the course of academical education, in the present times, is supposed to exact from those who aspire to its distinctions. In the first year of his residence at Cambridge, symptoms of disordered health, especially in the circulatory system, began to show themselves; and it is by no means improbable, that these were indications of a tendency to derangement of the vital functions, which became ultimately fatal. A too rapid determination of blood towards the brain, with its concomitant uneasy sensations, rendered him frequently incapable of mental fatigue. He had indeed once before, at Florence, been affected by symptoms not unlike these. His intensity of reflection and feeling also brought on occasionally a considerable depression of spirits, which had been painfully observed at times by those who watched him most, from the time of his leaving Eton, and even before. It was not till after several months that he regained a less morbid condition of mind and body. This same irregularity of circulation returned again in the next spring, but was of less duration. During the third year of his Cambridge life, he appeared in much better health.

" In this year (1831) he obtained the first college prize for an English declamation. The subject chosen by him was the conduct of the Independent party during the civil war. This exercise was greatly admired at the time, but was never printed. In consequence of this success, it became incumbent on him, according to the custom of the college, to deliver an oration in the chapel immediately before the Christmas vacation of the same year. On this occasion he

selected a subject very congenial to his own turn of
thought and favourite study, the influence of Italian
upon English literature. He had previously gained
another prize for an English essay on the philosophical writings of Cicero. This essay is perhaps too
excursive from the prescribed subject; but his mind
was so deeply imbued with the higher philosophy,
especially that of Plato, with which he was very conversant, that he could not be expected to dwell much
on the praises of Cicero in that respect.

" Though the bent of Arthur's mind by no means
inclined him to strict research into facts, he was full
as much conversant with the great features of ancient
and modern history, as from the course of his other
studies and the habits of his life it was possible to
expect. He reckoned them, as great minds always
do, the groundworks of moral and political philosophy, and took no pains to acquire any knowledge
of this sort from which a principle could not be
derived or illustrated. To some parts of English history, and to that of the French Revolution, he had
paid considerable attention. He had not read nearly
so much of the Greek and Latin historians as of the
philosophers and poets. In the history of literary,
and especially of philosophical and religious opinions,
he was deeply versed, as much so as it is possible
to apply that term at his age. The following pages
exhibit proofs of an acquaintance, not crude or super-
ficial, with that important branch of literature.

" His political judgments were invariably prompted
by his strong sense of right and justice. These, in
so young a person, were naturally rather fluctuating,
and subject to the correction of advancing knowledge
and experience. Ardent in the cause of those he
deemed to be oppressed, of which, in one instance,
he was led to give a proof with more of energy and
enthusiasm than discretion, he was deeply attached
to the ancient institutions of his country.

" He spoke French readily, though with less elegance than Italian, till from disuse he lost much of

his fluency in the latter. In his last fatal tour in
Germany, he was rapidly acquiring a readiness in
the language of that country. The whole range of
French literature was almost as familiar to him as
that of England.

" The society in which Arthur lived most intimately, at Eton and at the University, was formed
of young men, eminent for natural ability, and for
delight in what he sought above all things, the knowledge of truth, and the perception of beauty. They
who loved and admired him living, and who now
revere his sacred memory, as of one to whom, in the
fondness of regret, they admit of no rival, know best
what he was in the daily commerce of life; and his
eulogy should, on every account, better come from
hearts, which, if partial, have been rendered so by
the experience of friendship, not by the affection of
nature.

" Arthur left Cambridge on taking his degree in
January 1832. He resided from that time with the
Editor in London, having been entered on the boards
of the Inner Temple. It was greatly the desire of
the Editor that he should engage himself in the study
of the law; not merely with professional views, but
as a useful discipline for a mind too much occupied
with habits of thought, which, ennobling and important as they were, could not but separate him
from the everyday business of life; and might, by
their excess, in his susceptible temperament, be productive of considerable mischief. He had, during the
previous long vacation, read with the Editor the
Institutes of Justinian, and the two works of Hein-
eccius which illustrate them; and he now went
through Blackstone's Commentaries, with as much
of other law-books as, in the Editor's judgment, was
required for a similar purpose. It was satisfactory
at that time to perceive that, far from showing any
of that distaste to legal studies which might have
been anticipated from some parts of his intellectual
character, he entered upon them not only with great

acuteness, but considerable interest. In the month of October 1832, he began to see the practical application of legal knowledge in the office of an eminent conveyancer, Mr. Walters of Lincoln's Inn Fields, with whom he continued till his departure from England in the following summer.

" It was not, however, to be expected, or even desired by any who knew how to value him, that he should at once abandon those habits of study which had fertilized and invigorated his mind. But he now, from some change or other in his course of thinking, ceased in a great measure to write poetry, and expressed to more than one friend an intention to give it up. The instances after his leaving Cambridge were few. The dramatic scene between Raffaelle and Fiammetta was written in 1832; and about the same time he had a design to translate the *Vita Nuova* of his favourite Dante; a work which he justly prized, as the development of that immense genius, in a kind of autobiography, which best prepares us for a real insight into the *Divine Comedy*. He rendered accordingly into verse most of the sonnets which the *Vita Nuova* contains; but the Editor does not believe that he made any progress in the prose translation. These sonnets appearing rather too literal, and consequently harsh, it has not been thought worth while to print.

" In the summer of 1832, the appearance of Professor Rossetti's *Disquisizioni fullo spirito Antipapale*, in which the writings of Arthur's beloved masters, Dante and Petrarch, as well as most of the mediæval literature of Italy, were treated as a series of enigmas, to be understood only by a key that discloses a latent Carbonarism, a secret conspiracy against the religion of their age, excited him to publish his own Remarks in reply. It seemed to him the worst of poetical heresies to desert the Absolute, the Universal, the Eternal, the Beautiful and True, which the Platonic spirit of his literary creed taught him to seek in all the higher works of genius, in quest of some temporary historical allusion, which could be of no interest with posterity. Nothing however could be more alien from his courteous disposition than to abuse the license of controversy, or to treat with intentional disrespect a very ingenious person, who had been led on too far in pursuing a course of interpretation, which, within certain much narrower limits, it is impossible for any one conversant with history not to admit.

"A very few other anonymous writings occupied his leisure about this time. Among these were slight memoirs of Petrarch, Voltaire, and Burke, for the Gallery of Portraits, published by the Society for the Diffusion of Useful Knowledge.[1] His time was however principally devoted, when not engaged at his office, to metaphysical researches, and to the history of philosophical opinions.

"From the latter part of his residence at Cambridge, a gradual but very perceptible improvement in the cheerfulness of his spirits gladdened his family and his friends; intervals there doubtless were, when the continual seriousness of his habits of thought, or the force of circumstances, threw something more of gravity into his demeanour; but in general he was animated and even gay; renewing or preserving his intercourse with some of those he had most valued at

---

[1] We had read these Lives, and had remarked them before we knew whose they were, as being of rare merit. No one could suppose they were written by one so young. We give his estimate of the character of Burke. "The mind of this great man may perhaps be taken as a representation of the general characteristics of the English intellect. Its groundwork was solid, practical, and conversant with the details of business; but upon this, and secured by this, arose a superstructure of imagination and moral sentiment. He saw little, *because it was painful to him* to see anything beyond the limits of the national character. In all things, while he deeply reverenced principles, he chose to deal with the concrete rather than with abstractions. He studied men rather than man." The words in italics imply an insight into the deepest springs of human action, the conjunct causes of what we call character, such as few men of large experience can attain.

Eton and Cambridge. The symptoms of deranged circulation which had manifested themselves before, ceased to appear, or at least so as to excite his own attention; and though it struck those who were most anxious in watching him, that his power of enduring fatigue was not quite so great as from his frame of body and apparent robustness might have been anticipated, nothing gave the least indication of danger either to their eyes, or to those of the medical practitioners who were in the habit of observing him. An attack of intermittent fever, during the prevalent influenza of the spring of 1833, may perhaps have disposed his constitution to the last fatal blow."

To any one who has watched the history of the disease by which " so quick this bright thing came to confusion," and who knows how near its subject must often, perhaps all his life, have been to that eternity which occupied so much of his thoughts and desires, and the secrets of which were so soon to open on his young eyes, there is something very touching in this account. Such a state of health would enhance, and tend to produce, by the sensations proper to such a condition, that habitual seriousness of thought, that sober judgment, and that tendency to look at the true life of things—that deep but gentle and calm sadness, and that occasional sinking of the heart, which make his noble and strong inner nature, his resolved mind, so much more impressive and endearing.

This feeling of personal insecurity—of life being ready to slip away—the sensation that this world and its ongoings, its mighty interests, and delicate joys, is ready to be shut up in a moment—this instinctive apprehension of the peril of vehement bodily enjoyment—all this would tend to make him " walk softly," and to keep him from much of the evil that is in the world, and would help him to live soberly, righteously, and godly, even in the bright and rich years of his youth. His power of giving himself up to the search after absolute truth, and the contemplation of Supreme goodness, must have been increased by this same organization. But all this delicate feeling, this fineness of sense, did rather quicken the energy and fervour of the indwelling soul—the τι θερμόν πρᾶγμα that burned within. In the quaint words of Vaughan, it was "manhood with a female eye." These two conditions must, as we have said, have made him dear indeed. And by a beautiful law of life, having that organ out of which are the issues of life, under a sort of perpetual nearness to suffering, and so liable to pain, he would be more easily moved for others—more alive to their pain—more filled with fellow-feeling.

"The Editor cannot dwell on anything later. Arthur accompanied him to Germany in the beginning of August. In returning to Vienna from Pesth, a wet day probably gave rise to an intermittent fever, with very slight symptoms, and apparently subsiding, when a sudden rush of blood to the head put an instantaneous end to his life on the 15th of September, 1833. The mysteriousness of such a dreadful termination to a disorder generally of so little importance, and in this instance of the slightest kind, has been diminished by an examination which showed a weakness of the cerebral vessels, and a want of sufficient energy in the heart. Those whose eyes must long be dim with tears, and whose hopes on this side the tomb are broken down for ever, may cling, as well as they can, to the poor consolation of believing that a few more years would, in the usual chances of humanity, have severed the frail union of his graceful and manly form with the pure spirit that it enshrined.

"The remains of Arthur were brought to England, and interred on the 3rd of January, 1834, in the chancel of Clevedon Church in Somersetshire, belonging to his maternal grandfather Sir Abraham Elton, a place selected by the Editor, not only from the connection of kindred, but on account of its still and sequestered situation, on a lone hill that overhangs the Bristol Channel.

" More ought perhaps to be said—but it is very difficult to proceed. From the earliest years of this extraordinary young man, his premature abilities were not more conspicuous than an almost faultless disposition, sustained by a more calm self-command than has often been witnessed in that season of life. The sweetness of temper which distinguished his childhood, became with the advance of manhood a habitual benevolence, and ultimately ripened into that exalted principle of love towards God and man which animated and almost absorbed his soul during the latter period of his life, and to which most of the following compositions bear such emphatic testimony. He seemed to tread the earth as a spirit from some better world; and in bowing to the mysterious will which has in mercy removed him, perfected by so short a trial, and passing over the bridge which separates the seen from the unseen life, in a moment, and, as we may believe, without a moment's pang, we must feel not only the bereavement of those to whom he was dear, but the loss which mankind have sustained by the withdrawing of such a light.

" A considerable portion of the poetry contained in this volume was printed in the year 1830, and was intended by the author to be published together with the poems of his intimate friend, Mr. Alfred Tennyson. They were however withheld from publication at the request of the Editor. The poem of Timbuctoo was written for the University prize in 1829, which it did not obtain. Notwithstanding its too great obscurity, the subject itself being hardly indicated, and the extremely hyperbolical importance which the author's brilliant fancy has attached to a nest of barbarians, no one can avoid admiring the grandeur of his conceptions, and the deep philosophy upon which he has built the scheme of his poem. This is however by no means the most pleasing of his compositions. It is in the profound reflection, the melancholy tenderness, and the religious sanctity of other effusions that a lasting charm will be found.   A commonplace subject, such as those announced for academical prizes generally are, was incapable of exciting a mind which, beyond almost every other, went straight to the furthest depths that the human intellect can fathom, or from which human feelings can be drawn. Many short poems of equal beauty with those here printed, have been deemed unfit even for the limited circulation they might obtain, on account of their unveiling more of emotion, than consistently with what is due to him and to others, could be exposed to view.

"The two succeeding essays have never been printed; but were read, it is believed, in a literary society at Trinity College, or in one to which he afterwards belonged in London. That entitled *Theodicæa Novissima*, is printed at the desire of some of his intimate friends. A few expressions in it want his usual precision; and there are ideas which he might have seen cause, in the lapse of time, to modify, independently of what his very acute mind would probably have perceived, that his hypothesis, like that of Leibnitz, on the origin of evil, resolves itself at last into an unproved assumption of its necessity. It has however some advantages, which need not be mentioned, over that of Liebnitz; and it is here printed, not as a solution of the greatest mystery of the universe, but as most characteristic of the author's mind, original and sublime, uniting, what is very rare except in early youth, a fearless and unblenching spirit of inquiry into the highest objects of speculation, with the most humble and reverential piety. It is probable that in many of his views on such topics he was influenced by the writings of Jonathan Edwards, with whose opinions on metaphysical and moral subjects, he seems generally to have concurred.

"The extract from a review of Tennyson's poems in a publication now extinct, the *Englishman's Magazine*, is also printed at the suggestion of a friend. The pieces that follow are reprints, and have been already mentioned in this Memoir."

We have given this Memoir almost entire, for the sake both of its subject and its manner—for what in it is the father's as well as for what is the son's. There is something very touching in the paternal composure, the judiciousness, the truthfulness, where truth is so difficult to reach through tears, the calm estimate and the subdued tenderness, the ever-rising but ever restrained emotion; the father's heart throbs throughout.

We wish we could have given in full the letters from Arthur's friends, which his father has incorporated in the Memoir. They all bring out in different but harmonious ways, his extraordinary moral and intellectual worth, his rare beauty of character, and their deep affection.

The following extract from one seems to us very interesting :—" Outwardly I do not think there was anything remarkable in his habits, except *an irregularity with regard to times and places of study*, which may seem surprising in one whose progress in so many directions was so eminently great and rapid. *He was commonly to be found in some friend's room, reading, or canvassing.* I dare say he lost something by this irregularity, *but less than perhaps one would at first imagine.* I never saw him idle. He might seem to be lounging, or only amusing himself, but his mind was always active, and active for good. In fact, his energy and quickness of apprehension did not stand in need of outward aid." There is much in this worthy of more extended notice. Such minds as his probably grow best in this way, are best left to themselves, to glide on at their own sweet wills; the stream was too deep and clear, and perhaps too entirely bent on its own errand, to be dealt with or regulated by any art or device. The same friend sums up his character thus :—" I have met with no man his superior in metaphysical subtlety; no man his equal as a philosophical critic on works of taste; no man whose views on all subjects connected with the duties and dignities of humanity were more large, and generous, and

enlightened." And all this said of a youth of twenty
—*heu nimium brevis ævi decus et desiderium!*

We have given little of his verse; and what we do
give is taken at random. We agree entirely in his
father's estimate of his poetical gift and art, but his
mind was too serious, too thoughtful, too intensely
dedicated to truth and the God of truth, to linger long
in the pursuit of beauty; he was on his way to God,
and could rest in nothing short of Him, otherwise
he might have been a poet of genuine excellence.

> " Dark, dark, yea, ' irrecoverably dark,'
>   Is the soul's eye ; yet how it strives and battles
> Thorough th' impenetrable gloom to fix
>   That master light, the secret truth of things,
> Which is the body of the infinite God !"

> " Sure, we are leaves of one harmonious bower,
>   Fed by a sap that never will be scant,
> All-permeating, all-producing mind ;
>   And in our several parcellings of doom
> We but fulfil the beauty of the whole,
>   Oh, madness ! if a leaf should dare complain
> Of its dark verdure, and aspire to be
>   The gayer, brighter thing that wantons near."

> " Oh, blessing and delight of my young heart,
>   Maiden, who wast so lovely, and so pure,
> I know not in what region now thou art,
>   Or whom thy gentle eyes in joy assure.
> Not the old hills on which we gazed together,
>   Not the old faces which we both did love,
> Not the old books, whence knowledge we did gather,
>   Not these, but others now thy fancies move.
> I would I knew thy present hopes and fears,
>   All thy companions with their pleasant talk,
>   And the clear aspect which thy dwelling wears :
> So, though in body absent, I might walk
>   With thee in thought and feeling, till thy mood
>   Did sanctify mine own to peerless good."

> " Alfred, I would that you beheld me now,
>   Sitting beneath a mossy ivied wall
> On a quaint bench, which to that structure old
>   Winds an accordant curve. Above my head
> *Dilates immeasurable a wild of leaves,*
> Seeming received into the blue expanse
> That vaults this summer noon."

" Still here—thou hast not faded from my sight,
Nor all the music round thee from mine ear;
Still grace flows from thee to the brightening year,
And all the birds laugh out in wealthier light.
Still am I free to close my happy eyes,
And paint upon the gloom thy mimic form,
That soft white neck, that cheek in beauty warm,
And brow half hidden where yon ringlet lies:
With, oh! the blissful knowledge all the while
That I can lift at will each curved lid,
And my fair dream most highly realize.
The time will come, 'tis ushered by my sighs,
When I may shape the dark, but vainly bid
True light restore that form, those looks, that smile."

"The garden trees *are busy with the shower*
That fell ere sunset: now methinks they talk,
Lowly and sweetly as befits the hour,
One to another down the graffy walk.
Hark the laburnum from his opening flower
This cherry creeper greets in whisper light,
While the grim fir, rejoicing in the night,
Hoarse mutters to the murmuring sycamore,[1]
What shall I deem their converse? would they hail
The wild grey light that fronts yon massive cloud,
Or the half bow, rising like pillared fire?
Or are they fighting faintly for desire
That with May dawn their leaves may be o'erflowed,
And dews about their feet may never fail."

In the Essay, entitled *Theodicæ Novissima,* from which the following passages are taken to the great injury of its general effect, he sets himself to the task of doing his utmost to clear up the mystery of the existence of such things as sin and suffering in the universe of a being like God. He does it fearlessly, but like a child. It is in the spirit of his friend's words,—

" An infant crying in the night,
An infant crying for the light,
And with no language but a cry."

[1] This will remind the reader of a fine passage in *Edwin the Fair*, on the specific differences in the sounds made by the ash, the elm, the fir, &c., when moved by the wind; and of some lines by Landor on flowers speaking to each other; and of something more exquisite than either, in *Consuelo*—the description of the flowers in the old monastic garden, at " the sweet hour of prime."

> "Then was I as a child that cries,
>   But, crying, knows his father near."

It is not a mere exercitation of the intellect, it is an endeavour to get nearer God—to assert His eternal Providence, and vindicate His ways to men. We know no performance more wonderful for such a boy. Pascal might have written it. As was to be expected, the tremendous subject remains where he found it—his glowing love and genius cast a gleam here and there across its gloom; but it is brief as the lightning in the collied night—the jaws of darkness do devour it up—this secret belongs to God. Across its deep and dazzling darkness, and from out its abyss of thick cloud, "all dark, dark, irrecoverably dark," no steady ray has ever, or will ever come,—over its face its own darkness must brood, till He to whom alone the darkness and the light are both alike, to whom the night shineth as the day, says, "Let there be light!" There is, we all know, a certain awful attraction, a nameless charm for all thoughtful spirits, in this mystery, "the greatest in the universe," as Mr. Hallam truly says; and it is well for us at times, so that we have pure eyes and a clean heart, to turn aside and look into its gloom; but it is not good to busy ourselves in clever speculations about it, or briskly to criticise the speculations of others—it is a wise and pious saying of Augustin, *Verius cogitatur Deus, quam dicitur; et verius est quam cogitatur.*

"I wish to be understood as considering Christianity in the present Essay rather in its relation to the intellect, as constituting the higher philosophy, than in its far more important bearing upon the hearts and destinies of us all. I shall propose the question in this form, 'Is there ground for believing that the existence of moral evil is absolutely necessary to the fulfilment of God's essential love for Christ?' (*i.e.*, of the Father for Christ, or of ὁ πατηρ for ὁ λογος.)

"'Can man by searching find out God?' I believe not. I believe that the unassisted efforts of man's reason have not established the existence and attributes of Deity on so sure a basis as the Deist imagines. However sublime may be the notion of a supreme original mind, and however naturally human feelings adhered to it, the reasons by which it was justified were not, in my opinion, sufficient to clear it from considerable doubt and confusion. . . . I hesitate not to say that I derive from Revelation a conviction of Theism, which without that assistance would have been but a dark and ambiguous hope. *I see that the Bible fits into every fold of the human heart. I am a man, and I believe it to be God's book because it is man's book.* It is true that the Bible affords me no additional means of demonstrating the falsity of Atheism; *if mind had nothing to do with the formation of the Universe, doubtless whatever had was competent also to make the Bible;* but I have gained this advantage, that my feelings and thoughts can no longer refuse their assent to *what is evidently framed to engage that assent; and what is it to me that I cannot disprove the bare logical possibility of my whole nature being fallacious? To seek for a certainty above certainty, an evidence beyond necessary belief, is the very lunacy of scepticism:* we must trust our own faculties, or we can put no trust in anything, save that moment we call the present, which escapes us while we articulate its name. *I am determined therefore to receive the Bible as Divinely authorized, and the scheme of human and Divine things which it contains, as essentially true.*"

" I may further observe, that however much we should rejoice to discover that the eternal scheme of God, the necessary completion, let us remember, of His Almighty Nature, did not require the absolute perdition of any spirit called by Him into existence, we are certainly not entitled to consider the perpetual misery of many individuals as incompatible with sovereign love."

" In the Supreme Nature those two capacities of Perfect Love and Perfect Joy are indivisible. Holi-

ness and Happiness, says an old divine, are two
several notions of one thing. Equally inseparable
are the notions of Opposition to Love and Opposition
to Bliss. *Unless therefore the heart of a created*
being is at one with the heart of God, it cannot but
be miserable. Moreover, there is no possibility of
continuing for ever partly with God and partly
against him : we must either be capable by our nature
of entire accordance with His will, or we must be
incapable of anything but misery, further than He
may for awhile ' not impute our trespasses to us,'
that is, He may interpose some temporary barrier
between sin and its attendant pain. *For in the Eternal*
Idea of God a created spirit is perhaps not seen, as
a series of successive states, of which some that are
evil might be compensated by others that are good,
but as one indivisible object of these almost infinitely
divisible modes, and that either in accordance with
His own nature, or in opposition to it. . . .

"Before the gospel was preached to man, how
could a human soul have this love, and this consequent life? I see no way; but now that Christ has
excited our love for Him by showing unutterable
love for us; now that we know Him as an Elder
Brother, a being of like thoughts, feelings, sensations, sufferings, with ourselves, it has become possible to love as God loves, that is, to love Christ,
and thus to become united in heart to God. Besides,
Christ is the express image of God's person : in
loving Him we are sure we are in a state of readiness
to love the Father, whom we see, He tells us, when
we see Him. Nor is this all : the tendency of love is
towards a union so intimate as virtually to amount
to identification; when then by affection towards
Christ we have become blended with His being, the
beams of eternal love falling, as ever, on the one
beloved object, will include us in Him, and their returning flashes of love out of His personality will
carry along with them some from our own, since
ours has become confused with His, and so shall we

be one with Christ and through Christ with God.
Thus then we see the great effect of the Incarnation,
as far as our nature is concerned, *was to render human
love for the Most High a possible thing*. The Law
had said, ' Thou shalt love the Lord thy God with all
thy soul, and with all thy mind, and with all thy
strength;' and could men have lived by law, ' which
is the strength of sin,' verily righteousness and life
would have been by that law. But it was not possible, and all were concluded under sin, that in Christ
might be the deliverance of all. I believe that Redemption '' (*i.e.*, what Christ has done and suffered
for mankind) '' is universal, in so far as it left no
obstacle between man and God, but man's own will :
that indeed is in the power of God's election, with
whom alone rest the abysmal secrets of personality;
but as far as Christ is concerned, his death was for
all, since His intentions and affections were equally
directed to all, and ' none who come to Him will be
in any wise cast out.'

'' I deprecate any hasty rejection of these thoughts
as novelties. Christianity is indeed, as St. Augustin
says, ' pulchritudo tam antiqua;' but he adds, ' tam
nova,' for it is capable of presenting to every mind
a new face of truth. The great doctrine, which in
my judgment these observations tend to strengthen
and illumine, *the doctrine of personal love for a personal God*, is assuredly no novelty, but has in all
times been the vital principle of the Church. Many
are the forms of antichristian heresy, which for a
season have depressed and obscured that principle of
life : but its nature is conflictive and resurgent; and
neither the Papal Hierarchy with its pomp of sys-
tematized errors, nor the worse apostasy of latitudinarian Protestantism, have ever so far prevailed, but
that many from age to age have proclaimed and
vindicated the eternal gospel of love, believing, as
I also firmly believe, that any opinion which tends to
keep out of sight the living and loving God, whether
it substitute for Him an idol, an occult agency, or a

formal creed, can be nothing better than a vain and portentous shadow projected from the selfish darkness of unregenerate man.''

The following is from the Review of Tennyson's Poems; we do not know that during the lapse of eighteen years anything better has been said :—

'' Undoubtedly the true poet addresses himself, in all his conceptions, to the common nature of us all. Art is a lofty tree, and may shoot up far beyond our grasp, but its roots are in daily life and experience. Every bosom contains the elements of those complex emotions which the artist feels, and every head can, to a certain extent, go over in itself the process of their combination, so as to understand his expressions and sympathize with his state. *But this requires exertion;* more or less, indeed, according to the difference of occasion, but always some degree of exertion. For since the emotions of the poet during composition follow a regular law of association, it follows that to accompany their progress up to the harmonious prospect of the whole, and to perceive the proper dependence of every step on that which preceded, it is absolutely necessary *to start from the same point,* i.e., clearly to apprehend that leading sentiment of the poet's mind, by their conformity to which the host of suggestions are arranged. *Now this requisite exertion is not willingly made by the large majority of readers. It is so easy to judge capriciously, and according to indolent impulse!*''

'' Those different powers of poetic disposition, the energies of Sensitive, of Reflective, or Passionate Emotion, which in former times were intermingled, and derived from mutual support an extensive empire over the feelings of men, were now restrained within separate spheres of agency. The whole system no longer worked harmoniously, and by intrinsic harmony acquired external freedom; but there arose a violent and unusual action in the several component functions, each for itself, all striving to reproduce the regular power which the whole had once enjoyed.

*Hence the melancholy which so evidently character-
izes the spirit of modern poetry;* hence that return of
the mind upon itself, and the habit of seeking relief in
idiosyncrasies, rather than community of interest. *In
the old times the poetic impulse went along with the
general impulse of the nation.*

"One of the faithful Islâm, a poet in the truest
and highest sense, we are anxious to present to our
readers. . . . He sees all the forms of Nature with
the '*eruditus oculus*,' and his ear has a fairy fineness.
There is *a strange earnestness in his worship of
beauty*, which throws a charm over his impassioned
song, more easily felt than described, and not to be
escaped by those who have once felt it. We think
that he has *more definiteness and roundness of
general conception* than the late Mr. Keats, and is
much more free from blemishes of diction and hasty
capriccios of fancy. . . . The author imitates nobody; *we recognize the spirit of his age, but not the
individual form of this or that writer.* His thoughts
bear no more resemblance to Byron or Scott, Shelley
or Coleridge, than to Homer or Calderon, Ferdusi or
Calidasa. We have remarked five distinctive excel-
lencies of his own manner. First, his luxuriance of
imagination, and at the same time his control over
it. Secondly, his power of embodying himself in
ideal characters, or rather modes of character, with
such extreme accuracy of adjustment, that the circumstances of the narration seem to have a natural
correspondence with the predominant feeling, and,
as it were, to be evolved from it by assimilative force.
Thirdly, his vivid, picturesque delineation of objects,
and the peculiar skill with which he holds all of them
fused, to borrow a metaphor from science, in a
medium of strong emotion. Fourthly, the variety of
his lyrical measures, and exquisite modulation of
harmonious words and cadences to the swell and fall
of the feelings expressed. Fifthly, the elevated habits
of thought, implied in these compositions, and im-
parting a mellow soberness of tone, more impressive,

to our minds, than if the author had drawn up a set of opinions in verse, and sought to instruct the understanding *rather than to communicate the love of beauty to the heart.*"

What follows is justly thought and well said.

" And is it not a noble thing, that the English tongue is, as it were, the common focus and point of union to which opposite beauties converge? Is it a trifle that we temper energy with softness, strength with flexibility, capaciousness of sound with pliancy of idiom? Some, I know, insensible to these virtues, and ambitious of I know not what unattainable decomposition, prefer to utter funeral praises over the grave of departed Anglo-Saxon, or, starting with convulsive shudder, are ready to leap from surrounding Latinisms into the kindred, sympathetic arms of modern German. For myself, I neither share their regret, nor their terror. Willing at all times to pay filial homage to the shades of Hengist and Horsa, and to admit they have laid the base of our compound language; or, if you will, have prepared the soil from which the chief nutriment of the goodly tree, our British oak, must be derived, I am yet proud to confess that I look with sentiments more exulting and more reverential to the bonds by which the law of the universe has fastened me to my distant brethren of the same Caucasian race; to the privileges which I, an inhabitant of the gloomy North, share in common with climates imparadised in perpetual summer, to the universality and efficacy resulting from blended intelligence, which, while it endears in our eyes the land of our fathers as a seat of peculiar blessing, tends to elevate and expand our thoughts into communion with humanity at large and, in the ' sublimer spirit ' of the poet, to make us feel

> " That God is everywhere—the God who framed
> Mankind to be one mighty family,
> Himself our Father, and the world our home."

What nice shading of thought do his remarks on Petrarch discover !

" But it is not so much to his direct adoptions that I refer, *as to the general modulation of thought, that clear softness of his images, that energetic, self-possession of his conceptions, and that melodious repose in which are held together all the emotions he delineates.*"

Every one who knows anything of himself, and of his fellow-men, will acknowledge the wisdom of what follows. It displays an intimate knowledge both of the constitution and history of man, and there is much in it suited to our present need :—

" *I do not hesitate to express my conviction, that the spirit of the critical philosophy, as seen by its fruits in all the ramifications of art, literature, and morality, is as much more dangerous than the spirit of mechanical philosophy*, as it is fairer in appearance, and more capable of alliance with our natural feelings of enthusiasm and delight. Its dangerous tendency is this, that it perverts those very minds, whose office it was to resist the perverse impulses of society, and to proclaim truth under the dominion of falsehood. However precipitate may be at any time the current of public opinion, bearing along the mass of men to the grosser agitations of life, and to such schemes of belief as make these the prominent object, *there will always be in reserve a force of antagonist opinion, strengthened by opposition, and attesting the sanctity of those higher principles, which are despised or forgotten by the majority.* These men *are secured by natural temperament* and peculiar circumstances from participating in the common delusion : but if some other and deeper fallacy be invented ; if some more subtle beast of the field should speak to them in wicked flattery ; if a digest of intellectual aphorisms can be substituted in their minds for a code of living truths, and the lovely semblances of beauty, truth, affection, can be made first to obscure the presence, and then to conceal the loss, of that religious humility, without which, as their central life, all these are but dreadful shadows ; if so fatal a stratagem can be successfully practised, I see not what hope remains for a people against whom the gates of hell have so prevailed."

" But the number of pure artists is small : few souls are so finely tempered as to preserve the delicacy of meditative feeling, untainted by the allurements of accidental suggestion. The voice of the critical conscience is still and small, like that of the moral : it cannot entirely be stifled where it has been heard, but it may be disobeyed. Temptations are never wanting : some immediate and temporary effect can be produced at less expense of inward exertion than the high and more ideal effect which art demands : it is much easier to pander to the ordinary and often recurring wish for excitement, than to promote the rare and difficult intuition of beauty. *To raise the many to his own real point of view, the artist must employ his energies, and create energy in others: to descend to their position is less noble, but practicable with ease.* If I may be allowed the metaphor, one partakes of the nature of redemptive power; the other of that self-abased and degenerate will, which 'flung from his splendours' the fairest star in heaven."

" *Revelation is a voluntary approximation of the Infinite Being to the ways and thoughts of finite humanity.* But until this step has been taken by Almighty Grace, how should man have a warrant for loving with all his heart and mind and strength? . . . Without the gospel, nature exhibits a want of harmony between our intrinsic constitution, and the system in which it is placed. But Christianity has made up the difference. It is possible and natural to love the Father, who has made us His children by the spirit of adoption : it is possible and natural to love the Elder Brother, who was, in all things, like as we are, except sin, and can succour those in temptation, having been Himself tempted. *Thus the Christian faith is the necessary complement of a sound ethical system.*"

There is something to us very striking in the
words " Revelation is a *voluntary* approximation of
the Infinite Being." This states the case with an
accuracy and distinctness not at all common among
either the opponents or the apologists of *revealed
religion* in the ordinary sense of the expression. In
one sense God is for ever revealing Himself. His
heavens are for ever telling His glory, and the firmament showing His handiwork; day unto day is
uttering speech, and night unto night is showing
knowledge concerning him. But in the word of the
truth of the gospel, God draws near to His creatures;
He bows His heavens and comes down :

> " That glorious form, that light unsufferable,
>   And that far-beaming blaze of majesty,"

He lays aside. The Word dwelt with men. " Come
then, let *us* reason together;"—" Waiting to be
gracious;"—" Behold, I stand at the door, and
knock; if any man open to Me, I will come in to him,
and sup with him, and he with Me." It is the father
seeing his son while yet a great way off, and having
compassion, and running to him and falling on his
neck and kissing him : for " it was meet for us to
rejoice, for this my son was dead and is alive again,
he was lost and is found." Let no man confound
the voice of God in His Works with the voice of God
in His Word; they are utterances of the same infinite
heart and will; they are in absolute harmony; together they make up " that undisturbéd song of pure
concent;" one " perfect diapason;" but they are distinct; they are meant to be so. A poor traveller,
" weary and waysore," is stumbling in unknown
places through the darkness of a night of fear, with
no light near him, the everlasting stars twinkling far
off in their depths, and yet unrisen sun, or the waning
moon, sending up their pale beams into the upper
heavens, but all this is distant, and bewildering for
his feet, doubtless better much than outer darkness,
beautiful and full of God, if he could have the heart

to look up, and the eyes to make use of its vague light; but he is miserable, and afraid, his next step is what he is thinking of; a lamp secured against all winds of doctrine is put into his hands, it may, in some respects, widen the circle of darkness, but it will cheer his feet, it will tell them what to do next. What a silly fool he would be to throw away that lantern, or draw down the shutters, and make it dark to him, while it sits " i' the centre and enjoys bright day," and all upon the philosophical ground that its light was of the same kind as the stars', and that it was beneath the dignity of human nature to do anything but struggle on and be lost in the attempt to get through the wilderness and the night by the guidance of those " natural " lights, which, though they are from heaven, have so often led the wanderer astray. The dignity of human nature indeed ! Let him keep his lantern till the glad sun is up, with healing under his wings. Let him take good heed to the " sure " λόγον while in this αὐχμηρῷ τοπῷ—this dark, damp, unwholesome place, " till the day dawn and φωσφόρος the day-star—arise." Nature and the Bible, the Works and the Word of God, are two distinct things. In the mind of their Supreme Author they dwell in perfect peace, in that unspeakable unity which is of His essence; and to us His children, every day their harmony, their mutual relations, are discovering themselves; but let us beware of saying all nature is a revelation as the Bible is, and all the Bible is natural as nature is : there is a perilous juggle here.

The following passage develops Arthur Hallam's views on religious feeling; this was the master-idea of his mind, and it would not be easy to overrate its importance. " My son, give Me thine heart;"— " Thou shalt *love* the Lord thy God;"—" The fool hath said in his *heart*, There is no God." He expresses the same general idea in these words, remarkable in themselves, still more so as being the thought of one so young. " The work of intellect is posterior to the work of feeling. *The latter lies at the foundation of the man;* it is his proper self—the peculiar thing that characterizes him as an individual. No two men are alike in feeling; but conceptions of the understanding, when distinct, are precisely similar in all—the ascertained relations of truths are the common property of the race."

Tennyson, we have no doubt, had this thought of his friend in his mind, in the following lines; it is an answer to the question, Can man by searching find out God?—

> " I found Him not in world or sun,
>   Or eagle's wing, or insect's eye;
>   Nor thro' the questions men may try,
> The petty cobwebs we have spun:
>
> If e'er when faith had fallen asleep,
>   I heard a voice ' believe no more,'
>   And heard an ever-breaking shore
> That tumbled in the godless deep;
>
> *A warmth within the breast would melt*
>   *The freezing reason's colder part,*
>   *And like a man in wrath, the heart*
> *Stood up and answer'd, ' I have felt.'*
>
> No, like a child in doubt and fear:
>   But that blind clamour made me wise;
>   Then was I as a child that cries,
> But, crying, knows his father near;
>
> And what I seem beheld again
>   What is, and no man understands:
>   And out of darkness came the hands
> That reach thro' nature, moulding men."

This is a subject of the deepest personal as well as speculative interest. In the works of Augustin, of Baxter, Howe, and Jonathan Edwards, and of Alexander Knox, our readers will find how large a place the religious affections held, in their view of Divine truth as well as of human duty. The last-mentioned writer expresses himself thus:—" Our sentimental faculties are far stronger than our cogitative; and the best impressions on the latter will be but the moonshine of the mind, if they are alone. Feeling will be best excited by sympathy; rather, it cannot be excited in any other way. Heart must act upon heart—the idea of a living person being essential to all intercourse of heart. You cannot by any possibility *cordialize* with a mere *ens rationis*. ' The Word was made flesh, and dwelt among us,' otherwise we could not ' have seen His glory,' much less ' received of His fulness.' '' [1]

Our young author thus goes on :—

" This opens upon us an ampler view in which the subject deserves to be considered, and a relation still more direct and close between the Christian religion and the passion of love. What is the distinguishing character of Hebrew literature, which separates it by so broad a line of demarcation from that of every ancient people? Undoubtedly the sentiment of *erotic devotion* which pervades it. Their poets never represent the Deity as an impassive principle, a mere organizing intellect, removed at infinite distance from human hopes and fears. He is for them a being of like passions with themselves,[2] *requiring heart for heart, and capable of inspiring affection because capable of feeling and returning it.* Awful indeed are the thunders of his utterance and the clouds that surround his dwelling-place; very terrible is the vengeance he executes on the nations that forget Him : but to His chosen people, and especially to the men ' after His own heart,' whom He anoints from the midst of them, His ' still, small voice ' speaks in

[1] *Remains*, vol. iii. p. 105.
[2] " An unfortunate reference (Acts xiv. 15), for the apostle's declaration is, that he and his brethren were of ' like passions ' (James v. 17);—liable to the same imperfections and mutations of thought and feeling as other men, and as the Lystrans supposed their gods to be ; while the God proclaimed by him to them is not so. And *that* God is the God of the Jews as well as of the Christians ; for there is but *one* God. Hallam's thought is an important and just one, but not developed with his usual nice accuracy."
For this note, as for much else, I am indebted to my father, whose powers of compressed thought I wish I had inherited.

sympathy and loving-kindness. Every Hebrew, while his breast glowed with patriotic enthusiasm at those promises, which he shared as one of the favoured race, had a yet deeper source of emotion, from which gushed perpetually the aspirations of prayer and thanksgiving. He might consider himself alone in the presence of his God; the single being to whom a great revelation had been made, and over whose head an ' exceeding weight of glory ' was suspended. For him the rocks of Horeb had trembled, and the waters of the Red Sea were parted in their course. The word given on Sinai with such solemn pomp of ministration was given to his own individual soul, and brought him into immediate communion with his Creator. That awful Being could never be put away from him. He was about his path, and about his bed, and knew all his thoughts long before. *Yet this tremendous, enclosing presence was a presence of love. It was a manifold, everlasting manifestation of one deep feeling—a desire for human affection.*[1] Such a belief, while it enlisted even pride and self-interest on the side of piety, had a direct tendency to excite the best passions of our nature. Love is not long asked in vain from generous dispositions. A Being, never absent, but standing beside the life of each man with ever watchful tenderness, and recognized, though invisible, in every blessing that befell them from youth to age, became naturally the object of their warmest affections. Their belief in Him could not exist without producing, as a necessary effect, that profound impression *of passionate individual attachment* which in the Hebrew authors always mingles with and vivifies their faith in the Invisible. All the books of the Old Testament are breathed upon by this breath of life. Especially is it to be found in that beautiful collection, entitled the Psalms of David, which remains,

---

[1] Abraham " was called the friend of God;" " with him (Moses) will I (Jehovah) speak mouth to mouth, even apparently,"—" as a man to his friend;" David was " a man after mine own heart."

after some thousand years, perhaps the most perfect
form in which the religious sentiment of man has been
embodied.

" But what is true of Judaism is yet more true of
Christianity, ' *matre pulchrâ filia pulchrior.*' In addition to all the characters of Hebrew Monotheism,
*there exists in the doctrine of the Cross a peculiar
and inexhaustible treasure for the affectionate feelings.* The idea of the Θεανθρωπος, the God whose
goings forth have been from everlasting, yet visible
to men for their redemption as an earthly, temporal
creature, living, acting, and suffering among themselves, then (which is yet more important) transferring
to the unseen place of His spiritual agency the same
humanity He wore on earth, so that the lapse of
generations can in no way affect the conception of
His identity; this is the most powerful thought that
ever addressed itself to a human imagination. It is
the πον σ ω, which alone was wanted to move the
world. Here was solved at once the great problem
which so long had distressed the teachers of mankind,
how to make *virtue the object of passion,* and to
secure at once the warmest enthusiasm in the heart
with the clearest perception of right and wrong in the
understanding. The character of the blessed Founder
of our faith became an abstract of morality to deter-
mine the judgment, *while at the same time it remained
personal, and liable to love.* The written word and
established church prevented a degeneration into un-
governed mysticism, but the predominant principle of
vital religion always remained that of self-sacrifice
to the Saviour. Not only the higher divisions of moral
duties, but the simple, primary impulses of benevolence, were subordinated to this new absorbing passion. The world was loved ' in Christ alone.' The
brethren were members of His mystical body. All the
other bonds that had fastened down the Spirit of the
universe to our narrow round of earth were as nothing
in comparison to this golden chain of suffering and
self-sacrifice, which at once riveted the heart of man

to one who, like Himself, was acquainted with grief. *Pain is the deepest thing we have in* our nature, and union through pain has always seemed more real and more holy than any other." [1]

There is a sad pleasure,—*non ingrata amaritudo*, and a sort of meditative tenderness, in contemplating the little life of this " dear youth," and in letting the mind rest upon these his earnest thoughts; to watch his keen and fearless, but child-like spirit, moving itself aright—going straight onward " along the lines of limitless desires "—throwing himself into the very deepest of the ways of God, and striking out as a strong swimmer striketh out his hands to swim; to see him " mewing his mighty youth, and kindling his undazzled eye at the fountain itself of heavenly radiance : "

> " Light intellectual, and full of love,
> Love of true beauty, therefore full of joy,
> Joy, every other sweetness far above."

It is good for every one to look upon such a sight, and as we look, to love. We should all be the better for it; and should desire to be thankful for, and to use aright a gift so good and perfect, coming down as it does from above, from the Father of lights, in whom alone there is no variableness, neither shadow of turning.

---

[1] This is the passage referred to in Henry Taylor's delightful *Notes from Life* (" Essay on Wisdom ") :—

" Fear, indeed, is the mother of foresight : spiritual fear, of a foresight that reaches beyond the grave; temporal fear, of a foresight that falls short ; but without fear there is neither the one foresight nor the other ; and as pain has been truly said to be ' the deepest thing in our nature,' so is it fear that will bring the depths of our nature within our knowledge. A great capacity of *suffering* belongs to genius; and it has been observed that an alternation of joyfulness and dejection is quite as characteristic of the man of genius as intensity in either kind." In his *Notes from Books,* p. 216, he recurs to it :— " ' Pain,' says a writer whose early death will not prevent his being long remembered, ' pain is the deepest thing that we have in our nature, and union through pain has always seemed more real and more holy than any other.' "

Thus it is, that to each one of us the death of Arthur Hallam—his thoughts and affections—his views of God, of our relations to Him, of duty, of the meaning and worth of this world, and the next,—where he now is, have an individual significance. He is bound up in our bundle of life; we must be the better or the worse of having known what manner of man he was; and in a sense less peculiar, but not less true, each of us may say,

——" The tender grace of a day that is dead
Will never come back to me."

——" O for the touch of a vanished hand,
And the sound of a voice that is still!"

" God give us love! Something to love
He lends us; but when love is grown
To ripeness, that on which it throve
Falls off, and love is left alone:

This is the curse of time. Alas!
In grief we are not all unlearned;
Once, through our own doors Death did pass;
One went, who never hath returned.

This star
Rose with us, through a little arc
Of heaven, nor having wandered far,
Shot on the sudden into dark.

Sleep sweetly, tender heart, in peace;
Sleep, holy spirit, blessed soul,
While the stars burn, the moons increase,
And the great ages onward roll.

Sleep till the end, true soul and sweet,
Nothing comes to thee new or strange,
Sleep, full of rest from head to feet;
Lie still, dry dust, secure of change."

Vattene in pace, alma beata e bella.—Go in peace, soul beautiful and blessed.

" O man greatly beloved, go thou thy way till the end, for thou shalt rest, and stand in thy lot at the end of the days."—DANIEL.

———

" Lord, I have viewed this world over, in which
Thou hast set me; I have tried how this and that
thing will fit my spirit, and the design of my creation,
and can find nothing on which to rest, for nothing
here doth itself rest, but such things as please me for
a while, in some degree, vanish and flee as shadows
from before me. Lo ! I come to Thee—the Eternal
Being—the Spring of Life—the Centre of rest—the
Stay of the Creation—the Fulness of all things. I
join myself to Thee; with Thee I will lead my life,
and spend my days, and with whom I aim to dwell for
ever, expecting, when my little time is over, to be
taken up ere long into Thy eternity."—JOHN HOWE,
The Vanity of Man as mortal.

Necesse est tanquam immaturam mortem ejus de-
fleam: si tamen fas est aut flere, aut omnino mortem
vocare, quâ tanti juvenis mortalitas magis finita
quam vita est. Vivit enim, vivetque semper, atque
etiam latius in memoria hominum et sermone versabi-
tur, postquam ab oculis recessit.

The above notice was published in 1851. On sending to Mr. Hallam a copy of the *Review* in which it
appeared, I expressed my hope that he would not be
displeased by what I had done. I received the
following kind and beautiful reply :—

"WILTON CRESCENT, *Feb.* 1, 1851.

" DEAR SIR,—It would be ungrateful in me to feel any
displeasure at so glowing an eulogy on my dear eldest son
Arthur, though after such a length of time, so unusual, as you
have written in the *North British Review*. I thank you, on
the contrary, for the strong language of admiration you have
employed, though it may expose me to applications for copies
of the *Remains,* which I have it not in my power to comply
with. I was very desirous to have lent you a copy, at your
request, but you have succeeded elsewhere.

" You are probably aware that I was prevented from doing
this by a great calamity, very similar in its circumstances
to that I had to deplore in 1833—the loss of another son, equal
in virtues, hardly inferior in abilities, to him whom you have

commemorated. This has been an unspeakable affliction to me, and at my advanced age, seventy-three years, I can have no resource but the hope, in God's mercy, of a reunion with them both. The resemblance in their characters was striking, and I had often reflected how wonderfully my first loss had been repaired by the substitution, as it might be called, of one so closely representing his brother. I send you a brief Memoir, drawn up by two friends, with very little alteration of my own.—I am, Dear Sir, faithfully yours,

"HENRY HALLAM.

"DR. BROWN,
    "Edinburgh.'

———

The following extracts, from the *Memoir of Henry Fitzmaurice Hallam* mentioned above, which has been appended to a reprint of his brother's *Remains* (for private circulation), form a fitting close to this memorial of these two brothers, who were "lovely and pleasant in their lives," and are now by their deaths not divided :—

" But few months have elapsed since the pages of *In Memoriam* recalled to the minds of many, and impressed on the hearts of all who perused them, the melancholy circumstances attending the sudden and early death of Arthur Henry Hallam, the eldest son of Henry Hallam, Esq. Not many weeks ago the public journals contained a short paragraph announcing the decease, under circumstances equally distressing, and in some points remarkably similar, of Henry Fitzmaurice, Mr. Hallam's younger and only remaining son. No one of the very many who appreciate the sterling value of Mr. Hallam's literary labours, and who feel a consequent interest in the character of those who would have sustained the eminence of an honourable name; no one who was affected by the striking and tragic fatality of two such successive bereavements, will deem an apology needed for this short and imperfect Memoir.

" Henry Fitzmaurice Hallam, the younger son of Henry Hallam, Esq., was born on the 31st of August,

1824; he took his second name from his godfather, the Marquis of Lansdowne. . . . A habit of reserve, which characterized him at all periods of life, but which was compensated in the eyes of even his first companions by a singular sweetness of temper, was produced and fostered by the serious thoughtfulness ensuing upon early familiarity with domestic sorrow.

" ' He was gentle,' writes one of his earliest and closest school-friends, ' retiring, thoughtful to pensiveness, affectionate, without envy or jealousy, almost without emulation, impressible, but not wanting in moral firmness. No one was ever more formed for friendship. In all his words and acts he was simple, straightforward, true. He was very religious. Religion had a real effect upon his character, and made him tranquil about great things, though he was so nervous about little things.'

" He was called to the bar in Trinity Term, 1850, and became a member of the Midland Circuit in the summer. Immediately afterwards he joined his family in a tour on the Continent. They had spent the early part of the autumn at Rome, and were returning northwards, when he was attacked by a sudden and severe illness, affecting the vital powers, and accompanied by enfeebled circulation and general prostration of strength. He was able, with difficulty, to reach Siena, where he sank rapidly through exhaustion, and expired on Friday, October 25. It is to be hoped that he did not experience any great or active suffering. He was conscious nearly to the last, and met his early death (of which his presentiments, for several years, had been frequent and very singular) with calmness and fortitude. There is reason to apprehend, from medical examination, that his life would not have been of very long duration, even had this unhappy illness not occurred. But for some years past his health had been apparently much improved; and, secured as it seemed to be by his unintermitted temperance and by a carefulness in regimen which his early feebleness of constitution had rendered habitual, those to whom he was nearest and dearest had, in great measure, ceased to regard him with anxiety. His remains were brought to England, and he was interred, on December 23rd, in Clevedon Church, Somersetshire, by the side of his brother, his sister, and his mother.

" For continuous and sustained thought he had an extraordinary capacity, the bias of his mind being decidedly towards analytical processes; a characteristic which was illustrated at Cambridge by his uniform partiality for analysis, and comparative distaste for the geometrical method, in his mathematical studies. His early proneness to dwell upon the more recondite departments of each science and branch of inquiry has been alluded to above. It is not to be inferred that, as a consequence of this tendency, he blinded himself, at any period of his life, to the necessity and the duty of practical exertion. He was always eager to act as well as speculate; and, in this respect, his character preserved an unbroken consistency and harmony from the epoch when, on commencing his residence at Cambridge, he voluntarily became a teacher in a parish Sunday-school, for the sake of applying his theories of religious education, to the time when, on the point of setting forth on his last fatal journey, he framed a plan of obtaining access, in the ensuing winter, to a large commercial establishment, in the view of familiarizing himself with the actual course and minute detail of mercantile transactions.

" Insensibly and unconsciously he had made himself a large number of friends in the last few years of his life : the painful impression created by his death in the circle in which he habitually moved, and even beyond it, was exceedingly remarkable, both for its depth and its extent. For those united with him in a companionship more than ordinarily close, his friendship had taken such a character as to have almost become a necessity of existence. But it was upon his family that he lavished all the wealth of his disposition

—affection without stint, gentleness never once at fault, considerateness reaching to self-sacrifice :—

> " Di ciò si biasmi il debolo intelletto
> E' l'parlar nostro, che non ha valore
> Di ritrar tutto ciò che dice amore.
>
> H. S. M.
F. L."

THE END